EMPIRE & ORACLE

TIME CRIME BOOK 2

EMPIRE & ORACLE

CARNEGIE OLSON

HUMBLE HOGS PRESS

Humble Hogs Press

© Carnegie Olson, 2022

First Edition, First State

ISBN-13: 978-1-7342832-2-8 (eBook)
ISBN-13: 978-1-7342832-3-5 (paperback)
ISBN-13: 978-1-7342832-5-9 ("cloth" hardcover)
ISBN-13: 978-1-7342832-7-3 (case laminate)

Mothman empress illustrations: Kevin Ewing
Wolf illustration: C.O.
Maps: Christopher Fowler
Book design: Looseleaf Editorial & Production
Editing: Looseleaf Editorial & Production

Print edition typeface is Freight Text.

This is an AI-free novel.

To Angie
For cocktails in the afternoon.

To Kevin
For making it crazy.

TABLE OF CONTENTS

And you play your part, not withdrawing from the world when you realize how horrible it is, but seeing that this horror is simply the foreground of a wonder, a mysterium tremendum et fascinans.[1]

—J. Campbell

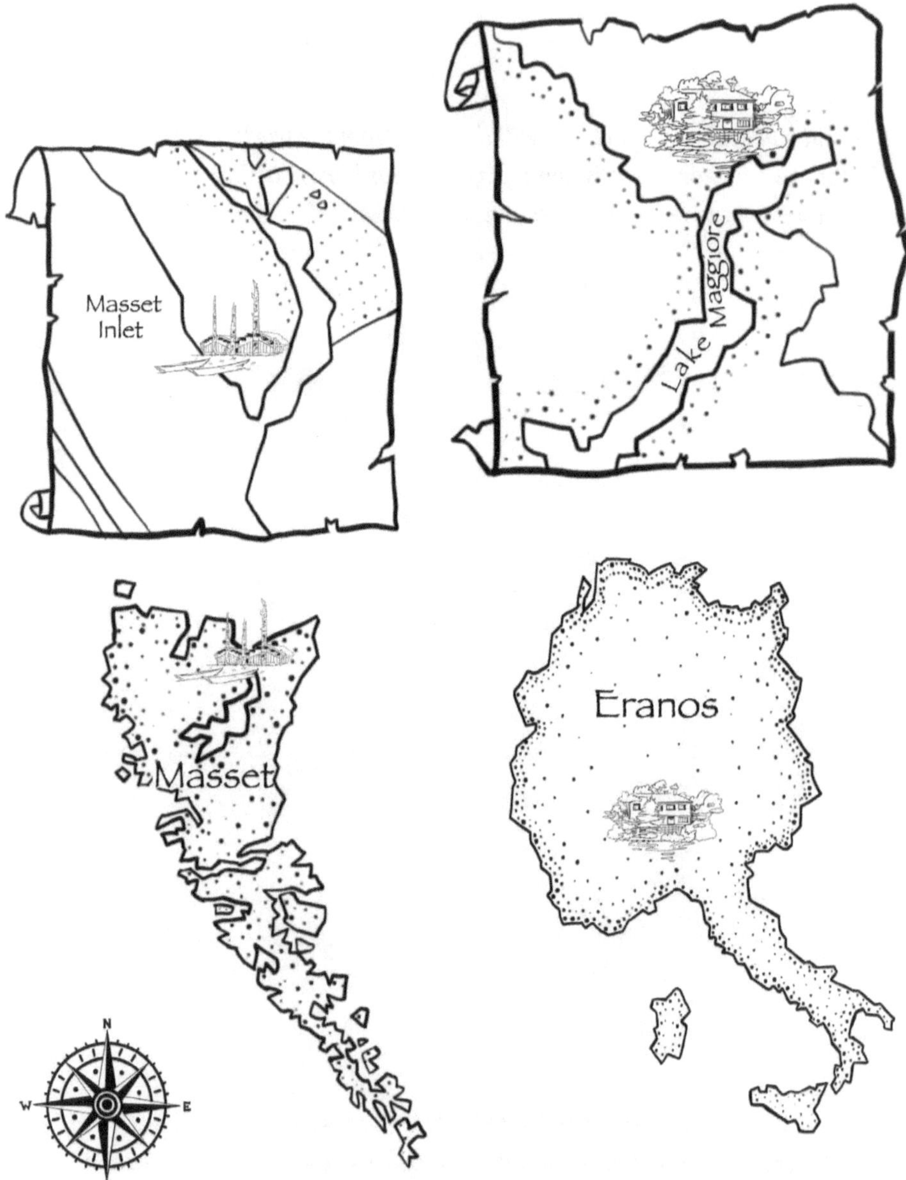

Masset Inlet
Lake Maggiore
Masset
Eranos
N
W
E
S

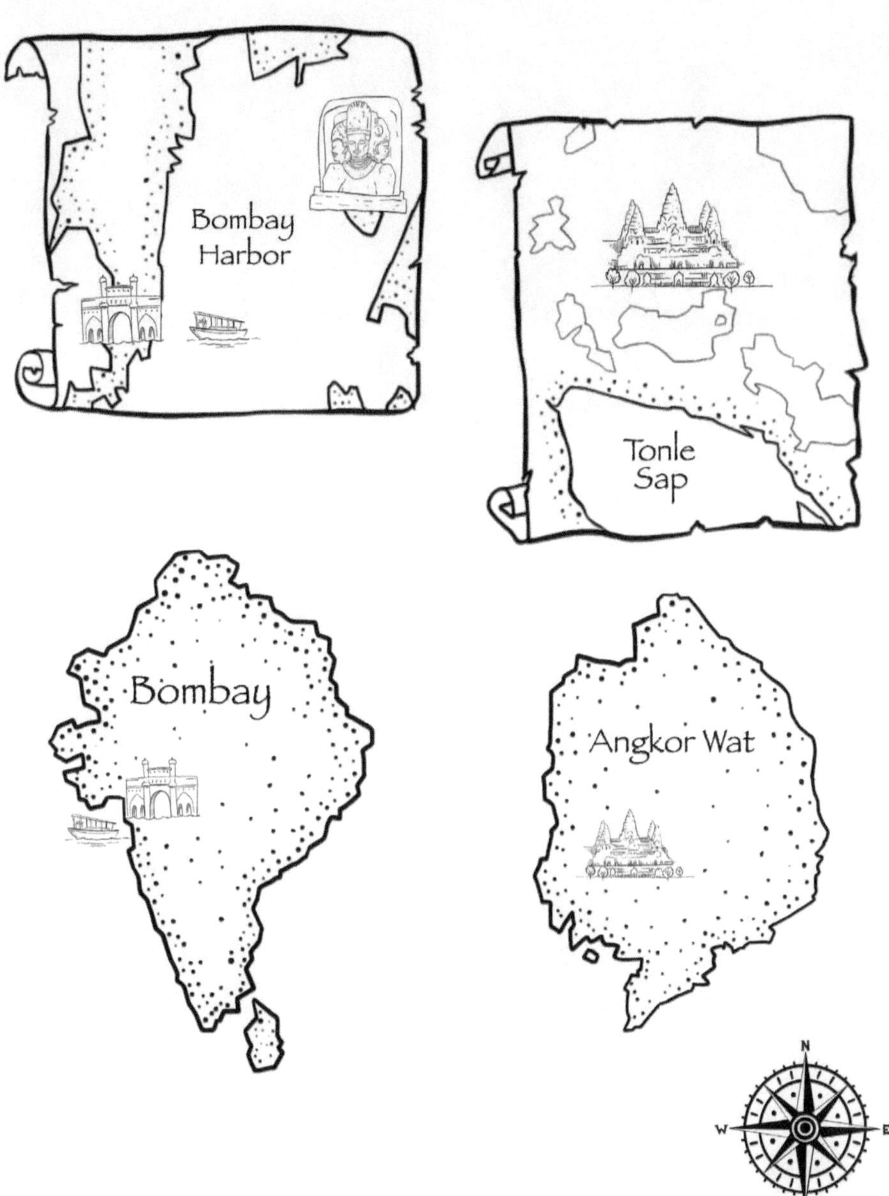

Bombay Harbor
Tonle Sap
Bombay
Angkor Wat
N
W
E
S

ANGKOR, 1144 CE

"Your skirmishes with the Cham have squandered manpower and resources. Your generals and captains die in the fields alongside their warriors, horses, and elephants. Your women and children are taken slaves. The hydraulics are neglected. The rice is not harvested. The tax is not collected. Energy for building is wasted in war. Because of you, the completion of the temple is made impossible."

"Great Lord," said the king. He lay facedown upon the floor of the shrine with arms outstretched, prostrate in the Khmer manner of obeisance, and reached further toward the feet of the three mole-men engineers, his voice muffled by the sandstone blocks. "Holy Trimurti, forgive me. I have not properly understood. Instruct me. What alms will appease you? What sacrifices? Is it your will that the Cham destroy us?"

"Fool," said Zero-Seven. "You *have* understood. From the beginning. Thereafter, all these months, you have lied, and you are lying now."

"Lord?" The king craned his neck and looked up, his pained expression made vaguely hideous by his reddened teeth and the smudged discoloration of his lips.[2]

---

2   Like many Khmer, the king avails himself of the famous betel chew, an alkaloid-rich masticatory comprised of the berry of the areca palm tree

Zero-Seven tweaked the resolution of his autotranslator. Always there was the annoying possibility of misapprehension, of the colloquial Khmer words confounding the translation of the royal language. He prepared to repeat himself.

"Wait," said Four-Alpha. "Suryavarman.[3] We have bestowed upon you the power to rule. Likewise, we have blessed the Khmer with the engineering to control the waters and increase the yield of rice. And the architectural means to embody the celestial city here, at the center of this world." He winked at Zero-Seven and rolled his eyes. "Your salvation and that of your people is maintained by us. Hence, the Cham is not of your concern. Neither the Vietnamese. Nor Siamese. Nor even the Chinese."

Suryavarman forgot himself and sat up. "But Lord! Oh, my gracious Lord, the Chinese buy our kingfisher feathers, elephant tusks, rhinoceros horns, beeswax, incense, pepper. And their merchants bestow gold, silver, and silks, the finely glazed pottery, the tin goods, sandalwood, musk, linen, iron pots, copper trays, and freshwater pearls. The ballistae[4] for war."

"War," said Six-Naught-Six, "is nothing but childish aggression disguised as purpose. The Aztecs, Greeks, and Romans at least had their sport as an occasional substitute. As for the rest, trinkets. Luxuries. Indulgences of betel, wine, women, and slaves. You are like one of your jungle crows, transfixed by sparkling objects of no utility at the cost of everything that matters. Get up, Suryavarman. And call your rājahotar from his hiding place."

Suryavarman scrambled to his feet. He snapped his fingers and

---

mixed with slaked lime (calcium hydroxide) and wrapped with *Piper betle* leaves that is used as a stimulant throughout Southeast Asia.

3   Referring to Khmer king Suryavarman II (1113–1150), builder of Angkor Wat.

4   A weapon consisting of two opposing bows, designed to be mounted upon an elephant or wheeled vehicle, that shot arrows with tremendous force.

waited. They all waited, as usual, while the venerable high priest—a slightly built, almost toothless crag of a man who appeared to be at least thrice the age of the king—hobbled from behind his embroidered curtain and assumed his deferential place an arm's length behind Suryavarman.

Six-Naught-Six toggled off his transponder and addressed Zero-Seven and Four-Alpha in the engineering tongue. "Testing, one, two," he murmured. Satisfied the translator was disabled, he proceeded. "Our predicament is plain enough. The Khmer are flawed. Humans are flawed. But these Khmer in particular lack sufficient intelligence and discipline. They lack the will to work. Suryavarman himself is lazy, stupid, and distracted by his own petty self-interests. And this priest of his? Upon whom we have been foolish enough to bestow the additional title of engineer? He is nothing but a snake charmer. Cunning enough, I will give him that, to have wrangled a career of priestly authority through the reign of, what, three kings including this one? Meanwhile, an engineer priest is nothing but a contradiction in terms.

"We have squandered three Earth years upon this charade," he continued, "teaching these fools astronomically relevant mathematics, the basics of stonecutting, monumental architecture, and hydraulic engineering. The diamagnetic advantage of an equatorial orientation for the clock component is now beside the point. The temple is not complete. It was the singular advantage we maintained over the Maya and Giza experiments. Alongside the breakthroughs in hyperdimensional resolution, our failure only makes the irony more keenly intolerable."

"Irony?" sneered Zero-Seven. "Which irony? That we, the Angkor team, were the statistical favorites over the Maya project clods and their sprawling geographical mess and the Giza project, which wasn't even expected to survive their first round of funding? Or that a three-millennia cultural head start transformed us from frontrunners to also-rans? The Maya team failed as the bureaucratic money pit we all anticipated. Giza ought to have flopped as a hopeless one-man show. Yet here we are. It is not merely intolerable; it is humiliating."

"Regardless," said Six-Naught-Six, "we have failed."

Four-Alpha stood scowling. "Five-X and that slipshod crew of his. Are we to allow him the victory in Giza? No. I say we assume control. Smash the Cham ourselves, make an example of this little tin toy of a king and his senile priest and drive this wretched populace like the chattel they are."

"A tactic," said Six-Naught-Six, "that will distort the future beyond our control. And guarantee that each of us is court-martialed. No. We have accomplished nothing besides bleeding moleman secrets into this stinking Khmer soil. And you, Four-Alpha, you would do things differently now? You allowed this petty tyrant his little egomaniacal indulgences. You allowed him to muster his army yet again and antagonize the Cham."

"You blame me?" Four-Alpha stomped his foot. "What in blazes have I done short of my duty?"

"You have addressed this puny ruler as an equal. And you have taught him enough of our language that he is likely deciphering enough of this conversation to put us at risk of a mutiny."

"Mutiny? What would you know of such a thing? Lounging within the cloaked zone, chatting with mission control, growing fat on our rations. While I risk my neck every day on the scaffolds and in the excavations? Directing the foremen, enduring this despicable weather and the horrible ultraviolet and the biting insects and disgusting food? I gnaw upon roasted fruit bats and pick maggots from my spoiled rice alongside the laborers. I am in the trenches. If there were talk of mutiny, I would know it. No. I am sorry to say the only mutiny is within this room. Amongst ourselves."

"Enough!" said Zero-Seven. We stand here infighting because this neurotic tyrant of a king, a human that is too young to acknowledge anything but his own feckless passions—he is barely an adult according to the biology of his race—and like any youth of any race, he is too bold for his own good, too self-serving, too inexperienced. He heeds nothing besides what hangs between his legs and glorifies his ego. Nevertheless, he has bamboozled us into assuming the temple has been his focus. Six-Naught-Six, Four-Alpha. Both of you imply that instead of kid gloves we ought to have wielded an iron fist. So be it. If Suryavarman believes we are the godhead, he nevertheless clearly believes himself to be our equal. Nay, our superior. What is his Hinduism to him, after all, besides a storybook full of warring deities and lusty goddesses? And an engine of superstition to convince the masses they deserve less than the squalor they already endure?"

"Then you agree," said Four-Alpha, "to forgo diplomacy and request the occupation force?"

"No," said Zero-Seven. "Our mission is to coerce the completion of the temple architecture. To win the people over by way of empowering their ambitions to a better life. To enlist this planet of its own volition in the promulgation of our engineering vision."

"And meanwhile," said Six-Naught-Six, "to risk space-time alterations that may in fact compromise our own present. The longer this Angkor Cell project drags on and the more insidiously our beliefs inculcate the populace, the greater the probabilities of skewing the architecture of our own dominance. Compassion, inclusion, and pedagogy are the hallmarks of every great civilization. Likewise, ruthless meritocracy and the rule of law. This Khmer boy king merely demonstrates that truth."

"This debate is not for us to resolve," said Zero-Seven.

"Who then?" said Four-Alpha. "The bureaucrats at Mega City One? They know nothing of what we've endured here. No one does. I want to go home, dammit. I haven't seen my children in three Mega City One orbits."

"We have all suffered," said Six-Naught-Six.

"Then I say we all go home," said Zero-Seven. "I say we forfeit what's left of the timetable. Why not? If we have failed, as you say, Six-Naught-Six, if the outcome is inevitable, then why squander another moment of our lives in this backwater?"

"Because you will be disgraced, Six-Naught-Six," said Four-Alpha. "As leader of this debacle, are you afraid your long career will end in humiliation?" He glared at Six-Naught-Six. "What of me? What of my career? Over before it has even begun, that's what."

Six-Naught-Six returned his attention to the Khmers. "Suryavarman. Divākara. You are to complete construction of the central shrine before the next zenith passage, or we will refuse to inhabit the temple. The sighting tube must be tested as soon as possible. The rainy season zenith passage is too late."

"But Lord," said Divākara, "the outer galleries remain incomplete. Our artisans strive to beautify them on your behalf. I beg of you, bestow us more time."

"How much?"

"One year. In this way completion of the engineering and beautification will coincide. A proper festival can be planned. Your blessing of the king's sarcophagus will then be auspicious."

"Sarcophagus? Blessing?" Six-Naught-Six appeared astonished. He glanced at Zero-Seven and Four-Alpha, but they merely shrugged.

"As Shield of the Sun," said Suryavarman, "I am empowered to receive the light—the light of the passage—beyond my death."

"How dare you?" said Six-Naught-Six. "You are empowered to receive nothing more than what we deem to bestow. The sacred deposit, white sapphires, and gold leaf—the light of the sun and the moon themselves—the divine legitimacy of this celestial city is empowered by us, the Trimurti."

"I shall inhabit the temple with you," said Suryavarman. "My ashes will reside with the sacred deposit. The column of light shall illuminate and empower my eternal sovereignty at each passage. I shall be as the sacred fire."

"Illuminate you? Eternal sovereignty? Sacred fire? At fifty-four cubits below the statue of Vishnu there will be no light illuminating anything, least of all your ashes. This is not a mausoleum, Suryavarman. You are arrogantly mistaken. Divākara, are you behind such insolence?"

The chief priest's only sign of deference, owing to his infirmities, was to bow his head. "The abode of Vishnu, akin to the Lord himself, resides within Heaven and Earth. We come to know Heaven by way of the Earth, and Earth by the way of Heaven. We come to know you, Lord, in our humble manner, by way of your trine aspect, manifested before us here." Divākara gestured contritely toward the molemen, his gaze respectfully averted, and brought his hands together over his chest as if in prayer. "And we maintain the sacred fire in your absence, in your honor. But the neak ta, the spirit sovereigns of the land from which this temple has come and upon which it resides, must also be appeased or the Khmer will suffer in life and in death. We will fail to inspire the beatitude of the temple and you, Lord, will abandon us. Interring the earthly essence of the king, then, alongside the sacred deposit, will assure the heavenly maintenance of your abode."

"That," said Four-Alpha, untranslated, "is quite a deft little speech, isn't it? And an example of how this sly human magician has propagated the advantages of his rank well into his decrepitude."

"The request is absurd," said Zero-Seven, likewise untranslated. "But to agree to it; to find a place for the king's ashes within the shrine, costs us nothing in terms of engineering."

As if sensing the tone of the molemen's otherwise unintelligible responses, or perhaps merely responding to the silence that ensued, Suryavarman spoke up. "The Khmer will not complete the temple, least of all in time for the coming zenith passage, unless it is also understood as the resting place of Paramavishnuloka."

Six-Naught-Six clenched his fists and the rubbery creak of the fabric of his gauntlets against themselves was the only sound in the room. He relaxed his grip and sighed quietly. "White sapphires. Gold leaf. Images of their puny moon and unsightly sun. The absurdity of wasting years carving their worthless myths into the walls of this unsightly construct. Perhaps it is fitting. An entire temple monument reduced to a reliquary for a doomed nation and the ashes of their petty king. Paramavishnuloka. What is he talking about?"

"A posthumous title," said Zero-Seven. "Uniting him with the so-called god-king. *He who has rejoined the realm of the supreme Vishnu.*"

"If it is all that is required to drive completion of the CCC[5] architecture and the sighting tube, then so be it. You are right, Zero-Seven, it will cost us nothing."

"As if we have any choice, besides," growled Four-Alpha. "Priests and politicians. In the end, one is nothing but a version of the other."

Six-Naught-Six toggled his autotranslator. "Suryavarman. Divākara. Your boldness is as tedious as it is insufferable. Such

---

5   Cosmic Clock Component. See Glossary.

disobedience invites your destruction here and now. But then humans will perhaps always much better demonstrate the demonic than the divine. Tomb and temple, then. So be it."

"Thank you, Lord," said Suryavarman. "Thank you." He once again prostrated himself facedown upon the sandstone blocks and reached out beseechingly.

Divākara remained, as always, flagrantly upright.

"Spare us your insincere obeisance," demanded Zero-Seven. "You will be held to the timeline. Fail us again, and we will abandon the Khmer to the hell of your own making. Be gone."

The priest and the king remained as they were.

"But, the Cham," said Divākara. "Our spies report of their mustering for war. You, Lord, possessed of unlimited sight and wisdom, witness their encroachment upon our borders. We cannot both defend ourselves and devote sufficient labor to the completion of the temple."

"Indeed, Great Lord," added Suryavarman. "Please. Bestow upon us the power to defeat our enemies."

Zero-Seven made to toggle his autotranslator, but Six-Naught-Six silenced him with a gesture. "Expedite a festival. All the sacrifices. Including slaves. A day for each face of the Trimurti. Do you hear? Only when the oblations are sufficient will the Khmer be made invincible. By my word. Meanwhile, know that you have tried my patience for the last time. Now, go!"

They watched the king and the high priest shuffle toward the exit and vanish behind the curtain door.

"You cannot be intending to assist them against the Cham?" said Zero-Seven.

"That would indeed require an occupying force," said Four-Alpha.

"Of course not," said Six-Naught-Six. "It is merely to buy a little time. The golden ball. You have established a secure contingency location? A hiding place that will secure it from the thieves, tomb robbers, and vanquishing armies of the future?"

Four-Alpha nodded.

"Secure it, then. Zero-Seven, begin decommissioning our command center."

Zero-Seven scratched behind his ears. "This Khmer festival. Three days. But how long do you think it will take them to prepare? A day? Two? Three? How much time does that leave us to disembark?"

Six-Naught-Six was studying his transponder intently. "It doesn't matter. HDT our command center to Mega City One as soon as possible."

Zero-Seven nodded. "I can configure the transport within twenty-four hours."

"Four-Alpha," said Six-Naught-Six. "That gives you more than enough time to engineer the safe haven for the ball."

"Yes. But all this haranguing between ourselves and then Suryavarman and his priest. I don't understand. We are going home? Within twenty-four hours?"

"I don't understand either," said Zero-Seven. "What has happened?"

Six-Naught-Six thrust his transponder at them both. "*This* has happened." He strode purposely across the stone floor of the temple enclosure and paused halfway outside the curtain door. "See for yourselves. I have just received new orders from Mega City One. After all this time and all our misery and now our maddening disagreements, the irony is indeed acute. And complete. As far as I am concerned, at least. We are to leave the Khmer to their fate, to their nightmare of history. Immediately."

CHAPTER 1

WOMAN IN THE MOON

"Duff?" It was late and the light was failing. Vixy blew into her hands and rubbed them together, her fingers stiff with cold. "Duff! Come!" It was her own fault—she knew better than to work so late in the forest. But she'd made so much progress, for once, with the data. The deluge was deepest right here. It *had* to be. All her work pointed to these coordinates. First the earthquake. Then the tsunami. The waters retreated, hauling the ruined land back across itself, scraping it raw, all the way to the coast. The saturated land drained. Evaporation did its part. Things dried up and grew again. An eon passed in ecological terms. The forest reestablished itself.

But not here. Not right away, anyway. A new lake had been left behind. And it was big. Huge. At 75,000 square kilometers, it was almost comparable to Lake Superior in Michigan, which at 82,103 square kilometers was the largest freshwater lake in the world and contained 10 percent of the Earth's freshwater. And this lake was deep. At an average of 400 meters, it was too deep, dark and in contrast to the Great Lakes, too poisoned with salinity for anything dependent upon fresh water to survive. Things died and decomposed and piled upon each other. Geologically significant magnitudes of time passed.

Meanwhile, no one cared. People were busy rebuilding. For a while there were more than enough resources elsewhere, even if it meant importing lumber from forests in China and Indonesia and

Russia and wherever else. Folks would have harvested trees from the moon if it had any. That, and this lake was in the middle of fucking nowhere. Even now, after seemingly every square centimeter of the planet had been scanned, marked, categorized, evaluated, and contextualized according to its perceived value, places like this still got lost. Overlooked, at least. Abandoned and forgotten.

Lost Lake, then. That's what she decided to call it. Lost to the ages and public consciousness, for it hadn't been a lake for at least a thousand years. It had transformed from a little inland sea to wetland, marsh, bog, meadow, scrub, and finally forest. Now it was as if nothing but forest had been here all along.

Hence, the treasures it concealed—the little remnants of the past—would have remained untouched, buried beneath the heavy silt and soil. Buried deeper and deeper with each passing season. Enough time passed and you got a recognizable layer. Sprinkle in another earthquake or two, some minor and major tremors here and there, and it was like stirring geological cake batter—the layers blended into one another, got turned over and mixed up.

"You can't, therefore, read this land in traditional archaeological terms," Mr. Z. had told Vixy. "It isn't that easy. And the quirky geophysics makes the anthropology that much more challenging to discern. Context is everything. But what is the context? That's why you're the exact person for the job. Your talent is multidisciplinary. Anthropological archaeology, yes. But your intuitive talents go beyond that, Vixy. You also grasp the mythology. Awe, cosmology—"

"Awe, cosmology, sociology and pedagogical psychology, yes, I know, I know," she'd told him. And he had smiled that impossibly tolerant smile of his—the one that used to make her crazy. Maybe it still did. How could she know? She hadn't seen him in—what had it been, over a year? Whenever he came to mind now it seemed crazy that she'd been so childishly in love with him. She'd been nothing but a silly schoolgirl then.

Meanwhile, devoting herself to her studies over the past two years had mostly taught her how much she didn't measure up, how much she had to learn. Her field was rife with talent. And while she'd been keen to maintain her connection to the Time Detective Contingent, working on this or that little project from home—nothing on site, no HDT—her contemporaries had had their noses full time to the academic grindstone. But she knew enough, possessed enough intuition, to seek and find a place like this. Ironically, so close to home. Hell, it *was* home. Everything she needed, a life's work, was here.

So much of the mythology of the Northwest Coast, her own Haida culture included, had been lost. Because nothing had been written down. At one time they just used to carve, but never wrote. It was the Northwest Coast's version of the myth time. Preliterate. And the undocumented past of this place somehow seemed to call to her. Her home. Undocumented, yes, but not necessarily unrecorded. For the images were rich and led deeply into the past. And if most of the physical evidence had literally disintegrated—the conditions were virtually the opposite of those within, say, the arid sands of Egypt—there were still clues to be had. It just took patience and hard work. An eye for things. And a nose. And some luck, of course. To find things. Bits and pieces. That was part of the allure of her work, that she could search and find and piece things together and tease them apart and the story of the past would unfold before her. Without her destroying it.

The selfish fools who sought to deregulate HDT made her furious. The idea of trudging through history to collect their firsthand accounts of it in the name of their own egos and careerist ambitions? Their shortsightedness was staggering. "Leave no trace" meant nothing to them, and neither did the reality of their scandalous transformations. As if the architecture of space-time were a means to an end and not something sublime and infinitely complex and sacred. Sacred, yes. Divine? Perhaps. Time crime was alive and well. And the TDC needed all the help it could get.

Still, she wished sometimes that she understood more about what she was doing and why so she could better foresee outcomes. And not waste time. And effort. And get to where she wanted to go with things. Wherever that was.

Listen to your heart, Vixy, her father had told her. *And if sometimes you don't know what it's telling you, well, hell, then follow your nose.*

She scrolled through her data one last time, saved her changes, and stowed the machine. She hurried to rewind the sounding cable and cringed at the mud clinging to the alignment sheath. Cleaning the thing later was going to suck. But darkness was falling. Quickly, always too quickly, like a blanket over a cage. This particular cable-core would have to do for now. Meanwhile, she'd have to hurry to get back to the all-wheeler or risk stumbling through the understory using nothing but her headlamp and trek mapper.

"Duff, goddammit!" She listened hard for him, rubbed her hands together again, briskly, desperately, as if conjuring a spell to hold back the old anxiety, the sense that she'd overstayed her welcome in the woods. She had never been lost, never had to signal for evac like so many of the amateur treasure hunters in this vast taiga. Never.

Never in the woods, at least.

She shivered and typed hurriedly:

> [March 21, 18:46. Field Day 3. Grid Nexus: 54.0115 ° N, 132.1472 ° W—Masset, Haida Gwaii (Historical nomen-clature: Queen Charlotte Islands), British Columbia]: Taiga unblemished. Post-tsunami ecology is diverse and flourishing. Magnetic imaging results negative. Relic readings dispersed but promising.

She shut down her device, shoved it into her pack and stood peering into the dimming forest. "Dammit, Duff, where the hell are you?" She whistled hard but the forest gobbled up the sound. "Duff! Come!"

A rustling noise startled her, and Duff materialized from behind the trunk of a tree, ears pricked, panting, his tail drifting back and forth, the picture of enthusiastic canine innocence.

"God, you crazy dog! Where have you been!" She caught her breath, yanked her pack chair from the ground and stomped toward him. "What are you doing?" He blinked happily at her. He was filthy up to his elbows. His belly too. Even his haunches were caked with moist earth. "What the hell, Duff!"

Duff lowered his ears at her for a moment—his attempt at defer-ence—then resumed his panting and tail-wagging eagerness.

Vixy tromped past him and immediately came upon the hole he'd dug, a deep gash in the earth so black she could hardly see into it. But she could smell it. The composted, almost decadent bacterial and fungal and otherwise biological richness of the soil. The smell of the infinite mystery of life.

"Jeezus, Duff."

Duff skulked toward the other side of his excavation and lay down, his tongue lolling and his breath steaming into the chill air.

"Since when did you become a digger?" Vixy peered warily into the hole, expecting the worst—something decomposed or otherwise disgusting—but there was only black earth, some exposed roots, an uprooted fern, and a sprinkling of dead leaves and pine needles—all the detritus of the forest floor. She circled the hole and clasped Duff's leash to his collar. "You're getting a bath when we get home, you know that?"

She looked upward into the soaring cathedral of trunks and branches, the treetops themselves burnished by the last of the day's long light, a tender illumination that always evoked for her an unsettling sense of longing and loss, of time slipping away. And goodbyes. It made her anxious to return to the all-wheeler. Nevertheless, there was Duff's hole to consider. She shined her flashlight into its depths, and something glittered. She knelt, leaning into the opening, keen to clear away the soil.

Gold? Her heart skipped a beat. Or merely *golden*? It was a medallion or a brooch, or perhaps a pendant. She used her trowel and her fingers to pry it carefully from the earth, wiped away the muck, and examined the thing as best she could under the harsh electric light. It was a shiny, gold-toned face no larger than the palm of her hand, with wide-set eyes skillfully inlaid with what appeared to be abalone—but she had no time to analyze for authenticity. The face had high cheek bones and an open mouth, deeply sculpted, and the image was set within a ring of yet more inlaid abalone. Fake or not, the piece was accomplished.

She dug into her pack for a marking flag and plunged it into the spot where she'd found it. She hauled out her device again and photographed the face and the flag. "Field Marker," she said. She hated using speech recognition but her hands were too filthy and cold to type. "Gold Face." The icon appeared upon the coordinate grid within the display—her first find! She slipped the face into a plastic sample pouch, got up, and made for where she'd parked the all-wheeler. "Come on, Duff," she said, tugging on the leash, her heart pounding. "Let's go!"

The thrill of her discovery heightened her sense of everything—of her breath in the chill air, of their shuffling through the understory, of the sharp silence and penetrating dimness. It was the same dimness that usually spooked her out of the woods by late afternoon.

But the face! Don't get carried away, she told herself, the piece is probably nothing—another hunk of contemporary jewelry, a trinket somebody lost while camping. This part of the country—the archipelago, the coastline, and for hundreds of kilometers inland—was strewn with them.

Straight ahead, the all-wheeler's reflectors glowed unmistakably. "There it is," she told herself, quickening their pace. "C'mon, Duff!"

She loaded her pack and her folding chair onto the all-wheeler, climbed aboard, jabbed at the ignition, and revved the hydrogen converter, glad for the reliable hum of the machine. It was strange, her fear of the motor not starting, of getting stranded in the woods. She'd loved the forest all her life and had only rarely been spooked by it. No more than anybody else, at least. But ever since Egypt and that blasted HDT nightmare, the idea of getting lost, well, she pushed such thoughts aside and made room for Duff. He hopped in, wedged himself into his favorite spot between the drive cowling and the wing stub, and flopped onto the rubberized floor mat. "Ready?"

She feathered the clutch and revved the motor. The all-wheeler rolled forward, its fat, knobby tires at home in the squishy, springy, sloppy ground. They climbed up and over the rotting hulk of an ancient red cedar, so large it evoked the broken hull of a grounded ship. After crawling along for another one hundred or so meters, Vixy stopped and looked straight up again into the treetops. No more sun, it was behind the trees, but she could see a patch of bright blue sky where the branches were thinnest. That was her way in and out of here.

She glanced at Duff. He lay with his eyes half closed, tongue lolling. She shifted into vertical, throttled the thrusters and hovered low, perhaps two meters off the ground, testing her yaw, pitch, and roll controls—the jets had been misfiring this morning. But now they sounded strong. She eased the craft higher and higher until they cleared the treetops, relieved at the light and the treetop expanse. She set the coordinates, shifted into flight-drive, and accelerated toward home.

———

THEY SPED ALONG, AND THE sun dipped below the dark tree line. The scattered clouds were a vivid orangey pink, the cockpit saturated with a tender, changing light. Vixy glanced down at Duff curled up on the floor mat, asleep. "We left just in time," she said quietly. She disliked flying the all-wheeler after dark. Something about the little craft's visceral quirkiness, so charming and jaunty on a day trip, made it seem temperamental and tedious at night, whether on the ground or in the air. But the thirty minutes nevertheless passed quickly, uneventfully, and the cottage came into view with light still in the sky.

———

VIXY SHOULDERED HER PACK AND skirted the vegetable garden, enticed by the aroma of dinner wafting from the house—beef chili and cornbread. She stomped up the steps, kicked off her boots and reached for the door. Duff clamored in ahead of her, trailing muddy paw prints across the kitchen floor. "Dammit, Duff! He needs a bath, Mom. He got into something—you should have seen the hole he dug."

Her mother donned her oven mitts and hauled a cast iron skillet to the kitchen counter, her face flush from the heat, then turned the cornbread out onto a plate. "What was it?"

"What?" said Vixy. She was hurrying to get out of her coat. "I'm starving!"

"You said Duff got into something."

"Oh, I'll show you. Where's Dad, downstairs?" She opened the basement door and hollered at him, "Dad!"

Duff barreled down the steps.

"Dad, Duff is dirty, he needs a bath, I'll take care of it!" She hung up her coat, padded down the hallway in her socks and set her pack in her bedroom, which doubled as her office. She donned her slippers, clambered back down the hallway and into the basement, shuffled past her father at his worktable, and made her way to the laundry sink. "Duff, come!"

"Got into something, did he?" He frowned intently at the fly he was tying. One hand held an otherwise invisible thread taut, and the other brandished a pair of scissors.

Vixy ran the water, rummaged through the collection of bottles, tubes, jugs, and jars in the storage cabinet, and snatched at the dog shampoo. "Duff! Let's go! Where are you?" Vixy stood waiting, testing the temperature of the water with her finger. "Dad? Is he out there?"

Her father arrived at the laundry sink carrying Duff in his arms.

"Oh, Dad, I was gonna get him—now you're all dirty, too."

"Go get changed and ready for dinner, Vixy. I'll take care of the dog."

Vixy rushed off. "Thanks, Dad," she said over her shoulder. "He's better with you anyway."

Her father shook his head and lowered Duff into the sink. "Children and dogs," he murmured.

———

VIXY CAME TO THE TABLE in her pullover, lodge pants and slippers. She tied her hair back with a flexible band. "Mmm," she said, reaching for a slice of cornbread.

Her mother feigned slapping at Vixy's hand and sat down across from her. "Wait for your father." She eyed her daughter. "And your hair. If it's that shaggy, you ought to make an appointment to get it cut."

"Shaggy?" Vixy scowled. "Where's the butter? You think my hair looks shaggy?"

"Where is your father?" said her mother. "What would happen if he didn't take care of your dog for you? You'd make a mess of this house, that's what."

"He volunteered, Mom," said Vixy, nibbling at her food. "And he'll get it done better than I could and in half the time, you know that. I make Duff nervous in the tub." She got up to retrieve the butter dish.

Heavy footsteps clomped up the basement steps and her father appeared, his shirt front and sleeves darkened with water. "Let's eat," he said, rubbing his hands together.

Duff barreled past him and shook himself in the middle of the living room, rolling onto his back and making a squirming drama of his condition. He jumped onto his paws, shook again, made a circuit of the room, as if he could perhaps outrun his damp fur and finally plopped down upon the rug before the hearth fire.

"Oh!" said Vixy's mother. "Hot sauce. I forgot the hot sauce. Victor?"

Victor snatched it from the cupboard and took his place at the head of the table.

Vixy's mother ladled out the chili, shoved a container of shredded cheese into the center of the table, and stood to straighten her apron.

"Sit, Eleanor," said her father. He held out his hands to the women.

Vixy put down her cornbread, and they all clasped hands. Vixy's mother shut her eyes tightly. The hearth fire crackled quietly.

Her father winked at her. "We thank you, Lord," he said.

Vixy grinned at the sonorous, formal affectation of his voice, as if it weren't merely his wife and daughter listening.

"We thank you, Lord, for this food, this house, and the well-being of us all."

"Amen," said her parents, together.

"Amen," said Vixy quietly, to herself. She watched her mother open her eyes and regard the table setting afresh, possessed of the lingering piousness that seemed so much a part of her. Her parents unclasped their hands, then her father reached for the ladle and her mother unfolded a napkin onto her lap.

To Vixy they seemed as innocent and naive and wise as always. Except she sensed for the first time the span of years. She suddenly felt hardened and grown-up, her parents older, more vulnerable, more precious than she ever could have imagined. It struck her that one day they would die and . . . what would happen then? She would be alone.

"Wouldn't you know?" said Eleanor. She used her spoon to dab at her chili. "I saw Daniel Cramer at church this week."

Vixy cringed.

"He graduated from university at the same time you did, remember?"

Vixy sprinkled shredded cheese on her chili, shook the tiny bottle of hot sauce vigorously and tipped a few drops into her bowl. She stirred, the spoon clattering against her bowl as if it were the only sound in the room. "I don't know, Mom. I mean, I don't remember any Daniel Cramer."

"He said he remembered you. The Cramers are the ones who moved to Vancouver, and Daniel's father, he was the coach of the high school soccer team. Wasn't he, Victor? Anyway, Daniel seemed very nice."

"You're going to tell me that church is a good place to meet people." Vixy spread more butter on her cornbread. "Because you met Dad there." She fidgeted in her chair, ashamed of her impatience but powerless to overcome it.

"It's true, Vixy," said her father.

"But Dad—"

"I'm not a churchgoer, everybody knows that. That's where you get it. From me, Vixy. You and I, we get our religion out of doors, you could say." He glanced at his daughter and tore at his hunk of bread. "And me and your mother? It was, I don't know, a zillion years ago. And I just happened to be in the church for a couple of weeks working on the pews—some basic carpentry they needed done. And since I was young and penniless and the church was paying and feeding me lunch, there I was for two weeks with this job to do. And there they were. All the pretty girls in the choir, that is."

"Dad," said Vixy, gulping down her chili.

"It won't kill you to hear this story again. Anyway, there they were, these girls, practicing a few days a week. And your mother—besides having a nice singing voice as far as I was concerned—she used to clean up around the place too. Most days it was just us and that old, rugged cross together in that little church. Isn't that what it's called in that hymn you girls sang? 'Old Rugged Cross'?" He shrugged and chomped into his bread. "So, we got to know each other from a distance, you might say. And the rest is history."

"'Old Rugged Cross,'" said Eleanor, shaking her head at him. "Victor." She sat staring into the distance for a moment, one hand in her lap and the other holding her spoon. "I'd forgotten all about it."

"Are you telling me nobody sings it anymore? 'Old Rugged Cross'? At church?" Victor went about his meal, reaching for more chili and tearing at the bread again. "Well, they ought to. But then nobody keeps up on the Haida songs either, I suppose. The good old songs. It all gets forgotten. Until somebody like Vixy at a university goes digging after it. Right, Vixy? Let me see." He chomped away for a moment, frowning as if trying to remember. Then he broke into song, his careful, quiet, tuneless baritone somehow evocative of his theme:

> On a hill far away, stood an old, rugged Cross
> The emblem of suff'ring and shame
> And I love that old Cross where the dearest and best
> For a world of lost sinners was slain[6]

Victor cleared his throat, beaming mildly, and sipped at his ale.

Eleanor blushed and got up from the table with her plate. She ambled into the kitchen.

"What do you think, Ellie? Are you ready for me to sing in your choir?"

"Victor, I've nothing to say about you joining the choir. But that's a beautiful hymn. You never told me you liked it."

"Hmm, well, I don't know about liking it or whatever. I just re-member you and me and the church and that music somehow. Weird, huh?" He raised his eyebrow at Vixy.

Vixy hunched her shoulders, placed her hands in her lap and nodded politely. "Yes, Dad." Why did her father's silly old story

---

6   "The Old Rugged Cross," composed by George Bennard in 1912, is a famous Methodist hymn and country gospel song first made popular by Ernest Tubb in the early 1950s. Public domain.

and that silly old hymn strike her now as poignant and wise? They'd always been her nutty family, so backwards and naïve. And her mother's response, that there could be something she didn't know about her husband after all their years together? It was touching, and she endured, again, the sense that she had been living as a child until now. She sprinkled more cheese and hot sauce onto her chili.

"You never used to dislike going to church, Vixy. Not until you went away to university."

Vixy resisted the urge to roll her eyes and instead sat with a spoonful of chili in her mouth and glared at her father.

"Eleanor," he said. He only referred to her as Eleanor when he was being demonstrative.

Vixy swallowed her food. "It's okay, Dad. I know Mom is only trying to be helpful. Trying to marry me off or something. Right, Mom?"

Her mother pursed her lips. "There's blueberry pie."

"And ice cream?" said Victor.

"Vanilla," said Eleanor.

"I'll get it."

"None for me, Dad," said Vixy.

"Oh, come on, girl," said her father.

"No, Dad. I don't want to have to run it off tomorrow."

Her mother doled out the plates. "Vixy, how was it in the woods today? You said Duff got into something?"

"Yeah, dirt," said Victor.

"Well," said Vixy, "I found something. I think. A face." She got up and hurried down the hallway into her bedroom.

Victor and Eleanor listened to her rummaging through her things. Her voice boomed from down the hall, "Actually, it *was* Duff who found it."

Duff looked up at the sound of his name, blinked sleepily in Vixy's direction, lowered his head, sighed, and promptly went back to sleep.

Vixy padded back into kitchen in her slippers, clutching the pouch. "It's dirty. Let me show it to you in the living room."

"Not if it's dirty," said Eleanor.

"It's not that dirty, Mom, I just need something to set it on. Like a dish towel or something."

Eleanor untied her apron, draped it across her kitchen chair, and frowned at Vixy, then handed over her dish towel. "This will have to do. Maybe you should wait and you and your dad can look at it in the shop."

"No, Ellie, we are all going to look at it right here."

They made their way into the living room with their pie, and Victor spread the towel on the coffee table. "C'mon now, Vixy, right here."

Her mother sat in her own easy chair, put on her glasses, switched on the lamp beside her, and reached for the novel she'd been reading.

Vixy began unwrapping the face.

"Ellie." Victor bent over the object and shoved a forkful of pie into his mouth. "Don't you want to see this?"

Her mother shifted. "I can see it," she said. "You'll have to explain it to me anyway."

"It might not be anything," said Vixy. "It was getting dark, and I just wrapped it up."

Her father was looking at the piece intently. "Hmm." He picked it up and hefted it. "Heavy for its size. No corrosion. And the abalone inlays, beautifully done . . ." He tilted the face toward the firelight.

Vixy handed him a magnifier.

"It could be Haida, couldn't it?" said her father.

Vixy stood up and tugged on her pullover as if the question made her feel awkward. "Or Tlingit or Nuxalk. Or just a copy."

Her father frowned at the thing. "A good copy, then, I'd say. But the strength of that face."

"Either way," said Vixy, "it's no older than twenty-first century. Otherwise, it'd be copper and not gold. The revival artists were the ones who experimented with nontraditional materials."

"The Tlingit were farther north and inland," said her father. "And the Nuxalk straddled the Bella Coola River."

"But that's prior to the twenty-first century," said Vixy. "Remember, Dad, the tsunami picked everything up and dumped it back down again wherever. Willy-nilly. Nothing is where it should be. I can't be sure of its provenance until I get it to the lab."

"I know, I know," said her father, frowning at the thing. "It's archaeological chaos from Seattle to Saint Elias, I understand. But this is the woman in the moon. And the woman in the moon is classic Haida."

"The woman in the moon is Northwest Coast mythology in general," said Vixy, affecting a supercilious air. "Not just Haida."

Her father feigned deference, handed the object to Vixy, and slapped his knees. "You're the expert."

Vixy shrugged. "I'm just learning, Dad."

"Your father is convinced our newfound tribal ancestry is the only thing that matters about your project, Vixy," said her mother. "There's more to the past out here than the Haida, Victor, for heaven's sake."

Her father reached for his pie plate. "I need some ice cream for this." He touched his wife's arm and ambled toward the kitchen. "Me Haida, you no Haida," he said in a theatrical voice.

Vixy sat on the hearth and finished her pie. For all his clowning, she understood her father's interest in her work, how the genealogical component of the anthropology appealed to him, how it reinvigorated his already intense devotion to his carving and his sense of connection to this watery archipelago.

Victor closed the refrigerator door, sampled his ice cream, and looked around the kitchen as if he'd lost something. "A little whiskey would be good. That Kentucky mash stuff you got me, Vixy. Who wants one?"

"Rye," said Vixy.

Victor held the bottle to the light and searched the cupboards for a shot glass. "That's right."

Vixy gathered her medallion, yawning as she talked. "I've got some work to do." She padded past her father at the refrigerator, snatched the shot glass of rye he held, and made her way to her room. "Thanks for giving Duff a bath, Dad."

***

VIXY SIPPED AT HER WHISKEY, grimaced at its bracing earthiness, and settled into her desk chair, rereading her work from the night before:

What becomes of a culture when the land and resources

that have sustained it for millennia are quite literally swept away?

The so-called Big Wave, the massive tsunami that in the late twenty-second century ravaged the landscape of the Northwest Coast, scoured the Earth's mantle clean in one direction, made a slurry of the entire geological surface, then backwashed that slurry upon itself as the water retreated into the sea. What remained didn't resemble at all what was there before.

As we now know, the documented 500-year cycles of Cascadian Subduction Zone (CSZ) and megathrust fault disturbances went rogue, shattering all predictions and expectations when a full-margin, 11.2 moment magnitude (Mw) CSZ rupture with its epicenter near Seattle combined with an undersea 10.9 Mw quake to unleash hydraulic pressures capable of displacing billions of metric tons of seafloor and a likewise mindboggling magnitude of land into an upheaval best described in volumetric and kinetic terms as biblical.

Then the mile-high tidal wave arrived, crashing inland, flooding half of Washington, half of Oregon, the top tenth of California, almost the entire coast of British Columbia including Juneau in Alaska, under a half mile of seawater for an hour and under several meters of seawater for a week. It left the land saturated like a sponge for over a year.

On the other side of the northern Pacific Ocean, Japan took advantage of the tsunami's ten-hour travel time west from the CSZ to fully engage its world-class earthquake defense plan, deploying its Tsunami Bubble—an enormous polymer dome—for what it expected to be the duration of the wave, keen to emerge high and dry and otherwise apply its resources to what the nation expected to be a minor land-based infrastructure cleanup. But the intensity and duration of the seismic violence displaced the Bubble's gasket along the length of the island nation's eastern seaboard and fractured the dome itself, a piece of which carved a half-kilometer-deep, twenty-kilometer-wide, two-hundred-kilometer-long gash in the Earth before shattering under the hydraulic strain and, in layman's terms, allowing the flood to "sink" Japan. The wave, thus weakened, still contained enough kinetic energy to flood the whole of Korea and inflict damage upon the coasts of Siberia and mainland China.

Ultimately, by the time the waters had receded and the land on both sides of the North Pacific drained into something resembling arable condition, three years had passed, ten million people had lost their lives, and hundreds of millions had lost their livelihoods.

Meanwhile, as always following a disaster, humans redoubled their efforts at controlling the uncontrollable and applied untold resources into lowering the risk of such disasters in the future. Eastern Eurasia and the Northwest Coast transformed their interpretations of risk management to include, in so many words, cosmic forces. Generations passed and the psychological scarring—the legacy of individual human trauma—faded. But it was not forgotten. The story of the Big Wave transformed into legend. Legend transformed into myth.

And like many myths, it lives on as a kind of true fiction in our hearts and minds, perhaps within our collective unconscious, wielding a mysterious power that some say affects the future. It happened, we can say, because recorded history tells us so. But then again, somehow, it didn't. Because it never happened to *us*.

Hmm, she thought. Not bad. But what would Mr. Z. think? He'd tell me it didn't matter what he thought, I bet. But it sounds like something he might have written.

The door hinge squeaked—it was Duff nudging his way into her room. He shuffled across the floor to his dog bed under the window and flopped onto the cushion with a sigh.

Vixy rubbed her hands together as if conjuring her inspiration and typed.

> The islands of Haida Gwaii were likewise scraped clean by the Big Wave and its population decimated—swept away—to an extent comparable only to the colonial period, when 90 percent of the people perished from European-borne smallpox. Within another century or two after the Big Wave, they had lost their language. The Big Wave could have destroyed what remained of what it means to be Haida. Some say that it did, that the Haida are extinct, that only their ancient symbols remain. And so be it, things come and go, everything must pass. No culture is too sacred. And the symbols are not enough.

"Ugh," she said aloud. What was she trying to say? She struggled against her nagging sense of inadequacy. Who am I to be writing a book? She repeated the title to herself for what seemed the millionth time. *Never Swept Away*: *The Legacy of the Big Wave upon Haida Culture*. She still liked it. She could do this, dammit. She looked at the time. Almost midnight. The hours flew past whenever she wrote. Meanwhile, tomorrow was Sunday, and she had nothing planned. She could sleep in for once. And then write all day.

She got up and clomped drowsily into the bathroom, surrendering to the exquisite fatigue that only a vigorous day of outdoor activity—all the fresh air and sunshine—could bestow. She made perfunctory efforts at washing her face and cleaning her teeth, plunged into bed, and turned out the light.

CHAPTER 2

ISLANDS AT THE BOUNDARY OF THE WORLD

"Vixy," said her father—he spoke through her bedroom door. "*Vixy.*"

She half opened her eyes at the persistent knocking. There was light in the sky, but the sun hadn't risen. Her parents wouldn't be leaving for church service for hours yet.

"Vixy, someone's here to see you."

She sat up, leaning groggily on her elbow. "What is it?" She frowned, her thoughts jumbled. She huffed and threw the covers aside. "Just a minute. Let me put something on." She paused on her way into the bathroom. "Who the hell is it, Dad?"

But her father's voice was down the hall. "She's getting ready. It might be a minute. Make yourself comfortable."

"Good morning, Vixy," said Mr. Z. He set his coffee cup aside and addressed her with an awkward familiarity. "It's too early, I apologize. I ought to have waited."

"Nonsense, Mr. Z.," said Victor. "You're welcome anytime."

Vixy clasped her robe around her neck, confused by her clashing intuitions—she felt compelled to hug him and, at the same time, to run into her room and shut the door behind her. Instead, she bent to scratch at Duff's ears.

"It's all right, Mr. Z.," continued Victor. "You know how Vixy likes her coffee before anything else in the morning. Ellie?"

Her mother was in the kitchen, already dressed in her Sunday-morning uniform of a conservative sapphire skirt, a pink blouse, earrings, and blue flats that she liked to wear to church service, which wasn't for another hour and a half. Her imitation patent leather purse lay upon the living room end table, near the door. At the sound of her husband's voice, she tied her apron and clattered the coffee mugs onto a tray.

"Let's sit," said her father. He ushered them into the kitchen and pulled out a chair for Mr. Z. "We'll get some breakfast going. Maybe Mr. Z. hasn't had anything to eat."

"Thank you, Victor," said Mr. Z., "but please, don't go to any trouble on my account."

Vixy's father beckoned for Mr. Z. to sit. "It's no trouble, Mr. Z. No trouble at all. Is it, Ellie?"

Ellie paused, wringing her hand towel as if struggling to resolve Mr. Z.'s presence. "No, certainly not." She scurried to the refrigerator. "Vixy"—she held out a container of heavy cream—"take this."

Mr. Z. sat down and scooted his chair closer to the table carefully, as if to prevent it making a sound.

Vixy set the little carafe before Mr. Z., then frowned. "You're the only one who takes their coffee with cream, Mom." She forced herself to look Mr. Z. in the eye—her self-consciousness was making her a fool.

Mr. Z., for his part, sat quietly, keen to regard her without pretense.

Vixy retreated to her usual place at the end of the table opposite her father and clutched at the back of her chair, reluctant to sit. She watched her mother bustle toward the stove, shove a pan of bacon into the oven, set about cracking eggs, and cut a pat of butter for the pan. "Do you need any help, Mom?"

"You can get the pancake batter from the refrigerator. Put it here beside the stovetop."

Vixy obliged.

"Now go and sit down." Her mother turned her back on her, engaged the kitchen fan, and set to work.

"I bake my bacon in the oven too," said Mr. Z., seemingly glad for the noise. He took a long, careful draught from his coffee, as if to provide Vixy time to sit without being stared at.

"Because it tastes better and cooks without a mess," said Vixy's father. "Right, Ellie? As good as any radiation press. Somebody's always trying to invent the answer to time and temperature. Which is what proper cooking is, isn't it, Mr. Z.? I remember Vixy telling us how you liked to do your own cooking. But people don't want to do the work it takes. Or to take the time. In anything. Someday there'll be just a pill to swallow for everything, a button to push. As if life is a science fiction book or something."

"There have been meal pills for a thousand years, Dad," said Vixy. "And we've got a meal-maker machine."

"And that was the biggest waste of hard-earned money on my part. Ellie doesn't use it—do you, Ellie?—and I don't blame her."

Ellie turned from the oven to respond, thought better of it, and returned to her preparations.

"But I'm old and stubborn," said Victor, shrugging.

They sipped their coffees and Victor half rose from his chair to welcome his wife's platter of pancakes with both hands. "Meanwhile, Ellie knows her way around a kitchen—she was a professional chef when I met her."

Vixy's mother set a jar of maple syrup on the table and dashed back to the stovetop to stir the eggs. "A cook, Victor. I was never a chef."

Vixy cupped her hands around her coffee cup and watched her father dole out the plates and flatware. Duff plopped down beside her, his elbows clunking onto the hardwood, and she glanced discreetly at Mr. Z. He appeared the same as always. Or at least as she'd always remembered him. And why wouldn't he? What was wrong with her? Mr. Z.'s trench coat lay across the back of the living room sofa, and she used it as an opportunity to escape the table for a moment and go to the closet for a hanger. She listened to the men talking straightforwardly to each other.

"Yes," said Victor, "the weather here has been cool and clear. How about New York? Or did you come from the university?"

"No, I've come from Queens," said Mr. Z. "It was rainy. A little cold, I'd say, for this time of year."

"Right. But you didn't drive your cruiser all the way from Queens, did you?"

"No. I took a teleporter, which I never like to do."

"Hmm. Then a taxi and then the ferry?"

"That's right." Mr. Z. couldn't disguise looking a bit weary.

"That's a tough ferry ride. At night, I mean. It's been years for me, but the ocean at night, well, that's a lot of tough travel."

Vixy hung up the coat and returned to the table. Her father topped off Mr. Z.'s coffee. Her father could make anyone feel at home. And Mr. Z.? He projected the same impossibly courteous demeanor that never quite eclipsed his raffish intensity. An intensity that used to thrill her because she never quite knew what to expect from him. But now the unexpected seemed a dangerous thing.

She sipped her own coffee at length, set her cup down, and rubbed her eyes with both hands long enough and with such self-absorption that it made her father glare at her.

"Now," he said, directing his voice at Vixy so that she stopped rubbing and looked past her hands at him. "What brings you here, Mr. Z.? It's been the better part of a year and a half, hasn't it, since you and Vixy—well, since Vixy said she retired from the TDC."

"Excuse me, just a moment, Mr. Z.," said Ellie. She held out a steaming tray of scrambled eggs. "Vixy, serve the orange juice, please. And the bacon's done too." She sprang to fling open the oven and haul the sizzling pan onto the stovetop.

Soon the table was crowded with food. Vixy's mother hovered beside the table, frowning at everything and wiping her hands fretfully on a dish towel. "Oh! The maple syrup!"

"Right here, Mom," said Vixy. "And soft butter for the pancakes if anyone would like some."

Vixy's father patted the chair beside him. "Sit, Ellie." He reached for Mr. Z.'s plate and piled on food. "How about some of everything, what do you think?"

"Certainly, thank you, Victor. Mrs. Velure, this is a wonderful banquet. Pancakes, of all things. There's nothing like a hot breakfast, and I never take the trouble. Thank you."

Vixy's mother wiped her brow with the back of her hand and sat down, flushed, a moist strand of her curly graying hair pressed against her forehead. "Call me Ellie, Mr. Z.," she sighed. "Please. And none of this is any trouble—I always prepare a big breakfast on Sunday. Not that we wouldn't have gone to some trouble had we known you were, well . . ." She trailed off.

"I could've had one of those bush pilots fly you over from the mainland," said Victor. "Saved you the ferry ride at least. Hell, I could've run my jalopy over and picked you up myself."

Mr. Z. grasped his fork but checked himself when Vixy's mother closed her eyes and crossed herself, placing her hand upon her husband's.

Victor likewise closed his eyes and they prayed together aloud, "Bless our company, oh Lord, and bless this food, amen."

Mr. Z. glanced at Vixy and was touched by the expression of steadfast affection she clearly bestowed upon her parents. Then their eyes met, and her face betrayed a wary anxiousness and darkened intuition, as if she knew his presence here was somehow fraught.

Victor regarded the repast happily. "Let's eat!"

Mr. Z. waited until everyone had been served, then enjoyed a mouthful of pancakes and eggs. He was stabbing his fork into his bacon when he paused, set down his fork, and sipped from his orange juice. He swallowed before addressing Vixy's father. "Victor, you asked what brings me here. Well, as I said, I've come from Queens. From the T.E."

Vixy's father kept chewing without looking up and nodded before plunging his fork into his stack of pancakes.

Vixy's mother nibbled at her food.

Vixy gripped her fork and stared at her plate. She had yet to eat.

"I've come for help," said Mr. Z. "Vixy's help." He resisted the impulse to glance at her and focused upon her mother and father.

Vixy's mother set her fork down and regarded Vixy with concern.

Vixy shifted in her chair and shoved at the food on her plate.

"Hmm," said her father, gulping down orange juice. He concealed a belch and focused sternly upon Mr. Z. Then he glanced at Vixy. "If anyone can help you, Mr. Z., I'm sure my daughter can. Despite all she's been through."

Vixy's mother clasped her husband's hand hard enough that her knuckles whitened.

"It's okay, Ellie. Vixy can speak for herself. But Mr. Z. has come all this way, traveling all night, and I for one am very interested in how we can be of help. Tell us, Mr. Z."

"Victor," said Ellie, "maybe it's not for us to be asking."

Victor shrugged. "Top secret, Mr. Z.?"

Mr. Z. forced a smile. He had tried to anticipate this exchange. "Well—"

"I'm working," interrupted Vixy. "On my research." She cut into her pancakes as if it were an imperative. "My dissertation is due soon."

There was a silence and Victor, for his part, seemed keen to honor it. He ate quietly.

"You're writing about the deluge," said Mr. Z. finally. He glanced at Eleanor and Victor. "About the Big Wave and the Haida's heritage, I know. Under contract. Congratulations, Vixy."

Vixy tossed her hair back and squared her shoulders, trying her best to look at him as determinedly as she could. There wasn't ever going to be a day, she swore, that he couldn't make her anxious and self-conscious just by looking at her.

"I wouldn't presume to interrupt your project, Vixy," said Mr. Z. "You have no obligation to the TDC, of course. I'd never have come, in fact. It's just that, well, when I spoke to your father"—he and Victor exchanged glances—"I'll say it plainly." He folded his napkin and placed it on the tabletop. "There is trouble at Eranos."

Vixy slowly chewed.

"The entire campus was attacked. Invaded, I should say." He paused as if to measure his words. "By terrorists. Thirty-six hours ago. It was a well-organized assault. A systematic siege. Efficient. Effective. Brutal. From exactly where, we don't know. By whom, we don't know either. Not yet. Somehow, they penetrated the security force—you know how formidable it is. Nothing like the T.E.'s, of course, but there was even a new Vanguard-Seven robot on duty. Destroyed. The human force, overpowered. The Eranos employees, the handful of them on duty, were made hostages. The terrorists have locked down the buildings. They've cut off communications. They've even appropriated the airport at Lugano."

Victor and Eleanor clasped their hands together.

Vixy stared at her food, and her toe tapped silently against her chair leg. She looked down at Duff, asleep, and resisted her impulse to gather him up and flee the room. She'd tried so hard to forget that part of her life, as a time detective. Ever since coming back. Ever since almost never coming back. From Egypt. From elsewhere. She chewed her lip and forced herself to speak matter-of-factly. "You said 'brutal.' What have they done?"

"Perhaps we should speak in private," said Mr. Z.

Eleanor made to get up.

Vixy looked at her parents, met their gazes.

"It's all right, Mr. Z.," said Victor. He was addressing Vixy. "Ellie and I can leave you two to talk. Ellie, we can go on to church early, can't we? Just give us a minute or two to get ready."

"No," said Vixy. "Dad. Mom. I want you here."

Mr. Z. looked hard at her, seemed to sense her resolve and her vulnerability. "That's fine. You should know that I'm here unofficially, Vixy." He took an affected breath and fiddled with his fork, fumbled with the food on his plate. "I've already broken . . . well, the captain—"

"You've already broken protocol," said Vixy. "And the captain doesn't know you're here."

Mr. Z.'s eyes glinted with veiled affection at her sharp tone, and he nodded gracefully, as if relieved to encounter something of the Vixy of old.

"What do they want?" she said. "These terrorists. Something ridiculous, I assume. And symbolic."

"Money," said Mr. Z. "Everything in the Bank of Zurich. All its global and off-planet holdings. Trillions of dollars, what have you." He shook his head.

"They're just thieves?" said Vixy. "Then why Eranos? If you're going to rob a bank, why not just rob it?" She scowled. "You don't believe they're just looking for money, do you, Mr. Z.?" Then she dismissed the whole idea in a huff. "Who cares? Eranos, the Bank of Zurich, what's the difference? Murderers, crooks, tyrants. It goes on. Everywhere. All the time."

"Vixy!" hissed her mother. She glanced at Mr. Z.

Vixy was unperturbed.

"This group," said Mr. Z., "they've killed twelve of fourteen people at Eranos. Including the entire security force."

Vixy remained silent, seemingly tempered but brooding. "I don't get it. What does the TDC have to do with it? And what the hell can I do?"

"It's Laron," said Mr. Z., and waited, his eyes upon her. "Émile Laron is the leader."

"Oh my God," said her mother, covering her mouth. "Victor. Vixy can't . . . she's been through enough—"

"Let them talk it out, Ellie," interrupted Victor. "Let Mr. Z. finish what he's come all this way to say." He looked hard at Vixy. "Go ahead, Mr. Z."

"Émile Laron has issued a ransom for the entire campus of Eranos. He's threatened to kill the two hostages and destroy the paintings, sculptures, library books, and objet d'arts piece by piece until he gets what he wants."

"What about the IMC?" said Vixy. "They've put a lot of money into Eranos. And they have plenty of resources beyond that. A peace-keeping military, even. Haven't they?" She struggled to temper the anxiety in her voice. It was as if this conversation and Mr. Z.'s visit were suddenly costing her far too much. "What does the TDC have to do with it? Where's the time crime?" Duff nudged at her arm with his wet nose and looked up at her, his innocent expression making every-thing seem even more maddening. "What does it have to do with *me*?"

Mr. Z. tapped his finger noiselessly on the table. This discord,

Vixy's anxiety—he'd anticipated her reticence. He knew she'd struggled since the HDT event out of Egypt, that she had refused the TDC's routine psychiatric help and instead sought refuge here, in Old Massett. Insisted upon quitting the contingent, even upon the cusp of being granted full-time detective status. Post-traumatic stress disorder, perhaps.[7] Or heightened GAD.[8] He understood. In his way, at least. Nevertheless, he needed her help, needed her resourcefulness and resilience. He needed someone he could trust and rely upon. He needed her experience. But perhaps it was too much to ask. He glanced discreetly at everyone, aware of Victor's protective pride of his daughter and Eleanor's fraught concern. He watched Duff nudging at Vixy's elbow, felt himself diminished by the dog's untrammeled devotion. He should not have come.

"I'd left Neutic behind at Eranos when I went for you," he said. "In Egypt. And it so happens that after the Olympic Theater attack, the T.E. expedited their search for a new location, and they assigned Neutic the task of researching the logistics, seeing as he'd become familiar with the place. Eranos itself was the front-runner for the next T.E. deployment, as you probably remember. Anyway, we don't know exactly what happened except that Neutic was there, on duty, when the terrorists struck. He attempted to resist the siege—he transmitted from inside one of the campus buildings when the terrorists moved in, just before they managed to sever communications. He apparently was holding a couple of them at bay, holding out until Laron himself detonated a high-explosive grenade on the grounds and Neutic . . ." Mr. Z. paused as if collecting himself.

"What, Mr. Z.?" murmured Vixy. "What happened?"

"The T.E. had a reconnaissance drone circling the campus. At least before Laron and his thugs managed to shoot it down. And

---

7   Post-traumatic stress disorder (PTSD) symptoms are generally grouped into four types: intrusive memories, avoidance, negative changes in thinking and mood, and changes in physical and emotional reactions. Symptoms can vary over time or vary from person to person.

8   General anxiety disorder.

believe me, it makes zero intuitive sense that Laron, given what we know about him, is anything but a lackey for what I assume are Scarab Club operatives. And motives. But we've heard nothing from anyone other than Laron himself since."

"Nothing from mister Neutic?" said Ellie.

"Video shows Neutic drawing Laron away from the campus. Dodging the rounds. And firing back, waiting until Laron himself came after him. Neutic could've perhaps escaped. But he must have been using himself as bait. It worked. Laron pursued him into the open. We couldn't do anything. Nobody at the TDC, nobody at the T.E. could get through in time. All we could do was trace them into the mountains. Then we detected an HDT tremor and we lost them. Thereafter, well, there has been nothing from Eranos. Except . . ."

Vixy went to the kitchen sink and stood over it. "Except what? Laron is alive, then. And what about Neutic? What do you think happened to him? Is anyone trying to find him, to help him?"

"He must still be alive. He's not in possession of his device, we can't verify proof of life. Neither the T.E. nor the TDC has yet deployed anyone—"

Eleanor rose from her chair and hurried into the kitchen. She grasped Vixy's hand.

Vixy hung her head. "What are they waiting for? I still don't see what it has to do with me. I can't help even if I wanted to. Even if I still wanted to be a time detective."

Mr. Z. stared into his plate and pushed it away. "Laron wants you."

Vixy laughed ruefully. "What?"

The sky had brightened outside the kitchen windows, but now a dreadful pall settled upon the room.

Mr. Z. stood up. "Laron is asking for you in exchange for Neutic. In exchange for Neutic's life."

CHAPTER 3

BLOOD EYE

Neutic huddled breathlessly against the iron stanchion of the narrow, swaying footbridge, mustering his courage. Should he cross? The forest towered on either side of the roaring, tumultuous river, almost to the edge of the craggy banks. His foot slipped—damn street shoes!—and he clutched at the support cable that disappeared into the trees across the swollen, riotous torrent.

"Stop behaving like a fool!" Laron yelled, but his voice was weak and far away, smothered by the cacophony. "You have nowhere to run!"

Perspiration trickled from Neutic's nose and chin, and he shivered despite the springtime sun upon his back—such was the frigid rawness cast up by a river full of glacial melt. Cross the bridge. Or don't, dammit, and keep running. Where? Higher up the mountainside? Into the trees behind him? Back down, in the direction of Laron himself? He'd been a fool to think he could draw Laron off for any length of time. A fool, too, to think he'd somehow survive. If only he still had his pistol.

He shuffled warily forward. The thin slats of the bridge swayed and pitched with each shift of his weight. He made it only halfway when he dropped to his knees to steady himself. He glanced back, glimpsed Laron's glide-pad some fifty meters downriver—the man was hugging the rocky bank, probably desperate to stay out of the trees. But the machine careened back and forth, pitching and rolling with Laron wrenching at the controls—he seemed unable to negotiate the swirling clash of atmospheres over the water and the rocks.

One of Laron's thugs emerged from the trees beyond, breathing hard and swiping at his face. The man smirked when he saw Neutic struggling.

Laron, meanwhile, had managed to ground his glide-pad upon a flat-surfaced boulder. When he saw Neutic watching him he shrugged, feigning exasperation, gripping the pad's handlebar with one hand and gesturing with his plasma pistol with the other. He shouted, "Are you quite satisfied, Mr. Neutic? Trying to be a hero? You have no weapon! Now, come down from there! Stop being ridiculous! I will let you live!"

Neutic shifted his weight, the bridge swayed, and he nearly fell. Laron's man on the other side—a blocky, brutish hulk with the posture of an ape and apparently as agile—stomped toward him heedlessly, a maniacal smile on his face as he yanked at the cables, apparently enjoying every stomach-churning tilt and sway of the bridge.

Neutic gathered himself and ducked beneath the cable, clinging to it, his body poised half over the water. He stared down.

"No!" shouted Laron. "Don't!"

Laron's plea snuffed out when Neutic let go. He struck the frigid water and hurtled downriver like some hapless, floundering fish. The cold was shocking—it took his breath away and he panicked. His body grazed rocks, boulders. He flailed but couldn't right himself, had no sense of the surface. His lungs were on fire, he gulped water, slammed against something hard, felt his strength vanish and the water engulf him. He was blacking out. Finished. Hettie's face. Hettie! She reached out to him as if in a dream. Hettie! She drifted away from him, arms outstretched, her expression fraught, and he knew that he would die.

"THAT'S ABSOLUTELY CORRECT, CAPTAIN," SAID Laron. "It's about time you took me seriously."

"We'll see," said the captain. "It's a ridiculous sum. You're a fool to think you can extort that kind of money even if we had access to it—"

"You have twenty-four hours," interrupted Laron. "After that, each hour of delay will cost you—will cost the world—at least one artifact from this charming campus. Hell, it will cost you and the world several artifacts each and every time I feel you are trying to drag your feet and manipulate me. Perhaps I ought to add another hostage to the list of precious casualties? Would that prevent your stalling?" With his elbows on the tabletop, Laron lowered his head and began to rub his boney skull with both hands. He reached for his cigarette, and his long fingers quivered over his narrow lips as the tip glowed red. "Now," he said, exhaling with an exhausted effort. "Regarding the exchange for Mr. Neutic."

"But, Boss, what are you talking about? We lost him."

Laron snapped his hand over the receiver and struggled to locate the mute button. He poked at it with a frustrated flourish and spun in his chair, his eyes bulging behind his shiny beak of a nose. "Shut up, Shields!" He turned his back on his hapless assistant. "Shut your stupid mouth before you single-handedly ruin everything! Dead or alive or on the goddamn fucking moon, it doesn't matter who or what or where that worthless shit of a time detective cadet managed to—" Laron cut himself short. "I've told you. We have only so much time. When the T.E. and the TDC and whomever else realize their precious Neutic is indeed dead—they'll have a reading on his biomass soon enough, I'm sure—they'll call our bluff, won't they?" Laron paused to regain his composure. "And there is not a worthless relic in this stinking mausoleum that will bring Vixy Velure to me like that man could have. He was what you call a high-value target, do you understand?"

Shields rolled his eyes, cracked his knuckles, and flopped onto the couch. "You're the boss. But we've still got those two other hostages tied up in the kitchen. High value or not." He toyed with the ivory charms that comprised the centerpiece of the low table before him, holding one close to his face with thick-fingered, grubby hands and peering at it with a disgruntled expression as he sipped from a bottle of beer. He smacked his lips and scowled at the taste. "You said this was supposed to be beer! It tastes like, I don't know what. Like piss!"

Laron, disgusted, returned his attention to the control panel. "You would know. Now shut up." He pressed the mute button and removed his hand from the receiver, affecting a lilting, smart-aleck cheerfulness. "Captain? Are you still there? I am terribly sorry, there must have been some interference. I was saying, regarding the exchange—"

"What exchange?" said the captain. There was venom in his voice. "What kind of beasts do you take us for, that we'd agree to such a thing?"

"Beasts," said Laron. He reached across the table to tap the ash from his cigarette. The ashtray itself seemed to catch his attention and he picked it up, squinting at the details. It was in the image of a serpent with a lion's head coiled around what appeared to be a winged goddess of some type. He set it down with a clunk. "Vixy Velure for Herman Neutic. That's all. Along with the money, of course. Those are the conditions."

There was a pause.

"Do you hear?" said Laron. "Don't think I'm not capable of—"

"I don't care what you think you're capable of. You can't bully us into anything."

Laron jabbed at the control panel and the hologram camera flickered to life, projecting the image of the captain into the room.

Shields sat blinking at it.

"Well then," said Laron. He snatched at the ashtray, produced a claw hammer from his overstuffed duffel, and proceeded to flail at the object, smashing it into the tabletop, bits of ceramic flying about. He tossed the hammer aside and made a demonstration of brushing the debris from his shirt front.

"Jeezus!" said Shields. He ducked away with his knees up and his arm covering his face. "Boss, what the hell?!"

Laron looked about wildly, spied the ivory figurines on the tabletop, and raised the hammer again.

Shields cowered.

Wham! Wham! Wham! One by one, Laron pulverized the ivory figurines upon the tabletop, gouging hideous dents into its polished wooden surface. Finished, he gloated for a moment, then tossed the hammer on top of the mess.

"We've only just begun here, Captain," he said, wiping his hands. His face was gaunt and bloodless except for his pinkish, glistening eyes. They were red-rimmed, almost throbbing with a facinorous enmity—eyes that seemed to consume his entire bodily ration of hemoglobin.

Shields sat up, warming to the lusty, debased shamelessness of it all. He snatched at the hammer himself and looked avidly about the room.

Laron waggled his finger at Shields and rested his feet, muddy hiking shoes and all, upon the console. "Now, Captain. Shall we continue?" He lit a cigarette, inhaled deeply, and talked impudently through the exhaled smoke. "Or shall I gather my worker bees and proceed with more gusto on behalf of our remodeling?" He gave Shields a knowing glance to keep him quiet.

The captain waited.

"No?" said Laron. "No response, Captain? Playing the tough guy, as usual, are you? All that army experience you've been keen to apply to your big civy job there at the mighty TDC?"

"Vixy Velure is no longer part of the TDC cadet program," said the captain. "She is a private citizen. I am happy to admit that I don't even know where she is."

"Liar," said Laron. "*You are a liar!* I know for a fact that the TDC can locate Miss Velure in a heartbeat, private citizen or otherwise. And it would not surprise me if she were indeed sitting right there beside you."

"Believe whatever you want, Laron. You know you can't hope to get away with any of this. Not the murders, not the taking of hostages, not the money. Extortion at this level—you've merely doomed yourself and your cronies to imprisonment or death. You can't think we won't wait you out. We'll starve you out if nothing else. The TDC and the T.E. deal with terrorist scum like you every day of the week."

Laron puffed his cigarette and spoke to the ceiling. "This is all so . . . exhausting. *You*, sir, are tiring. I am not some uneducated, desperate sociopath. I am not an amateur. Neither am I without the means to render my continued existence a happy one. You have no idea, Captain, how overmatched you and the T.E. actually are. And this isn't a debate. It is a declaration. You are being a wicked, unreasonably bad man. And you have underestimated me. Well, then. Let's move on. I have a surprise for you. You'll see. Twenty-*three* hours, tick, tick, tick. Because you have chosen to waste this past one. Get me the money. And get me Vixy Velure. Or else." He jabbed at the console, and the hologram of the captain vanished.

CHAPTER 4

SEA BEAR

"My God, Z," said the captain, "Rosa de Cosmos. And her husband, Nick. I knew them both. You knew them, Z. Vixy, you too. Murdered. It's unthinkable. If I'd known Laron was capable of it, I never would've allowed him any leeway, any room to move." He pounded his fist on the table. "I would've called in a strike force and leveled the place! Goddamn Eranos and its priceless archives to hell! I'd have pulled the trigger myself, blown it all to bits, blown that evil bastard coward sky high!"

Mr. Z. and Vixy stared blankly at the transponder.

"What about the son?" said Vixy. "Nick II."

"Safe at home," said the captain. "He was in transit, on his way to work at Eranos when the compound and the airport were invaded. We got to him, thank God. Though if it were me, I don't know how a young man is supposed to live through such a thing. Losing his mother and father? I swear, I don't know."

"Indeed," said Mr. Z.

Vixy got up from her seat across from Mr. Z. and ambled toward the water. She slumped onto the gravel beach and contemplated the purplish clouds stretched against the orangey, setting sun. Masset Inlet seemed dark and swollen and restless. And the dimming sky close enough to touch.

This was when she most loved this place. At days end. She cherished the mornings and embraced the afternoons, but she loved the evenings, which were painterly like nowhere else she'd ever been and evoked everything that meant most to her. The sea and sky. The rich forests. The memories of her childhood. The birds and beasts that still roamed the woods, swam in the waters, and flew overhead. Whales— minke and humpback. Orca. Porpoises. Seals. River otters. Black bear. Falcons, petrels, owls, woodpeckers, jays, eagles, oyster catchers, and cormorants. And of course, the ravens. Even the spooky bats flitting and chirping overhead. She sighed at the fleeting sense of everything, at the powerful mythic sense of her special island life. How could she ever again consider leaving?

She snatched at a pebble and flung it down the length of the shoreline. In the distance a raven soared over the surf and in a behavior peculiar to the species, tucked its wings and flopped upside down in midair, plunging toward the water as if it had perished in midflight. It was no surprise to Vixy when, just as it seemed doomed to crash headlong into the sea, it righted itself, outstretched its wings, and swept low toward the gravelly beach. It strutted amongst the pebbles and tilted its head this way and that. Trickster. Thief. Blindly self-important. Lusty, impatient, insatiable. Creator of the land and sea. Bringer of the sun, moon, and fire. Discoverer of humanity. Few animals so embodied their mythic attributes. She envied its self-possessed indifference and blithe, transformative courage.

"Goodbye, sir," she heard Mr. Z. say. He was strolling toward her, one hand digging into his pocket and the other carrying her vest. Something about him seemed uncharacteristically awkward and dark.

"What's is it?" said Vixy. "What's happening?"

"They can't get to the bodies," he murmured. "Nick and Rosa. It's despicable. Reconnaissance images confirm they've been left hanging. By their ankles, for heaven's sake. From the Yggdrasil Ash, of all things."

"My God." The so-called Yggdrasil Ash was the enormous, beloved tree near the center of the campus. Vixy hugged her knees at the horror of the image and stared into the distance. The sound of the sea lapping against the pebbly shore, so familiar, struck her now as strangely troubling—an unintelligible yet evocative language.

Mr. Z. watched Vixy watching the water. How could he be doing this to her? Bringing horror to this tranquil place, her island home, her refuge? He glanced up at the tortured skeleton of the shipwreck half buried in the gravel. It had resided here for he didn't know how long. Vixy never seemed to notice it. Neither did Victor or Eleanor, for that matter. To the locals it was a commonplace landmark, something that endured the tides and witnessed the sun and the moon and the passing of the seasons as if it were a natural thing and not a manifestation of man. And perhaps his hubris. He suddenly felt like an intruder. He handed Vixy her vest.

"Thanks." She zipped it up greedily and pulled her legs farther against her chest, then rested her chin upon her knees.

He sat down beside her, and they stared past the bay.

"The axis of the world," said Vixy.

"Hmm? Oh, Yggdrasil, yes." Mr. Z. gnawed his lip at what had to have been Laron's intentionally vicious irony.

"It's the place of the thingstead," she said, never taking her eyes off the water. "Where the Nordic clans met. Where they balanced the injuries against their dead and mutilated relatives."

It struck Mr. Z. that she was reciting something from one of his classroom lectures. "That's right."

"And it *is* despicable," she said, "what's happening at Eranos. Unimaginable. And it's just like Laron to make it even more so by insulting the mythology."

The raven, which Mr. Z. had not noticed before, beat its wings once, twice, and lifted itself heavily from the beach before flapping and drifting off like a dark spirit into the trees. He watched Vixy watching the bird. She's as pretty as ever, he thought. Womanly now too. Her prickly self-consciousness and bravado things of the past. He had to admit that perhaps he had no right to behave as if he really knew her anymore. Yet he recognized her willful expression, her look of determined confidence, that flash of unpredictable obstinacy that endeared her to him. He had no heart to place her in harm's way ever again. "Vixy," he said.

But she interrupted him. "I bet you're surprised I remembered something from class." A clever grin flashed across her face, then a shadow too, and she lowered her eyes. She ran her manicured hands over her thighs, curled them into loose fists, then shoved them into the pockets of her vest, hunching her shoulders against the clammy damp that seemed to rise from the beach. The gentle neap tide had ebbed, and Vixy sought the moon through the treetops. Her longing made her feel sullen. No, not sullen. Unsettled. Anxious.

Soon the sky would be swimming with stars. But the stars themselves would be fraught. For out there somewhere was the Great Conflict. That other nightmare. A war of worlds. Space and time and life itself were always fraught, weren't they? Always besieged. There seemed no place for peace, not even here. She sensed the ground beneath her feet, listened to the water caress the shore, inhaled the briny ocean breeze, and embraced with her whole heart this place that was her home. "Among the Haida we have our own version of the axis mundi. And Ttsaamuus—Snag—he guards it."[9]

"It's the original house pole too," said Mr. Z.; "Snag's stone post at the bottom of the sea."

"I love it here, you know? It saved me. I don't understand how I could ever have left it." To Mr. Z. she seemed self-possessed and vulnerable and brave.

"Vixy."

"My mother gave me this years ago," she continued, "when I graduated from high school." She withdrew a slender silver necklace from beneath the collar of her blouse. On it hung a tiny black carving, which she displayed upon the back of her hand.

"Argillite," said Mr. Z., squinting at it. "Sea Bear?"

---

9   Among the Haida, Snag is an alternative form of Taangghwanlaana, the One in the Sea, and is also intimately associated with Sea Wolf, Sea Bear, and Beaver. In Haida sculpture, Raven is a close relation and Snag below and Raven on top is a common arrangement on Haida poles. Cheryl Shearar, *Understanding Northwest Coast Art: A Guide to Crests, Beings and Symbols* (Vancouver: Douglas & McIntyre, 2000), 98.

Vixy nodded. "I never used to wear it. As a kid, you know. I thought it was silly. Haida heritage, Indigenous culture, and all that. It seemed old-fashioned. Something that would hold me back. I don't know. It's strange how we are when we're young, isn't it?" She laughed softly. "As if I have to tell you, being a teacher and all. Anyway, I read up on it. The mythology. How Snag and Sea Bear, they're akin to each other. I've read up on a lot of things, lately, I guess." She trailed off.

"It's a fine charm, Vixy," said Mr. Z. "And it's fine too, you know, more than fine, that you want to stay here. For your work. Well, for everything."

Vixy slipped the necklace back under her blouse. "They say that to wear a Snag motif indicates an acceptance of responsibility." She looked to the horizon. "Responsibility for supporting the world."

Responsibility for supporting the world, thought Mr. Z. He felt a pang in his heart. She would thrive here in her new life. Her future was here. "I'm sorry I came, Vixy." He stood up, and his shoes grated upon the gravel. He shoved his hands into his pockets.

She looked up at him, her eyes glistening in the failing light. "No. I'm glad you came. I was afraid at first. But you had to come, I know." She likewise stood and zipped her vest all the way to her chin. She folded her arms and shivered once against the chill air. Then she turned to Mr. Z. and cleared her throat quietly. "Tell the captain I want to help. Tell him I'm ready."

CHAPTER 5

INTO THE VALLEY

THE CARGO-BAY DOOR OF THE stealth transport dropped away. The whine of the jet engines became a roar, and a chill wind blasted into the fuselage. The jumpmaster corporal, bathed in green light, dropped to his knees at the platform's edge, grasped the handhold, and peered steadfastly down into the gaping night.

Vixy's stomach churned, and she glanced at Mr. Z. He winked at her and adjusted his oxygen mask nonchalantly, as if they were exiting a cab on a city street and not about to jump out of a plane at an altitude of 10,670 meters.[10]

The jumpmaster raised his free hand above his head and communicated the thumbs-up.

Vixy gulped. Thumbs-up meant stand by. She grasped her oxygen manifold coupling with one hand and snapped her visor closed with the other, shifting her weight. A goddamn old-fashioned nighttime HAHO[11] jump. She focused hard upon the jumpmaster's upraised arm. He glanced at his altimeter, geodata readout, and chronometer,

---

10   Approximately 35,000 feet.

11   High Altitude High Opening: military low-signature (clandestine) infiltration parachuting terminology that describes canopy deployment at altitudes up to 8,230 meters (27,000 feet) and distances 30 miles or more

brought his hand to his chest, and finally thrust his arm straight out, gesturing emphatically at the open bay door once, twice, three times. GO, GO, GO!

Vixy's adrenaline surged and she yanked herself free from the oxygen manifold. She breathed deeply to verify flow from her canister and waddled to the edge of the platform, her kit bag wedged awkwardly between her legs. The jumpmaster nodded, then she stepped forward and plunged into the night. The plane vanished behind her and she tumbled earthward, orienting herself against the wind from below and her view of the vivid moon. Thank God for a clear sky! Because now she was even more convinced that freefalling on instruments alone would have been the death of her.

She peered at her altimeter and counted down—the counting kept her nerves at bay if nothing else. That, and she'd never trust her automated ripcord release.

Eight thousand two hundred thirty meters, eight thousand two hundred thirty meters, eight thousand two hundred thirty meters. She repeated it like a mantra because she had to. To keep from pulling her ripcord early, let alone late.

She looked skyward, searching desperately—there! Mr. Z., thank fucking God! He was diving, using his shoulders like rudders. He hurtled past her—as navigator he'd lead them to the target. Mr. Z. leveled out just below and away, and she glued her eyes to her altimeter. Rip cord at 8,230 meters . . . PULL!

Her chute pack emptied, the harness straps dug deeply into her flesh, and she endured the hard deceleration. She reached for her chute toggles and spied Mr. Z.'s canopy below, its taut fabric gleaming in the bright moonlight.

They drifted into the dark valley and Vixy worked to align herself with Mr. Z.'s flight path. Easy does it—stay clear of his turbulence! She reflexively glanced at her altimeter and remembered to check

---

from the target with the objective of eliminating detection of aircraft or personnel from the ground.

her navigation system. Fifty kilometers to target, south by southwest. Just be patient, goddammit. Just follow Mr. Z. . . .

And maintain radio silence. Émile Laron, for all his bungling incompetence, had managed to establish a formidable HDHS[12] net. And now it was all about risk minimization—getting in without being seen. Hence, this archaic style of infiltration.

Mr. Z.'s navigation system was programmed to cut out automatically in—she checked her altimeter again—two thousand meters. After that, he'd be on mag-lenses and a manual topo map, heaven help them both. She was glad the responsibility was his.

They soared through the valley, down, down, down, and she felt herself relax a bit, getting the pace of the descent, the responsiveness of her controls, and the reliability of their trajectory. She began to discern the emerging geography. The Alps—breathtaking, and unearthly in the moonlight. Like the stomping grounds of the gods. She suddenly longed to stay aloft forever, to fly amongst the miraculous peaks and never endure life upon the fraught surface of the Earth again.

Her altimeter pulsed. Five thousand meters, four thousand, three, two, one hundred fifty meters. Jettison the kit bag! The ground suddenly rushed toward her. She saw Mr. Z. touch down—stay clear of his canopy! Brake hard, brake hard, pull, pull, pull—touching down . . . now!

"Argh!" She came down awkwardly upon her ankle, turned it, and stumbled. The wind filled her canopy, and she toppled—"Oof!"— and got hauled overland on her backside. Release! Release! God, she was jammed in the rocks, goddammit!

She snatched her knife from her thigh sheath and slashed desperately at one riser, then the other. She tumbled fitfully to a stop and tore her mask away. She lay panting, her heart pounding, afraid to move. Was she injured? How badly? She felt battered and bruised but no sharp pains. Nothing seemed broken.

---

12 Hyperdimensional hyperspectral (HDHS). Referring to the propagation of the electromagnetic energy spectrum into hyper-dimensional physics. See glossary.

She looked downwind and saw Mr. Z. working hard to gather up her loose canopy.

She disconnected her harness, stripped it off. She waited for Mr. Z. to approach with the wadded-up chute and addressed his look of concern.

"I'm fine. I'm okay." She snatched the canopy from him, shoved it under her arm, and started hauling in her kit bag. "Just a rough ride at the end, that's all. Thanks for getting my chute."

Mr. Z. was breathing hard. "What about your ankle? You're limping."

"I landed on it a little bit. And then my releases jammed. But I'm okay."

Mr. Z. toggled his night vision and scanned the landscape behind him. He pointed. "Let's muster at that outcropping. Thirty meters out, or so. See it?"

"Yes."

They stowed their kit bags, doing their best to hide them under the rockface, and flopped down side by side. Mr. Z. yanked off his helmet and peered at the transponder strapped to his wrist, his eyes darting from the display to a point in the distance. "We're on target and on time. Sunrise at Eranos in two hours. Here in the mountains, it won't happen for another three or so." He stuffed his helmet out of sight alongside his kit bag.

Vixy hefted her pack, careful of her bruised backside. "It doesn't get any more nerve-racking than that. Not for me. They can keep their damn nighttime HAHO bullshit." She snugged her pack straps gingerly and looked around. "And I still can't believe Laron was capable of maintaining an HDHS net this far from Eranos. All the scanners and data processing required, to say nothing of the maintenance—it's not like he has a team of technicians at hand. This Scarab Cult or whatever he belongs to—how are they acquiring the technology? Where in hell were Bruggs and Laron getting the funding and the technology in the first place? Not from selling Egyptian antiquities." She tore off her helmet and ran her hands through her hair.

"Hmm, yes," said Mr. Z. "The Scarab Cult." He hefted his plasma pistol, ejected the cartridge, squinted at it, shoved it back into the magazine, and toggled the safety. He shoved the weapon into his body holster. Then he yanked at his survival knife, hefted it, and returned it to its sheath. "It seems like all we can do to keep up with the next threat."

Vixy pursed her lips and looked out. "Which way?"

Mr. Z. checked his transponder and gestured into distance. "That way." He led them from the outcropping, and they trudged along wordlessly for perhaps a quarter mile, pausing at the top of a steep hiker's trail. "At the bottom we'll head north, traverse the moraine, and make our way into the mountains. We ought to be over the pass before nightfall with Ticino[13] at our feet."

---

13   Ticino is Switzerland's Italian-speaking canton situated south of the Alps. The areas around its two lakes, Lago di Lugano and Lago Maggiore, enjoy a Mediterranean climate where palms and citrus trees grow, figs, olives, and vineyards are cultivated, and other subtropical vegetation flourishes.

CHAPTER 6

UNGUARDED MOMENT

Neutic shivered himself awake with his head pounding and the sun blazing in his face. What was he doing sprawled upon this patch of mud? With torn clothing? Beside a roaring river? And amid these huge, fractured boulders? He felt groggy. His bones ached. And he was goddamn freezing.

"Argh." He gathered himself and sat up stiffly. Sunlight warmed the mucky, stony washout where he lay, but frigid air poured from the river. He squinted at the sky—the angle of the sun seemed to indicate something like midmorning. But where was he?

The woods on both sides of the river were dense, and the gnarled tree trunks abutted the stony shoulders of the riverbank as if the water had split the land like a seam. "How long have I been laying here?" He looked around. "Ouch," he said, clutching at his neck. He groped at the back of his head, following the soreness until he found the tender, swollen welt. He checked for blood on his fingertips. Nothing.

A scene thrust itself upon him. That crazily precarious bridge. The roaring river below and the icy air uprushing. Laron and his brutish lackey. He himself had jumped. But then what? He shivered uncontrollably now, teeth chattering. Get warm. Get away from this damn water, goddammit.

He scrambled over the craggy rocks, finally arriving at a grassy berm some fifteen or twenty meters from the river, where the air was distinctly warmer. He flopped onto his back and turned his face toward the light and heat, absorbed the warmth on his back from the grassy earth.

His shirt and pants were tattered in places but mostly dry. How he escaped the river was beyond him. He must have somehow drug himself from it. Or been thrown clear and then collapsed. It had been late afternoon when he was running from Laron. That meant he'd spent the night and the better part of the morning unconscious. Shit. No shoes. He stared at his whitish, naked foot, and the other adorned with the ragged remains of his sock. He patted his pants pocket for his device and discovered the fabric hanging open, torn from his thigh. Of course. He'd lost it. Then a wave of panic. No way to know where he could be besides downriver. But how far downriver? And where did the river even lead to?

Stop panicking. Think, for fuck's sake. How far could the river have possibly carried him? He strained to stand and looked up through the trees—the snowy peaks of the mountains were there, high above. Not that he'd recognize one peak from the other. Nothing looked familiar. Of course it didn't. Just the roaring goddamn river and the trees and the mountains and the fucking blue sky. He was lost. Lost!

His composure promptly fled, and he scrambled up as if possessed, compelled to run upriver, back to wherever he'd come from, to find someplace he could recognize. He hurried through the grass, leapt over a boulder, struggled over another, stumbled, then changed his mind. The effort of scrambling amongst the shattered rocks alone was impossible. He peered into the trees. Yes, through the woods might be easier. He dashed toward the trees—a forest of pines—and stopped again, breathless. There were obstacles of all sorts. Namely, besides the dense woods themselves, there were fallen trunks and deep depressions heavy with brush. In short, no clear way through any of it. He was trapped and lost. Lost!

He was panicking. Just like in all the stories of all the fool people who got themselves lost. But he couldn't help feeling breathless. His breathing was the only sound in the woods, in fact. He glanced toward the river. "I *am* lost," he said aloud. "Completely lost. And running will only get me more lost." That was the wisdom. He'd spent time in the woods back home. If you ever got lost, everyone understood, stay put. Then people can find you. You have to resist the compulsion to run and find your own way out. Or back. There is no going back. The river could've carried him, well, he had no idea how far it could have carried him. He gritted his teeth. Stay where you are. Wait it out. Wait to be found.

But this was different than getting lost in the woods close to home or near some trail in a national park. This was no camping trip. This was the middle of nowhere. Pure wilderness. There was no one to help him.

Besides Mr. Z. and the captain. Yes, of course the TDC would look for him. Eventually. Meanwhile, night would fall. The temperature would drop. A killing cold, perhaps. He was screwed. By the time anyone at the TDC would look for him, let alone find him, he could die of exposure. He needed shelter.

The idea of spending the night in these woods terrified him. He made his way back into the sunlight, compelled to abide for a time in the open space between the trees and the river. He blinked at the sun and took stock, trying to see something, anything at all that would suggest . . . anything. He either had to keep moving, or he had to construct some sort of shelter. A lean-to if nothing else. He'd need branches and . . . he couldn't think.

Stay warm, first off. He could stay warm by moving. But where to? He couldn't stay here, could he? He couldn't cross the damn river either, and why would he? What else could he do? Upriver seemed pointless. Downriver, then. It would be difficult, but not impossible, to make his way as far as he could. But it seemed like it was late enough in the afternoon that he ought to commit to building a lean-to. Or commit to somehow getting to open country.

That was it! There are clearings beyond these trees, perhaps. Maybe a valley. He had to get farther from the mountains. The river, by God, he could follow the river down. Because rivers goddamn flow down from the mountains. Into valleys. Into frigging towns and cities.

Screw the lean-to idea for now. Stick to the fucking river. Follow it down for as long as seems reasonable. Until . . . he didn't know—until he was too tired to go on. Or he had to fucking stop and bivouac and the night came and he lost his fucking mind. Just go!

Easier said than done. The terrain was vexingly erratic. The shore was a jumble of broken and shattered boulders, sharped-edged gravel, and spiny, ragged tree stumps. The forest? Dark. Cold. Impossibly dense. He convinced himself it was the riverbank, or perhaps the edge of the forest if that proved easier—he would have to try both, perhaps. He might be a fool to move. He might be guaranteeing that he'd die out here. He was going against all the wisdom, all the advice. So be it.

<hr>

He'd been struggling along just clear of the riverbank for what seemed hours, sweating, agonizing at the pain in every limb—it was if he'd careened against every rock in the river before it spit him onto shore like a cherry pit. You're alive, he told himself. Nothing broken. Quit whining.

Nevertheless, his lack of progress was maddening—it was all he could do to keep from gouging the soles of his feet on practically every pebble, pine cone, twig, or gnarly root. He scrambled toward a smooth rock that hung low over the river and dangled his aggravated feet in the icy water. The irony of it—enduring near hypothermia one moment then dehydration and heat stress the next. He was a blistered, shoeless, sweaty mess. He sprawled upon the rock and splashed the frigid water onto his face and neck. He drank too, damning the risk of the water being contaminated with God knows what.

He tried again to gain his bearings, peering into the trees for any sign of a clearing. None. He tried to ascertain the movement of the sun across the sky. He ought to be capable of discerning something of his compass directions. Think now, goddammit. The sun was setting, but it hardly set directly west, especially in the spring. Dammit, if he had his device, he would simply bring up a map. And what would he see? He tried to imagine the map. He knew the Alps ran more or less east and west across the continent. The sun was setting more or less in the west. Eranos was more or less to the south. Mountain rivers upon this side of the Alps, then, would flow toward it, roughly to the south. What else could be the source of Lake Maggiore, for instance, but snow melt from the mountains?

He guessed he'd been moving west, then, and this river would likely as hell be meandering in a southerly direction.

His stomach growled. And to say his energy was flagging was an understatement. He ought to begin constructing some sort of shelter because it would likely take him hours. Oh, Hettie. I'm tired. And lost. No food, no shelter. Visions of himself huddled dead amongst the rocks or somewhere under the trees assailed him. His body, picked apart by wolves and buzzards and he didn't know what. Were there wolves in the Alps? Or buzzards? What about bears?

What did it matter? He'd die here, lost like the ignorant, citified fool that he was, never having tracked down Hettie's murderers, failing to do anything to avenge her death. "I'm sorry, Hettie." His voice sounded strange to him, absurdly inconsequential beside the rushing waters and the impenetrable trees and the goddamn implacable mountains. "T.E. attaché. Time detective cadet. Lost in wilderness. Body never found." He almost laughed.

Too footsore and tired and despondent to continue, but nevertheless panicked at the thought of nightfall, he resolved himself to the idea of a shelter. He peered into the trees for a suitable place, as if he had any idea what that meant. He'd built a so-called lean-to once, as a child on a school-sponsored field trip. After brief instruction by an outdoorsman, they'd spent part of a day meandering about the woods with the direction to use fallen limbs and pine branches and whatever else to construct something akin to an overnight shelter, something that might protect them long enough to be found. Who could've believed that he'd be the one kid who'd actually have to do it for real?

What about fire? The idea almost thrilled him. Besides the heat, there would be the light—it would keep him safe and sane. But how to start one? How to goddamn start a fucking fire?

He had no idea. Rubbing two sticks together? He snatched up a finger-thick twig, snapped it in two, stupidly regarded the sticks. He made a halfhearted effort to rub them against each other. Pathetic. He knelt, jammed one stick into the ground, and furiously sawed at it with the other. Nothing. No heat. Let alone smoke. Fuck!

He sat back, dismayed at his own incapable ignorance, at the forest's soulless, infinite impenetrability. He longed for open space. To somehow get his bearings. He stood up, compelled to redouble his efforts, to hurry up and get somewhere, to run. To escape this goddamn river and the goddamn motherfucking trees. "Argh!"

What the hell is that? Sunlight? A bright gleam, yes, angling through the trees perhaps a hundred meters into the forest. Open space, it had to be. He scrambled away from the shore, left the roar of the river behind him, padded along on a blissfully soft bed of pine needles, and finally arrived at an incalculably marvelous view of the lower valley.

His sense of relief was so profound that he felt reborn—he was dead a minute ago. Dead. Now? His heart leapt and he rushed forward to take in the sundrenched expanse of the valley. Green. Lush. His eyes followed the slope of the land, assessing the massive gouge of the moraine. He searched surrounding foothills for some sign, some orienting landmark. He scanned the hillsides and flowery vales for a sign of anyone, anything, any sign of habitation, be it farmer, hiker, cow, or sheep.

He strained into the distance so intently and for so long that when he finally came to himself, he felt lightheaded and exhausted. He'd seen nothing. Nothing but the grassy, flowery valley and the rock-strewn hills. But look, there! A narrow hiking trail like a dark, spindly thread traversing the entire length of the valley, broken only by the rocky desolation of the moraine that bifurcated the valley floor. He collapsed onto the turf battling a new despair: should he descend into the valley and follow that trail? Where did it lead? It seemed to lead west, away from where he'd decided he ought to be going. Don't do it. Follow the river. But now he couldn't see the river. What about nightfall? The sun was low. It would disappear behind the mountains in what, an hour or two? Where in hell was he, goddammit?

Something caught his attention. Down in the valley, moving across the moraine—could it be? He blinked at it, straining to make it out. Yes! Two people. Hikers, perhaps. Making their way toward his side of the valley. They were, what, perhaps a kilometer away? He watched, mesmerized, afraid to look away lest they vanish.

Get after them! Go! He strode forth, unsteady on his sore feet and stiff legs, and scrambled down the slope. He'd not gone fifty meters when he realized how far away they were—the distances across such large expanses were deceiving. Panicking, he jammed his index fingers into his mouth and whistled, blowing with all his might. But his call seemed to dissipate as soon as it left his mouth. He tried again. Impossible.

The hikers were still visible, their movements barely discernable, but they'd turned after emerging from the moraine, angling obliquely away from him. Hurry! He made to run after them and immediately lost his footing, falling on his behind, sliding down the grassy slope. "Argh!" He rolled to a stop, his shin abraded and smarting, looked up for his hikers, and began again. He'd never catch them. But he *must!*

Yell, for fuck's sake. He stumbled desperately down the slope, trying to close the impossible distance. "HELP!" Encountering a rise, he lost sight of them and panicked, forced himself to leap blindly up it. They were still there, thank God! He stood hunched over, gasping for breath, his hands upon his knees. He was about to hurry down the hill when something moved near the bottom of the slope, perhaps twenty-five or so meters away. Bear cubs? God, yes, two of them!

The animals frolicked in the tall green grass, oblivious to him. His curiosity dissipated almost as soon as it had arrived. He must get to those hikers. He strode down the slope, determined to make a wide berth past the animals, when it struck him. The mother. She had to be—and suddenly there she was. Not twenty meters distant, lumbering toward him, or toward the cubs—he was too close, dangerously close.

His heart was in his throat at the sight of her—a hulking, broad-shouldered specimen. The animal's flesh rippled beneath her shaggy, blackish-brown hide. She stood upon her hind legs, her toothy snout held high, her heavy-taloned paws poised at her chest, and she seemed to have tripled in size. She looked askance at him with her jaws agape and her black lips curled above her hideous canines. Her snout quivered, as if she'd indeed caught scent of him. Was he upwind or downwind from her? What did it matter? He was too goddamn close. What if she charged? Where could he run?

Back up. Just back away. Slowly. No. She'd charge him for certain. She could outrun him. He was dead if he moved. And he was dead if he didn't. He glimpsed the hikers in the distance, saw the cubs wrestling in the grass, endured an agonizing forestalling of his destiny. He glimpsed the horror and savagery of his own demise. Another way to die. But whether his fatigue dulled his senses or the terror itself was simply too profound, a strange calm possessed him and he stood quietly, come what may.

The sow grizzly snorted, dropped to the ground, and rose again, as if agitated. She rolled her eyes and opened her mouth to the sky in a silent roar, her great paws with their hideous talons at her chest. She dropped to all fours again and shook her mighty shoulders as if gathering herself.

KAPOW!

The sow started and froze, but the cubs seemed oblivious, rolling about in the grass, wrestling.

Neutic stood stock still. Gunshot?

KAPOW!

Neutic flinched and the sow scurried through the grass, compact and nimble now, nosing her cubs together up the slope in the direction he had come. She leapt ahead of them, turned back once as if to lure them onward, and all three animals disappeared over the rise as if they had never existed.

The hikers rushed toward him, making their way closer and closer as if in a dream. For he must be dreaming. There was the soft grass beneath his feet, a sweet breeze in his face, and the long light of the sun that struck everything with a tawny clarity and warmth. He could not believe his eyes.

"My God, Neutic!" said Vixy. She rushed at him, breathless, and stood staring, as if he'd risen from the dead.

Neutic felt as if he had and stared back, incredulous.

Mr. Z. followed, breathing hard, his eyes keen and searching. He stripped off his pack and gripped Neutic's shoulders. "Remarkable! My God, Neutic!"

Neutic could only manage to blink at them. "Yessir."

Vixy looked him up and down. "Are you okay? Are you hurt? I

mean, your clothes and . . . well, you look like hell." She stifled a laugh and paused to look him straight in the face. "And that bear, it was as big as a Kodiak or a grizzly from home! But Mr. Z. recognized you. He was scanning the valley with his binocs and I thought he was crazy when he said he saw somebody that looked like you. I mean, how could it be you? Oh, Neutic, I'm so glad it is." Her expression changed, suddenly full of pathos. She rushed forward to embrace him, held him tightly for a precious moment, then stood back, scowling. She swiped angrily at a tear upon her cheek. "You bastard! What were you trying to do? Laron. His thugs. They would have killed you."

"Yet here you are," said Mr. Z. "Alive and well. Relatively speaking, that is. Let me look at you. Your clothes. Your shoes! What happened to them? For God's sake what happened to *you*? But don't let's hear anything about it until, for heaven's sake Neutic, you must be hungry and thirsty and—"

Neutic nodded, made a clumsy attempt at brushing himself off. "Yessir. Yessir, I'm okay, I just, well—" His emotions welled up so that when he tried to laugh, he coughed instead, covering his mouth with the back of his hand, straining to compose himself.

Vixy dropped her pack and began digging through it. "Jesus. You've been out here on your own with nothing." She tore open an energy gel and shoved it at him alongside her canteen. "It's getting cold. Hell, it will be dark soon. Mr. Z. has a flight jacket you can wear, don't you Mr. Z.? But jeezus, your feet."

Mr. Z. had already unpacked his jacket and draped it over Neutic's shoulders. "I've got an extra pair of socks and these tech shoes, for climbing. They're not really intended for walking, let alone hiking, but they may fit you well enough."

Neutic donned the jacket and flopped onto the grass to shove his feet into the socks and shoes, wincing as he worked the cinch straps. Mr. Z. tossed him a knit cap and Vixy knelt to offer him another energy gel. "Drink and eat. I've got more."

Neutic fumbled with the packages.

Vixy helped him tear away the foil. "Neutic, you look like you've been in a traffic accident. Your face is all bruised. Your eye, it's black and blue. And swollen. Look at your hands. Your clothes are all torn. I mean—"

"Are you certain you're not injured?" interrupted Mr. Z. "For God's sake, Neutic, tell us what happened. Can you?"

Neutic shook his head. "No," he mumbled, then washed down the gel with the water. "I mean, no, I'm not hurt. Just sore. And for the life of me, I don't know what happened. After I jumped off the bridge, that is. Into the river. I woke up on shore and I still don't remember anything in between."

"You jumped into a river?" said Vixy. "It looks like you've been in a cage fight." She reached to lift the back of his jacket, but Neutic pushed her away, suddenly embarrassed.

"I'm okay. Really. Much better now, let me tell you. I thought I'd be spending the night out here." He sucked at the last of the energy gel and swallowed hard, shoving his debris into his pockets. He adjusted his cap and gestured at Mr. Z.'s shoulder. "Rifle? If you hadn't fired, I don't know. I was convinced it was the end."

"We didn't fire," said Vixy. "I mean, Mr. Z., he had his rifle out, but those detonations were bear scares."

Neutic frowned at her.

"Like big firecrackers," said Vixy. "A big bang to frighten a bear away. We couldn't have shot at the thing from that distance. Way out of range."

"Right." Neutic swallowed hard. "But, sir, what are you both doing here? I mean, your gear and everything."

"Our mission is to end the siege," said Mr. Z. "To infiltrate Eranos and shut down Laron."

"We're going to kill that asshole if we have to," said Vixy. She looked blanky at him. "Wait a minute. Mr. Z.? I don't get it. The captain told us that Laron wanted to trade Neutic for me. If Neutic had already escaped by then—"

"Then Laron was lying," said Mr. Z. "One of his demands, besides all the money in the Bank of Switzerland, was to force us to agree to swapping you for Vixy."

Neutic scowled. "What does he want with Vixy?"

"I know," said Vixy. She smiled at him. "But I'm worth a hell of a lot more than you are, aren't I? Oh, Neutic, it's all crazy. Laron, he's already killed—" She shut her eyes and shook her head.

"He's killed Rosa and Nick," said Mr. Z.

Neutic stood up creakily and zipped his jacket. He frowned at them. "I can't believe it."

"Yes," said Mr. Z. "Maria de Cosmos and her husband. Two of the kindest, most innocent souls I've ever known."

"It's unspeakable," said Vixy. "And that sonofabitch couldn't stop there. He hung their bodies on the Yggdrasil Ash by their ankles, as if to . . ." She put her hand over her mouth.

"It's pure physical and psychological terrorism," said Mr. Z.

Neutic looked stricken.

"Steady now." Mr. Z. reached for him. "I'm sorry, my friend. You've been through your own hell. Vixy, call for the rescue transport." He hefted his pack and tightened his straps. "You and Vixy will be safe and sound at the T.E.'s temporary headquarters within the hour."

"What?" Vixy had been examining her transponder, her finger poised over the display. "You mean Ascona? No." She tapped her device and scowled. "I mean, we're all going to wait here, aren't we? Together. For Neutic's transport. And then I'm going with you."

Mr. Z. turned his wrist to glance at his timepiece and peered into the direction they'd been heading. Vixy's eyes followed his.

"No," said Mr. Z. "That's an order, Vixy. Your role in this mission is already accomplished. We've found Neutic. Alive, beyond all hope. Both of you have done more than could've been expected. You both have gone above and beyond."

He stepped away from them, his expression stoic, his resolve unflinching. Then he forced a wry smile. "Watch out for that damn bear now, you two. Stay safe. Get to Ascona. There's plenty that needs to be done for us to get Eranos back." He saluted them casually and they all managed smiles. He turned and strode away briskly, waving at them blindly with his arm above his head.

Vixy let her pack fall to the ground. "Goddammit, Z." But Mr. Z. had already hiked out of hearing range. She tapped at her transponder and focused upon Neutic. "Transport will be here in forty-five minutes. But we've got to hike several kilometers that way"—she gestured—"east, back the way Mr. Z. and I came in. To clear Laron's interference web. I know the last thing you want to do is hike. But can you make it?"

Neutic nodded. "Mr. Z. is going after Laron by himself? I feel like we ought to—"

"Forget it, Neutic." Vixy sighed. "There's no convincing him. I swear I always feel like he's either leaving me behind or I'm chasing after him." She shouldered her pack ruefully.

They both stared after Mr. Z., but he'd already disappeared into the foothills.

Vixy dug into a pocket of her jumpsuit. "Cigarette?"

Neutic didn't answer. It was as if the fatigue of his ordeal was flooding over him. He felt leaden, almost woozy with exhaustion. He tried filling his lungs, still focusing into the distance where Mr. Z. had gone.

Vixy eyed him closely, placed her hand upon his shoulder, and peered into his face. "Sit." She yanked something from her pack and knelt before him, then tapped at her transponder. "Here," she said softly, pushing a capsule into his mouth. "Take this. Meganutrient, painkiller, antibacterial, antiparasitical, all in one. You probably drank your share of that river water, didn't you? I'm changing our transport coordinates. You're in no condition to hike." She held the tip of a squeeze bottle to his lips, forcing him to drink from it. "Exposure. Trauma. I'm not so sure you didn't suffer some form of shock. Maybe a concussion. That meganutrient will help keep you going until the rescue gets here. Screw Laron's HDHS net. Mr. Z.'s going to have his work cut out for him, and so do we, so be it."

From then on, Neutic's experience was a dream state, as if events happened to someone else, including the roaring, percussive flutter of the rescue transport, the craft's blustery, roaring landing and someone—Vixy?—clutching a blanket round him. Then he was hauled up, and there were men in uniforms and helmets strapping him onto a gurney, talking to him loudly, and him unable to answer. Then a view of the darkening valley from high above and the dimming, pink-orange sky with the pinpoint stars emerging, and the bracing silhouette of the mountains fading into the distance.

CHAPTER 7

THINGSTEAD

VIXY SAT QUIETLY AT THE conference table paging through the book her father had sent her; namely, an ancient collection of Northwest Coast imagery published in the twenty-first century that he discovered at an estate sale in Vancouver. She liked to think she'd seen all the old photographs, but her father, ever on the lookout for items related to Haida history, had a knack for digging up things she'd missed in her research. She scanned one of the black-and-white images into her device. A house pole depicting Raven. Snag, on the bottom, clutching salmon twins. Circa 1885. But what startled her was the accompanying text. *Twins are magical,* it read, *and people must be careful and conscientious in handling them, for twin power may be harmful or beneficial.*

The captain frowned at her and drummed his fingers upon the table.

Neutic eyed the captain and nudged Vixy's arm.

She intentionally ignored him and kept reading. "1885," she repeated aloud, as if to herself. Then it struck her. Salmon twins. Neutic himself was a twin.

"Earth to Miss Velure."

She glanced at the captain. "Sir?"

"1885?" said the captain.

Vixy appeared flummoxed.

"BCE, sir," volunteered Neutic. He shifted in his seat, cleared his throat, and continued. "Vixy was just suggesting that it was 1885 BCE, or thereabouts, when the Harappans[14] inhabited India. Before it was India. In their late Bronze Age period."

"Harappans," said the captain flatly. "Neither one of you are making any sense. What's any of this have to do with the HDT event and losing track of Mr. Z. and Laron?"

"No, captain," interrupted Professor Wilhelm, "I think they are indeed making sense. The Harappans. An important Indus Valley civilization. Their history may be relevant. Inasmuch as a culture from the northwestern part of that country can be said to have an influence upon the islands of Bombay, as the city eventually came to be named. In its golden age, that is." She sat with her elbows on the tabletop and pressed the palms of her hands together beneath her chin, accentuating the slender elegance of her fingers and immaculate manicure. "Before it was renamed time and again, of course. Meanwhile, Captain, weren't you suggesting that 1954 Bombay is an operational nexus?"

"For the Scarab Cult?" The captain made a face and scratched his head. "Well, bronze age, golden age, whatever age, I'm just running with your idea that if Bombay in 1954 was experiencing some sort of cultural awakening or newfound global relevance, it would make the place that much more attractive for foreigners with controversial big ideas. They might think they could blend right in. Avoid criticism. Avoid detection. Get a foothold for their agenda."

"You mean hide out until they make a play to get their way," said Vixy.

"Hey," said the captain, "it's a cult, isn't it? Self-described. A

---

14   The Bronze Age on the Indian subcontinent began around 3300 BCE with the beginning of the Indus Valley civilization, also known as the Harappan culture. The Harappans developed new techniques in metallurgy and produced copper, bronze, lead, and tin. The Late Harappan culture, which dates from 1900 BCE to 1400 BCE, overlapped the transition from the Bronze Age to the Iron Age.

small group with controversial philosophies, that's what a cult is. Or controversial politics. What's the difference?"

"Bombay in the 1950s would indeed have been ripe for a flourishing of ideologies," said the professor. "Cultish or otherwise. And to our point, it would therefore be easier to round up members. And as the captain suggests, gain momentum."

"For their damn cause," said the captain. "Exactly."

"Laron," continued the professor. "If he and the late Professor Bruggs—wasn't that his name, the German Egyptologist?" She glanced at her notes.

"You mean the black-market antiquities operative, don't you?" said Vixy.

"That too, yes," acknowledged the professor. "Meanwhile, if Laron and Bruggs could manage to operate a faction of the Scarab Cult within 1881 Cairo, it doesn't prevent another faction from simultaneously operating in 1950s Bombay. Or anywhere else, for that matter. Does it?"

"So, now what?" said Vixy. "I mean, we can request permission from the Time Guard to run an infiltration trace. Laron and Mr. Z., their HDT trail is plenty warm to generate the precise coordinates in 1950s Bombay so Neutic and I can HDT and find them. Find Mr. Z., at least. I mean, who knows what he's up against on his own? That Shields character is vanished from Eranos too, isn't he? Probably with Laron."

The captain squeezed his eyes shut and rubbed his head. "Z has a knack for arriving in the middle of the action. Without allowing for proper backup. Or support. Or anything that would involve actual planning and proper operational procedure." He waved his hand. "But anyway. Shields. That he escaped to Bombay with Laron is one idea that makes sense, yes. Shields, like any lacky, can't be said to maintain any loyalty to the cause. Especially when the going gets tough. He's going to go with the winner. Or try to win everything for himself. That's his psychological profile. He's a hired gun type, that's all. Not exactly a mercenary. More a mercenary wannabe." The captain glanced at his own notes. "Well, given his less-than-spectacular record. Zero military experience. All the intelligence on him indicates he's never been involved in anything but extortion and petty ransom. Although he tends to get around. Twenty countries in ten years."

"The Scarab Cult sure likes their cheap thugs," said Vixy.

"You said he gets around, sir," said Neutic. "And he's not from Earth, if that means anything."

"That's right," said the captain. "And it does mean something. Because it brings me to my point." He collected his papers and turned to squint at the projection. "Look here. There's a minor planet some twenty light-years from Polaris, and damned if I can't think of its name right now. It was discovered goddamn eons ago. Anyway—"

"Twenty light-years from Polaris, sir?" Neutic typed as he talked. "Dhruva Minor."

"That's it," said the captain. "Dhruva Minor. Population. . ." He dove back into his documents, running his finger down the page. "Three billion or so. A benign culture, of no political consequence, inhabiting a planet orbiting the dwarf star Polaris B."

"In Hindu mythology, the Pole Star is called Dhruva," said the professor. "And in Chinese mythology, Emperor Zhuanxu is mentioned as a god of the Pole Star." She appeared thoughtful. "It's no wonder, then. That is to say, it's remarkable, actually. . .." She trailed off.

"Remarkable," said the captain. "How so?"

"Mr. Neutic," said the professor, "please, you've a knack for databases—can you bring up something on the association between Earth's Eastern mythology and the Pole Star? Polaris. The North Star. All these terms, they are going to come up—"

Neutic's fingers flew over the keyboard, and he squinted at his display. "There's a brief technical description that seems useful. Except it's a bit of a word salad."

The professor gestured for him to proceed.

Neutic held forth: "Polaris is a multiple star, comprising the main star, UMi Aa—which is a supergiant—and two smaller companions, namely, UMi B and UMi Ab, and two distant components, UMi C and UMi D."

"When does axial precession point Earth to a new pole star?" said Vixy.

"Axial precession," repeated Neutic, typing. "Ten thousand years, when the pole star position will be occupied by Vega. And there's a bunch of mythological references here too, except they're all Egyptian." He looked to the professor.

"Ancient Egyptian mythology does well, arguably, to syncretize an Eastern and Western perspective, a perspective that may indeed be applicable here. Go ahead—is there anything more?"

Neutic read carefully. "The Pharaoh Khufu ruled Egypt around 2550 BCE and was entombed within the largest of the Giza Plateau pyramids. During his reign, Thuban, also known as Alpha Draconis, was planet Earth's pole star"—he acknowledged Vixy with a glance—"around which all other stars revolved. Two narrow shafts bore outward from the king's burial chamber, and for decades, scholars assumed they were merely airshafts. But in the 1960s, astronomers found that they have an astronomical purpose; namely, that one of the shafts pointed directly toward Thuban. The other was aimed at the belt of Orion, which symbolized Osiris. As the stars near to the pole never set, the Egyptians described them as 'imperishable' or 'undying.' Khufu expected that when he died, he would join not only with the sun, but with Thuban as well, maintaining order in the celestial realm, just as he had on Earth." He peered more closely into his display. "And regarding China, there's more. A lot more."

"Ancient Chinese astrology is centered upon the Pole Star," said the professor. "It is referred to as, let me think, the Honorable Lord of the Heavens. Or some such thing."

"That's right," said Neutic.

"Argh," mumbled the captain. "Astrology." He scratched his head with both hands. "Where are we going with this, Professor? I mean, Mr. Z. would likely be on board with this stuff right now, this theorizing and, what does he call it? Mythological syncretization? But if we're going to help him, or at least expedite trying to find him, we've got to take action. The HDT trail was sketchy to begin with—Laron employs a damn aggravating HDT smoke screen—and we all know that hyperdimensional transport residues decay rapidly. I say we go with 1954 Bombay." He clacked away at his keyboard. "I'm putting in the request for the tracer net. Around the whole damn Bombay Island. Or islands. Or archipelago, whatever it is."

"It was an archipelago before 1845 CE, sir," said Neutic, summarizing what he saw on his display. "It was referred to as the Seven Islands of Bombay. But a series of land reclamation projects engineered it into a single landmass."

"The Isle of Bombay, then," said the captain. He hammered at the Enter key. "Done. If that's where Z is pursuing Laron and Laron is merely a pawn in the Scarab Cult chess game, then maybe we'll finally get inside this thing."

"And get a motive?" said Vixy. "For the Scarab Cult? Because I still don't see it. Or the connection to the molemen. I don't get that either. I mean, did the molemen even know that Bruggs and Laron were part of this cult?"

"Let's just get on the ground in Bombay," said the captain. "In 1954. Vixy, you and Neutic, you're going together. If Neutic clears his medical, that is. Let me see . . ." He squinted at his display and tapped a key. "Yes, it says here that you've cleared. Okay then, Neutic, congratulations. Welcome to full-on time detective work. You've been a cadet for, what, six months? And now you're going to be a shellback. When you get back, we'll throw you a shellback party, or whatever they do. Vixy knows. Meanwhile, there is no time to lose, folks. Let's assume the TDC will get Z's coordinates nailed down pronto. They better."

"But where in Bombay?" said the professor. "That is, where do you propose that Vixy and Neutic begin? That's an enormous geographical area, even in 1954."

"Well, let's see. How about starting at the bottom and making your way up? The Gateway to India. Right there at the southern tip. A dawn arrival, at the foot of that monument." He made a show of striking keys. "Done. Coordinates submitted. Seventy-two-hour urban infiltration, that's all I can arrange on short notice. You'll both report to the transport bay in, let's see"—he glanced at his display—"I'll give you four hours. And Neutic, I'm issuing you a standard cadet transponder. No HDT capability. Limited communication clearance. Vixy, you get to see how Neutic here is going to hold up. Neutic, Vixy is the transport leader. That means she's the boss. You do what she tells you, do you hear?"

Neutic nodded. "Yessir."

Vixy appeared anxious and shifted in her seat.

The captain scooted his chair closer to the table and addressed Vixy and Neutic in a careful tone. "Find Z. That's job one. Neutralize Laron. That's job two. Job two only happens if Mr. Z. is there to help you. It goes without saying that if he's in trouble—"

"We call for help," said Vixy.

"You call me, that's right. I am online twenty-four seven when you two are on HDT, okay? You both are my personal responsibility." And if the TDC can't trace Mr. Z. by the time you land, well, you're both going to be earning your pay, let's put it that way."

CHAPTER 8

BOMBAY, 1954

MR. Z. SQUINTED INTO THE clammy heat. He felt nauseous and lightheaded—an HDT hangover worsened by the difficult climate. Whether it took him a day or a week to acclimatize it was time he didn't have either way. Because every second Laron was on the run was a crime against time. He'd had Laron in his sights—literally within his crosshairs—at Eranos but he had hesitated. Now, this.

He breathed the overripe ocean air, winced slightly at the whiff of rot and excrement that drifted up from the streets, and coughed at a wisp of automobile exhaust. A cluster of street vendors were set up near the entrance of the museum, each of them hawking bric-a-brac. Mostly shamelessly garish Hindu imagery—a hackneyed painting here, a gaudy statuette there. He accepted a pamphlet from a vendor and paid the man his rupees. "The Prince of Wales Museum," he read, "is one of Bombay's prized British Raj–era structures."

> The museum is built in the Indo-Saracenic style of architecture—a blend of 15th to 16th century Gujarati and Islamic design—in addition to English brickwork. The structure is adorned with an impressive Mughal white dome that adds splendor to its appearance, and the building is bordered by lavish green gardens. The

galleries display works within the areas of natural history, archaeology, and art.

"Well, if it isn't Alfred Salmony!"

A man's voice rang out, clearly American, and Mr. Z. turned to look. A trim, middle-aged gentleman in short sleeves and khakis enthusiastically approached a group of three others—two Caucasians, similarly attired, one significantly older than the other, and a dark-skinned Indian gentleman in a kurta, a short-collared suitcoat, a white cap, and leather slip-on loafers.

"Joe Campbell!" said the older man, clearly a bit astonished. His scruffy black shoes, drooping white socks, and shortened pants cuffs lent him an air of unselfconscious professorial awkwardness. He smoothed the thin gray strands of his pate, smiled, and reached out to accept Campbell's handshake.

"A small world, indeed!" exclaimed Campbell. "But my God, Salmony, what are the odds?"

The two acquaintances laughed at each other, and Mr. Z., intrigued, drifted through the passersby, drawing nearer but careful to maintain a discreet distance.

"Joe," said Salmony, "this is Jason Grossman. And this is Kashi, our bearer and guide."

Grossman, an olive-skinned, broad-shouldered man with thick dark hair and boldly framed eyeglasses smiled amiably and accepted Campbell's hand. Kashi, a slightly built man in comparison, nodded energetically and raised his hand palm outwards, then performed a short bow.

Campbell was tanned and trim, perhaps fifty, and had his hair pomaded in the style of the times. With a camera strapped across his shoulder, he seemed poised and considerate. In fact, all three foreigners appeared, to Mr. Z.'s eyes, to exude the self-possessed nonchalance of having been in country for some time.

"Well," said Salmony, patting his pockets. "Would you like to join us? We were just going in for a little museum tour. Before my lecture."

"Lecture?" said Campbell. "Why, well done, Al."

"Yes, it's after lunch—at one o'clock. In the art section some-where."

"That's great, Al," said Campbell, "really. What's the topic? What-ever it is, I'd like to hear it. Ha! I still can't get over the coincidence." He laughed.

"I'm actually here on research," said Salmony, "but I agreed to a lecture in exchange for access to a private collection. You know how it is." He affected a grimace.

"I do, Al. I'm not quite in your boat this time, though. I'm likewise here on research, courtesy of Eranos, but no lectures to do. Not yet, anyway." He crossed his fingers and smiled.

"Eranos? I have just had an essay published, in hard cover, as it happens, out of Ascona. More coincidence, I suppose. We arrived . . . when?" He glanced at Grossman. "Two weeks or so ago. How about yourself?"

"Four months, I think. With two left to go."

"Well now, that sounds like a worthy sabbatical. What do you make of it so far? India, I mean."

"Besides being enormous? Hmm, I'd say its bounties are utterly unique."

"Without a doubt. You intended to visit the museum, then?"

"Indeed," said Campbell.

"Well," said Salmony, checking his watch. "Shall we?"

They entered the museum lobby, and Mr. Z. followed, pausing here and there within sight but not always within hearing distance of the men, feigning his own interest in the occasional artifact. He knew that he risked committing a severe leave-no-trace violation, for he recognized the names of two of the four men—Salmony and Campbell—as notable, published scholars whom he himself had read. Salmony was perhaps the more obscure and the more academically situated. Campbell had already published what was to remain his most famous book. And if he wasn't mistaken, Salmony would in fact live a mere four or five more years—the man would suffer a heart at-tack upon another of his research expeditions, dying at sea. In terms of the leave-no-trace protocol, it was knowledge like this—personal familiarity and foreknowledge of a man's demise—carried into the past and, worse yet, in direct proximity to the subjects themselves, that was to be plainly avoided.

He ought to leave. He ought to cut short this entire encounter. And the temptation to remain and cater to his curiosity was exactly the reason an HDT event was so dutifully and thoroughly vetted prior to approval. Because the temptation to interact and even intervene—to influence—even for the most highly trained and strong-minded time detectives who knew better, was almost impossible to resist while in the grip of such an encounter. It was human nature to experience an almost irresistible compulsion to further the interaction. It was akin to being starstruck, yet also different and more sinister, for the compulsion hinged upon a seductive sense of the power of one's influence.

Mr. Z. understood perfectly well, then, that even his thoughts possessed the potential to skew the future. And he could not unthink them. Hence, the trace effects loomed impossibly large. The risk was acute. Walk away, then. Leave now. Seek Laron elsewhere, clear his head, at least.

Nevertheless, and profoundly against his better judgment, he found himself following the party into the heart of the museum. Why? Intuition. And the sense of synchronicity—the experience of an acausal yet meaningful coincidence that Jung described. Something about Kashi, especially. And the configuration of this unlikely coincidence of people and place and circumstance that heightened Mr. Z.'s sense that Laron himself was mysteriously entangled in these circumstances. This was legitimate time detective work. But with potentially diabolical space-time fallout. Don't get carried away, he chided himself. Be careful. Be careful as hell.

They arrived at an especially quiet, dimly lit alcove deep within the museum. Its focal point was an old, folio-sized codex laid open within a display case, its parchment manuscript pages agleam with illuminations and dense with elaborately inscribed Sanskrit text.

Grossman and Kashi seemed uncomfortable in the cloistered room and retreated to the main hallway, where they meandered listlessly.

Campbell studied the codex closely, and Salmony lingered nearby, as if curious himself.

"Hmm," said Campbell. "this is a copy of the *Panchatantra*. Attributed to a fellow named Vishnu Sharma, it says here. It's a Hindu work in five interrelated books, if I recall. Animal fables in verse and prose."

Salmony leaned over the case and looked down his nose at the book.

Campbell smiled patiently at Salmony. "You know, there's an interesting tale in here entitled, let me think, 'The Story of the Crows and the Owls'—a kind of treatise upon war and peace and, anyway, bear with me, Al. The crows and the owls are traditional enemies, they're at war. One of the crows pretends to be an outcast from his own group to attain entry into the rival owl group. Yes, that's it, I think. He learns their secrets and vulnerabilities. He later summons his group of crows to set fire to all the entrances to the cave where the owls live, and the poor creatures suffocate to death."[15]

Salmony raised his bushy eyebrows.

"But what I find especially interesting," continued Campbell, "is a point about the imagery. While the story can be interpreted as referring to crows, it's just as probable that the author is referring to ravens. There's a subspecies, *Corvus corax subcorax*, I think it is, present in India, particularly the northwest region of the country. It could be here, then, in India, that the raven first appears in recorded myth. Long before it appears in North American lore. Which is remarkable, isn't it? Another case for dispersion, don't you think?" He smiled wryly at Salmony, as if keen to bait the man's criticism.

"Dispersion of migratory tribes from the Asiatic continent," interrupted Salmony, "across the so-called land bridge of the Ice Age, yes, yes, Franz Boas and the Jessup Expedition and all that. You know the subject of my lecture is a discussion of my new book—an essay, really—concerning the dispersion and diffusion of symbology. The antler and tongue motifs, specifically as they occur in China."

---

15   Referring to Vishnu Sharman, *The Five Discourses on Worldly Wisdom [Pa], Book III,* trans. Patrick Olivelle, (New York: New York University Press & JCC, Clay Sanskrit Library, 2006).

Salmony peered at his watch, then placed his hand on Campbell's shoulder. "The mythography, my friend, is your area, but you really might find my topic interesting."

"Ahem, excuse me, gentlemen." It was Kashi. He gestured at the display. "This text, they are animal fables. And it is also a discourse upon political science, what is termed a *nīti śāstra*."

Campbell and Salmony each regarded Kashi with mild surprise.

"From oral traditions," continued Kashi, his voice growing impassioned, "that are as old as we are able to imagine." He seemed to swell with a measure of national pride. "It has been said the *Panchatantra* is the most frequently translated book in all of India. Perhaps the most translated Hindu text in the world."

As old as we are able to imagine, thought Mr. Z. Where in hell have I heard that before?

Salmony seemed impatient. "Hmm," he said. "Indeed. Very excellent, Kashi, thank you." He turned perfunctorily toward Campbell. "What do you say to lunch, Joe? I've been told the cafeteria is decent."

Campbell seemed quietly bemused by Salmony's indifference but nevertheless nodded. "Whatever you say, Al. That sounds fine."

Mr. Z., his back to everyone, waited until the two scholars had exited the room and then intentionally bumped into Kashi. "Oh, I am terribly sorry. I didn't see you." He grasped Kashi's shoulder as if to steady the man, glanced after Salmony and Campbell to make certain they'd continued down the hallway, and dug his fingers into Kashi's arm, forcing him away from the doorway. He hissed into Kashi's ear, "I know who you are."

Kashi squirmed and stomped his feet, scowling. "Excuse me, sir!" He attempted to collect himself, producing a white handkerchief with which he dabbed at his brow. He affected an air of wide-eyed befuddlement.

"*As old as we are able to imagine*," growled Mr. Z. He forced Kashi's arm behind him, twisting and pulling so the man gasped and made to claw at Mr. Z.'s face. Mr. Z. turned away and caught Kashi's hand in his own, then bent the fingers back. Kashi's knees buckled, and Mr. Z. relented, hauling him up again. "That was a quote from a monograph, *Problems, Myths and Stories* by Doris Lessing." Mr. Z.

tightened his grip, his nostrils flaring. "It is a very fine piece, except that it won't be written for another forty-five years."

Kashi's eyes flashed, and he made to pull away. Mr. Z. held fast and shoved him against the wall, pressing his free hand over Kashi's mouth. The little man glared fiercely, continuing to struggle. Beads of perspiration trickled down his temple.

Mr. Z. spoke with calm severity: "You will introduce me to your friends. Salmony. Campbell. Grossman will have a car available for all of us to return to the hotel after Professor Salmony's lecture." He half revealed his plasma pistol so Kashi was forced to glance at it, then eased the firearm back into his shoulder harness. "Do you understand?" He gestured toward the door, and Kashi relented.

They entered the hallway just as Grossman peered at them from around the corner. "Kashi," he said with surprise, "we thought we lost you. Who's this?"

Mr. Z. pinched Kashi's arm.

Kashi hesitated, forcing a pained smile. "Oh, Mr. Grossman," he laughed, "I am so sorry, certainly." He wrung his hands. "No. No, I was not lost. I have just been speaking to this interesting man. His name is, ah . . . Mr. . . . ."

"Jones." Mr. Z. stepped forward to shake hands. "My name is Jones."

Grossman shook. "Hello, sir."

Mr. Z. affected a cheerful nonchalance. "I teach in the United States. I'm visiting the museum for the first time. I happened to overhear—it is Kashi, you say, sir? Your name, I'm sorry." When Kashi hesitated, Mr. Z. glared at him.

"Yes, yes, my name is Kashi. I am the bearer and guide for these gentlemen."

"Oh, I apologize, then," said Mr. Z. "For being a bother. But you see, I just couldn't help overhearing a portion of your conversation about the *Panchatantra*. Fascinating. I study folklore as an amateur. I'm enjoying my first visit to the museum and I understand from Kashi that you are with Professor Alfred Salmony. I happen to be familiar with his journal, *Artibus Asiae*, and his scholarship on behalf of, let me think, Chinese jade, is it?"

Grossman seemed taken aback at Mr. Z.'s sudden effusiveness until Salmony and Campbell appeared from around the corner.

Mr. Z. affected an earnest smile and waited. When neither Grossman nor Kashi made to introduce him, Mr. Z. spoke up. "Good afternoon, gentlemen. You, sir, must be Professor Salmony." He extended his hand.

Salmony shook it and smoothed the wisps of hair upon his scalp.

"I go by Jones," said Mr. Z. He offered Campbell his hand. "Very nice to meet you as well, sir."

"Campbell. Joe Campbell." He shook Mr. Z.'s hand heartily.

"Mr. Jones has apparently read *Artibus Asiae*," volunteered Grossman. "And your publications on Chinese jade?" He glanced sideways at Mr. Z., who addressed Salmony with an amiable nod.

Salmony's wary dubiousness evaporated, and he cleared his throat. "Well, yes. Thank you. You subscribe to *Artibus*?"

"No, sir," said Mr. Z. "That is to say, I have come across it via my university library. You are the editor-in-chief, as I recall. But forgive me, I am interrupting your lunch."

"Mr. Jones," said Grossman, "perhaps you're aware of the professor's lecture this afternoon?"

Mr. Z. feigned embarrassment. "Lecture? Oh, I hadn't realized, but what a remarkable coincidence. Had I known—"

"It's here in the auditorium," offered Campbell. "At one o'clock." He addressed Salmony. "I assume it's open to the public?"

"Certainly," said Salmony.

"Why, thank you," said Mr. Z.

"Until then, sir," said Kashi boldly. "Meanwhile, lunch is within the museum cafeteria. And it has no doubt begun." Kashi glanced at his wristwatch and distanced himself from Mr. Z., forging down the hallway.

"Cafeteria? I'm afraid I don't know my way around. And I'm famished. Do you mind if I tag along?"

"Not at all," said Salmony. "A friend of *Artibus Asiae* is a friend of mine."

THE CAFETERIA RESEMBLED AN AMPLE private room or a club lounge, replete with a slightly downtrodden hodgepodge of British Colonial furniture—burnished ebony occasional chairs and tables, botanical-themed upholstery patterns, a healthy display of rattan and even a well-traveled leather trunk or two. The pale plastered walls had not been painted recently, and the billowing white drapes seemed slightly threadbare and a bit dingy at the hems. The darkly stained wooden shutters, while sturdy, were here and there missing a slat. The room evoked a fading gentility and a blithe indifference to the bygone raj of its origins.

Mr. Z. regarded the two ancient, double-bladed fans turning lazily overhead like unmeshed gear teeth, as ineffectual against the clammy seaside atmosphere as against the passage of time itself. Twice removed from yesterday, he thought. It was the time detective's curse, feeling doubly displaced.

A pedestaled plaster bust of a mustached man with heavy features and a commanding visage dominated the center of the room. He sported a fez and an open-collared uniform adorned with medals. Evocative of the previous century. I ought to know this man, thought Mr. Z. Indian Army, perhaps?

"This isn't the cafeteria, is it?" said Grossman. "It seems more like a hotel lounge."

"It is indeed a cafeteria, sir," said Kashi, his voice stiff with pride. He snapped his fingers repeatedly and raised his voice. "Hello! Hello!" There was the clumsy clatter of kitchenware from a half-open door, and Kashi stomped toward it.

Mr. Z. restrained himself from following. What kitchen in the world didn't possess a back door for deliveries? But it wasn't as if he could go barreling after the man and not throw himself into suspicion. But if Kashi went through those double doors . . .

Campbell ambled toward the center of the room and stood face-to-face before the bust, rubbing his chin at it. "Syed Ahmad Khan? Do you think? He wrote something about—what was it—the Indian Rebellion?[16]

---

16   Referring to an essay entitled "The Causes of the Indian Mutiny," Syed Ahmad Khan's critique of British policies that he blamed for causing the

A hundred years ago. He was loyal to the raj. Supported the Islamic rationalists, if I recall."

"The Mu'tazila," said Salmony.

"That's it," said Campbell.

"Here!" barked Kashi. He had remained just outside the kitchen and clapped sharply at the doors. "We are a group of five, if you please! Jaldee se!"[17]

A shabby-looking maître d' shuffled forth. He was a dark-skinned Indian in an ill-fitting European-style white jacket, black slacks, and a limp bowtie. A pair of lighter-skinned adolescent boys in undistinguished kurtas, churidars, sandals, and aprons followed, each of them struggling to hold one end of a platter piled with teetering tableware.

"The largest table," bellowed Kashi. He gestured stiffly toward the center of the room. "That one there! We will all be seated there!" He seemed suddenly keen to shift everyone's attention to the table.

Mr. Z. watched him eye the swinging kitchen doors and glance back warily into the room.

"Stop!" shouted Mr. Z. and rushed after him. "Stop him!"

"What in God's name?" exclaimed Grossman.

Kashi burst into the kitchen and Mr. Z. followed, crashing against the heavy inertia of the doors, but nevertheless in hot pursuit.

Kashi skittered around a long prep table at the rear of the kitchen, and it was all Mr. Z. could do to squeeze past two prep cooks dicing vegetables and avoid stumbling face-first into the flaming stove before him.

"Ullu ka pattha!"[18] uttered one of them. "Yahaan se chale jao, Yah paagalapan kya hai!" exclaimed the other.[19]

---

revolt. He believed Muslims were threatened by the rigidity of their own orthodox outlook, and he promoted Western-style scientific education by founding schools and journals and organizing Muslim entrepreneurs.

17   In Hindi, "Hurry up!"

18   In Hindi, "Son of a bitch!"

19   Likewise, "Get out of here, what is this madness!"

Mr. Z. made the turn and ducked—pots and pans hurtled over his head, then a chef's knife whizzed past. Mr. Z. slipped upon the greasy floor and caught himself. Kashi dove through the delivery door, and Mr. Z. sprinted after him.

———

THE DOOR BURST OPEN ONTO a loading dock. Mr. Z. leapt down the steps, squinted into the sunlight, and scanned the grounds for Kashi. There! A man on the run, heading for the main entrance.

Mr. Z. sped after him and despaired when Kashi disappeared around the balustrade that ran the length of the property and divided it from the streets of the city. He skidded to a stop upon the museum drive and looked about wildly. Where in hell did the man go? There!

Kashi was dashing through the pedestrians and the glut of parked automobiles and British-style double-decker tourist buses—there were even several incongruous, horse-drawn carriages awaiting fares.

Dammit! Mr. Z. cringed when Kashi piled into a taxicab—a nondescript American sedan, black with a white top, perhaps a Dodge or a Plymouth or a Chevrolet—and Mr. Z. almost immediately doubted which vehicle it was. There were so many identical cars, mostly taxis, and all of them black with white tops! No, Kashi's taxi was missing its right rear hubcap and sported a gash across the fender. There it was, crawling through the congestion of vehicles toward the main road.

Mr. Z. pulled up short, breathless and sweating. "Taxi!" he bellowed, and flagged down the nearest able-looking machine.

"No, sir, I am sorry!" The driver waved him away enthusiastically.

"I say, sir, excuse me!"

Mr. Z. found himself shoved aside.

"Bloody hell, can't you see this is our taxi?"

A middle-aged man in a business suit and his scowling wife in a dowdy dress elbowed their way past.

"Bloody hell, yourself!" murmured Mr. Z. Every damn taxi was suddenly accepting passengers at once. Kashi's cab still crawled through the congestion, and in a moment or two it would reach the main road and vanish into the city streets.

"Englishman?"

"What?" Mr. Z. turned to look.

"Are you English?" An Indian man sporting a wiry beard straddled what Mr. Z. recognized as an auto rickshaw.[20] Except this version, a prototype perhaps, more accurately resembled a modified three-wheeled motorcycle than anything—no cockpit for the driver and merely an ad hoc, open-air cabin and bench seat for a single passenger.

"Is this a cab?"

"Hmm," said the man, twisting his beard. "American."

"I'll pay you!"

The bearded man peered at the rupees Mr. Z. held out. "Goddammit, man!" said Mr. Z. "You speak English, don't you?"

"Goddammit, I do, sir." The bearded man smiled broadly at himself. "Yes. And you are wanting to follow that Plymouth taxi with the missing hubcap and the gash upon the fender. I have been observing you just as you have been ignoring me." He kick-started his motor and gestured Mr. Z. aboard.

Mr. Z. clambered in. "Hurry!"

The driver cranked on the accelerator. Black smoke belched from the exhaust, and the machine launched them into traffic, tires squealing. The contraption shimmied past the larger vehicles, made a hard right into the traffic circle surrounding Wellington Fountain, and pitched onto two wheels. Mr. Z. nearly tumbled into the street—he clutched at the doorframe to right himself.

"Hold on, sir! I see them!" The cabbie leaned upon the accelerator, and the motor rattled and sputtered and coughed. Yet when they sped into the Queen's Road heading north, they were nevertheless gaining ground on Kashi's taxi. The cabbie hollered over his shoulder, "Who are you, sir? What is your name?"

---

20 Bajaj Auto claims to have introduced the country's very first auto rickshaw in 1959. But it can be assumed that prior to mass manufacturing and official bureaucratic regulation as a taxicab, the city's entrepreneurs had invented their own versions.

"Z!" Mr. Z. shouted into the wind. "My name is Z!"

"I am Dev!"

"There!" Mr. Z. pointed ahead. "There he is!"

"Yes, yes!" shouted Dev. "I see it!" He squawked his horn and cranked the accelerator.

Mr. Z. hurtled back into his seat, and they spilled onto Esplanade Road, barreling west along the south side of the fort, then angled north, speeding past the University of Bombay, the landmark Rajabai Clock Tower, and the Bombay High Court in quick succession until Dev suddenly slowed. They were at the junction of Elphinstone Road and Woodby Street and Dev looked about wildly, seemingly uncertain.

"There!" cried Mr. Z. "That way!"

Kashi's taxi was slowed by a line of heavy traffic surrounding the Victoria Terminus. "Tatti!"[21] said Dev, gesturing at the vehicles. "If the VT is not the busiest rail station in all of India, then I am an elephant's asshole!"

They cleared the station and veered north and spied Kashi's taxi some hundred meters up Hornby Road. Dev bleated his horn, attempting in vain to pass vehicles. The *Times of India* building zipped past on their left, and to the right the dusty rail yard spread its blackened tendrils toward the docks.

Mr. Z.'s resolve waned as they ambled north and Dev seemed to lose heart for the chase.

"The traffic will only get worse near the bazaar, sir, I am sorry."

"Bazaar?" said Mr. Z.

"The Chor Bazaar. Street shops. How do you call it, a flea market? Clothes. Crafts. Pots and pans. Car parts. Food. Junk. The works. Parts for my engine, I find there. You have lost something in Bombay today? They say you find someone selling it in the Chor Bazaar tomorrow. It is not called the thief bazaar for nothing!"

Mr. Z. envisioned a shabby congestion of dingy shop fronts shoulder to shoulder, overflowing with worthless trinkets. Hawkers

---

21 A Hindi expletive equivalent to *shit*.

haggling with customers and so on. And it struck him that Kashi might try to lose himself there. But the thought of pursuing a man through the shuffling shoppers and the makeshift shop fronts left him exasperated. The city suddenly seemed sprawling and, at the same time, impenetrably dense. "The bazaar, how far is it from here?"

Dev shrugged. "Straight to Mutton Street, that way, a few blocks. Turn right. You will see and hear everything."

"Stop here, Dev. Let me out."

Dev halted in the middle of the street, indifferent to the ensuing mayhem of passing vehicles and honking horns.

"Here!" Mr. Z. thrust a fistful of rupees at Dev and extricated himself from the rickshaw with his arm thrust out defensively against the traffic. "Dhanyavaad!" he shouted. *Thank you.* It was the only Hindi phrase he knew. He dodged the traffic until he'd finally left the roadway behind him, then looked back, somehow compelled to get a last glimpse of Dev. But the forthright Hindu and his crazy rickshaw had disappeared into the busy street.

It was late afternoon and the light had changed; the withering white heat now diminished to a golden warmth that burnished the cityscape with what seemed a pensive melancholy. Foreign lands and unfamiliar cities—travel in general—mostly enlivened him. But he was tired, hot, and hungry. To say nothing of parched. He felt encrusted with the sweat and dirt and dust of his exertions. All apparently futile.

The city looked shabby and impenetrable. But this Kashi fellow was just a man. On the run. And bound to make a mistake.

On the street corner across from him sat a line of beggars, and he noticed a younger couple, desperately thin, huddled shoulder to shoulder with an emaciated child lying drearily upon the pavement between them. The child's face was painted with pale ash, its forehead marked with a smudged bindi.[22] The father, if that's who he

---

22 An ornamental dot traditionally worn by Hindu women in the middle of the forehead or between the eyebrows, made of colored sandalwood paste, kohl, or other pigment and having various religious and social significance.

was, stared blankly. The mother clutched a begging dish that rested upon the pavement, as if it were too heavy to hold.

Mr. Z. moved farther from the main road. The vehicular traffic gave way to a milling throng of men and women of all ages, many of whom bore candles and tiny oil lamps. Others seemed intent upon stringing small electrical lights of all shapes and sizes onto storefronts, the facades of buildings, and streetlamps. A festival? Men dangled from ladders to drape strings of paper pennants onto awnings and street signs. Women leaned out of windows to decorate the window frames.

Mr. Z.'s spirits lifted a little. It must be Diwali—the Festival of Lights. An annual Hindu celebration. Five days of it, if he recalled correctly, representing re-creation and rebirth, the victory of light over darkness, and the appreciation of the good things in life. Lakshmi was its attendant deity, but the festival was enjoyed as much in secular as in religious terms. It was an opportunity for everyone to enjoy family and bestow gifts, to eat sweets, set off fireworks, and forget one's cares. His heedless pursuit of Kashi seemed suddenly less, well, heedless. It was a search now. He must approach it like the detective work it had become. Think. And observe.

He headed west, determined to discover Mutton Street. But he hadn't gone a block along the bustling sidewalk when he encountered a vendor serving hearty-looking, intensely aromatic hot sandwiches. He stood awash in the smoky allure. The cook and his food stall seemed clean and efficient, professional, and the queue of customers lent credence to the quality of the food. Sandwiches—toasted and cut into four sections—were the theme. So-called Bombay sandwiches, yes. He recalled having listened to someone speaking English near the Taj Mahal Hotel when he'd arrived, something about the unlikely ingredients—buttered white bread stuffed with slices of beetroot, boiled potatoes, cucumbers, tomatoes, onion rings, and mint chutney. He found himself next in line, pointing to the sliced bread sizzling upon the grill.

The proprietor nodded.

"And tea?" Mr. Z. made a motion as if drinking from a cup.

Soon enough, Mr. Z. had paid his rupees and was alternately

chomping at his sandwich and gulping down his tea. Better piping hot than cold, despite the weather—after all, the cleanliness of the water here was not to be relied upon.

A bit restored, he surveyed his surroundings. Further up the block, a robust crowd occupied an entire intersection. This must be the bazaar. He caught sight of a street sign—Mutton Street, yes. He angled into the crowd, making for the center of things, and was immersed in a crush of people vying to inspect an incongruous profusion of merchandise, none of it new, and much of it unidentifiable to his Western sensibilities. Containers? Or were they décor? Or both? Were these utensils or tools? Perhaps weapons? What he *could* recognize were dusty old transistor radios, dull brass images of Hindu gods and goddesses, and racks upon racks of brightly colored clothing. One busy stall seemed crammed with a bit of everything, from garish framed paintings and embroidered pillows to car parts— every type of gear, spring, cylinder head, gasket, connecting rod, piston, etcetera. Also, cameras, clocks, pictures, hand tools, musical instruments, lamps, books, maps, furniture. The detritus of the entire mid-twentieth century on display, name your price.

Ahead, he noticed a middle-aged man shuffling in and out of a narrow storefront before which were stacked enormous muslin sacks—each half as tall as a man. Coffee beans. But there was something about the man's complexion, his eyes, and the shape of his face. And his finely tailored, apparently raw silk garment. Mr. Z. ambled toward the stall, pretending to examine the coffee beans. He dallied amongst the baskets of dried dates and nuts—almonds, peanuts, and cashews. He lingered before a steaming brass pot and enjoyed the intensely rich aroma of coffee. Then it struck him: Egypt. This vendor was Egyptian. He watched the man sip ruby-colored liquid from a small, crystal glass.

"Karkadeh?"[23] said Mr. Z.

The man glanced sidelong at him while tending to another customer.

---

23 A well-known tea beverage within Egypt made from hibiscus flower and served hot or cold.

Mr. Z. examined a date, turning it in his fingers patiently. "These are Medjool," he said. He moved on to a basket of darkened, almost black versions. "And these are Hayani?"[24]

The Egyptian settled with his customer and turned to Mr. Z. "The very best Hayani, yes. Try them." He watched Mr. Z. chewing. "And the best Medjool dates too. Moroccan."

Mr. Z. chewed and nodded in agreement. "I'll take some of both."

The Egyptian prepared two small wax paper pouches, one for each handful-sized portion of dates, and Mr. Z. prepared to surrender his rupees.

"Wait here, please." said the man. He ducked into the shop and reemerged with what appeared to be a shot-glass portion of the red tea. "Karkadeh," he said. "You are correct. Nobody here knows it. Hibiscus. From Upper Egypt. Very fine. Too expensive for these streets."

Mr. Z. sipped, then smacked his lips quietly. "Lovely flavor, thank you."

"How is it that you know of karkadeh? You are English. Perhaps American?"

Mr. Z. lay his rupees upon the tabletop. "I have fond memories of Cairo. And the Fayoum." They regarded each other for a moment. "It so happens that I am looking for something," said Mr. Z. "A heart scarab."

"Jewelry? Not here, sir. Jewelers and craftsmen, they are mostly in the southern part of the city. Sheik Memon Street. The Jain jewelers. Diamonds. Gold. Silver. Bangles." The Egyptian studied Mr. Z. more closely. "But a heart scarab? If you seek something authentic, you ought to know there is nothing of significance in a place like this."

A glimpse of someone moving about in the tiny, dark, enclosed space behind the stall made Mr. Z.'s blood quicken. Something about who it was—this entire encounter seemed strangely ominous. "I am looking for artifacts."

"Then you ought to go to a museum."

---

24 A type of date commonly planted in Egypt.

Mr. Z. shrugged and absently reexamined the sacks of fruit and nuts. "The pharaohs," he said, as if speaking to himself, "were buried with scarabs of green stone etched with magic words and placed over their hearts. For the heart was weighed at the time of death against a feather, in the presence of Osiris, and a true heart would not unduly tilt the balance." He readdressed the Egyptian in a quietly theatrical tone. "*O my heart, rise up not against me as a witness . . .*" He shrugged when the Egyptian remained stoic, unrevealing. "By way of a heart scarab, one could buy one's way into heaven."

The Egyptian's expression darkened. "Hrmph! Magic spells," he said. "What is your name?"

"Mr. Z."

"I am Abanoub." He collected his rupees. "Thank you for your business, Mr. Z. And good luck to you, finding your artifacts."

They took casual measure of each other again, and Mr. Z. turned to go.

"Wait."

Mr. Z. glanced back.

"Wait, sir!"

An elderly man emerged.

"Grandfather," said Abanoub, "you ought to be resting."

The old man's bearing was dignified despite his stooped shoulders and stiffened affectations. And he cocked his head at Mr. Z. in an unfocused manner that indicated his vision was lacking. "Abanoub," he whispered, "describe him to me."

Abanoub seemed impatient but nevertheless regarded Mr. Z. anew, looking him up and down. "Well, I don't know, Grandfather, he is dressed like an Englishman. Or American. Pants. Jacket. Collared shirt. Taller than me. Slender."

"I know all that by his voice. Except the clothing, of course. I have heard your name before, Mr. Z. A very long time ago. When I was a boy. After that, I traveled far and had many adventures. Across the Mediterranean. And all the way to London and back again. But the woman who raised me, in Cairo, she told stories to me that I still remember. Her name was Amu." The old man paused, as if for effect, and patted Abanoub's shoulder.

"Grandfather," said Abanoub. "I am sorry, sir, my grandfather, his memory—"

"My memory sustains me," interrupted the grandfather. "And one of the stories I remember best is the story Amu told me of a mysterious man named Mr. Z. And a young woman named Miss Vixy. Who traveled through time."

CHAPTER 9

DAISY CUTTER

THE PLASMA WHEEL DETONATED, AND the dismembered bodies of four thousand molemen soldiers toppled into the trench from which they'd just arisen or sprawled in nightmarish pieces upon the ruined, incinerated earth. The land steamed and smoked. Rivulets of blood pooled and simmered. The flesh and bones of the molemen bodies cooked, and the ground itself lay fissured and glistening like broken glass upon either side of the impact corridor.

Cog rolled over, gasping, into the sulphureous stench and smoke. His ears rang, and his respirator and plasma saber had been torn away by the percussive blast. He raised his face shield, inspected his textile armor, and grasped at his torso and legs. Intact. He touched his face. Not burned. Lucky. He had been far enough away. Shielded by the rocky outcropping too. But what did that mean in the face of the unholy carnage before him? Two regiments of molemen soldiers destroyed. Twenty molemen flash cannons annihilated.

Where was General Ten-Square? *Sergeant* Ten-Square now, of course, just as Cog had been reduced to corporal. He squinted into the haze. There, perhaps ten meters distant. He scrambled toward a crumpled heap face-down in the muck.

"Sir," croaked Cog. But he couldn't hear himself. He couldn't hear anything but the maddening ringing in his ears. He dropped to his knees and grasped Ten-Square's shoulders with both hands. "Sir!" He felt himself shouting, felt it in his throat, but the general—he would always be a general, dammit!—would never hear anything again. Cog knelt beside the body and stared blankly at the bleak landscape. Once a fertile farmland zone, now it might have been the lifeless surface of an asteroid or some naked moon.

"Argh."

That he could hear astonished him. "General?" Yes, he could discern his own voice. Cog watched the general's body heave. "General!"

Ten-Square hauled himself onto his knees, grimaced, and swiped at the muck caked upon his chin. He tried to stand and stumbled.

"No!" said Cog, "Stay down!" He strained to look overhead, deep into the sky, searching for the inevitable postblast strafing fighters.

"Damn the fighters to hell," mumbled Ten-Square. He sat quietly for a moment, looking about him, brooding upon the desolation and carnage. "If the Central City is enduring anything like this . . ." His uniform was saturated with brackish earth and silt. The ground had been almost liquefied by the energy, and silica dust had impregnated his textile armor, making it glisten in the diminishing daylight. "Daisy cutters,"[25] he said. "Where in hell are they getting the technology?" He glanced at Cog. "Are you hurt?"

"No, sir. I don't think so. Am I talking too loudly? My hearing is pretty wrecked." He jammed his fingers into his ears and wriggled them forcefully.

"Bastards," said Ten-Square. He coughed painfully into his elbow and scowled at the scene. "Mothmen sons of bitches." He dragged his forearm across his face, spit at the ground, scrambled to his feet, and flung the muck from his hands. "Engineers, my ass! They don't know

---

25   The twentieth-century Earth example was an American conventional weapon system (bomb) used in Vietnam and known for its ability to flatten a section of forest or jungle into a helicopter landing zone. Later it was used in Afghanistan as an antipersonnel weapon and as an intimidation weapon because of its large blast radius combined with a visible flash and sound audible at long distances. In comparison, the moleman version is an order of magnitude (approximately ten times) more powerful.

who they're dealing with. They're getting help from somebody, Cog, goddammit. It's a conspiracy. A damn conspiracy that we failed to rat out. But who is it? Who in their right minds would align themselves with these barbarians?"

Cog tried not to look at the bodies. "I don't know, sir. Maybe it's the alliance. Perhaps we underestimated . . ." He trailed off. "We've got to find cover, sir. And transmit, somehow. Contact headquarters."

"They won't be back," said Ten-Square. "The mothmen. They probably figure they got us all. I wouldn't waste ammo and fuel and time strafing a wasteland if I were them." He peered at the sky. "We're in it now, aren't we? You and me. Getting what we deserve for our failure with Giza." He made a halfhearted attempt to brush detritus from the front of his uniform. He stomped his feet and straightened his clothes, looked about for his helmet, snatched it up, swiped at its silica-blasted surface and heat-warped face shield, and tossed it aside. "You know, Cog," he said, tugging at his gauntlets, "I can't get the idea of Five's transponder out of my head." He rubbed his face and ears and eyed the horizon intently. "That it never came back, you know? That the cleanup drone never recorded it as inventory."

Cog didn't respond.

"You know what that means, Cog, don't you? It means the damn TDC has it. In the name of all engineering, I swear if that son of a bitch Z and those goddamn meddling time detectives, if they've aligned themselves with the mothmen . . ."

"Sir, do you really think the TDC would abandon their non-aggression mandate?"

"Hell no," said the general. "I mean, yes, hell yes, they would abandon their nonaggression mandate. They'd just make it look like the T.E. or some other IMC member nation with the chutzpah and military know-how to put up a fight is doing the dirty work. Subterfuge. Espionage. Geopolitics. Intergalactic political gamesmanship. Misinformation. Propaganda, when it fits the bill. Whatever it takes to gain an advantage, damn the idea of honor all to hell. All the cowardly, tedious, underhanded shit that goes on behind the proper business of war. It's never been any different, and I've no mind for it, Cog. You know that. It was bureaucratic tedium and backslapping and trying to please clueless administrators and career bureaucrats that handcuffed us with the Giza Cell. Otherwise, we could have . . . hell, if I was in command of this battalion, for instance. . . Ack!" He waved his words away and examined the rent in the earth and the mutilation that extended for as far as they could see. "But this was something I'd never have predicted, Cog. This is a surprise. This mothman military prowess. That's why I say there has to be something behind it, something nefarious and twisted. Meanwhile, we've been distracted. By the Cosmic Clock Project, for one thing. But we'll turn this around, this war, and crush the mothmen soon enough. And complete the CCP too. Now that we know what we're dealing with. The mothmen scum and whoever is behind them are going to pay. Anyone fool enough to stand in our way is going to pay. The *will* is the way, right, Cog?"

Cog fumbled with his transponder, swiped at the display, shook the thing, and tossed it aside. "Dead," he said. "Like everything else."

"Never mind, Cog. It's just as well. Those hills." He gestured into the distance. "Field command is that way. If they survived the assault, they'll be asses and elbows organizing a counterstrike. Meanwhile, we might get in there and get ourselves some hot chow, a shower, and a change of clothes. And some damn sleep, even. I haven't had a good night's sleep since we've been stationed out here in this hellhole. Let's move out."

The thought of food struck Cog as ludicrous in midst of the hideous carnage. And a good night's sleep? He doubted he'd ever have one again. But the general had seen combat before, while Cog had not. He'd been an administrator. A technician. An ideas guy. You could get used to anything, he supposed. And he couldn't deny that he was hungry. "Here's to being alive."

"What's that, Cog?"

He hadn't realized he'd spoken aloud.

Ten-Square rubbed his index fingers into his ears and grimaced. "Goddammit, my ears are still ringing."

Cog raised his voice. "Here's to being alive, sir."

"Damn straight, soldier." Ten-Square looked into the hills through his field glasses, ignoring the one shattered eyepiece. "We'll hit that

M.A.S.H. unit at Zero Hill. Range . . . ah, blast it!" He thrust the field glasses from his face, shook them, knocked them against the palm of his hand and tried again, squinting hard into the eyepieces. He gave up, made a motion to toss them aside, reconsidered, and clipped them to his belt. "Nine or ten klicks, I'd say. We might make it before nightfall. Let's just pretend we've lost our dog tags and we don't know what the hell has happened to us. That we're a little shell shocked. Which I'd say we goddamn are. And we don't know our names. We'll play dumb that way, Cog. We might be presumed dead already. I'm serious. And I'm thinking it might be to our advantage. At least for a while. To maybe figure out something about what the hell is going on in this bloody war behind the scenes."

"What about the Pole Star Lattice?" said Cog. "If the mothmen are getting help; if they've made a new alliance—I don't know, it's a multiple star, lots of moons, lots of asteroid belt obfuscation. Or it's possible our interplanetary reconnaissance missed something."

"No, Cog. Don't be second-guessing the reconnaissance. Espionage? Subterfuge? Yes and yes, that could be. But the recon? It's like the engineering. Solid. Nobody hides from the molemen, Cog."

They trudged along in silence for a time. And Cog's sense of relief at being alive quickly deteriorated into fatigue and a nagging desperation. Things seemed futile. He felt old and tired. As if he were impossibly disconnected from Ten-Square's resolve. This damn war. Another Great Conflict. Years of military nonsense ruling the day. Rationing, blackouts, air raid drills, and nonstop relocation from this command center to that one and back again. To say nothing of casualty reports and pro-war and anti-war skirmishes within the populace. He was too old for this shit. And the irony was brutal. Him always wanting to get off-planet and to be where the action was. Now? He was going to die off-planet. In the damn center of the action.

"Listen to me," said Ten-Square. He seemed to sense Cog's failing resolve and slowed a bit. "Buck up, Corporal. This is your sergeant giving you an order. You and I both are going to get off this rock." He kicked a stone out of his path. "Think of this as the beginning of our comeback. You and me, dead to the world and born again. And therefore free to get to the bottom of things. You watch. First thing,

I want to find out what happened to Five's transponder. I want us to get to the bottom of what the hell the TDC knows. This war is beside the point for you and me, Cog. We'd be discharged on medical, no doubt, after all this." He gestured as if to encompass everything around them. "Our job now? It's the same as it's always been. The Cosmic Clock Project, that's what I say. The bigger picture. It isn't at all over with, I'm telling you. Let's just be dead for a while. As long as it takes to get under the hood and dig through the guts of all this. Ghosts in the machine, you know that phrase? Well, you don't have to believe in ghosts to see how it just might be to our advantage to act like one."

CHAPTER 10

THE EMPEROR'S HAND

EMPEROR CHANGPU SAT POISED UPON his wicker throne in his usual manner, upon a firm pillow and seated as far forward as he could safely manage. The posture provided, first and foremost, ample clearance for his sword and sheath. Secondarily, it relieved the strain upon his knees. And finally, he had learned long ago that it forced his attention upon the outside world. Not his own thoughts or those of everyone else. The temptation to merely scan the thoughts of his advisors—and for that matter, the populace themselves—and dispense with conversation and verbal inquiry or declaration, well, it was just that. A temptation. Because he himself did not like to speak. Mostly because the articulation of thoughts somehow skewed them. Very few individuals deftly spoke their minds. He knew, because he read them. Thoughts were actions in themselves, and their influence could be as poisonous or pure, as destructive or productive, as anything corporeal. Ack. His knees ached, regardless. He shifted his weight, breathed a deep sigh, and tried to listen.

"Therefore, Your Imperial Majesty," continued the empress, scanning the faces of the seven advisors seated across from them, "the oracle bestows favor upon our plans." She gathered her yarrow stalks, and the silken folds of her garments rustled against each other. Her precise movements mesmerized the members of the court.

Indeed, the empress's articulate, pale hands were perhaps the most expressive thing about her. They still appeared youthful to him, her flesh still smooth and unblemished, her fingers slender, straight, and lustrously manicured, today in vivid ebony. But it was her tender voice that evoked his fascination. Like birdsong at a distance. Or the lyrical enticement of the bow upon the string. Beguiling? It beguiled everyone. Always and everywhere they bent their ears to it.

And she alone possessed a mind he could not penetrate. Not fully. So he was required to listen to her words and observe her expressions and attempt to decipher her affectations. Hence, she remained a mystery to him, more or less, and attractive in all manner of ways.

Observing her thus beside him, watching her deft hands manipu-late the yarrow stalks, listening to her, observing her composed and intelligent face, the fineness of her features, it never failed to evoke his memory of their courtship years, so long ago now, so innocent and naively promising. When he claimed for her the twin moons and stars and she indulged his vain declarations. Ah, youth.

"Advisors," he said. He eyed the members of his court. "Adepts. Everything furthers. Our Mythological Revitalization Initiative proceeds as planned. In accordance with the oracle." He gestured respectfully toward the empress. "The Cosmic Clock Component is within our grasp. Thereby we approach salvation. For to rescue the Arrow of Time from the clutches of the molemen infidels is to invoke the salvation of the Way."

The emperor paused. He knew their thoughts. He understood who followed and who fought him. Who sought to help and heed and who sought to impede, even destroy him. He knew their scan-dalous ambitions and ruthless desires. It was akin to understanding a portion of the future, but only in the sense of better predicting their actions. To know a person's thoughts was not to know what they would do next. Or think next. That required wisdom, amongst other faculties. Intuition. And keen knowledge of mothman nature.

His knees ached and he longed to stand. Or sit properly. Press on, he told himself. Think not of the trivialities of my bodily dis-comfort. "Hold to the empress's oracle. Embody the Way. And each of you will be rewarded. How so? Each with a hectare of land within the Pearl River region of the Prime Realm. Meanwhile, your work is far from over. It is merely the end of the beginning. For despite your achievements in coercing, redirecting, and manipulating the hyper-dimensional trajectory of the young time detectives, Mr. Z. himself, under the protection of the wolf, remains outside our influence. And the golden ball remains at large."

"Your Excellency, what of the war?"

Advisor Shan, again. Earnest in his inevitably self-serving manner. Loyal to the idea of the throne but in the end, in his mind, beholden only to the empress. And a fool to have convinced himself that the empress reciprocated his perverse affections. Like so many before him, he was infatuated with her, and therefore weakened, ultimately doomed to be cast aside. The empress suffered no fools. For now, Shan's ambitions and knack for the engineering set him apart in terms of usefulness.

"The outcome of the Great Conflict has been foretold. The distractions of the moment, then, the petty difficulties we face, well, each of you has been bestowed with the tools and training to execute your duties. Attend to them. Take mindful refuge within your work for its own sake. Do not grasp at outcomes. Do not kowtow to your fears. In this manner, each of you is empowered to embody the Way."

He clapped his hands upon his knees in a self-satisfied manner and gestured toward the door of the imperial meeting hall. "You are dismissed. Return to your temples and factories and laboratories and farms. Redouble your commitment to the protocol. Implement the science. Devote yourselves to the demands of your psychospiritual powers. Be assured, I know your thoughts. Remember, then, that to fail me is to fail the Way. To fail the Way is to forfeit your life. For your life is the Realm."

The empress watched the advisors bow to the emperor and one by one shuffle from the room. She savored the silence for a moment, then dismissed her courtier with a gesture. "Sire. Husband."

The courtier bowed and backed away, then paused. "Empress, I beg your pardon, please. Will you and His Excellency dine here tonight, within the Hall of Ritual, or within your private rooms?"

"Neither," snapped the empress. "Have you forgotten my anniversary? The emperor and *myself* shall dine in the courtyard between the

Hall of Origins and the Hall of Supreme Beatitude." She smoothed her robe, plucked a stray thread from the embroidered image—a white crane beside a green river.

The courtier bowed and hurried away.

"In the courtyard?" said the emperor.

"The weather will be cool and clear," said the empress. "Auspicious."

The emperor resigned himself with a shrug and strained to get up.

The empress touched her husband's sleeve. "We shall dine and drink and listen to the crickets in their cages."

"Hmm," said the emperor." He grimaced at the pain in his knees. "It has been years."

"It is our anniversary." The empress clasped her hands around his sword hand, smiling faintly, tenderly, and helped him down the steps. Then her expression darkened. "The hexagram was a changing one. I deemed a full interpretation before the advisors to be inappropriate."

The emperor cocked his eyebrow at her. "Tell me."

The empress's eyes darted about warily.

"I sense no intrusion of mind," said the emperor. "No subterfuge within these walls."

"Nevertheless, espionage takes many forms. Telepathy, even yours . . ." She drew her robes closer, tightened the sash about her waist. "How can you know for certain?"

"Nothing is for certain. Despite the wisdom of the oracle. Divinations demand interpretation, do they not?" He had never seen her so fretful. "Just as men's thoughts do. There is a mystery within all things, indeed. We attempt to mitigate the risks, that is all. By holding to the Way."

"*Standstill*," she said. "The same oracle cast by one hundred emperors before you. In times of trial. You cast it yourself barely a year ago."

"So be it," said the emperor. "We have lost the Way. Our mythology is broken."

"Therefore, I have cast another oracle. Asking not what is to come of our conflict with the molemen, for to ask again is to tempt fate and insult the Way. Rather, what is to become of the Realm under our rule? Ta Yu, possession in great measure. However, the change is to Po, splitting apart."

The emperor took a careful breath. "The book instructs us not to be unduly influenced by the first flush of interpretation. Is that not what you yourself advise?"

Her silence betrayed her uncertainty.

"What is it, then?"

"The inferior, dark forces overcome what is superior and strong, not by direct means, rather, by undermining it gradually and imperceptibly, so that it finally collapses."[26] The empress examined his reaction.

The emperor closed his eyes against the intensity of her regard, his only recourse whenever she was in possession of the oracle. "Continue. Withhold nothing."

"The leg of the bed is split," said the empress. "Those who persevere are destroyed. Misfortune." She appeared diminished for a moment, as if her dismay was a physical burden. "You are a true son of heaven," she said. "You possess the merit of essential nature and heavenly dao. Hence you are worthy." She bowed her head.

He grasped her hand. "I am no more or less afraid than any man," he said. "No more or less afraid than you."

She clasped her hands around his and spoke with conviction. "Within the oracle there is a nine at the top. A large fruit containing the seed of the future is still uneaten. The house of the inferior man is split apart, he ends up useless, while the superior man, when he gives generously and is not proud, receives the support of the people."

"Hence, everything furthers," he said. "Is that not correct?"

She nodded, her head still bowed.

"He who has faith preserves his heavenly nature," said the emperor. He touched her chin, lifted her face, looked into her eyes. Their

---

26 Richard Wilhelm, *The I Ching or Book of Changes*, 3rd ed., trans. Cary F. Baynes, Bollingen Series XIX, (Princeton: Princeton University Press, 1990 [1967]), 93. Republished with permission of Princeton University Press; permission conveyed through Copyright Clearance Center, Inc.

plans for winning the war, for wresting control of the Cosmic Clock from the molemen, for restoring the Arrow of Time and the sanctity of the Way would not fail for lack of faith. Neither would it fail for lack of technology. Nor lack of the power of vital force, of ming. For he had worked to cultivate all these things. He had educated the people. Provided resources. Advanced the science. Empowered each component of their military. "The oracle is fortuitous, and the war will be won." He clapped his hands, and a concierge emerged from behind a screen. "I must inspect our troops and meet with our generals." He rose stiffly, clacked down the shallow steps of the dais in his wooden geta, and ambled toward the door. He paused to glance back. "Oysters. Tonight. And crickets." He forced a smile and hobbled from the room.

The empress could not bear to return to her quarters. She felt too anxious, and instead bowed her head and clasped her hands together, listening again to the silence as if it contained the wisdom she sought. For the oracle was ominous. Fraught. And she had not been forthcoming to the emperor. She had hidden the danger as foretold. Only she understood the oracle that was cast by the emperor in all its dreadful detail. Indeed, a changing Ta Yu. But the change was six in the fifth place. A shoal of fishes. The yin power manifests. And represents neither prince, nor king, nor emperor. But rather queen. Or empress.

CHAPTER 11

DESTROYER

THE CONCRETE JETTIES EXTENDED THEIR shabby, unflattering welcome into the murky waters of the harbor, and Mr. Z. beheld the low shoulder of land beyond. He felt careworn, and he longed for the sun to finally set, if only to cancel its ruthless white heat. But then, he did not look forward to a sweltering tropical darkness either. Especially in a place like this.

Elephanta Island. Many centuries before the attentions of the future rendered it not only restored but once again a sacred place of active Hindu worship. If the island had indeed started as a Buddhist stronghold, it soon enough embraced Hinduism to the extent that in the sixth century CE or so, the famed Shiva caves were hewn into the low, basalt cliffs occupying the island's mangrove-choked interior. A staggering effort of devotion and a remarkable aesthetic accomplishment. And the carvings transformed a pitifully nondescript, out-of-the-way nub of volcanic rock within the nether regions of a deep-water bay into a sacred place that transcended millennia of humanity's folly and pervasive spiritual indifference.

And this place had certainly endured its share of such indifference. Vandalism by colonializing Portuguese soldiers. Inevitable theft of the pieces of heritage by collectors. There was an inscribed stone, recalled Mr. Z., said to have been absconded in 1540 or so on behalf of a Portuguese viceroy for the purpose of deciphering its text. But its words were never transcribed, and its story was lost to history. What did that stone say, if anything, about the vivid symbols and ambitious architecture that lay beyond this crude shore? It was exactly the type of mystery that sparked Mr. Z.'s longing for an investigation, an authorized HDT exploration to recover what was lost and illuminate the motivations and explanations—the whys and wherefores—of what empowered such a magnificent mythological vision and the execution of it.

Meanwhile, Bombay Harbor itself seemed graceless and defiantly unpretty. It was windblown and choppy, a hazy marine middle ground strewn with cargo ships, tankers, tugs, and globetrotting sailing vessels. The ferry lumbered closer and docked. Mr. Z. stood aside, allowing the tourists—mostly Hindu families with children, the men in their kurtas and churidars, a few in Western-style shirts and suit coats, the women in their saris or ghagra choli—to scurry ahead of him. He scanned the muddy beach and patches of scraggly marsh, the desiccated inland grasses and low, unkempt hills strangled with palm, mango, and tamarind trees. It was as if the route to the famous temple caves demanded a mental austerity commensurate with the stark inhospitality of the island's wilderness.

He finally disembarked beside a bespeckled man and his wife. The man was in traditional white trousers, waistcoat, and a dark cap, his wife adorned in a Victorian-style blouse beneath her gara saree. They sported Western-style shoes too. Clothing communicating significant wealth for the time. If Mr. Z. had to guess, he would consider them Parsis. He took in the expanse of the island. "Ah, Shiva," he breathed to himself.

"The destroyer," chirped the Parsi man. He smiled gamely at Mr. Z.

"Hmm? Oh, yes. I'm sorry. The destroyer, indeed. And the great ascetic."

The Parsi nodded and squinted into the knotty, greenish hills. "Indeed. Commensurately austere, then, isn't it? For a temple to the god. Hello, sir." He offered his hand. "My name is Ardeshir. This is my wife, Bachu."

Mr. Z. shook hands. The man's English contained only the slightest accent. He paused to allow the remaining handful of passengers to shuffle past. "I'm . . . Jones."

"Mr. Jones. You are an Englishman? Wait!" He looked Mr. Z. up and down with his full attention. "You have the bearing of an American. And there is your pronunciation. But then you have not spoken much, ha!"

Mr. Z. couldn't hide his bemusement. Here was a man who appreciated the habit of observation.

"And I do not intend an insult by any means, Mr. Jones. Your Americanness. It is merely an observation. All the nationalities tend to comport themselves with their undeniable idiosyncrasies. Would you agree?"

Perhaps it was the strain of his mission and his anxiety over the absence of Vixy and Neutic, or the HDT lag, or his long damn day chasing the scummy Kashi, but Mr. Z. found himself at a loss.

"Please," said Ardeshir. He motioned for Mr. Z. to step ahead.

They were at the shore and stepped down from the dock. He forced himself to search the landing and the path ahead for any indication of Kashi.

Ardeshir had been watching him. He nodded with a theatrical gravity. "And you are wondering what brings my wife and I, being Zoroastrians, to this Hindu sacred site?"

Mr. Z.'s courteous expression, or perhaps merely his silence, seemed to inspire Ardeshir.

"I am a scholar. Of religion. With an interest in Hindu symbology."

"Hmm," murmured Mr. Z. "I likewise study religion. And I teach comparative mythology."

"Well then, sir, we are indeed the same. Religion. Mythology. One and the same. From my perspective. And such a coincidence really isn't one, the two of us with identical interests arriving together here. First of all, seeing as this is perhaps my . . . let me see." Ardeshir pressed his index finger against his temple for effect. "My tenth or eleventh visit to this island."

"Twelve," said Bachu, feigning wifely exasperation.

"My wife is always correct. Twelve times. With much research left to uncover, certainly. Hindu and Buddhist, both."

They stood at a crossroads of sorts where the path approaching the caves began and the start of the small-gauge railroad, complete with puffing engine and open-air passenger cars, was accepting tourists.

"You will be walking or riding, Mr. Jones?"

"Walking."

"And we will be riding"—Ardeshir gestured at the train—"because my legs are old and weak." He smiled. "I look forward to perhaps encountering you at the caves, sir. And if that is not to be, then Bachu and I have enjoyed meeting you." He touched his hand to his hat and tipped his head in a discreet bow. "To Shiva."

"Indeed," said Mr. Z. "All the best in your work." He watched the two Parsis settle into their train car. They exchanged waves, and he made his way up the trail, suddenly reflective. Shiva was the cosmic dancer, after all. The greatest ascetic. And the destroyer. All these aspects of the great god both comforted and unnerved him. More than any other deity, this one invoked in him the terrible, unlimited, ruthless sublimity of the universe. All evils, all suffering perceived as legitimate and necessary as its opposite.

He paused, looking about. Whatever Kashi intended by fleeing to a mostly barren island was an illogical mystery. There was the proximity of the mainland to the east, but there were any number of less tedious and restrictive routes. Meanwhile, where could anything but a wild monkey hope to disappear into for any length of time in a place like this?

Zizo had explained that this island still supported a thousand or so inhabitants—the families of rice farmers, fishermen, and shipwrights. Kashi couldn't expect to ingratiate himself to the extent that any of them would conceal him. He'd be a hopeless fugitive. Unless there were an outpost of some type, some terrorist cell or secret refuge attached to whatever group Kashi belonged to. It would perhaps require only a little money to keep the natives quiet. But even if Kashi was simply on the run, he could not be acting alone. Laron *must* be involved. He felt it in his guts. And when Zizo recalled Laron's name from the stories Amu told him, that he'd heard rumors of a man named Laron and a Scarab Cult too, well, it was no surprise. So as incongruous as it seemed, as much as his common sense told him that Laron could be anywhere within the sprawling megalopolis of Bombay, his intuition told him that Kashi was leading him directly to the man.

He breathed the clammy sea air with its whiff of diesel from the train and redoubled his pace, leaning into the elevation change and delving into the reddening hills. If he could only find Kashi before nightfall, he could perhaps call for reinforcements. Before spending the night out here on his own.

He struggled to remain on task. Think, dammit. Assume that Kashi would make for the temple caves like everyone else. And if he wasn't seeking the caves, there was nothing to be done about it, because then both Kashi and Laron had managed to escape.

The path rose steeply as it approached the grand entrance to the main hall from the north. Here and there macaques attempted to ply the tourists for food. The path itself was paved with bricks interspersed with sections of low staircase, and the accumulated change in elevation was significant. Mr. Z. wiped his brow and turned back to the darkening waters of the harbor.

"I remember Amu," Zizo had told him, "as a strong-hearted, capable woman of Coptic descent. She told me stories, legends. Even into my adolescence. One in particular, about how Cairo got its name, I enjoyed very much. There was a kingly warrior and soldiers on horses and priestly astrologers reading the stars and planets and so on. It was a tale I was convinced that I had forgotten until you came."

They had sat face-to-face in the small, shaded room behind the food stall, taking the measure of each other, the old man astonished and breathless and Mr. Z. himself rapt. The coincidence was impossible. Yet, there it was. Zizo recalling Vixy's Amu, and Amu telling a tale of Vixy herself. All during their chat, as with his encounter with Campbell and Salmony, he reminded himself about leave-no-trace protocol, that he ought to have left then and there, requested an HDT evacuation, and filed his report.

"Nothing is too fantastic for a young boy to believe," Zizo had continued. "And then you turn around and one day you are old— the years have flown. And perhaps you find yourself not so much believing in anything."

Mr. Z. recalled Zizo's searching eyes.

"Bombay," Zizo had said. "The City of Gold, some call it. Because men dream of riches and find them here."

Mr. Z. resisted engaging in conversation, though he'd found it impossible not to hold Zizo's gaze and search the man's face. But each moment left a trace. Each action, each thought. The idea had felt like a torture then, as if time itself cried out for him to stop, to goddamn get up and walk out and not look back. He cringed at his indiscretion. He'd fallen victim to the shimmering allure of coincidence and the compelling sense of serendipity and synchronicity and portent. To the seduction of time travel.

"You talk of scarabs," Zizo had continued. "There is a rumor of a cult. One obsessed with scarabs. And riches. They perform rites in the Shiva caves."

Scarab Cult! It was all he could do not to blurt the words. "Rites? When?"

Zizo had merely shrugged. "I don't know anything about them."

They'd parted in silence. No handshake. No wink. No nod of acknowledgment. He'd made sure of it. Yet he'd felt the old man's gaze upon his back like the heat of the sun. Perhaps Zizo somehow understood. Oh, the accursed taboo of such an encounter! He fought his compulsion to someday tell Vixy—to admit to her that he'd encountered someone from her HDT past. It was exactly such an alluring notion—the entanglements of time travel—that he was never to indulge. Never. And he wouldn't. The risks were too great. Meanwhile, Zizo had implied Laron's ultimate destination here in India—forbidden fruit in LNT terms. But fruit that had nevertheless fallen upon the ground by its own accord. And there wasn't a time detective alive that would not snatch it up.

The Shiva caves, then. That Kashi had fled here, well, the pieces fit. But the odds of Laron himself being here too? If the TDC had managed to trace Laron, the captain would have communicated it. They hadn't. And the situation with Vixy and Neutic, if there was one, was perhaps keeping the captain busy enough. Meanwhile, he himself was following protocol for once and refraining from transmitting. Who knew, after all, if Laron and company weren't even now attempting to track him? If this was a Scarab Cult base of operations? Of course, he could have it completely wrong. But there was nothing else for it, except giving up and going home. And his guts told him to see this through.

It was half past four o'clock. The light was fading, and the caves, according to the posted signage, were to be closed to tourists at five o'clock. Hence, for anyone interested in anything beyond a frivolous walkthrough of the temples, this last ferry trip to the island would have seemed a worthlessly hurried consideration. Why, then, would a man like Ardeshir, for instance, if he were indeed a scholar conducting field research, have chosen to arrive here without enough time to accomplish anything besides perhaps taking a handful of photographs? And the man had brought his wife along.

The idea nagged at him, and Mr. Z. looked for evidence of the train or the caves themselves. He recalled something about one hundred and twenty steps comprising the path, and while he hadn't bothered to count them, it seemed the caves ought to be coming into view. Yes. There. Straight ahead. Finally, a level courtyard of sorts, and beyond, the cave entrance with its massive stone pillars that strained beneath the raw rock overhang.

Now it struck him, watching the tourists milling about and experiencing the crudeness of the environs, that on the outside chance that Kashi and perhaps even Laron were or had been here, they may have established their own field headquarters away from the busy caves, hidden within the mangroves. In which case, he'd never find them.

Then again, there remained the idea of hiding in plain sight. It seemed ludicrous. This main cave was large. And there were two others—the eastern and western sanctuaries, both significantly smaller.

Argh. Belaboring everything was a waste of energy. The other caves were easily accessed via the main hall. It would have required a troublesome overland trek around the cliff face to get to either of them otherwise. No. If any of the caves were a destination for anyone, by common sense they would enter from the north and proceed into the main hall.

A train whistle trilled. The diminutive engine had chugged its way to the station, such as it was. It was a mere concrete platform. Mr. Z.

found himself scanning the disembarking passengers for Ardeshir and his wife, but he failed to spy them. And a gesticulating guide ushered the handful of tourists into the cave. "Please! The caves are closing soon! It will be dark! The last ferries depart in less than one hour. If you wish to see, then follow me quickly."

Mr. Z. thought he ought to see what there was to see while a little daylight remained. He followed a clutch of tourists up the steps and reached discreetly into his jacket for his plasma pistol. He compulsively checked the safety and that the weapon wasn't hung up on anything—that he could draw it quickly—and guided it back into the holster.

He brushed past the mangled yet still noble sculpture of the Yogishvara Shiva, its arms and legs missing, to their left. Carved into the opposite wall of the entrance was the figure of the Natajara, the so-called Dancing Shiva. But the mighty god had long ago been likewise mutilated, his torso broken at the thighs and all but one of his many arms fractured at the elbows. Nevertheless, there remained his stony visage: resolute, profoundly meditative, bestowing the indomitable glory of his contemplative bliss.

Mr. Z. knew the images. He'd studied them. He knew the rough dimensions of the main hall—it formed a rectangle approximately forty meters by twenty-seven meters. He had intended to visit these caves in person within his own time, of course, and not merely by way of video tours. It was essential to be here firsthand. But the permits required had not been granted. Millennia hence, the accumulated vandalism—tourists scrawling graffiti, the shameless chipping away of the carvings for mementos, or the millennia of people treading upon the floors and influencing the atmosphere within the caves by their respiration and the chemicals left behind by their touch—had rendered the carvings at risk. Hence, visitation required a lengthy application that was often refused without the support of an influential insider. His research had been confined to text and photographs. Now, because of the LNT protocol, he would be precluded from communicating whatever came of his firsthand impressions. So his aspirations to publish on the topic were dashed.

He moved further in. Hewn into the south wall, deep within the cave and directly ahead, would be the renowned Trimurti, the magnificent tri-imaged statue of Shiva, the Great God in his three aspects, towering a full six meters and forming the massive focal point of the chamber. On the western end of the hall would be the Sanctuary of the Lingam, its four stone entrances flanked by sculpted guardians.

He peered past the sturdy stone pillars, suddenly compelled to see for himself the Trimurti. The others in the group seemed reluctant to continue, as if wary of the dim, low-ceilinged confines. He watched a young man regard his timepiece, shrug indifferently into the darkness, and turn to the young woman beside him expectantly. She eyed the cave depths warily and drew her silk scarf more closely around her face. Rather than proceed, she drew back, tugging at the man's arm as if to leave. And suddenly everyone in their little group seemed of similar mind. Mr. Z. watched each of them move toward the entrance and hurry down the chamber's steps.

Mr. Z., meanwhile, stood poised near a pillar within the center of the Great Hall. He watched the remaining tourists drift toward the exit. If he were to leave, then he ought to do it now. That, or duck farther within and hide until everyone had gone. He'd be stranded here overnight if he stayed. Yet the idea of giving up and returning to Bombay seemed almost as off-putting. The thought of giving up his pursuit of Kashi made him grind his teeth. He had his flashlight and his plasma pistol. He could tough it out on the island, the sweltering night and monkeys and mosquitoes be damned.

The guide hurried past, rattling off something in Hindi, then English. "Please! Everyone! The time is to go! Everyone must leave! Hello! The caves are now closed! You must leave to the boats!" He made a cursory circuit of the darkening hall, seemingly keen to round up his charges as if they were lost sheep.

Mr. Z. did his best to become one with the nearest pillar, pressing his back against it.

Soon enough there were no more voices or footfalls, and a strangely unsettling silence engulfed the hall. Mr. Z. couldn't help reconsidering his plan. What made him think he could endure a night upon this island, let alone within these forbidding caves?

It was then that he spied something—or somebody—scrambling

up the entrance steps, hugging the far wall. Yes, a man, practically tiptoeing into the hall.

Mr. Z. hid behind his pillar and craned to peer round it, his eyes almost aching for a nuance of light. Kashi. It had to be.

It was too quiet. There ought to be footsteps. And the confounded darkness of this cave—how was Kashi, or whoever it was, managing to get around in here? Mr. Z. reached for the tactical lantern on his belt. No, don't turn it on, stay hidden, for God's sake. Just wait. What he wouldn't give for his damn night vision!

He listened. Nothing. He'd be forced to switch on his lantern, dammit. Count to a hundred first. But he hadn't begun to count when he heard something. Outside the hall. Voices. Hushed. A moment later there was light—several lanterns!—and a commotion near the entrance. There were twenty or so men, women, and a handful of children in various casual dress—they appeared no different than tourists.

"Okay, ready now? We lift him on the count of three."

It was a man's voice outside, perhaps upon the steps.

"One, two, three, up!"

Two men in shirtsleeves and khaki slacks awkwardly hauled someone in a wooden wheelchair—he appeared elderly—up the staircase. The others made their way deeper into the temple cave, their lanterns casting a feeble glow, as if the light were powerless against the penetrating dark.

There was the smell of kerosene and the quiet shuffling of the visitor's feet over the rough floor. Mr. Z. peered round his pillar. The group gathered before the massive Trimurti and arranged their six or so lanterns below it, so the famous three-headed image was illuminated from below and their little group was framed in light. He counted twenty of them. They seated themselves casually side by side, legs crossed, some availing themselves of thin grass or bamboo mats, others merely seated upon the hard rock. A handful stood in the rear alongside the man in the wheelchair.

And it was one of these men who donned a pale, cassock-alb–style garment. A priest! Of course! What else could this little gathering be besides a ceremony of some type? And the implied secrecy of it all? Without a doubt he had been right to pursue Kashi here. Where was the little rat?

The priest took his position before the congregation, such as it was, with the shadowy visage of the Trimurti looming behind him. At the priest's feet was a modest, shoebox-sized fire altar or some such contrivance. It housed several pillar candles, discreetly aglow, and Mr. Z. saw that the priest's attire was featureless except for a matching rope cincture for his cassock-alb and a modestly proportioned, pale-colored miter on his head. The miter was adorned with a shimmering insignia, but there wasn't light enough for Mr. Z. to discern it.

A reverent silence permeated the cavern, and Mr. Z. pressed himself against the pillar, straining to see. The priest knelt to adjust his fire altar, and the insignia upon his miter caught the light—a scarab! Golden.

The priest collected himself and assumed a prayerful pose, his hands pressed together beneath his chin. "We believe the past is a living thing and that only the chosen are bestowed the power to change it. *We are the chosen.* We hereby receive the divine benediction by way of the Two Partners. Amen."

"Amen," intoned the congregation.

"Peace be with you," said the priest.

"And also with you."

The priest, perhaps middle-aged, stood tall and projected an air of poise and quiet authority. His voice was warmly, charismatically sonorous. Priestly in all the right ways, thought Mr. Z.

The man continued. "Welcome to this remarkable palace. Welcome to this stronghold and treasure trove of ancient Shaivite devotion. It is a stirring place. A sanctuary set apart from civilization. Isolated. Embraced by nature. Unembellished except by the inspired hands of its original spiritual craftsmen, who, by way of their remarkable work, evoked the tenets of their faith and the powerful mystery of existence itself. And our struggle within that mystery. Here, carved into the living rock, we encounter the symbols of time and eternity. Of light and darkness. Birth and decay. Life and death. Creation and destruction. Think for a moment, if you will, what the experience must have been like in the fifth and sixth centuries CE, as we refer to it within these times, when the work was new and all these images, these magnificent symbols, were physically intact. It seems a unique achievement now, and it must have seemed a transcendent achievement then.

"Behind me, as I am sure you know, is the Sadashiva—the Supreme Being—a Shaivite version of the Trimurti that expresses what we may interpret as the trine aspects of the single Shaivite deity. Within other sects, of course, the Trimurti acknowledges the individual aspects of Brahma and Vishnu, also. Here upon your right, then, is the god's western visage, Brahma, the creator, also expressing Shiva's female aspect. Upon your left, the eastern visage, is Shiva's terrifying destroyer aspect, his chaos-creator iteration, and the central image communicates Vishnu, the sustainer of the cosmos.

"Now, imagine making the pilgrimage that you have made, but some twenty-five hundred years ago. Before power boats and trains. Before bulldozers and backhoes. Before machines. Before electric light. You would sail to this place in your little boat, and the remoteness would be part of the experience. An arduous journey on behalf of the divinity being its own worthy sacrifice, an end in itself, akin to the journey of life. Moreover, within this context, traversing the waters of the harbor may be interpreted as a symbol of ablution, of cleansing and purification. Fire, too, is yet another symbol of purification.

"The mythological images, then, the metaphors here at hand— this massive Trimurti—they are as potent and effective and affecting as any other that speaks to the Mystery. Open yourselves to them. But remember, we seek to syncretize but not to homogenize the wisdom. Allow the images here to do their work upon you in their own manner. Experience within the local symbols, as they may be termed, the universal truths."

The priest raised his hands. "Rise. Make your offerings. But do not linger. Our ferry is waiting."

It was only at this point, as a queue formed before the fire altar, that Mr. Z. observed that each member of the congregation possessed a pale slip of paper. More than a handful of them scribbled hurriedly upon and folded it, and one by one they approached the priest, their hands pressed together and heads bowed in prayer, waiting. The priest touched their offering to the scarab insignia upon his miter, and when he handed it back to them, they bent to incinerate it upon the little fire altar. The service apparently concluded, and everyone drifted toward the exit.

Mr. Z. hesitated, his instinct to retreat into the courtyard conflicting with his intuition to observe more of the priest's postservice activities. Who was this man? Was he indeed merely a priest? Who were the congregation themselves? If this were indeed an iteration of the Scarab Cult, why were they all here? Were they all from identical space-time coordinates? And the brevity of the service struck him. Had they made such a journey only to depart almost as soon as they had arrived?

But the theology and the symbols, the call to *syncretize but not homogenize the wisdom*. Of Shaivites? Syncretize with what, exactly? On the face of it, it was inarguably egalitarian. And innocent, even naive. Too innocent. Too naive. As if the kicker to their ideology had been left out on purpose. The mystery of the—what did the priest call it? The two aspects? No. The two *partners*. Yet if this was all there was to it—if the Scarab Cult were nothing more than religious triteness and spiritual platitudes . . . No, there must be more to it. Did they somehow know they were being observed? Was this merely theater? A show? Even a trap? And where in hell was Kashi?

The departing members had availed themselves of all but one of the lanterns, and Mr. Z. took advantage of the deepening darkness to creep closer and observe the priest with his lone lantern and quiet little fire altar. Immediately, he caught a glimpse of something else—a shadow, approaching. Kashi! It had to be!

"Father."

It was a breathy whisper that Mr. Z. could barely discern. But the priest's response was unequivocally forthright and loud.

"Fool!"

Mr. Z. watched Kashi cower and glance warily about him.

"But *Father*!"

"Enough! You have failed!"

"I . . . the mission. You cannot know how it was! Something went wrong, someone—"

The priest waved Kashi away, yanked his miter from his head, and stuffed it into a pocket of his cassock-alb. He stooped to extinguish the candles and strode toward the lantern. Kashi shuffled after him. The shadows of the two men danced against the cave walls.

"It is the time detectives!" cried Kashi. "I swear! I am being followed. I am in danger. You must help me!"

The priest brushed past Kashi, then hesitated. He set down the lantern, wrung his hands, and tore off his robe. He folded it roughly and shoved it under his arm. "It is out of my hands. You are a fool and a liability. As I suspected. You will answer to Laron. Now get out. Or stay, dammit, what do I care? Just do not attempt to follow us to the boat!"

The priest again turned his back upon Kashi and bent to gather the fire altar within the fabric of his cassock-alb. It was then that Kashi leapt at him, his knife flashing.

"Argh!" The priest cried out and fell back. The lantern clattered to the floor. They struggled.

But Kashi's hand was over the man's mouth and then all was still. The priest sprawled at Kashi's feet, and the only sound was Kashi's labored breathing. Kashi seized the lantern and darted away, not toward the main entrance but west.

The western shrine? But why? Mr. Z. hurried to follow him, as closely as he dared, and when he gained the stairs, Kashi was already scrambling across the open courtyard.

"Kashi!"

The voice boomed, reverberating against the rock like a thunderclap. Each man froze.

Mr. Z.'s mind reeled—who in hell? Laron, it must be. He scrambled for the cover of the nearest rock wall, holding his breath. Footsteps! Two men—one tall and lean, the other less so—emerged from the darkness of the northwest entrance to the courtyard, from the direction of the trail back to the train depot. They lit the courtyard with a powerful, autofocusing floodlamp—the kind Mr. Z. would have liked to have packed—and illuminated every darkened corner with flashlights.

Kashi skidded to a halt near the middle of the courtyard and hesitated. Mr. Z. watched him hurl his lantern aside and dash in the opposite direction, retreating into the Great Hall.

Blam! Blam!

Mr. Z. flinched at the blasts. Plasma pistols. He drew his own and ducked low behind his pillar, fighting the urge to peer out.

"Aiee!" A muffled shriek from within the hall.

"Finish him, Shields. Pour l'amour de Dieu![27] Do not make me track the little fucker all over this miserable island in the dark."

Mr. Z. peered out from his hiding place and waited. He watched Shields—a stocky, heavy-limbed ogre of a man—lumber up the temple steps following the beam of his lantern. Laron sauntered several meters behind, aiming his lantern before him with one hand and swinging a plasma pistol at his side with the other. "My little shiny-haired Indian man. Kashi. Nervous as a chicken. Where are you?" Laron paused at the staircase and wiped at his brow. "Shields!" He shouted into the emptiness of the temple entrance. "Dammit, you clod! Do I have to come in there? Shields!"

Mr. Z. crept toward Laron at a careful distance. The main hall was illuminated enough by the lanterns. But neither Kashi nor Shields nor Laron himself was visible because Mr. Z. could not risk mounting the stairs.

"Gut shot. Hmm." Shields's voice was coarse and flat. "It didn't take him long to bleed out."

"Spare me your hunter-gatherer colloquialisms," said Laron.

"Huh?"

"Just haul him into the bushes. Or something. Get rid of him. And where is that damn priest? Just like a fucking Egyptian to disappear as soon as there is work to be done."

Mr. Z. crept up the steps, crouching, hugging the rock wall. He slipped a stun grenade from the clasp of his belt, armed his plasma pistol, and tried to see inside. The men were side by side, some distance from the lingam shrine.

---

27   "For the love of God!"

"Ack!" shouted Shields, "what the hell is that?"

A furious scuffling ensued, and Mr. Z. ducked away from it, then caught a glimpse of something leaping out the other side of the sanctuary, scurrying into the blackness of the western exit.

Shields aimed his pistol at it.

"Leave it!" hissed Laron. "It's nothing but a monkey—this place is crawling with them. Now get moving. Get rid of this goddamn body, goddammit."

Mr. Z., a stone's throw from the men, let fly with his stun grenade. It skittered across the irregular stone floor.

"Grenade!" hollered Shields. He shoved Laron aside and charged toward the device, lantern ablaze. He swiped at it with his foot, sending it careening toward the eastern entrance.

Mr. Z. ducked and covered his ears, watched Shields leap behind a pillar.

Bang! The device detonated with a brilliant flash at the far end of the temple hall, and Mr. Z. caught sight of Laron fleeing for the main entrance. He leapt after him, immediately realized he'd never catch him, knelt, aimed in the direction of Laron's careening lantern light, and fired.

"Argh!" Laron crumpled, and his lantern skittered down the steps. "Shields! Help! Goddammit, Shields, for fuck's sake, I'm hit!"

Blam!

Mr. Z. ducked, and shards of stone stung his face. He lunged instinctively toward the stairs, then thought better of it—he'd be sandwiched between two armed men. He scrambled toward the protection of the lingam shrine and dove across the threshold, hauling himself into a corner. He lay there, gasping, his heart pounding.

"I know it's you, old man!" hollered Shields. "Z! You rat coward!"

Blam!

Rock splintered outside the lingam shrine. Shields was coming for him. But from where? He crawled to the northern opening and fired blindly, then retreated to the western opening. He exited, hurled another stun grenade toward the center of the hall, covered his ears against the concussion—boom!—and ran like the devil for the main entrance.

He dove headlong down the darkened steps only to find the stairway empty and Laron gone. The moon had risen, bathing the courtyard in a planetary glow, a blessing. He barreled across the courtyard stones and passed through the northwest opening in the rock. He skidded to a stop, hugging the rock face outside the caves, and waited, listening for Shields.

Nothing.

Then a wavering light along the opposite wall of the courtyard—Shields, still coming. Mr. Z. fired a desperate shot at the light and broke into a run, half stumbling, half running along the footpath toward the tiny railway line. The jetty was perhaps one and a half kilometers down the hillside toward the ocean. Laron had to be making for it.

The moonlight, though a godsend, wasn't enough to inspire confident footing—the ground was uneven, rocky, and dotted with low scrub while the silvery, shadowless light flattened his perspective. He stumbled along, sweating, breathing hard, struggling to make headway while keeping a lookout for Laron ahead and Shields behind. There, straight ahead, a light! It moved in the direction of the jetty. But too quickly. It couldn't possibly be Laron, let alone an injured Laron. Somebody else, then? But who? Or maybe it was a trick of the moonlight. Perhaps he misjudged the distances and it was a boat, a vessel on the water?

He strained to see, but it was no use. Damn, no trek goggles! He hurried over the rugged ground, keen to track the wavering light, but it was outdistancing him. Only something motorized could move that quickly, especially over this terrain. Then the wind changed, and he heard the roar of an engine—a damn glide-pad of all things. Only Laron would so shamelessly defy all HDT ethics and transport such a thing into 1954. He glanced back—no sign of Shields. Laron was getting away, outrunning him toward the twinkling lights of the jetty.

When he finally gained the beachhead, waves hissed across the pebbly shore, and the cooling sea breezes were both a relief and a curse. It was as if Laron had vanished. Across the water, somewhere within the black distance, was the Bombay shoreline. Was Laron already headed for it? Or had his HDT nexus been here, upon this island?

He peered fitfully out to sea. He scanned the shoreline, focusing on the jetty. Laron couldn't ride a glide-pad across the open water. But he might possess cloaking technology. Suddenly the sputtering yowl of a small engine—incongruously powerful and modern—interrupted the stillness. It came from down the shore. A jet-rider! Why did he think these scoundrels would bother with ferries?

The jet-rider swerved around in a frothing wake, engine whining. Mr. Z. glimpsed Laron's pale silhouette against the shimmering sea and cringed as the machine roared away.

He tapped his transponder—he'd had the sense to strap it into his shoulder pouch—and scrambled the last fifty meters or so toward the jetty. "Captain! Do you copy?" No response. The silence and the sense of his own bungling failure made him furious, and he tried again. "Z to Captain Chase." After what seemed an eternity with the indifferent ocean before him and the desolate island behind, the transponder crackled to life.

"Go ahead! Jeezus, Z, go ahead! The transmit ban . . . I wasn't expecting . . . goddammit Z, what's going on?"

Mr. Z. scanned the jetty wall for another jet-rider. There had to be one for Shields. Yes, there!—bobbing in the water on the opposite side, hidden from incoming ferries. The machine's sleek graphite hull gleamed in the moonlight.

"Z? Do you copy?"

"Yessir. I am chasing Laron. I need somebody to intercept him at the Gateway of India ferry port—he's traveling by jet-rider from Elephanta Island. Are Vixy and Neutic here? Can they help?"

"They're not, Z. Vixy and Neutic did not arrive. No transponder feed. We can't track their ghosting. Something about their HDT went to shit—geodesic deviation, curvature torsion, we don't know yet. They're alive, they're healthy—we've got proof-of-life data, but that's all. That, and that they're together. They made it through the manifold cleanly. We just don't know where and when they goddamn are! But look here, Z, I've mapped your vectors. Meridians, parallels, hypermeridians, all good, I can see your coordinates. But Laron, nothing. He's still obfuscating. You are on your own, Z. Just do what you can to stop him."

Mr. Z. grasped the handrail at the jetty wall. Beneath him the jet-rider bobbed wildly in the tossing sea. He drew a breath and prepared to clamber over the rail.

Blam!

A plasma shell struck the metal railing and Mr. Z. flinched at the stinging sparks. He leapt, crashing into the water, flailing at the choppy water, gasping and spitting.

"Z!" said the captain. "Z, what the hell!"

Mr. Z. groped at the jet-rider's hull and handlebars and hauled himself into the seat. He punched the ignition. "Start goddammit, start!" Nothing. He punched it again. "Shit!"

"Shit is right, you motherfucker!"

It was Shields, shouting at him from somewhere on shore. Breathless. Coughing a smoker's hack. "Shit is goddamn right, you bastard son of a bitch!"

Mr. Z. dove from the jet-rider and swam hard along the jetty wall, searching for a handhold. He tried hauling himself up. Argh! The sharp pain in his arm—his old injury from the Olympic Theater. He fell back, then reached up again, this time grinding the toes of his trek boots against the stones and straining with his legs. He flopped like a floundering fish onto the jetty's walkway, soaking wet and breathless. And in plain sight of Shields. But Shields was still searching the waters beside the jetty, aiming his lantern into the tossing sea.

Mr. Z. aimed his plasma pistol at Shields, trying desperately to steady his hand. No, too far, too dark. Shields lumbered toward him. Just wait. Wait for him to come to you. There. He aimed, finger upon the trigger. "Freeze! Don't move, Shields! Don't be a fool—I have you in my sights!"

Shields kept coming.

"Last chance, Shields! Stop, or I'll shoot!"

The waves crashed against the jetty, and the sea breeze whistled across the choppy water.

"Do it, Shields!"

"Fuck you, old man!"

Shields, like some cowboy in an ancient western, drew his pistol.

Mr. Z. fired twice, and Shields fell to his knees, staring wide-eyed, then flopped face-first onto the concrete.

Mr. Z. crept toward the body, holding Shields in his sights until he stood over him. He nudged the man's shoulder with his foot, grinding at the flesh. Nothing. He holstered his own gun, pried Shields's pistol from his dead hand, and shoved it into his belt. Then he rifled through the man's clothes, searching for a key, a fob, anything that might start the jet-rider. Nothing.

"Damn it all to hell," said Mr. Z. Shields's body and the jet-rider were perhaps thirty meters apart—there was no hauling the body or the machine around to try and get the man's finger pressed into the ignition keypad. Mr. Z. unsheathed his pocketknife, grasped Shield's limp hand, and paused. "I'm guessing you're right-handed." He spread the man's fingers onto the stony surface of the jetty and leaned onto his knife, crunching through the bone. He got up, Shields's index finger in hand, climbed back over the jetty railing, and lowered himself onto the jet-rider. He shoved Shield's fingertip into the identification pad, and the motor roared to life.

"Z! For God's sake, Z! Are you there!"

Mr. Z. shouted into the transponder over the noise of the motor. "Yessir! Yes, Captain!" He revved the engine and wheeled himself round to face the open water, idling. "Shields is dead. I've got to leave the body." He revved the motor, squeezed the handlebars, tucked his knees against the seat, and engaged the drive. The seawater churned fitfully behind him, the salt spray rushed past him, and he sped headlong toward Bombay.

CHAPTER 12

CASTAWAY

AN EMPTY WAREHOUSE WITH A *broad main aisle and typical high-strength flooring. Fiber-steel storage racks towering upon either side. Everything in immaculate condition, not a paint chip or scuff mark anywhere, as if the place had just been built.*

But wait, thought Five, there isn't any ceiling. The racks soar upward into . . . clouds? And there are many, many racks. They disappear into the distance in all directions. Where am I? What is this place?

He noticed the musky reek of machine oil. And the tang of electrical ozone. And the impenetrable quiet. And the light, which was suddenly brighter. He squinted at it. It was so bright that it hurt. And it made him anxious.

He strolled tentatively along the center of the pristine aisleway, looking this way and that down the aisles between the racks for . . . what? Molemen? Anybody or anything that would make sense of what was going on? An exit?

His pulse started racing. He felt himself perspiring. He had to get out of here. He spurred himself into an anxious trot. "Hey!" he gasped at no one. "Hey! Help!" But the limitless space gobbled up the sound. He couldn't help panicking at the sudden sense of things closing in upon him and everything being seized in a painfully fraught conflict. What was the matter with him?

Boom!

A thunderous concussion rumbled through the floor, as if a massive object had fallen. It frightened him, and he broke into a run. Something was coming. It was coming for him. He was out of his wits now. He had to get out, had to get out, had to—

FIVE WOKE WITH A START and snatched at the tiller. Asleep! How long had he been out? He checked the night sky in a panic, likewise his compass. He was heading a bit to the southwest, and he corrected his bearing. Whew! He had remained on course, despite himself!

He inspected his sails, rigging, and hull—he was always inspecting his sails, rigging, and hull. All good. And the trade wind was holding. But the moon was higher, and the circumpolar constellations were shifted—he'd slept perhaps thirty minutes. Fool! Nodding off would get him killed.

He rubbed his face and scratched at his ears, trying his best to clear his thoughts. He felt the coolness of the wind evaporating his anxious flush of perspiration. Crazy goddamn dream. Crazy falling asleep at the tiller. Stay awake!

The wind and the water rushed past, the moon and stars and wisps of cloud held sway above him, and he welcomed the sense of returning to himself and the task at hand. If his bearing was accurate, he would get there. And the sooner the better. He tried to get a feel for his speed. Twelve knots or so. But without gages or land-based references, he couldn't be certain. He had done his best to calculate his hull speed, but that was a theoretical maximum, and the reality had to do with any number of variables—from the inefficiencies of his primitive materials to his makeshift design-and-build techniques. He needed to reach the Mekong Delta in less than two days, before this whole contraption fell apart or he went crazy out here on his own or both. He imagined himself shipwrecked, clinging to one of the hulls, drifting upon the ocean current, waiting to die of exposure or thirst or, horror of horrors, to be eaten by sharks.

He toyed with the gennaker, tugging upon the sennit cabling he'd taken so much care to construct. He'd used it to lash together virtually every component of his catamaran. It had taken him weeks to find the dried coconuts, remove their stringy husk fibers, spin the fibers into twine, then lay the twine oh so tediously into rope. Strong stuff. But he'd never fully trust any of his handiwork. Not the sennit, not the hollowed-out driftwood hulls, not the strength of his mast nor the stability of his bridge deck nor the integrity of his tiller or rudders. It was one thing to craft his crude canoe that he used to traverse the archipelago and another thing entirely to engineer something truly seaworthy. He was no shipwright. Neither was he a damn sailor. Not by choice, anyway.

Meanwhile, he was experiencing too much true wind and not enough apparent wind.[28] He adjusted his gennaker, trying his best to sense when his speed had been maximized. It was tedious, and the focus exhausted him. So be it. Two days and two nights or sooner than that for sighting land, hopefully. Unless he'd misremembered the data, and then who knew? He forced himself to banish such thoughts. Have faith in the numbers. Two days and two nights at sea. And here his first day was already behind him and this first night had been uneventful so far. Unnerving at first, the idea of sailing at night. But there was moonlight and starlight and the wind and the water, and his catamaran had cooperated. So far, at least.

But dozing off like that? It drove fear into him like a nail. Sailing off-course for hours in a dead sleep could be the end of him. Perhaps he ought to tie off his tiller just in case? No. Neither the wind nor his equipment could be trusted. Sleep was out of the question. Just stay awake, dammit. Make all possible speed. Get through this night, and in the morning there would be land in sight and . . . then what? Now *there* was something to think about, something to keep his mind occupied: the trip upriver. How long would that take? If he made five knots sailing upriver, that would mean another two days

---

28 "True wind" is equivalent to wind speed, and for a sail mounted perpendicular to the wind, it defines the vessel's maximum speed. But with appropriate sail design, "apparent wind"—the pressure drop or airfoil effect across the portion of the sail opposite the wind—allows for sailing speeds that surpass wind speed.

or more to reach Angkor. Or at least the Tonle Sap Lake. And only if his navigational intuitions and what little he remembered about the nature of the continent and Cambodia itself were at all accurate. All that stuff from his cadet training may as well have been a different lifetime. Somebody else's lifetime. Perhaps it had been. So much had happened since those faraway days that he often couldn't reconcile the two versions of himself. The version before he abandoned the mission and the version after. And for that matter, the version of him hiding out in that hovel in the western desert before whatever happened, and whatever he was now. In a goddamn different time and place. So be it. It was crazy, this gambit to get home. It was crazy sailing into the middle of the South China Sea. But it seemed like crazy was all he had.

Five guzzled the last of the fresh water from his coconut-husk canteen and hurled it into the sea. He had made no provision for having to collect rainwater during his journey. Mostly because anything to do with that portended his being lost at sea, and he was frankly convinced he'd rather die than be a castaway again. He packed hydration for his two-day journey and an extra coconut or two as a reasonable contingency. Food, likewise—he had prepared just enough dried fish to keep himself going until he struck land. After that? He'd have to fish and forage, so be it.

Fixated upon the horizon, he longed for his first night at sea to end. He longed for a telltale glimmer of dawn, for the change in scenery it would bring, if nothing else. The moon rose merely two Earth hours or so before the sun. And it seemed to him that the barren little asteroid moon had been crawling up the sky for an eternity.

A gust of wind tossed sea spray onto his face, and he wiped it away irritably. Ack! Then another burst of spray and there they were again—the dolphins, four of them, shadowing him so closely that he could almost lean over and touch them. They cruised alongside, just below the surface, breaking only occasionally to breathe, barely moving their tailfins. They swam with such effortless ease that they seemed jet propelled. And their faces were shrouded in greenish phosphorescence, as if they'd arrived not from the deep, dark waters of this ocean but from another dimension. But then, this ocean was perhaps akin to another dimension, wasn't it?

He recognized a whitish scrape across the nose of one of them, the extra-stout back of another, and the two so similar in appearance they could be identical twins.

"Hello!" he shouted. The wind snatched his voice away, but who was to say they couldn't hear him? "Back again, are you?"

Talking to them seemed both thrilling and insane. Without losing a trace of momentum, they each surfaced, eyed him for a split second, snorted through their blowholes, and dove, vanishing into the depths. He endured a pang of longing at their leaving him, a biting loneliness inexplicably profound. He looked ahead, surprised by the horizon clearly delineated: dark ocean below, whitish dawn above. At last!

———

A WARM, SALTY BREEZE CARESSED his face, and Five savored the sweet fragrance of land—there was no better way to describe it. Before him, five hundred or so meters across the water, was the lush green shore of palms and tangled brush. He'd made it.

The water here was quite shallow, and he peered through its luminous, aquamarine clarity all the way to the sandy bottom. He sat paddling, the sea lapping quietly at the hulls of his vessel. As anxious as he was to get ashore and feel the stable earth beneath his feet, he endured trepidation at the thought of how to go about it. He still had to find the Mekong Delta, after all, and find a way upriver. He had a lot of sailing ahead of him. And risking the shore here, on behalf of a rest, meant risking having his craft battered upon outcroppings of reef or some such calamity. Screw it, just keep sailing.

Where was the delta? Or was this it? He couldn't discern any entry points. The jungle was so dense—virtually impenetrable. He squinted into the far distance, fully up and down the coast. A handful of sailing vessels—traders, they had to be—plied their way within sight of the shore. Junks, was that what they were called? Whatever they were, they would be seeking the delta as entry or exit to and from the Mekong and the villages upriver.

Humans. The possibility of encountering them filled him with dread. That and the weather. Ever since he'd sighted land, the sky had become overcast, foretelling inevitable rains. He recalled that the monsoon—six or so Gregorian months of it—bestowed precipitation that would flood the Mekong to such an extent that it would force its tributary, the Tonle Sap River, to flow backward, inland. This region had a curious hydroclimate, certainly. And if he were correct and it were indeed late August, the inflow of the Tonle Sap River into the Tonle Sap Lake would be at its maximum.

He couldn't envision the maps that indicated exactly where the Tonle Sap branched from the Mekong, but it hardly mattered. He just needed to begin heading up the Mekong. Getting to the Tonle Sap River, then to the lake and all the way to Angkor itself, let alone its namesake temple . . . well, one thing at a time.

He scratched at his ears. He missed his book. He'd open it this instant if he could, because there would inevitably be something within it, some analogy or metaphor—some mythic reference— that he could apply to his predicament to assuage his anxiety and help him know what to do. Oh, he'd tried to scrawl passages, mere sentences even, onto tree bark, into the sand, onto the skins of the fish that he caught. To help him remember the wisdom. And to write for its own sake. Because he needed to write. To feel like a civilized being, for shit's sake. But scraps of fish skin and tree bark and swaths of beach sand weren't a keyboard, and fish bones weren't even a stylus, and it was one thing to write things and another to remember things he had read, and it was as if the very act of trying to remember forced the memories away. Memories of everything. Like his mother and father. What they even looked like. Especially his father, dead so many years now. To lose him and then the memories of him too?

He bobbed along with the waves, paddling to maintain his position, and stared hard into the jungle. For that's what it was, jungle. Seemingly impenetrable. Yes, the waters spilled into the sea from any number of muddy estuaries and distributaries. There was no beach. No defined entry upriver. It all appeared entangled and forbidding. The hero enters the forest at its darkest, most entangled point, he reminded himself. At a point of his own choosing. He remembered that much from his book.

He tried again to remember what had happened after he'd dug himself in at the ruin in the desert between Giza and the Fayoum. His fraught trek, trying to bait the drones. His pathetic diversions against the inevitable pursuit. But he had never even seen any drones. He had been dug in, that's all. Waiting. For the end. And he had heard and felt that strange rumbling. And was seized by a horror that strangled his heart and destroyed his very thoughts. He remembered grasping at the hilt of his puny knife, scared shitless. And thinking of his father.

Then he had awakened to find himself sprawled upon the sand, but not the sands of Egypt. The sands were white. Immaculate. The sky was clear and blue but the wrong color blue—a vivid cerulean he'd never encountered in his life, not even in training simulations. A palm tree swayed above him, its shiny green fronds twisting indolently in the breeze. An ocean breeze. He had somehow awoken on a beach—an empty, strangely intimate white sand beach with nothing but ocean as far as he could see. And the blue surf hissing indolently up and back, up and back, as if to symbolize his imprisonment within eternity itself.

He thought he'd died. Gone to a kind of heaven. Of course, he had considered that he might be dreaming. Or delusional. Or permanently cracked off. But he rested there with the breeze upon his face and the taste of the sea upon his tongue, listening to the surf and the rustling of the palm leaves, and discovered that he couldn't have been dead. And that he couldn't have been dreaming either. Or if he were dead, or dreaming, then death and dreaming was identical to being alive. Because he'd had to piss, for one thing. And he had been thirsty. And hungry. And he was still wearing his uniform from the Giza mission. But no transponder. He had surrendered that to the human, to Miss Vixy.

And so he had pissed onto the trunk of the palm tree beside him, and thereafter struggled every single day to survive.

Fresh water had been a difficulty. He had been forced inland, through the overgrowth dominating the center of his island, and fortunate to come upon a depression retaining a reliable supply of what must have been rainwater. It was a lifesaving source that he had returned to time and again until, much later, he had finally engineered his own habitation—a palm leaf hut—replete with his rainwater collection system, a small cistern, dry food storage, and a workshop. He was in possession of his knife and trek goggles, his pack, until it had essentially disintegrated from hard use, and for everything else, well, he had been required to fabricate it.

He had scoured the island, which happened to be merely a cay, which he understood to be the sandy, low-elevation surface of an underlying coral reef, for sources of fruits and nuts and set his traps for fish and came to realize that he was still on Earth. By way of the familiar constellations he knew he was in the northern hemisphere, a fact further verified by the almost ceaseless northeasterly winds—the so-called trade winds.

He estimated his latitude by way of the north celestial pole, closely enough approximated within the perspective of this planet's space-time coordinates by Polaris, and his ad hoc, handheld inclinometer.

But longitude had been more difficult, for he had no timepiece. It was simple enough to establish solar noon by way of comparing the lengths of a shadow. Accounting for the difference between clock time and solar time was likewise straightforward enough by utilizing the equation of time. But having lost his precision celestial navigation tool in Egypt meant he had to rely upon the clumsy sextant attachments integrated into his trek goggles for his lunar distance calculations. Hence, the cumulative error within his spherical trigonometry calculations was significant.

Nevertheless, the mathematics placed him somewhere within the China Sea, which roughly defined the area of ocean between the Philippines and Southeast Asia. And if his mostly barren conglomeration of atolls, reefs, islets, and cays were mapped and had a name, well, his knowledge of the Earth's geography outside of lower Egypt was pitiful. Hence, he'd made up his own name, the Castaway Islands.[29]

---

29 Later, by way of communication with Cog, Five learns that he was occupying what in the twentieth century were named the Spratly Islands.

His original cay had turned out to be far and away the best in terms of food, fresh water, shelter, and safety from the monsoons— there was something about its orientation and proximity, perhaps to certain reefs, that kept the destructive waves at bay. In his little raft, then his canoe, he eventually explored much of the archipelago. Only to keep returning to his original and favorite cay, which he had christened, naturally enough, My Island.

And he soon enough resolved himself to living out his days as a castaway. And oftentimes he contemplated, in his despair, the means of his suicide. For what was there to live for? But he was a coward when it came to formulating a plan for his own demise, let alone carrying anything out. How to do it, after all? Drowning? Self-induced starvation? Dehydration? Exsanguination? He couldn't bear the idea of any of it. Likewise, he couldn't bear the idea of striving, alone and without hope of rescue, to attain old age and a natural death, what- ever that might be, stranded upon this worthless scrap of land in the middle of an insignificant sea, upon the surface of a doomed planet.

And so he devoted himself to engineering a plan, crazy as it may be, and the means, impossible as they may seem, to get back home. Which first entailed scouring his own mind—his memories and training—for any knowledge of Earth he had accumulated during his cadet training and hitherto dismissed as irrelevant in comparison to the requirements of his Giza mission. What did he know about this planet and its geography, history, flora, fauna, and its human population? He discovered, perhaps because he had little to distract him and all the time in the world, that he recalled a great many things about Earth. Some of which were inspired by his memories of his book. For within the myths and mythologies and the scholarship it contained lay much of the story of the entire planet. And its people.

Nevertheless, without his transponder, without any technology beside the essentially prehistoric, he could not dream of gaining the means to hyperdimensionally transmit, let alone hyperdimen- sionally travel to Mega City One. If anyone there besides his mother would even have him. And this Gordian knot, this insoluble dilemma of the technology and the engineering, somehow kept him busy minded and determined and creative and, well, sane.

Until one day, it occurred to him that the other Cosmic Clock Component projects, those that had failed as part of the legendarily ambitious engineering competition established by the molemen engineers to discover the best geographical location upon Earth to install the golden ball and initiate the inaugural CCP lattice point, might still contain their prototypes. The golden balls. And perhaps remnants of the diamagnetic suspension frames too, who knew? Mostly the stories of the failures had been reduced to half-remembered tales of misadventure and the data and analysis buried in forgotten archives—old news—in favor of promoting the accomplishments of the active Giza Cell project, the competition's winner. But if a golden ball, however hackneyed a version, existed within his space-time coordinates, then perhaps he could somehow find a way to get to it. And use it to get home.

He had heard tell of the Angkor Cell. Circa 1296 CE in Earth parlance. Angkor Wat was the temple, and the Cosmic Clock Component architectural monument the molemen engineers had conspired to convince the Khmer populace to build. If he was indeed somewhere in the South China Sea, then the appropriate coast was perhaps within a reasonable two or three days from My Island. The city of Angkor and Angkor Wat itself were another several days or so upriver from there. However absurd it initially seemed that he could build something to get him across the ocean and then upriver, well, even if he had to walk through the jungles of Cambodia once he got there, he would do it. If it meant he had any chance at all of finding the golden ball, if it were still there, then what did he have to lose? He would build a craft and get himself to Cambodia. And if he was somehow doomed to be in a time coordinate that predated or postdated the Angkor Cell project, so be it. He would travel there and find that part of the world empty of the temple, if not of pesky humans, or long since rendered a thoroughly pillaged, decrepit ruin, void of the ball. And that would be the end of it. The end of his hopes and the end of everything, and so be it.

The engineering of his double-hulled catamaran had been, given the circumstances, straightforward enough. He had experimented with various designs, made test voyages around his cays, and the long and short of it was that he had left the Castaway Islands behind him. He abandoned My Island in favor of a pure adventure of impossibly reckless aspiration. A fool's mission, but a life-affirming mission nonetheless. If he must age out or suffer some fatal illness or a calamity here, upon Earth, if this miserable planet was to be his fated end, so be it. But he would fight it. If he were fated to die within this space-time coordinates, he would nevertheless die fighting to get home.

But *when*, exactly, was he? And how did he get here? What had happened between that moment beneath the sands of the Egyptian desert in 1881 and when he found himself marooned upon My Island? Was he suffering from amnesia? Because no HDT science, no engineering could suggest an explanation.

The how of his otherwise miraculous transport, then, was something he set aside in favor of solving the problem of when. Could he simply observe his surroundings and ascertain a rough estimate of his Earth era? Even if he had been a scholar of Earth history, and he was far from that, the answer was no. First and foremost, he had very little besides the wildlife to observe. He once saw two sailing vessels pass at some considerable distance from My Island. Wind-driven, incredibly ancient-looking contraptions, more akin to enormous canoes possessing outriggers and a single mast with sail. He knew little of the history of this planet's sailing technology. Nevertheless, something about those ships—their coarse, hand-hewn quality, perhaps—suggested they may have originated within several centuries of the space-time coordinates of his Giza mission. Otherwise, the sea and sky, for their part, provided no clues.

Why not let it go? Why not embrace his freedom from the tick, tick, tick of time? He had tried. Sometimes, the shifting sands and rolling waves, the strange sun and the lonely moon seemed enough for a worthy life. But especially during those sleepless nights, when the sky was clear and he wandered the beach outside his hut, he could not bear the thought of surrendering to this life of exile in time and space. For the stars beckoned. Mega City One beckoned. It was out there, somewhere. His home. If he could only find a way.

Months passed. He watched his uniform and his gauntlets become so tattered that he'd had to weave his own textile patches from the native grasses. He considered going without his gauntlets or using them only when absolutely necessary, as if he could somehow spare them from dilapidation. But he had soon realized how foolish it was to try to save anything. From what, after all? And for how long? He might be marooned upon Earth forever. He might die here. Talk about leaving a trace. He ceaselessly pondered that irony—his leaving a permanent trace upon Earth via his own demise—as both cruel and comedic.

He came to regard his gauntlets as symbolic, somehow. Of who and what he used to be. A wannabe moleman engineer, for one thing. And the legacy of his father as his father would have perhaps preferred it. And of course, his race. Go without the gauntlets, he'd told himself. Who cares? You don't need them. But he did need them. When he went around barehanded, he felt somehow not himself.

So he soon enough wore them through. And wove several versions since and improved their fit and finish each time. But one night he determined to toss the handful of spare straps and fasteners stowed within his pockets and pouches, all of which had contributed in some large or small manner to his survival, into the sea. Yet he could not let them go either, when it came down to it, and instead stowed them in a special place within his hut, content to know that they were there. But that was all he kept. Oh, and his ten or twelve remaining toxicity test strips from Giza—early on they had allowed him to discern the things he could not eat (but not the things he ought to eat). Fish, mollusks, some nuts and berries, a root or two that he learned to boil into edible mush, a fungus he could tolerate, grubs, snakes, rodents, birds that he'd managed to snare. All of it terrible, unpalatable, alien dross. But he had thus survived.

Trek goggles, his knife, and a collection of bits and bobs. And his memories. That was what he had left of the past. Otherwise, he had gone native and worked to forget. Which only drove his memories deeper into his soul. Deeper, yes, and more burdened with yearning than he thought possible. He was forgetting details. And remembering only the strongest images and visions. And oftentimes he caught himself questioning the veracity of his memories—it was too often that he had the sense that he was mythologizing, for lack of a better term, his past. His life upon Mega City One, even his time in Egypt, it all seemed so distant, sometimes, and more distant every day. He could not properly inhabit the life he had once lived. There was this time and then there was his myth time. He had studied a bit about the phenomenon. Certain cultures indeed referenced an era, oftentimes only a generation or two past, that seemed remote from their immediate, day-to-day, personal memories. Myth time could represent an impersonal memory, a cultural memory of sorts.

And it was happening to him. Too many of his memories, so many of them not so long ago, if he were honest with himself, he found impossible to identify with. His time as a cadet, for instance. It had meant so much to him. It defined him. And it was slipping from his cognitive grasp. Into a deeper, troublingly remote, more and more intangible, ineffable condition. And it broke his heart to think of things this way.

Perhaps he was still a coward and a traitor. Perhaps he always would be. And perhaps this was the life a coward and a traitor deserved. And the death.

Sometimes he dreamed of starting over, of never having been a cadet, of never having had any crazy ambitions, of being a young moleman who would never do anything more troubling than read his banned books and someday write his own. He wanted to live. But not like this. And so here he was, living as a castaway in time and space. And dreaming up his own sliver of hope, his own farfetched mission to get home. Angkor. If the iteration of the ball was there, and he could find it . . .

He slapped at the water with his paddle and squinted at the Cambodian shore. He was wasting time.

THUNDER ROLLED FORTH FROM THE steamy throat of the delta and made the leaden dawn and grayish tributaries impenetrable and foreboding. Rain pitter-pattered upon the sea, slicked the bridge deck of the catamaran, and drip, drip, dripped from his conical, woven reed hat. Which he despised almost as much as he despised that kufiya from the Giza mission. It was uncomfortable, and he couldn't hear shit with his ears tucked beneath it. But what to do? An umbrella would not leave his hands free. A hood was more annoying and less effective as a disguise than an indigenously styled hat. And it was inevitable, once he began his journey upriver, that he would encounter humans.

He snugged his poncho closer around his neck and eyed the steady stream of rainwater dribbling from the boom of his mainsail. Even in a light rain like this, he could refill all his coconut canteens within perhaps thirty minutes. And here he'd been fretting about drinking water. If these monsoon rains kept up, he'd have more fresh water than he could bear, not including the blasted river itself.

Monsoons. Rainy seasons. To hell with this planet's confounding hydroclimate. At sea, the skies had been mostly clear. Now, the geography dictated its opposite. The sky was oversaturated, and the land too. Flooded. He guzzled from his coconut canteen and instead of discarding it, he took a moment to capture the rainwater from the mast boom, corked the canteen, and exchanged it for another. Fill this one and get going. Stop stalling.

He felt too weary and hungry and sick and tired of being confined to his catamaran to even try envisioning what it would be like to get upriver. Where should he start? This distributary seemed the broadest yet. But he had drifted past at least a handful of other potential entry points. How to know if any of them would lead him to the main body of the Mekong? They might just as well divert into a cluster of unnavigable dead-end marshes or rice paddies or what have you. River deltas. The Nile possessed one, but he'd seen it only by way of maps. Otherwise, he knew they were enormous, sprawling geographies of silt and marsh and labyrinthine wastelands. How far inland he would have to sail and how difficult would the sailing be, let alone the navigation, before gaining the true river? He needed the shortest, most reliably northerly route to Angkor.

He had already pondered the only three rational options. The first, give up utterly and allow himself to drift out to sea and into oblivion—suicide. The second? Flounder about on his own, guessing at what distributary to ply and hope it wasn't a dead end. Third?

The best idea. Namely, he could try to shadow a junk—Chinese, Javanese, what have you—upriver, putting his faith in the idea that the larger vessels would assuredly keep to the most reliable and navigable route inland.

Meanwhile, his fatigue had wrecked his perception of time. It was morning, that's all he knew. And that trader vessel on the coast? He could have slowed and followed it surreptitiously enough, hoping it would lead him to the Mekong and upriver, but who knew if it wouldn't stop at a different port? Then what?

There would be other ships, that's what. There *had* to be. His cursory training as a cadet had exposed him to the basics of Cambodian history, and those junks—flatbottomed, blunt-nosed vessels—likely placed him somewhere within Earth's twelfth or thirteenth century. So there, his place in time, within a reasonable doubt and acceptable margin of error was, remarkably, serendipitously, exactly what he needed! It was as if the cosmos themselves were trying to help him. And if he weren't so tired and miserably bound to this tiller, he would have backflipped with joy into the sea and celebrated.

He lashed the canteen alongside the others and hauled his mainsail taut. You enter the forest adventurous at a point of your own choosing, where the forest is densest and there is no path. For if there is a path, it is somebody else's path. This is what it means to be properly on the adventure. He was paraphrasing from his book. It struck him that he was perhaps transitioning from the waters of the unconscious to the forest adventurous and all his bullshit metaphors weren't going to get him anywhere unless he started paddling and got himself upriver.

He had only just begun approaching the nearest distributary when a sizable vessel drifted out of the mist. It possessed two masts, each rigged with the typical squarish, ribbed, dingy red sailcloth and what looked to be a pair of enormous oars jutting from its broad hull. Its earthy colors and dark sails almost camouflaged it against the backdrop of the land. He zoomed in, adjusted the focus of his trek goggles, frustrated at the pesky condensation within his lenses. The seals were not what they used to be. Meanwhile, the craft was pointed inland and looked to be low in the water, perhaps heavily burdened.

Yes. There were crates and bundles stacked on the deck—it looked to be full of cargo.

He hurried to stow his oar and catch a portion of wind. It happened to be gusting a bit inland, a lucky break. Because tacking upwind would be a misery—he had yet to master the technique—and to lose the opportunity to follow this ship, well, he may never catch the thing. This was his chance. Despite his stiff limbs and sore ass, he sat up, leaned into the tiller, and hauled his mainsail open to the wind.

In no time, he'd come within a hundred meters or so of the junk, which upon closer inspection had once been painted a vivid vermilion. Now the grain of the underlying wood planking was just as prominent. The weathered hull, oddly snub-nosed and sporting a high, square stern, appeared quite sound. But it was the raked sails that Five found himself examining with intense interest—their unusual, battened design with cross members of what appeared to be bamboo. The mostly reddish textile panels had been patched with paler material. The crew was hauling in the enormous pair of oars. Apparently, they had been negotiating the shoreline and were now again under sail and, yes, moving upriver!

How close to get? Would the crew become too curious about his catamaran? Would they find him threatening? Would they lower a dinghy and attempt to engage him?

Meanwhile, he employed his gennaker as a spinnaker, having furled his mainsail. There was plenty of wind off the sea, at least for now. He'd prefer, then, to simply tail this craft at an easy distance that allowed him to benefit from their navigation of the waterways. Always there was the risk of striking an unseen outcropping, a submerged rock or log or even the carcass of some wrecked vessel.

After some tedious fussing with his foresail rigging, he settled into a matching pace behind the junk, perhaps three or four knots, and he followed, carefully, patiently, unnerved at leaving behind the freedom of the open ocean in favor of the mysterious, smooth-surfaced confines of a forest-bound river. The broad waterway meandered its way into the surrounding hills, and the day brightened despite the overcast sky and persistent drizzle. He was glad for a gentle

downwind, enough to overcome the current, though he was forced
to trim his sail further to avoid catching the junk.

They sailed along for a time, and when he felt confident enough to
take his eyes off the junk and the river, he glanced back, astonished
to find that the jungle forest had already closed in behind him. The
ocean, gone! And now nothing but the jungle-choked riverbanks and
leafy foothills fore and aft. But where were the rice plains? He had expected flatlands and farms as they sailed inland. Were they indeed
headed north? He found himself doubting his compass. Stop making
assumptions, he told himself. There was nothing else for it except to
follow this junk and hope for the best. Enjoy the wind while it lasted.
He forced himself to relax and loosen his grip upon his rigging. He
sipped water and chewed on a strip of coconut meat, sucking at the
creamy, slightly sweet and salty pulp. If it felt like progress, it was.

WHAT SEEMED LIKE HOURS PASSED, the gray sky unchanging, except
that Five found himself adjusting the polarity of his trek lenses
to compensate for what had to be the changing intensity of the sun
crossing higher overhead. Occasionally, the winds shifted and both he
and the junk slowed, and he was busy tacking with his mainsail and
the gennaker and doing his best to keep pace with the junk, which
oftentimes lumbered along tediously. How he longed to simply attach
the catamaran to the junk by a length of rope and allow himself to
be towed along! He even fantasized about finding a way to clamber
aboard and stow himself away all the way to Angkor as a passenger.
Oh, to sleep a sound sleep!

They rounded a broad bend and came upon a plethora of watercraft, none that compared in size to the junk—they were without
exception variations of low, battered-looking barges, some covered,
some partially open to the weather, some with a mast and sail, some
with oars, including a type of oar that extended directly behind—a
stern sweep, if he recalled the term correctly—and still others with
nothing but poles in the hands of their crew, the women and children
included. Families, perhaps. Oh, and numerous roughly hewn rafts

whose sole purpose appeared to involve hauling a crate or two of cargo, crudely tarped against the weather. Dinghies too, paddling out from the rickety docks at the flooded shore to the barges and back again, apparently unloading or loading cargo.

Five peered past the docks, searching farther into the jungle for evidence of a village or some kind of trading post. After all, if there were docks here and commerce going on, there must be an accompanying village. But his junk did not tarry, despite receiving the attentions of a handful of the dinghies that paddled up beside it. Just don't paddle up to me, he thought. As if it mattered. Clearly, he possessed no cargo. Although somebody may assume he was in the market for something. But clearly no one found his catamaran even curious for its own sake, despite it being the only thing like it on the water. They'd either seen it all or were simply indifferent to yet another insignificant, one-man vessel.

The rain had stopped, and they sailed slowly out of view of the little port. Five availed himself of the opportunity to relieve himself over the side, drink heartily from one of his coconuts, set up another for rainwater collection, and stuff chunks of dried fish into his mouth. He had been doing his best to conserve his provisions, but if the trip upriver consumed more than another day, perhaps a day and a half, he would be forced to . . . what? Get ashore and forage? Fish from the catamaran? He pushed such thoughts aside. Just keep going, junk. Get moving. Get me upriver.

THE DAY DRAGGED ONWARD, AND the junk lumbered along within it. The river and the hills were unchanging. Once in a while the clouds cleared and allowed the sun to wink through, and with it an instantly sweltering humidity engulfed him. But soon enough the wind would change, the clouds would return, and the drizzle would resume.

When would they reach Angkor? Was his junk in fact bound for Angkor? It seemed unlikely. He had a sense that Angkor could not reasonably be the destination for such a large craft. Wouldn't it unload its cargo close to the sea and leave it to the smaller vessels to do the work of distribution that far upriver?

He felt suddenly anxious. He may be wrong, very, very wrong about all of this. His dates could be off by a millennia or more. Angkor Wat may not even exist yet. And all this would be for naught, and he'd be lost in time on this horrible planet for the rest of his life, and moreover within this stifling jungle. He longed for the open air and reliable isolation and fishing and coconuts of My Island. More irony. He never would have believed wanting to return to My Island.

The sky was darkening. Night was coming. He dreaded the idea. Would the junk moor itself for the night? Would it continue sailing? If it dropped anchor, it didn't mean he had to do likewise. He could keep sailing, couldn't he? But without the light of the moon and stars, it would be foolish. Likewise for the junk. Unless it knew its route so well that it didn't matter. Still, to sail a river by night? It will have to lay up. And if so, then him too. Oh, for the airy, dry safety of his grassy island hut!

It was then that he noticed an odd clunking noise, only to discover that it had to do with his own movements upon the cross deck. When he shifted his weight or the wind filled his sail in a certain capacity, there was the clunking. He crawled about his cross deck, hurrying to examine every last lashing.

Argh! Loose windings at the junction of his port side hull and the frame of his cross deck! Dammit! He leaned over the side, examined the joint more closely, and ground his teeth at the sight. Given the pounding this makeshift contraption had endured at sea, it was no surprise. But it was what he feared most, the idea of his catamaran falling apart. He jiggled the hull—a few centimeters of play. He checked the length of the hull fore and aft and crawled across the cross decking to do the same for the starboard hull. Hmm. Perhaps some looseness here and there. He'd lashed everything as tightly as he could manage, but with the water and the strain of sailing, it made sense he'd have to make repairs.

But dusk was coming on. What to do? He could hardly attempt to relash anything while afloat. He'd have to beach himself. Except there was no beach in sight. He had been diligent enough to pack several lengths of spare cabling, but he'd rather ride it out and hope for the best, to run to failure over getting bogged down with clumsy preventative repairs.

He returned to his tiller and allowed his sails to fill, then pondered what to do. Do what the junk does. Let that be the decision maker. If they anchored, he would anchor. If not, so be it; as long as this catamaran held together, take it all as it comes. If it wasn't broken yet, don't goddamn fix it.

The night came down, and likewise the rain. His fatigue gnawed at him, and he felt suddenly terrified of the darkness beyond his vessel, as if the darkness upon the water and the blackness of the forest shores and the hills beyond were full of menace. No. It was just the night. He would just keep going upriver. And then and there, just as he'd resigned himself to sailing in the darkness, the junk furled its sails and dropped anchor.

He could see a flickering onboard—they must have a fire pit of some type. How he longed to sit before a warming, drying, light-giv-ing fire. To eat proper food and not fret about rationing his water. To be under a roof, any roof. And sleep and not worry at all about the current, the wind, his anchorage, or the water.

He fought against his panic and hunger and the pain in his legs and arms and back and could not bear the idea of a night alone upon the water in this miserable monsoon weather. Could he paddle to shore and find a place to bivouac? Of course not. Not now, at least. If not humans, then animals, and if not animals, then perhaps swarms of biting insects, worse than he endured out here on the breezy river, would assail him. Stay here. Endure it. Lay down, pull your poncho over your head, and sleep. Sleep, and if he were lucky, he would perish in his sleep and not be forced to endure tomorrow. Since becoming a castaway, hardly a night passed that he didn't more or less hope to die in his sleep and have it all come to an end. None of it would matter then—the struggle and strain and ceaseless longing to get home.

They moored at a point in the wide river where a low island peeked above the water—there wasn't enough land to walk upon, but Five lassoed the catamaran to a tree stump. He allowed it to drift downstream a bit, tugging against the cable, and, assured of the secure lashing, laid himself down. He rested his hand upon the tiller, as a kind of comfort, and plummeted into sleep.

———

THERE WAS NO DAWN. RATHER, Five opened his eyes to the bright of day, groggy and disoriented, and immediately sat bolt upright, panicked that he was drifting out to sea. No. The catamaran was tethered to its humble stump. Yes, he'd stopped for the night and . . . where was the junk? Argh! He looked about, wincing at the soreness in his bones. The river was void of watercraft. On the eastern shore, a mere stone's throw from the bank of the swollen river, he noticed a tiny village—no more than several grass huts upon stilts—covered in mist. And upon the riverbank itself a motionless cluster of rafts and a tattered-looking barge. But no humans. Was everyone asleep?

That he hadn't noticed the village last night only aggravated his sense of disorientation, as if it had appeared out of nowhere. But it had been dark, certainly, and he had been exhausted—he was still exhausted. He simply hadn't noticed, that was all. But, dammit, where was the junk?

He relieved himself, drank from a canteen, shoved a handful of coconut meat into his mouth, and sat chewing and pondering. He had overslept, and the junk had shipped out, either upriver or downriver, it was that simple. And that little village with its boats had simply been obscured by the moored junk itself.

He sighed fitfully—what did it matter that he'd made some sense of things? He'd been careless. He'd been a fool.

It began again to drizzle. As if to add insult to injury. He scowled. A mild breeze buffeted his craft, and a corner of his furled mainsail flapped indifferently. He considered the hull with a fresh perspective. That lashing needed attention before he did anything. And he needn't haul the catamaran out of the water to make the repair, he merely needed to stabilize the craft and get off the cross deck— body weight prevented an efficient reworking of the joint. That meant wrestling the catamaran at least partially onto land. He considered and immediately rejected the idea of grounding himself upon the muddy riverbank—too great a risk of attracting the attention of onlookers, and how would they react to his appearance and his craft? No, just get this thing partially out of the water right here, dammit.

He swigged from his canteen in anticipation of his exertions, hauled upon his tether, and drew the catamaran as close as he could against the steep underwater beach of the islet. He tied off and scrambled onto the grassy shore, his legs wobbly. Dry land, at last! He hauled on the line as hard as he could and the vessel lurched from the water with surprising ease, sliding over the slick grasses, and Five fell onto his backside into the soft, saturated turf.

Whew! The catamaran sat poised with its hulls almost three-quarters out of the water. And as luck would have it, the torsion exerted upon the cross deck and hulls had crammed the joint in question firmly together. He slashed at the old, loose cord, tore it away, and hurriedly threaded the new cording, pulling hard against each winding, making certain all was as tight as possible, closed the knot, and stood huffing and puffing at his work. Good enough.

He noticed some movement on the far shore—humans. Meandering amongst their boats, perhaps beginning their workday. He had to hurry and get out of here.

He shoved at the catamaran, panicked for a moment when it wouldn't budge, then shoved more heartily, and the craft slid from the islet and drifted into the water. He freed his line, leapt aboard, raised his mainsail, used his paddle to shove off, and finally caught some wind. Not a following wind, but southwesterly enough that it carried him slowly upriver.

He wrestled with the rigging and the tiller and out of the corner of his eye watched the little village fade into the distance, still blanketed by its ceiling of mist. The rain picked up, so be it, and the dreary hills in the distance foretold nothing but the unsettling mystery of kilometer after kilometer of meandering river. But his compass indicated north, more or less, and it would have to do, one bend of the miserable Mekong at a time.

FIVE SHOVED THE LAST OF his dried fish into his mouth and sipped at his water to soften the flesh. The rain had relented, but the changing wind kept him busy with his mainsail and spinnaker. At times he enjoyed a blessed southerly breeze, but mostly he struggled to negotiate its neurotic nature, even tacking against the wind at times, trying and failing and trying again to maintain something of the required forty-five-degree angle for his sails. He was making fraught and exhausting headway. But it wasn't as if he could paddle upriver, even if he'd had the foresight to install a mounted pair of oars. The current was too significant.

How far had he come upriver? How far did he have left to go? His estimate of two and a half days sailing to Angkor had likely been grossly optimistic. If he was making the requisite five knots, he would be surprised. Then there was the meandering nature of the Mekong itself, adding perhaps kilometers to his route. That said, he might be closer than he had assumed, who knew?

The sky remained a stubbornly gloomy blanket of low, grayish, rain-soaked cloudiness that refused to provide him even a glimpse of blue sky, let alone the sun. He needed that sun. But what he would get was another night of starless, moonless, claustrophobically oppressive, rainy misery. Not sailing at night was killing his progress. He resolved then and there to continue through the night. Besides, he was low on provisions. He would need to go ashore soon and forage—the thought pained him, for he knew virtually nothing about what was edible or not within this geography. No, fishing was the rational option, if there were fish to be had in these waters.

Starvation had become his new enemy. That and losing his way, of course. Don't get too weak to get ashore and find food. Consider infiltrating a village and stealing, if necessary. That would be the protocol from the perspective of his cadet training, certainly, but his heart and soul simply longed to get where he was going. Don't be a fool, he told himself. Don't get impatient or it will cost you your life.

The current resisted his advance, the capricious winds frustrated his sailing, the rains were ceaseless, the river itself seemed endless, and he was weary beyond words. He longed to eat and rest and be dry and be off this confounded river and clear of this knotty, overgrown, festering, forest jungle wasteland! That his compass had him sailing mostly west-northwest and not directly north only increased his sense of despair. North was the way, wasn't it? On top of everything the day was fading and the awful night loomed.

He was busy gnashing his teeth and grousing about his predicament when he rounded a bend and beheld the river now widened by perhaps a third again of its width. And further ahead, another islet, or island, large enough that it seemed almost inhabitable. Could it be a peninsula? He tried desperately to recall something of the Mekong's route, but it was useless. The map in his head amounted to a nebulous memory, utterly unreliable. The hard reality was that he was being forced to the left or right. Which way, dammit! Did it matter?

He was making good speed, sailing downwind, and the river now seemed more like a large lake and behaved as such—the current had changed. It was no longer against him. In fact, the water eddied and swirled in great sweeping flows—he felt as if he were being borne as much by the current as the wind. And he bore down upon the islet or island or peninsula, what have you, itself. He experimented with his compass—the broader distributary was to the right and seemed almost directly north, whereas the slenderer lefthand leg would take him north-northwest.

Were there no other boats? As if that would help him at all. No, make a choice, dammit. Just then, an aggressive gust of wind filled his mainsail and spinnaker and the catamaran lurched forward, yanking the ropes from his hand and throwing him off-balance—he let go of the tiller to catch himself. He scrambled across the bridge deck for his lines, ducked the boom, crawled back to regain the tiller, and by the time he'd turned to resituate himself he found the craft being hauled crosswind to the left of the landmass by nothing more than the surprising strength of the current itself. He was traveling *with* the goddamn current instead of against it! This distributary was flowing backward in comparison to the Mekong!

Then it struck him. By the gods, it was the annual convergence! It had to be. And this must be the Tonle Sap River! He'd made it! The engorged, ocean-bound Mekong was driving this little river back upon itself—the water would empty into the great freshwater lake, the Tonle Sap. And unless he had it all wrong, the lake bordered the royal Khmer city of Angkor itself. The hydroclimate of this region was finally on his side.

For the life of him, again, he could not picture the exact geography. Let alone the distances. The northern region of the so-called Great Lake was somewhere south or southwest of the temple city, but the distance he would be required to trek through the jungle was a mystery. A kilometer or two? Or ten? Or more? Just get to the lake. Get to the lake and find food. In the water or on the damn land. Just get there.

———

FIVE LAY UPON HIS BELLY at the stern of the catamaran with his slender fishing spear poised, peering into the murky water. The waters of the Tonle Sap were calm. And murky. But full of fish. They rose to snap at insects at the surface almost by the minute. And he knew from his experience on My Island that the thrust of his spear ought not to be awkward and violent but rather fluid. Spy the fish, wait, gather himself, and in a single stroke, commit.

There! Five scrambled onto his haunches. He'd run the creature through at the stoutest part of its middle, and it flailed its tail. He jammed his fingers into the gills, yanked the spear free, lay the flopping fish upon the cross deck, and knelt upon its tail. With his free hand he clasped his knife and plunged it into the flesh behind the creature's gills, sawed through the backbone, and beheaded the thing. He scored the flesh at the tail and guided his knife toward the missing head, using the backbone as a guide. With the tip of his knife, he sliced a thumb-sized portion of the skin free from the thick flesh, secured the fillet against the deck using the flat of his blade, grasped the corner of skin firmly between his fingers and yanked at the skin in portions, adjusting the knife forward to keep from tearing the flesh. Soon enough, he had exposed the fillet. The creature had looked healthy—bright eyed, the skin clear of markings, a good weight for its size, all the hallmarks of good, safe eating—but nevertheless he eyed the flesh for imperfections. If he were cooking it, he would be less concerned about parasites and entirely unconcerned with the skin. But raw?

He plucked a few pin bones free of the flesh, eyed it all one last time for imperfections and bones, hacked the fillet into chunks, and tossed a piece into his mouth. Hmm. Decidedly murkier tasting than the saltwater version. But edible.

———

HE ESTIMATED IT WAS MIDDAY. The rain was a light drizzle. Five focused his trek goggles upon the bustle of activity at the northern shore of the Tonle Sap where a narrow tributary or distributary opened upon the wide, sparsely treed plains beyond. All along the little waterway, at least as far as he could see, were rickety houses upon stilts.

Such small fishing barges and the little canoes and rafts, well, he'd seen a handful of them on his journey upriver, but nothing like the cluster of activity here, close to the shore of the lake. Perhaps they had come from upriver? Perhaps they had sailed past him in the night? It hardly mattered. Such significant human activity, such considerable sign of civilization, suggested like nothing else could that what lay beyond was Angkor. And if not Angkor—if somehow he'd gotten off-course or misremembered the geography—then it didn't matter. Because as far as he was concerned, if he were to never see this catamaran or the river again, he could die satisfied that he had conquered them both. He had sailed far enough. If the jungle or the plains or the heat or the rain or starvation killed him, so be it.

With that he made directly for a place upon the shore within a reasonable trekking distance to this distributary. For it was a distributary—he spied canoes and boats heading further inland. Perhaps there would be a string of habitations, villages even, all attempting to thrive upon the economic activity bestowed by the Mekong, perhaps running all the way to the temple city itself.

Here, if need be, he could steal food and perhaps materials. After all, if he were indeed anywhere near the thirteenth century, and if he properly recalled his history, the smelting of iron would be an active undertaking in this region. Iron smelting meant iron tools. Tools that could perhaps help him build a shelter. And hunt.

But he was getting ahead of himself. Iron tools and weapons, and for that matter food, was hardly his immediate concern. He had to get ashore. But the flooded river, surging far beyond its dry-season banks, destroyed much of the usable shoreline in nautical terms—there was nowhere to disembark except directly into the stands of trees or bamboo or dense shrub. And too much of that lush greenery communicated merely the illusion of dry land. For hundreds of meters or more, the inland overgrowth would be at least partially submerged. It would resemble bayou or seasonal marsh or tributary and be impenetrable except perhaps by canoe. No, he must find a suitable landing place.

There. Just to the west of the little port, perhaps one hundred meters away, and conveniently sheltered behind an outcropping: a ridgelike rise populated with trees whose trunks did not appear wholly submerged at the base. He skirted the port at a distance that did not draw attention and worked his mainsail and tiller to aim for the inlet. He glided headlong toward the shore, thrust his oar into the water to feel for land, felt nothing, then barreled headlong and with too much ungainly speed into something hard.

His starboard hull struck first, violently twisting the catamaran and hurling him sideways—he lost the tiller, reached for the edge of the bridge deck, missed it, and plunged into the water.

He choked, flailed his arms, panicked at being separated from his craft. His limbs were stiff and weak, and only at the last moment did he manage to duck from his hat and slip from his poncho, or he would have been dragged under. He floundered, unable to gain a sense his own natural buoyancy. Use your arms and legs, dammit! Breathe, float, swim to shore!

His feet finally touched bottom, and it was as if his life had been saved. He groped and clawed and stumbled through several meters of shallow water, silty lake bottom, and difficult brush only to flop face-first and exhausted onto a patch of muddy, open ground. He lay gasping, his heart pounding, as vulnerable and defenseless as a stranded fish.

"Land," he breathed. "Goddamn land."

When he finally gathered enough strength to sit up, he rested upon his haunches and took stock of things. The nature of the jungle forest: on first impression, impenetrable. The catamaran, as if it mattered: the starboard hull askew, its prow gouged half a meter into the bank, the forward lashings snapped, the tiller aslant, and the rudder dangling at an impossible angle. The mast leaned forlornly aft, and the rain pelted the partially unfurled sail and dripped indifferently from the surface of the bridge deck. The poor vessel's hapless condition virtually compelled him to weep with despair. It somehow forced him to envision their entire journey together, and he found himself incongruously mourning the craft's demise. He had never named the thing, though it more than deserved a name. Their journey together had been incredible, after all. That was it: *The Incredible*.

He struggled back toward the catamaran, confident that he could get back to his mud flat. He gathered his string of coconut canteens, slung them around his neck, and looked about for his sandals. There, still lashed to the mast. What of his fishing spear? Likewise. Ought he to take it with him? He peered into the jungle. What he needed was a damn machete. The spear would be unwieldy. And he could always fashion another version.

He evaluated the condition of his goggles—they were fine— checked that his knife remained secured at his makeshift belt and felt for his autotranslator collar—of all things, the device seemed determined to remain with him through thick and thin. He regarded the catamaran, his hard-won handiwork, top to bottom and stem to stern one last time. Then he patted the hull affectionately and turned to make his way into the trees.

CHAPTER 13

LOST IN PLACE

"Where and when are we?" said Neutic. He shifted his weight from one foot to the other and stared at the mud oozing from beneath the soles of his trek shoes. "This looks like a floodplain or something." He shielded his eyes and squinted at the vivid green landscape, which was uniformly flat between large patches of jungle forest. In the far distance, through a veil of hazy atmosphere, a bluish stretch of low mountains struck him as ominous.

"That's because it is," said Vixy, frowning at her transponder.

"Is what?" said Neutic.

"A floodplain!" Vixy tapped furiously at the device. "Or something. Un-fucking-believable! This can't be happening!"

The sun was high, not quite overhead, and the air was hot and humid and so intensely rife with a vegetal pungency that Neutic felt as if he struggled to breathe. He checked his own device. "Twenty-nine degrees Celsius. Air quality, excellent. But humid as hell. Obviously." He looked askance at Vixy.

She clutched her transponder at arm's length, glaring at it. "Nothing," she said. "No response. No communication link to Mr. Z. No communication link to the TDC. It's as if we're goddamn unstuck in space-time." She shook her head at the transponder and locked eyes with him. "We're in fucking Cambodia, Neutic. My fucking transponder says fucking goddamn *Cambodia*!"

Neutic raised his eyebrow at her and ran his hand through his hair. "But when? And exactly *where* in Cambodia?"

"Near Angkor goddamn Wat. As it has yet to be called, apparently. Because we're in 1296 CE!"

The quaver in her voice made Neutic anxious. That, and the way she stared wide-eyed at him, her eyes glistening with tears.

"Why didn't we boomerang when the coordinates failed?" said Neutic. "I mean, can't we reconfigure? Or reboot? Whenever something goes wrong like this with an HDT, there's a contingency plan, isn't there? At least that's what the training—"

"Fuck training," said Vixy, feigning a laugh. She swiped at her tears. "Shit happens. That should be the training. I can't engage the retrip. Let alone the boomerang. Something's blocking it. Or interfering . . ." She scowled at her transponder again.

"That means Mr. Z. is in 1954 Bombay without us."

"I don't know. I can't see him. This thing is only referencing the here and now. Goddammit, Neutic." She looked at him beseechingly. "It's like I'm cursed. Me and HDT. And now I've cursed the both of us."

Neutic stared at his feet again. "Let me see, I remember the HDT bay, the verification of the coordinates, the countdown, everything seemed like it was going fine, things were—"

"Things *were* fine," said Vixy. "Everything was right. We were synced with the catapult. Synced with parallax contingency, synced with three-sphere. Our meridians, parallels and hypermeridians were locked."

The strain in her voice made his pulse race. If she didn't know what had happened, then he certainly didn't. He was just along for the ride. This, his first HDT. He replied with all the steadfastness he could muster. "It's okay, though, isn't it? I mean, there must be something we can do."

"I don't know. There are only so many goddamn contingencies I've been trained to handle. Christ, Neutic, it's fucking thirteenth-century Angkor Wat, are you kidding me?" She shoved her trek goggles onto her face, holding tightly to the arms for a moment as if using them to regain her composure. She tapped the rim to increase the magnification and carefully scanned their surroundings.

Neutic himself looked around with a newfound wariness.

"What would Mr. Z. do?" murmured Vixy. "He'd probably find it all goddamn fascinating. And an interesting opportunity or something." She snatched her trek goggles away from her face and addressed Neutic directly. "My first proper HDT and we end up lost. Or close enough to it. Angkor Wat. Jeezus."

"Isn't Angkor Wat some kind of temple? Or a monument, or something?" said Neutic. He instinctively tapped at his device.

"It's supposed to be the largest religious monument on Earth," said Vixy. She donned her goggles again and scanned in the other direction. "There! To the east about five kilometers. Look out there and tell me what you see."

He adjusted his goggles. "Well, it looks like a wall. Of stone, mostly. And some wooden huts, I think. Wow. Towers. Gleaming. Like gold."

"Yes," said Vixy. "That's the temple; that's Angkor Wat itself. It has to be. And somewhere north of here, that way through the jungle, maybe, is supposed to be Angkor Thom."

"Which is the Khmer capital," said Neutic, reading from his device. "No, wait. In 1296—you said we're in 1296, didn't you?"

Vixy nodded. "I'm telling you, Neutic, we're smack in between the ancient Khmer capital and one of the largest mythological monuments ever constructed. That has absolutely nothing to do with our mission."

Neutic read aloud from his device. "The last and most enduring capital city of the Khmer Empire was Angkor Wat. Established in the late twelfth century by King Jayavarman VIII"—he pronounced the king's name slowly and deliberately. "Covering an area of nine square kilometers."

"Angkor Thom came later," said Vixy. "It's the place with all the huge stone face towers. I remember that much from a class I had. But Angkor Wat. Let me think. It wasn't really ever abandoned, I don't think."

"It says here Angkor Thom became the capital in approximately 1200."

"Right," said Vixy. "But my point is that there will still be people at Angkor Wat. Living there. Maybe lots of them. And I'm not even sure whether they're Hindu or Buddhist at this point in history. I remember something from one of my undergraduate classes about a transition from Hinduism to Buddhism."

"You're right. It says here that Jayavarman VIII was allowed to abdicate after being deposed by his son-in-law Indravarman III, the first king to make Theravada Buddhism the state religion."

Vixy sighed as she looked about. A trickle of perspiration slid past her cheek, and she wiped it away with an air of exasperation. "I don't see a fucking soul, do you?"

"Nope," said Neutic.

"But we're not alone," said Vixy, "you can bet."

"That sounds like a line from a lousy horror film," said Neutic. He'd intended to sound bemused, but instead he sounded anxious. He hoped Vixy hadn't noticed. "You mean Khmer?"

Vixy looked at the sky and their surroundings with an air of resolution. "Khmer. Indigenous folk. Or, I don't know what. I mean, I don't have any idea how we've ended up here. Pure accident? To have an HDT misfire us beside Angkor Wat? I don't know, Neutic. I do know that I've no idea how in hell we're going to get back. Or to 1954 Bombay, where we're supposed to be. And it makes me wonder if Mr. Z. got to Bombay okay. Maybe he had a bad transport too? God, I swear Laron has something to do with this. Or the goddamn Scarab Cult. But how in hell are we going to get out of here?"

Neutic looked about them warily. "What about a—what do you call it?—an EIB?"

"Emergency immolation beacon? I'm not torching this transponder—or your device, for that matter—before we try to figure something out." She glanced about, hands on hips, her voice low, as if talking to herself. "What would Mr. Z. do? What in hell would he do right now?"

"What about supplies?" said Neutic. "We packed for an urban environment. If it were Bombay we would've had—"

"I know," barked Vixy. "We would've had provisions available. Now all we've got is emergency rations. And we can purify water. But otherwise, shit, I don't know."

Neutic squinted into the glaring sun. "What about a bivouac? It's already noonish. We should find a place to, I don't know."

Vixy looked toward the jungle. "You're right. We'll need shelter. And we need to stay out of sight. Leave no trace and all that. Until we figure out what to do. Neutic. Really. I'm having a hard time not freaking out."

Her admission steadied him. "You said we're between Angkor Thom and Angkor Wat. And that Angkor Thom—that's a smaller temple complex, right?—it's five kilometers north? I'm thinking that Mr. Z., if he were here, would get within sight of a civilized area. To observe the people and what they're up to, get a feel for things. All while staying hidden; out of sight, until . . ." He trailed off.

"Until what? Until he starved to death or died of malaria or something?" Vixy looked miserable. "But you're right. Mr. Z. would observe things. And not goddamn panic like I'm doing. Let's head that way. Out of the sun, at least. And out of plain sight. Toward the edge of the forest there. Maybe we can find a place to bivouac. And maybe work on this transponder somehow. Let's just walk."

They stomped through the mucky ground, squishing across the lush turf toward the woods.

"I don't get it," said Neutic. "The transponder only seeing our current space-time coordinates. And not having any communication capability, as if it's being blocked or something. I mean, is it transmitting and not receiving anything, or is it not transmitting at all?"

"I don't know," said Vixy. "It's not giving me any transmission status."

"You said you could work on it. How so?"

"I mean tinker with the archival data, run some diagnostics—there are a couple things I know how to do. But I can't get under the hood of this thing. You know what I mean?"

"Sort of. I mean, not really."

"I'm just not convinced this HDT glitch was a glitch. There's nothing—no hyperdimensional skewing, no spurious transport marginalia, no ghosting—that would indicate a technical malfunction. Everything points to a clean, traceable transport. I don't know. Microscopic anomalies inside the tachyon venturi tube—the polishing can comply with spec and then, during transport, somehow, stress fissures, surface imperfections can manifest themselves. At least that's what the gearheads told us in training. Who the fuck knows? I'm no goddamn engineer. It makes me wonder, though, Neutic. My transponder would've recorded a correction protocol and initiated a standard series of fail-safes automatically. Everybody in cadet school, it's the first thing they want to know: what happens if something goes wrong with a transport, will I be lost in elsewhere, how does anyone find me? And they told us. An automatic emergency trace is initiated, and it generates a robust error library that is used to boomerang back—inbound along the outbound route. That's if the original automatic reboot fails *and* the leapfrog to our proper coordinates, too." She scowled dismissively. "All this goes beyond any transport glitch, Neutic, I'm telling you."

Neutic wiped the sweat from his brow. "Leapfrog."

"Yes. Instead of ending up here, the HDT fail-safe would have calculated an alternate route, like for a ground car when you're in a traffic jam."

"So you're saying this wasn't an accident?"

"I'm thinking out loud, and I'm saying that a transport glitch like this doesn't seem like an accident as much as . . . goddammit, I don't know. Which freaks me out. Because who could possibly crack the encryption of our transport, let alone redirect it? But if someone wanted to skew our HDT, Neutic, that's the only explanation for the lack of an error library and the communication failure."

"If they could crack our HDT encryption and skew our transport, they could have just killed us instead. They could have shot us into elsewhere, like you said. So doesn't that mean somebody wanted us here? And now?"

"You're starting to think like a time detective, Neutic. Not that it makes me feel any better." Vixy stopped them short, grasping at Neutic's arm. "Hey, do you remember that business about the mothmen that Professor Wilhelm was going on about at the T.E.? And how the captain seemed like he didn't want to disagree with her like he usually does when he gets all skeptical about syncretizing mythologies and being intuitive and waiting for all the data and the facts?"

Neutic nodded. "He didn't say anything when the professor mentioned the mothmen using psi-power and technology to expedite their Mythological Revitalization Initiative, their MRI. Is that what she called it?"

"MRI, yes. The professor said she had a vision, Neutic. Literally. She saw something that wasn't a dream. Or it was a waking dream. Her and her damn adept powers—that woman is spooky as hell." She resumed walking toward the trees.

"She's quite a lady," said Neutic.

Vixy looked sideways at him.

Neutic shrugged at her. "I mean, a vision, yes. The professor mentioned the golden ball, right? And Egypt and the pyramids of Giz—"

"The Great Pyramid," said Vixy. "Khufu. That's where Five installed it. The golden ball was the key component of the molemen's so-called Cosmic Clock Project, you know all that. And then Five sabotaged the whole thing."

They walked along in silence for a time.

"But Five left the golden ball behind," said Vixy. "He *must* have. When he went into the Western Desert, he wasn't planning to . . . he *couldn't* have been planning to. . .." She trailed off. "That's where Mr. Z. said Five was headed when he last saw him. Into the middle of nowhere. And he must have known it was the middle of nowhere. His HDT nexus was at the Red Pyramid, after all. And if he were simply headed to the Fayoum, it would've taken him days to get there on foot. And what kind of food and water was he packing? And what good would the golden ball be to him, anyway? I was in possession of his transponder; he wasn't going to any alternate HDT nexus, he couldn't get home if he tried. He was doomed, Neutic. Mr. Z. said Five must have been using himself as a decoy or something. Because he knew the molemen engineers would never just let the mission collapse."

"And gold cannot HDT," said Neutic.

"That's right. *Gold cannot HDT.* Everyone knows that. Five couldn't have gotten home again with it if he'd wanted to. So it makes sense he just left it behind. Let it lie there beneath the pyramid."

"And there was evidence of HDT ghosting," said Neutic. "The captain mentioned it. That could've been someone, the molemen, perhaps, going back for it."

"I don't think so," said Vixy. "The surprise attack on Mega City One by the mothmen. On that harbor of theirs where all that carnage took place. And now the war. I don't think the molemen, despite all their scheming, all their pangalactic plans and ambitions, know which end is up right now."

"So, who then?" said Neutic. "The mothmen? It makes more sense that it's just the Scarab Cult keeping us from capturing Laron. But then, like I said, why didn't they just kill us?"

"Who could've screwed with our HDT? Think about it, Neutic." They arrived at the edge of the forest, and Vixy stripped off her pack and set it beneath the shade of a palm. "Let's sit for a minute. Here in the shade. God, it's so hot and humid, and I don't know about you but on top of that, HDT, it always makes me a little nauseous." She tried fanning herself with her hand and gave up. "When I'm the pilot or the driver, I'm goddamn fine, but when I'm not? Hell, I get seasick in my dad's canoe whenever the water's choppy."

Neutic watched her rummage through her pack, remove a medic lozenge, and place it on her tongue. She sipped at her energy drink.

"Ugh," she said, a miserable look on her face. "Me and my big dreams of becoming a TD and I can't even stomach the travel." She put a cigarette to her lips.

"Tobacco? How did you get that through?"

"One of the transport techs. Who shall remain nameless. He likes me. And this couldn't have skewed our transport, because I saw him enter it into inventory."

Neutic raised his eyebrows and unshouldered his pack, feigning indifference.

"Don't worry, I'm not going to light it. I just need to smell it. And taste it a bit. See?" Vixy returned the cigarette carefully to her pack. "What about you? How are you doing?"

"Fine," said Neutic.

"No headache, even?"

"Lucky, I guess." He sat down with his back to a tree across from Vixy.

"Sometimes the effects are delayed. So don't be surprised." Vixy handed him a portion of her ration. "But you might be one of those lucky ones, like Mr. Z." She offered him her energy gel. "We'll split our rations until we get our shit together. And then I don't goddamn know what."

Neutic chewed his food ruefully, and they passed the energy gel between them. He watched her put the package to her lips, noticed her flushed complexion, found himself admiring her smooth skin glistening with perspiration.

"I'm thinking the ball is here," she said.

"In Angkor Wat?"

Vixy shrugged and chewed her food.

"But why would the ball be here? Why Cambodia and why 1296?"

"Because the mothmen are trying to take control of the Cosmic Clock Project. Or the Scarab Cult is. I don't know."

"But why does it have anything to do with us? I mean, unless we've somehow gotten in the way. I just don't see what separating us from Mr. Z. would accomplish."

"Divide and conquer, I don't know." Vixy wiped a strand of hair from her face and closed her eyes as if exhausted. "It's just my intuition, that's all."

Neutic clenched his teeth and waited. He needed her to finish her line of thought. He'd come along with the intention of helping Mr. Z. in Bombay with whatever he needed done. Apprehending Laron, at least. Meanwhile, he considered himself on a steep learning curve that had begun back at Eranos. The arrangement had provided for any number of vocational opportunities. Captain Chase himself seemed to endorse his aspirations to become a more integral player in the goings on within the TDC. And this HDT expedition, his first, was privately symbolic of his commitment to the idea of acting against the kind of terrorism that killed Hettie. He was fighting, always fighting somehow, for Hettie. But now? He handed Vixy the energy gel. "You can finish it."

Vixy drank, crumpled the package, and stowed it.

Neutic listened to the sound of birds chirping and the breeze, what there was of it, rustling through the foliage. "I feel like I ought to know what to do. How to do something to help us." He got up. "And that sounded pathetic, I'm sorry."

"It did," she said. "Men. Always feeling like they have to save the day." She squinted up at him with a wry smile on her face. He stood with his back to her and couldn't see her grinning at him. For all his self-depreciation and self-possession and awkward, quirky sophistication, he had a way of appearing at home in whatever clothes he wore. As if he were a natural part of his surroundings. It didn't make any sense, but to her, Neutic seemed a natural at hyperdimensional travel. He might be a natural at being a TD, if it came to that. He looked the part, standing there in his TD uniform, the standard close-fitting, dark-colored slacks and synthetic black polo-style short-sleeve. She was glad he'd been issued a plasma pistol too, now that they might really need it. She was about to confess to him that she was terrified about their predicament when she noticed him staring at something.

"What in hell?" Neutic crouched low.

Vixy tried to follow his gaze. "What is it?" she whispered.

Neutic gestured. "Where we came from. Look."

Two men of smallish stature stood within the clearing she and Neutic had just left. They meandered about, bending over here and there to peer at something on the ground, pointing this way and that, shielding their eyes from the glare as they spoke to each other. They appeared to be looking for something in the distance.

"Get down," said Vixy. "All the way down."

They lay flat, side by side within the shade of the trees.

Vixy adjusted her magnification. "I don't get it."

"What?" said Neutic.

"It's like they're arguing with each other. Having a disagreement. And their clothing. Something's not right about it."

"Hmm," said Neutic. "You're right about the clothing. I'm pretty sure natives are naked to the waist, wearing nothing but a cloth round their waists, even the women. Except for royalty."

"How do you know that?"

"Something I read in college. An anthropology class. Something from a famous diary composed by some monk or diplomat or something. Buddhist, maybe. I think he was trying to get to India to gather original Buddhist texts or something. To bring back to China. I'd have to look it up. But it describes the natives."

"Don't bother," said Vixy. "Looking it up, I mean. I believe you. And that's exactly it, Neutic. These guys aren't Khmer. Their heads are covered. Hell, they're completely covered. Like they don't want to be recognized. Or noticed."

"Which only makes them more noticeable," said Neutic. "Look at that. One seems skinnier. The other one with the cane seems older. And it looks like he has a device! Look, he's trying to manipulate it under his robe as if he's hiding it." He shoved his trek goggles onto his forehead and turned to Vixy, incredulous.

Vixy was still peering at them. "And the one with the cane is pointing it right at us. Son of a bitch. We've got to get out of here, Neutic. We've got to go *now*. They're tracking us."

Neutic turned to her. "What? Why? I mean, how would they—"

"I don't know. I just know they're looking for us. I feel it." She crouched low and began stepping back further into the forest. "C'mon. They're coming."

CHAPTER 14

FENG & CHUNG

Advisor Chung allowed a drop of sweat to fall from his cheek. "With due respect to your technology, my young comrade, our quarry stood exactly here. Within the past hour, by way of the signs. See here?" He gestured at the ground. "And here and here? Footprints. Two sets. On top of one another. Modern footwear, of course. They were confused and dismayed at the perceived malfunction of their transport event. Hence, they stood here, debating what to do next. Then they made their way to the forest, there." He thrust his staff in the direction of the trees. "Seeking cover."

Feng attempted to examine the turf for himself, but the effort aggravated his nausea and lightheadedness. "Seeking cover, indeed." He straightened and breathed through his nose as if to keep from fainting. "From this awful sunlight and heat, if nothing else."

Chung regarded his fellow mothman's pasty complexion, unsteadiness, and bleary distractedness. Feng had insisted upon his own authority, the HDT had made him ill, and now he was an obstacle within the emperor's court and a liability on this mission. He imagined himself snapping the neck of this sickly, self-absorbed upstart with a simple swipe of his cane. "If I were likewise off-course, disoriented, frustrated, and afraid, I would seek shelter within the trees. Yet, vulnerable as they are, they will not remain so for long. Vulnerable, that is. As time detectives, they will ascertain their coordinates and work to reestablish communication with their contingent. They may indeed be observing us, fools that we are, standing here in the open, having followed them too closely—against my advice." He relished how Feng winced at the sound of his talking and stepped closer to irritate him further. "Our skills at so-called hyperdimensional travel leave something to be desired, do they not?"

"Sshh! If we are being watched, then do you also intend to have us be heard? And would you have me communicate your displeasure to the empress herself?" Feng squinted into the afternoon sun and dabbed his face with his handkerchief.

"Empress?" Chung eyed him suspiciously.

"Emperor," said Feng. "I meant say the emperor, of course." He shifted the folds of his tunic—an ill-fitting reproduction of the saffron-colored Buddhist version. "A mild bout of HDT sickness is commonplace, yet you nevertheless insist upon picking at me. Meanwhile, we have the golden ball to consider."

"We have the time detectives to consider first and foremost," said Chung. "And the indigenous Khmer themselves. We are to leave no trace. Infiltrating the temple grounds will require patience and forethought."

"The natives will do as I tell them," said Feng, "because they are defenseless against the powers of psi. The Cosmic Clock Component is virtually ours already. Your predilection for espionage is quaint but old-fashioned, Advisor. As for the leave-no-trace protocols, you ought to know they are merely a contrivance propagated by our enemies. The Arrow of Time is unassailable. But enough of this bickering—you are here to assist and protect, like any soldier. I should remind you that the Realm has many able warriors who would be eager to replace you."

Chung bit his tongue. This slimy bureaucrat. So certain of himself. So disrespectful of the Way. The man's weaknesses were his own punishment. "Let us make haste, then. And if leave no trace is of no concern, why not take the main road?" He gestured at the wide, muddy track some twenty-five or thirty meters distant and hobbled toward it.

Feng rummaged into his tunic for a coca leaf, placed it upon his tongue, and silently prayed that it would bring speedy relief. How did that old lout Chung endure this heat and humidity? And this damnable HDT nausea? Chung was a hideous goat and just as willful. Could the empress have misjudged Chung's constitution? She had described the mothman as a doddering old imbecile, his battlefield heroics mere embellishments, the emperor's favoritism mere naive sentiment. This HDT event was to have rendered Chung weak and worthless if not dead, but he seemed nothing if not physically sturdy, cognitively sharp, and psychologically impenetrable.

Feng put his hand to his forehead and sucked at the coca leaf. Younger, less decrepit mothmen initiates who volunteered for the HDT tests had in fact been killed outright or perished from the after-effects. Many others had endured chronic debilitating symptoms, psychological and physical. Yet Chung was apparently faring better than mothmen half his age, himself included. And Chung concealed something too. The man's expression at mention of the empress, for instance. Could it be that she indeed underestimated Chung's psi-resistance? But the empress did not misjudge. Or she would not have placed he himself in command of this transport.

He struggled after the impossible, cantankerous old warrior, comforting himself that he need only endure this hellish experience until he commandeered the ball . . .

CHAPTER 15

LOST & FOUND

"This is the month of January or February," grumbled Five. Or thereabouts. Within the thirteenth century. Or thereabouts. Not knowing exactly where he was on this forsaken planet was one thing. But never knowing exactly *when* he was? Torture.

If in cadet training he had found the Gregorian calendar at all interesting as an alternative space-time perspective, well, things had changed. He no longer interpreted the mess—the discrepancy between Earth's Latinate names for the last four months of their Gregorian year and their numerical position within the calendar itself, for example—as a charming relic of this planet's cultural idiosyncrasies.[30] The molemen calendar, properly based upon the age of the universe, was the accurate representation of reality.

His exile, then, had taken its toll. His sense of adventure and the thrill of the unknown had long since drained from him like the waters had been draining over the month since his arrival at Angkor Wat.

---

30   September originates with the Latin *septem*, meaning *seven*. *Octo*, *novo*, and *decem* mean *eight*, *nine*, and *ten*, respectively. For whatever reason, when the Romans added January and February to the calendar, a correction to the names of the last four months of the year never corresponded to a cultural imperative.

The water flowed from all the reservoirs and aqueducts and the damn Tonle Sap itself. And what remained of the hydraulic engineering his people had bestowed upon these backward humans was already suffering. No proper maintenance at all. Silt blocking the inlets and outlets. The aqueducts themselves crumbling, the stones left unrepaired and the waters bleeding into worthless swampy wastelands instead of the farmland. Idiots. He hated this place. He hated the maddening variety of this backward planet's myriad calendars. And he hated this blasted forest jungle. Meanwhile, where, where goddamn *where* was the fucking golden ball? "WHERE!"

Pull yourself together. For shit's sake, quit shouting. Not that anyone would hear him. And what if they did? Argh.

He tromped through the heavy undergrowth, sweating and panting in the stifling humidity, swatting mosquitoes and grumbling to himself. The rainy monsoon had been its own torture—water and wet everywhere—but this dry season? It was sweltering. And maddeningly buggy. It made him long for the cloudy, cool, watery ways of his river trip. Or even his oceanside days upon My Island.

And what he wouldn't give for a damn machete. He squinted into the canopy of tree limbs and tropical foliage and scrambled over the grotesquely intertwined roots. The impenetrable, riotous growth seemed determined to reach out and consume him. This part of the planet was virtually rotten with overdriven biology. Choking plants and fungi. Teeming microorganisms. Insects, mammals, birds, and reptiles everywhere. The snakes alone drove him mad, slithering underfoot, lounging obscenely upon tree limbs and dangling from branches. He routinely found them asleep in this or that corner of his bivouac.

And birds. Screeching, warbling, twittering, chattering birds. More species of birds and more otherworldly noise than he had ever imagined possible. Infinitely more varieties than frequented Egypt or My Island. And then there were the monkeys. Yowling at night, crashing boldly through the foliage during the day, they ceaselessly threatened his stores of provisions. They had stolen every morsel of his food more than once, forcing him to go to absurd lengths to secure and protect his provisions.

Yet it was perhaps the insects that ruled this place. Mosquitoes, gnats, flies, bees, hornets, wasps, spiders, scorpions, centipedes, beetles, cockroaches, ants. Seemingly all keen to feast upon his flesh and blood. Or bite, sting, or otherwise discomfort him. Or gnaw ceaselessly at his food and equipment, even his clothing. There were the harmless versions—butterflies, moths, crickets, and what have you—but what did he care? He was hardly an entomologist or even a naturalist. These creatures were unintelligent alien life on a desperately primitive alien planet.

Mega City One understood species engineering. The molemen had mastered the dynamic of life; it was merely a matter of applying the mathematics. Engineer out the bad—the troublesome and irrelevant—and engineer in the good—the beneficial and useful. Useful. Like a machete, if he only had one. Leave no trace. He spat at the thought of it. He ought to steal a damn machete out from under one of the village folk. And damned if he wouldn't at the next opportunity. He tore at yet another cluster of vines obstructing his path.

Ack! He'd closed his grip upon a bug-eyed lizard, as luminously green as the foliage. The thing darted away, and he paused to collect himself. He'd not bothered with availing himself of the otherwise effective protection of his gauntlets because they merely filled with perspiration and slipped from his hands.

He sipped from his coconut canteen, minding his intake, for he so hated the exhausting task of retrieving fresh water from this or that stagnant, evaporating pond or, because of the drought, the temple moat. It never goddam rained anymore. The once ubiquitous rivers and creeks and distributaries? He had to avoid them, shriveling as they were, because the Khmer too often used them as sewers.

He adjusted the polarity of his trek goggles and verified his coordinates. Five kilometers or so from the western entrance to Angkor Wat. And another half of a day wasted poking around inside the damn temple shrine, again, for the golden ball that wasn't there. And then he'd nosed around *outside* the temple, between the wall and the moat, for another couple of hours. A blasted waste. He was out of ideas. He'd gridded out his search protocol and engineered a methodical and systematic archaeological plan like some desperate moron Egyptologist looking in the exact wrong spot for some pharaonic tomb, and the northeast corner plot was his last chance. Months of work. And nothing to show for it.

Where would those goddamn Angkor Cell engineers have buried the thing? In all the carefully controlled historical records they'd been exposed to as cadets—the story of that failed CCC effort as written and told, versus the facts—and in all the rumors and data leaks, the one thing that was never anything but a wild speculation was where in hell those engineers hid the damn golden ball. The gold couldn't HDT, so it had to remain upon Earth, of course. But the engineers and the project managers and whoever pulled the strings at the top weren't going to allow that ball to fall into the hands of the humans. No. It was *our* ball, that was easy enough to understand. What had the humans done to earn the right to it? They'd just melt it down into silly baubles and trinkets. The project's legacy and the honor of the moleman race deserved a proper, secret burial. Just in case the Giza Cell project failed, for instance, and Angkor had to be fired up again.

Five understood. He understood the politics and the practicalities and the contingencies and most of all the pride involved. And then again, he didn't. He had just wanted to follow in his father's footsteps and become a moleman engineer and live the life he thought he ought to live. In spite of his crazy passions. The big picture and the space-time ambitions and the destiny of the moleman race? He couldn't really fathom it then, and now? Well, look what had happened. Look at what he had become. His life was a space-train wreck. It was no goddamn proper life at all.

And it was about time he moved his bivouac closer to the temple, because this ridiculous trek "home" every day was killing him.

He'd been marching for an hour or so, grumbling at everything and otherwise dutifully following what he believed to be the route to his bivouac, when he came upon an open space and, startled and confused, found himself face-to-face with a shabby stone statue. Where in hell was he?

He tapped at his handmade compass, and the needle shifted and his stomach along with it—dammit! He was always keen to verify that the needle was moving freely, and here he'd botched it and trekked into oblivion! How long had he been at it, plodding through the jungle like a directionless idiot?

"Argh!" He ground his teeth. His first order of business whenever he referenced his compass was to assure himself that the needle was not sticking. Being a handcrafted piece of shit, it was prone to do just that.

He looked about wildly for a moment, trying to gain something of his bearings. Don't panic. The needle had jumped only a degree or two. He just needed to retrace his steps until he recognized some-thing. Calmed, he regarded the curious monument in front of him.

It was a seated figure in a meditation posture, one leg bent at the knee and resting sideways upon the ground, the other with its foot planted and tucked closely against the statue's torso, supporting what must have been a forearm and hand, but all that remained was a fractured stump. The figure was badly damaged. Half of a foot was broken away too. Its expression seemed peaceful, its eyes mindfully closed and its smile curiously generous, betokening the intensity of its presumed bliss. Of Hindu influence? Or purely Indochina? Meanwhile, grotesque lichen growths garlanded the statue's head, arms, and portions of its legs as if it suffered from some extravagantly hideous skin disease. He tapped at the figure with his knife blade. Here, not even stone could resist the voracious appetite of the jungle.

A humid breeze tickled his face, and he caught a whiff of something wretched. Then he gagged. What in hell? He turned and caught sight of them. Vultures, not thirty or forty meters distant, near the edge of the clearing. And beneath the vultures, the scattered corpses.

The bodies appeared to be laid out. Or was there some sort of massacre? Whatever it was, these poor souls had been left to rot in plain sight. And be picked apart by the crouching birds and the pair of mangy dogs that tore at the loose flesh and bones, the animals squawking and growling and fighting with each other as they fed. Five gagged again and looked away.

The stone figure, then. It was Yama, that was it—the Hindu god of death. This was a cemetery. But without burials. The rumors attached to the Angkor Cell project were true. The engineers had witnessed all manner of unseemly Khmer mortuary practices—open cremation for royalty, and for the rest of the humble populace, this unspeakable abandonment.

But it seemed impossible that the Khmer would be the only culture within the cosmos who so despised or disrespected their dead. There must be a reason.[31] Then the stench and the harsh calls of the vultures assailed him. Just get out of here!

But then he spied something. Near the remains. Where the dogs had been clawing at the earth and the birds gouging at the ground with their beaks. The scene was unbearable, yet he was drawn closer. He buried his face into his elbow against the smell and approached, and the vultures flapped their greasy wings at him and the dogs fled into the trees. He rushed forward, holding his breath, tiptoeing as carefully as he could past the putrefying limbs and gas-bloated torsos and rotting faces, all of which writhed with clots of voracious maggots. The flies buzzed in maddening swarms, and the earth beneath his feet was sticky and black with blood. He averted his eyes from everything besides the thing he dared not believe was there.

He gasped and thrust his knife at the last deathly bird until it took flight and left him to it. Him and the flies and the seething swamp of putrescence that bestowed what he sought most. Gold.

Five kicked at the earth. Then he jabbed hurriedly at the thing with his knife to dislodge it. It was round. He snatched it up, damn the filth. And it was heavy for its size. He clutched it, unbelieving, and darted almost blindly from the horror toward the fragrant, quiet, welcoming verdure of the forest jungle. It was gold, yes. Solid gold. A golden ball.

———

Five sat within the quiet shade of his hovel, adjusted his goggles, and squinted through his magnifier at the nanotext etched into the otherwise dully polished surface of the ball. He could just make it

———

31 Exposure of corpses to the elements for the purposes decay and consumption by scavengers is known as excarnation.

out. Dimensions. Distances. Planetary geometries. He scrolled and scrolled. There! A mention of the zenith passage. And the Angkor Wat shrine. And here, the proposed length of the zenith sighting tube, the shaft that received the beam of sunlight and allowed it to penetrate to the sarcophagus of the Khmer king. Well, that was the story the Angkor Cell crew foisted upon the Khmer royalty, at least. It was designed to further or at least integrate their mythological obsessions. Twice each year, at each zenith passage event, when the sun within these geographical coordinates was directly overhead and would penetrate via the sighting tube to the king's ashes in the heart of the temple, his spirit would be empowered with divine solar energy. The king's posthumous title was "Shield of the Sun," and his rule within the afterlife would be sustained and would fortify the enduring majesty of the Khmer empire.

Of course, what the molemen engineers intended was entirely different. The sunlight was to strike not the ashes of the king but the surface of this golden ball, thus activating the quantum entanglement link that bound Earth to the other planetary components within the Cosmic Clock lattice. After it had been properly engineered, that is. Which was to say, honed within tolerance, just as the Giza ball eventually was by his father, and installed within its diamagnetic suspension frame at the proper distance from Earth's magnetic core. It was an x-ray reflector. The Cosmic Clock Component that never was.

To the Khmer, then, the golden ball was a mythologically empowered artifact bestowed by the Trimurti, its untarnishing perfection embodying the power of the sun during all the days the solar disc absconded from its zenith trajectory across the sky. To the molemen, it was another triggering mechanism within the pangalactic lattice that would allow them to harness space-time and control the past, present, and future—the very destiny—of the universe.

And for Five, it was his only way home.

Now, how to reengineer a prototype Cosmic Clock Component into a hyperdimensional transport machine? The answer was within the nanotext, namely, the semiannual zenith passage trigger. Its main purpose was to calibrate the component and maintain the precise, entangled accuracy of the lattice, but at the same time, by way of the synergistic science, it opened an HDT portal. A standard, run-of-the-mill, workaday wormhole between this planet and Mega City One. It was a maintenance route, of sorts, a purely utilitarian project management highway in the event an engineer or two was required to work repairs on site.

All this standard-issue cross-functionality was common knowledge to any wannabe Giza cadet. Each of them, himself included, had inculcated these general engineering precepts that served to marry each lattice component with the others. The prototype ball in his hands, then, useless as a Cosmic Clock Component because of its insufficient sphericity, its lack of mirror polish, and probably even its overall mass, might still function as an HDT device. It was a farfetched idea, Five had to admit. All manner of engineering requirements for the entanglement physics remained outside his grasp. But he had convinced himself that if nothing else, he could work toward functionality one step at a time, that he would discover the next solution by overcoming each challenge in turn. Something would come to him, the solution would arrive and he would discern it—a solution not yet within his grasp but attainable by way of his constant application of effort.

He would crack the science and conquer his limits. He had to believe that he could deliver his own salvation. He had nothing else to believe in. Nothing except himself and the practical legacy the ancient moleman engineers had bestowed upon him.

CHAPTER 16

CRACK THE SKY

LIGHTNING SLASHED ACROSS THE SKY. Cog waited, and when the thunderclap rocked the scorched earth beneath his boots, he barely flinched. Another cataract of rain fell, the trenches flooded, and a slurry of moleman body parts and corpses—all the meat and bones and putrid viscera of the fallen—disgorged itself upon the wounded land.

General Ten-Square lay motionless beside him, struck down, and the downpour pelted the poor man's backside. So much for their feigning death and getting to the bottom of this nightmare of a war. Only hours after having struck out on their own together, an MP transport, of all things, had picked them up, fed and watered and reoutfitted them, like animals, and redeployed them into this doomed outpost.

It's the end of the world, thought Cog, and he crouched behind the wrecked blast shield of the battalion's mighty energy cannon, covered his head with his arms, and buried his face against the muck-covered metal.

Not like this, he told himself. Get up. Die like a soldier and not a damn dog. He clawed at the gun's high-angle artillery gear and fumbled with the firing solution lever. His hands were stiff with cold. He hauled himself up further to press his face against the rangefinder. The display glowed. Still operational, go figure. So was the subterranean ammunition cell. Its firing deck was still primed, the indicator lamp flashing green. He pressed his face hard against the cloudy eyepiece— he could perhaps still trace the burn-line . . . yes. The orbiting moth-man gunship was poised in enfilade[32] just beyond the Karman Line.[33]

He twisted the turret control, and the motor chattered. Jammed. But only partially—he could still rotate the thing forty-five degrees either way. So be it. He shoved the loader control forward and felt the subterranean gun carriage rumble—a few rounds left. He set the firing sensor to halo-detect. When the mothmen gunners calculated their new firing solution, there was a chance they'd be overconfident, too assured of their victory; they may not take care to shroud the pre-ignition. It was worth a try.

The indicators flashed in sequence: red, yellow, green. The Big Gun was locked and loaded. He braced himself, his aching hands barely capable of grasping the mud-slicked bulkhead, turned his face away from the howling wind and slashing rain, and waited. This little moleman army satellite-planet outpost was a total loss. But he may yet do his part to give the main fighting force of Mega City One a chance to recover and regroup, to survive and fight. The super-dreadnaught attack ship of the mothmen had a weakness, after all—an Achilles' heel discovered by the molemen engineers. Its bombing hull lay exposed for more than sixty seconds prior to and immediately following a strike—the bay doors took that long to grind open and shut. And if the crew were up there waiting

---

32 Weapons fire *enfilades* a target when it strikes along the target's longest axis. A trench, for example, is in enfilade when it may be fired upon down its length.

33 The Kármán line, or Karman line, named after Theodore von Kármán (1881–1963), a Hungarian American engineer and physicist, is an astronautic term that originally described the boundary between the Earth's atmosphere and outer space at an altitude of 100 kilometers (62 miles) above the Earth's sea level. At the time of the Great Conflict, the term has been in use for millennia, cosmos-wide, to describe the near-space/outer-space boundary of all atmosphere-generating planets.

casually in orbit, unshrouded on top of everything, he just might get lucky . . .

He felt a tremor as the Big Gun responded to the halo-detection. The barrel swept up and over, and he counted aloud, the sound of his voice torn from his mouth by the maelstrom of weather. "Five, four, three, two . . ."

The earth quaked and the concussive cataclysm cracked the sky, transforming night into day in an instant—a direct hit! It had to be! The storm clouds parted, stripped away by the shock wave, and Cog prepared for the atmospheric fallout—he snatched at a battered helmet lying beside him and crammed it over his head. He dared not look out. He could only squirm farther beneath the warped armor-shield of the cannon and curl into a fetal ball before the blast of heat and light arrived and the shock wave swept everything away.

CHAPTER 17

HOUND OF HEAVEN

"I FLED HIM,"[34] MUMBLED LARON. His eyes were wild, his expression feverish. "I fled him." The sea spray stung his face and he cackled at it, at the searing pain in his leg, at the unraveling of his plans, at his insane predicament, at that meddling cockroach of a time detective. "Mr. Z.!" He spat the name into the wind, twisted the throttle, lolled his head back, and howled over the roar of the engine, driving his jet-rider headlong across the choppy water.

Soon the famous Gateway of India loomed before him and he cut the motor, swerved violently, and allowed the craft to wash sideways up the concrete slipway. The craft teetered there, the seawater backwashing down the ramp, and Laron half leapt and half toppled from his seat. "Argh!" He writhed upon the concrete, clutched at his leg, and when the machine tipped onto its side, he found himself partially pinned beneath it. "Merde! Putain!"[35] He shoved and kicked at the hull of the jet-rider until he'd freed his foot, hauling himself toward the pedestrian staircase that led to the street above.

---

34 From *The Hound of Heaven*, a poem by Francis Thompson, first published 1893. Public domain.

35 French. "Shit! Whore!"

"Oh, Maa!" The single dock attendant, an Indian, spoke in halting English as he rushed down the steps of the quay toward Laron. "My God, sir! What is it? Let me help!"

Laron swung at the man and stumbled to his feet, dragging his bad leg. "Get off! Get away, you idiot!" The man ducked and backed away, exasperated.

Laron forced himself up the steps toward the road, leaning heavily upon the handrail, swaying like a drunkard.

The dock attendant took one look at the weird machine and shouted after Laron. "Sir! My God, sir!" He gestured toward the incongruously futuristic jet-rider. "What is this? Whatever it is, sir, it cannot be left here! Sir!"

"I fled him," murmured Laron, oblivious. He moaned, clutched compulsively at his leg, then yanked at his tie and flung it onto the pavement. He coughed. What he wouldn't give for some fresh water. He felt sick. Feverish. A handful of pedestrians took pains to avoid him. He lurched past them.

"Down the nights. Down the days." He wiped at his face. "I fled him."

It was something he'd read, something about one's demons being in pursuit. He couldn't care less where the words came from. Nothing mattered now except getting to his HDT nexus.

"Down the night and down the days, I fled him."

The words fueled his rage, and his rage would see him through. To killing Mr. Z. And if not, then to his own escape, at least. He swiped at a lock of pesky hair in his face and lost his balance, then grabbed at the railing and held tightly to it, as if the ground beneath his feet were tilting. He scanned the still-busy streets, trying to shield his eyes from the glare of the headlights. "Cab! Cab, goddammit!" He waved blindly. "Caaab!"

A car swerved close to the curb and parked. "Cab here, sir!" The young taxi driver peered at Laron from behind the wheel of his vehicle. For all he knew, this teetering European was some drunken tourist. When he comprehended Laron's injured condition, he pulled closer, stopped, and leapt out. "Do you need the hospital, sir? If you have been drinking, you know, the police will bother you. But you do not look very well. Where is your hotel? I will take you home, at least."

Laron frowned, struggling to focus upon the man, then lumbered past him and piled headlong into the back seat.

The driver hurried back to his cab, slammed the door, and eyed Laron in the rearview mirror with a mixture of tolerance and impatience common to his trade. "Where do we go, sir?"

It was as if Laron's exertions had intensified his delirium, and he sat moaning, clutching at his wound. "Down the arches of the years," he mumbled.

"Down the arches of the years, sir, certainly. Now, where shall we go?" It was then that he noticed Laron's bloodstained pant leg. "By God, sir, there is blood! Blood!"

Another man—the dock attendant—hurried toward them, breathless and gesturing wildly. "Hey! Hey, there, cabbie! This man is crazy! Take him nowhere but the police!"

"Watch out!" said the cabbie. "Get back! Are you drunk yourself? Leave my customer to me!"

"You fool! He is much more than drinking. Dangerous. He tried to strike me! He left his crazy boat in a heap at my docks. Call the police!"

"Call them yourself!" The driver leapt into his cab. He stomped on the accelerator and swept the vehicle into traffic, oblivious of the car horns. He eyed the dock attendant's retreat through the window of his cab. "Sir, I cannot drive you around this traffic circle all night long. Please. You want nothing whatever to do with the police. You would not be much better off at the hospital if you are in trouble. Do you understand me, sir?"

Laron sat slumped, as if unconscious.

The cabbie was alarmed. "We are going there. To the hospital." He revved the engine and thrust at the gear shift.

"No!" groaned Laron. He hauled himself up, suddenly lucent. "The Asiatic Society! Of Bombay! Do you hear? Near Horniman Circle! What is wrong with you? Go, you fool! Get me there!"

"The RAS, sir? Do you mean the Royal Asiatic—?"

Laron nodded impatiently. "In the town hall building. The Royal Asiatic Society, yes, yes, just go, go!"[36]

The driver craned his neck at the traffic, spied his opening, then stomped on the accelerator. With a belch of blue-white smoke from the exhaust, they sped from the quay.

———

"C'MON, C'MON, DAMMIT!" MR. Z. forced himself to wait for the tracer function of his transponder to complete its calculation. He revved the jet-rider's engine and was about to shove the machine into gear when the data cleared. Finally! The Asiatic Society, of all places. Had Laron recruited them too? He mapped his route, scowling impatiently at the display. From the ferry port to the Asiatic Society was 1.4 kilometers—a five-minute drive in a taxi. If the trace was reliable—who knew if Laron could scramble even the location of his HDT nexus?—he had to hurry.

Mr. Z. ducked behind the wind screen, squinted into the spray, and wrenched on the throttle, hugging the seat tightly with his thighs so as not to be flung from the machine. Nevertheless, the acceleration and the sea chopping against the hull surprised him and he slowed, instinctively shifting his weight, trying to find a workable combination of navigational control versus speed. "Damn it all, I've got no time for this, just go!" With that, he scrunched closer to the dashboard, pinched his knees hard against the seat, and let the machine roar.

Faster was indeed easier—the machine possessed a planing hull, and the controls responded better when Mr. Z. feathered the airfoils.

———

36   The Asiatic Society of Mumbai (formerly Asiatic Society of Bombay), funded by an annual grant from the Central Government of India, is a learned society within the field of Asian studies. It can trace its origin to the Literary Society of Bombay, which first met in the city in November 1804 and was founded by Sir James Mackintosh.

He roared across the water with the throttle wide open, and in no time the lights upon the quay came into view and he spied the spillway. There! Laron's jet-rider! Alongside were several uniformed men—policemen, they had to be. But what would they make of the machine, of its technology? Leave no trace, dammit to hell. He slowed and steered wide of the spillway, keen to avoid being seen, and puttered along the seawall toward the vacant end of the ferry port, out of earshot and line of sight. He selected a spot that offered an outcropping of stone as a makeshift dock. He kicked at the scuttle plug, the craft immediately took on water, and Mr. Z. leapt from the seat. The craft sank quickly, gurgling and sputtering like a harpooned beast. He scrambled up and over the remains of the seawall and stood breathless, nursing his arm—the strain of the ride had aggravated his old injury. And here he was again at the Gateway of India. Dammit to hell, he was chasing Laron in circles!

———

LARON SPRAWLED UPON THE BACK seat of the cab, his chest heaving.

"Sir?" said the cabbie. "Wake up, sir!"

Laron groaned and mumbled something, and the cabbie scowled at him. "We are here, sir. At the Asiatic Society."

Laron thrust the door open and tumbled from the cab. He lurched to his feet, once again dragging his leg.

"Sir! My rupees!" The cabby was already out from behind the wheel of his vehicle, his door flung open, and a step behind Laron—it was not the first time one of his fares attempted to allude him. "Your payment, sir!" He clutched at Laron's arm, and they struggled.

"Get your hands off me!" Laron swung wildly. The cabbie merely ducked, and Laron toppled haplessly to the ground from his own momentum.

The cabbie reached for him. "I am sorry, sir. But you must pay! You must! Or I will call the police!" He glanced about at the empty city.

Laron dragged himself toward the society's broad marble steps.

"No, sir! My payment! Please!" The cabbie shook Laron's arm.

"Argh!" Laron shoved his free hand into his suit coat and flung a handful of coins. Pice, annas, and rupees clattered across the concrete.

"Kutte ki jat![37] You are crazy acting! Crazy!" He stooped to the snatch the coins, glancing warily over his shoulder at Laron. "Crazy European," he muttered. "I try to assist somebody, and this is the thanks I get! My good deed for the day, that's all it is. And good riddance to you, sir. Good riddance!"

Laron hobbled up the building's thirty-odd steps. He paused midflight, breathless, and focused blearily upon the building's pedimented portico, its eight softly illuminated Doric columns.

The cabbie shouted up from the street. "It is closed, sir! Ha, that teaches you! You will not get in! All such buildings in Bombay are closed at night!" He snatched a last coin from the pavement, scurried into his cab, and drove off.

Laron teetered on the upper steps. He swiped at his brow and scowled at the low moon. Yet his vantage point and the slight breeze returned him to himself for a moment, and he looked out upon his wide view of the cityscape, focusing first upon the Horniman Circle Garden, a large public park directly across the street. Then he glared at something farther out. "There," he murmured. "There it is. The oldest fire in this miserable shithole of a city."[38] He teetered a bit, caught himself, and half collapsed. "Parsis. Eternal fires. I would piss on it!" He coughed and spat. Wiped at his mouth with his sleeve. He turned to crawl pathetically up the remaining steps, his injured leg stiffened, the wound now festered and swollen. He leaned hard against the front door and pressed his disrupter against the lock.

---

37   "Breed of dog!" A Hindi expletive.

38   The Seth Banaji Limji Agiary, constructed in 1709, is close by—an eight-minute walk from the Asiatic Society—and perhaps within Laron's view. It is the oldest Parsi fire temple in the city and, in accordance with the Zoroastrian faith, maintains a perpetual and sacred fire within in its confines.

The sensor flashed and beeped, and he twisted the door handle and shoved himself inside.

He locked the door behind him, switched on his pocket lantern, and made his way laboriously to the Durbar Hall, his gasps and clumsy footfalls echoing within the dark.

"Stop," shouted Mr. Z. "Here! Stop right here!" Mr. Z. shoved his rupees at the cabbie, leapt from the vehicle, and sprinted headlong up the steps of the Town Hall building. He took two at a time, gasping at the strain, sprang at the central door, and twisted at the handle. Locked. Of course.

He scanned the building's facade for another entrance. Door upon identical-looking door. Something caught his eye. Bloodstains on the concrete. Yes. And smudged shoeprints beneath his own feet! The discovery rejuvenated him. Laron was here, dammit!

He stepped away from the door, aimed his pistol at the lockset, turned his face away and fired once, twice. He kicked at the door and burst inside, holding his breath, listening. No alarms. No sound of any guards, let alone Laron. No lights either—the place was as dark as a crypt. And he had no lantern. Where would the man have gone—an HDT nexus could be anywhere. Dammit to hell, he may already *be* gone!

He considered another scan—perhaps he could decipher the HDT location. Screw it. He could waste time fumbling around in the dark. He could do goddamn handstands and it would avail him nothing. Think!

He pricked his ears. What was that? The sound of something scraping heavily across the marble floor. Like furniture being shifted. Yet muffled too, as if behind a door. That way. He grasped his plasma pistol. He was virtually blind and resorted to the pathetically weak beam of his transponder. He crept toward the sound. There. A pale sliver of light peeped from between a set of double doors. He approached as quietly as he could, grasped the handle, and shoved. There, in the far corner of the room—Laron with his back to him.

"Laron!" Mr. Z. hurled a chair out of his way and leapt over a low table.

Laron spun about, clutching his transponder in one hand and aiming his pistol with the other.

Blam!

Mr. Z. dove beneath a conference table, scrambled between a phalanx of chairs, and struggled to his knees, prepared to fire.

"Ha!" Laron's laugh was maniacal. "Too late, you *fool*!"

Mr. Z. fired and Laron vanished. Mr. Z. braced himself for the HDT vacuum. A bluster of papers, debris, and dust swirled past him and whorled around the nexus where Laron had been.

Mr. Z. holstered his pistol and used the meager light from his transponder to clamber past the tables and chairs. He aimed his transponder at the spot where Laron had been. The display alternated between blue and white for a time, working at a trace. "C'mon, c'mon." Finally, it pulsed yellow, then green.

COORDINATES ACQUIRED.

"Goddammit, c'mon!"

DUPLICATED.

Steady green. Mr. Z. brought his feet together, shoved his device into his arm pouch, and stood ramrod straight, chin down, arms at his sides.

When the security guards appeared, ducking round the doorframe to peer warily into the darkened room, the gust of wind startled them, and they reached to turn on the lights. "Ma!" said one of them. "What the devil!" Chairs lay strewn about the room. "I smell smoke!"

The other guard coughed. "A gun," he gasped. "A gun has been discharged, I am certain. I told you I heard something like that. I told you, didn't I!"

Otherwise, they shrugged at the toppled chairs and disheveled furniture and stared at each other. "But there is no one here."

CHAPTER 18

INFLUENCE OF THE GODDESS

"WE DINE AT THE RISING of the second moon," said the empress. "The preparations must be exact, do you understand? Likewise, the service—no deviation from my instructions will be tolerated."

The servant bowed and departed, stepped quietly across the stones of the courtyard, and finally disappeared beyond the soft glow of the lanterns.

The emperor, meanwhile, stood hunched over his douzha,[39] clutching a delicate horsehair brush in one hand and fussing with the tiny bamboo screen with his other. Exactitude on behalf of the cricket ring's proportions was essential for fairness. This, and brushing away the tiniest fleck of debris. It was unfortunate that the empress herself regarded so many of his preparations undetectable. Otherwise, she could have lent credibility to this auspicious event. "You shall become the General tonight," he whispered heartily.

"Talking to crickets," said the empress. "The boyish interests of men never leave them. What if I told Advisor Chung that you are both starving and withholding water from his cricket to gain an

---

39 The oval ring designed for cricket fights (Chinese).

advantage?" The clear early autumn weather with the stars so close made her optimistic and cheerful. And the aroma of woodsmoke from the brazier spiced the air with both a magical nostalgia and the invigorating promise of the future.

"Chung's cricket," replied the emperor gravely, "has received every benefit of my tickling skills. See for yourself. He is vigorous and shiny. He enjoys the same licorice-infusion bath as the General."

"And honey for supper, I suppose!" said the empress. "I should be so well kept!" She affected a scowl.

"There is no honor in a contrived victory," said the emperor. "A fair fight is the only fight." He coaxed each cricket from its tiny, lacquered box and stood up, pressing his hands into the small of his back. "Ah!" he said, wincing.

"When will you learn to mind your back? There are servants to manage your precious crickets."

"Come," said the emperor. "You must witness the bout. To legitimize the outcome. Chung expects the long legs of his beast to ensure his victory. But long legs are no match for a thick neck and large teeth. You should be the one to remove the screen."

"Why me?"

"To verify that I have not influenced the outcome." He rubbed his hands together and waved her to him.

"You are being dreadful in your seriousness," said the empress, looking down her nose at him. But she nevertheless approached the douzha and grasped the tiny screen between her slender, powdered fingers, her blood-red nails vivid in the lantern light.

"Wait," said the emperor. He deployed Chung's cricket on one side of the screen and the General upon the other. "Now!"

The empress snatched the screen away, and they watched the ensuing standoff.

"They are doing nothing," she said. "Are they afraid to fight?"

"They are taking the measure of each other. The contestants first fence with their antennae"—the emperor gestured with splayed fingers as if to emphasize his point—"and only then display spread mandibles. Look there! When their jaws come together, the fight is on. He who retreats, loses!"

A period of intense observation ensued before the insects finally engaged each other, and then the emperor's exclamation resounded across the courtyard. "Victory! Victory to the General!"

"The one chirps," said the empress. "And the other . . ."

"The other is vanquished! My champion, the General, he sings in triumph!" The emperor's face beamed, and he bent to admire his insect. He yanked the jade cap from his gourd, carved in the ancient fashion with a motif of flowers, fruits and vines, and coaxed his champion inside. "Here you are, my brave General. You have earned your rest."

The empress shuffled across the stone patio toward the dinner table, speaking over her shoulder. "Poor Chung," she said. "He will be disappointed. How often is a cricket beheaded?"

"Hmm," said the emperor. "One usually retreats to end the match. But this indicates courage upon both sides. Chung's warrior fought till the last. An honorable death." He carried his gourd to the table and took his seat across from the empress. His servant stood quietly some paces away, fan at the ready.

Lanterns hung from the branches of the trees, and the night was easeful and warm. A servant swept her brush across the rough surface of a clay cricket cage some distance from the table, coaxing forth the limpid delicacy of the inhabitant's song.

The emperor sat listening. He rubbed his hands together again and brought his attention to the meal. "I smell the ocean. Shellfish? Oysters? Ah!" He waved the servants forward, eyeing the dishes.

"To the General's victory," said the empress, and raised her glass. "And to a fine harvest. The people are happy."

They toasted, and the emperor sipped heartily from his wine and patted his cricket cage.

The royal taster appeared, a young man of stoic countenance, and stood beside the table. The tray was set before them, and the empress, curiously, turned the dish when the taster reached to select an oyster. The empress glared sharply at him, but when the emperor looked up, she was once again cheerful. The taster swallowed, and the empress waved him away. She turned to the emperor. "He is impudent, attempting to select the best of them." She affected a gracious smile and served them both. "You shall eat at least as well as your cricket."

The emperor smiled at her absently. He was enjoying the influence of his wolfberry wine and allowed his gaze to drift toward the courtyard, into the lighted windows of the palace beyond, then upward, into the evening sky filled with stars. The second moon had indeed risen—an ample waxing gibbous tinged with gold. He felt his wife's gaze. The empress focused upon him in a startling, piercing manner. His impulse was to read her thoughts, but of course he could not. He watched her raise her cup to her luminous powdered face and striking painted lips.

He likewise sipped. "Hmm. Gouji jiu.[40] It has been ages, has it not?"

"Since we were married," said the empress. She set down her glass and looked at her hands.

The emperor sipped again. "What inspired it? The solstice?"

She tipped her head ambiguously.

"I know what it is. The Great Conflict has been preoccupying me. Preoccupying every member of the court. I have been ungraceful and negligent. Dishonorable. To you."

The empress dismissed the remaining servants with a gesture and they departed, bowing, into the shadows. She selected an oyster, cradled it with both hands, its ragged, stony texture a contrast to her tender flesh. She held it close to her face, her nostrils flared delicately, her eyelashes fluttering. She tipped the mollusk into her mouth, breathed it in with a tenuous, almost imperceptible inhalation. She swallowed and, curiously, wiped away a tear.

The emperor smiled at her, gulped at his wine, and reached for an oyster himself, guzzling the meat and slurping the liquor. He reached for another and another until he had consumed several in quick succession. "Mmm, excellent."

With that, a wave of potent drowsiness overtook him. The empress peered intently at him, and he rubbed at his face, for it felt flushed.

---

40 Gouji jiu is a Chinese alcoholic beverage made from wolfberry.

He tried to speak and managed only a clumsy groan. He grasped his throat, gasped, and clutched at the table edge. He teetered, made to rise, and instead slid from his chair into a heap, his eyes staring.

The empress stood over him, clutching her fan. When the emperor began to convulse, she snapped it open, hid her face behind it, and looked away.

The emperor reached out to her with his mind. *Help me. Help. Me.* Pain stabbed at his guts. Blackness enveloped him. No . . . *no!*

CHAPTER 19

AH, BAMBOO!

Ah, bamboo! Five admired the uniformity and order of the towering, healthy grove. Every culm soared straight and unblemished to its leafy crown. What a relief from the twisted, strangled chaos of the rest of the jungle!

He gripped a culm and looked up. The shafts were strong, and just young enough to retain some subtle flexibility. He may get the proper eighty millimeters inner diameter out of the top third of these stalks. And with so many spectacularly flawless examples to choose from, he could afford to be picky and select only the very best.

Because tolerances mattered. But he reminded himself that it wasn't as if he required anything close to Cosmic Clock Component levels of refinement. No. All he needed were HDT-quality tolerances.

He hacked away at the base of a culm with the saw blade portion of his knife until it snapped and toppled. Yes, perhaps ten meters of good shaft here. Two more culms and he'd have more than the twenty-five meters required for the shrine. The damn shrine. Hauling the culms overland to his bivouac, then dragging them into the temple, and finally into the central shrine? It exhausted him just thinking about it. He ought to cut a few extra culms in case one or two of them failed the drying process. Or if he botched carving out the diaphragms and needed to start over—diaphragm thicknesses varied significantly between culms, at least given his early experiments. All that, and a section may fail when he undertook the vac-boring itself.

He rapped upon a section of culm with the handle of his knife. He could feel and hear the strength of it. No, if he had any problems, it wouldn't be the fault of the bamboo. The risk of mechanical failure lay within the components of his makeshift vacuum pump. A chamber could fracture, or a seal could fail, and he'd have no time to fix it. Or he'd be discovered and . . . hell and blood, so many things could go wrong it made him crazy. Meanwhile, he had neither the time nor the workspace to run proper engineering trials.

He pondered the idea of boring only halfway down. Or a damn third. It would save so much time and effort. To say nothing of lowering the demand upon his equipment and the risk of a failure. But no. Anything less than all the way to the sacred deposit—24.69 meters from the floor of the shrine to the sarcophagus—and the beam of sunlight during the solar zenith would be dangerously fore-shortened. Mind the meridians. Pay attention to the parallels. Heed the hypermeridians. And dig deep or don't get home.

Moreover, within the context of this planet, an astronomical unit was 1.496×10^8 kilometers. Eight light minutes. But that was only the mean distance from the Earth to its sun. He also had to account for the orbital variation on the date of the two zenith passage events.

Which event to choose? According to the nanotext data, the Gregorian April 26 option occurred within the dry season, hence a greater probability for a clear day and the full power of the sunlight trigger. Best of all, it was sooner rather than later.

Either date would likely attract enthusiastic hordes seeking the spectacle of the illumination—the zenith passage itself—or the festival that would likely surround it. Perhaps for days, even weeks, who knew? So the Khmer themselves were perhaps his biggest obstacle to an effective transport. They presented the prospect of the temple city, the temple proper, and the tiny inner shrine space being packed with humans exactly when he needed it empty. To say nothing of his inevitable comings and goings through the temple galleries and courtyards during his preparations—the confounded shrine itself lay precisely and intentionally at the temple's least accessible point.

His engineering and equipment were within his control. The Khmer and their festivals and rituals were not.

Nevertheless, he needed to incorporate a significant distraction. Something significant enough to at least clear the inner shrine and allow him to barricade access while he made his escape from this shithole planet. He had no flares. But he could possibly get his hands upon some fireworks. The Khmer apparently loved their fireworks. Which they must be acquiring from the Chinese traders? Anyway, on their riverboats and in their little villages—even in the fields—he had heard the telltale snapping and crackling. More than likely it had something to do with banishing evil spirits.

Pilfering such luxury goods would be a risky project on its own. And then the Khmer would probably be getting their fill of fireworks the day of the passage anyway, so he couldn't know if the ruse would work.

He scratched irritably at his ears. It all seemed too damn complicated. There were too many variables, too many unknowns. And the entanglement physics still evaded him. It was, as usual, his weaknesses with the applied mathematics. *Just work the numbers,* his father would have told him. *Work the numbers and you can accomplish anything.* And so he had diligently slaved away at the calculations by day and goddamn pondered them all night until he finally managed to fall asleep.

But one thing at a time. Stick to the goddamn plan. Complete the sighting tube engineering. Leave the entanglement calculations—and the HDT radio mechanism, for that matter—to fate. The solutions would come to him. And he would engineer the practical applications. And everything just may work. Or damn it all to hell, he was doomed to die here!

Meanwhile, the idea of a religious festival intrigued him. How would the Khmer populace go about celebrating the zenith passage? Would it be a cloistered event limited to royalty, to the king's court, perhaps? Would the event occur in multiple locations, or exclusively at Angor Wat? Would there be a migration or pilgrimage of some sort from the far corners of this realm? Would there be temporary encampments? How large would the crowds be?

It wasn't as if anybody, any molemen at least, had done any research on the post-Hindu decline of Angkor and the Khmer's use of the temple. The mythology only mattered when it was still viable as the CCC. It was possible that the Khmer populace, steeped as they probably were in animistic beliefs and magic, had never heeded Vaishnavism to any extent. The knowledge that the king and his court, including his priests, retained about the nature of the temple's solar function may have been lost or mostly superseded since the interment of the king's ashes and the building of Angkor Thom. And then further obfuscated by the advent of Buddhism.

But it wasn't as if any of that—the human presence or not within the temple—mattered. Because he would have to prepare for the worst case. And it was going to take some luck, in the end, despite everything.

All this Five pondered as he hacked the culms to size. And the thinking invigorated him just as laboring in the sweltering heat and humidity exhausted him. He so missed his studies. His true studies, not these blasted mathematics and the entanglement physics. Rather, his references, databases, researches, and books. *The* book. What had happened to it? The cleanup drones would have destroyed it. Or it was disintegrating into the desert sands of the future. Whatever had or would happen, the book was lost to him.

Within an hour, he was finished. Four sturdy-looking, ten-meter lengths stretched out before him. Each of which would require at least six weeks, after carving out the diaphragms, to dry properly, given what he could make of the water content. Mega City One cured their hollow shaft forest lumber in huge kilns. Likewise, if he wanted to expedite the process, he ought to employ fire in some manner. But talk about tedious. And tricky. Roasting unwieldy lengths of bamboo culm over fire—his meager campfire—even if he could engineer a proper means of support for the process, would require turning the shafts by hand and moving them along their length over the heat at precisely the right holding time so as not to overheat them. If their moisture steamed away too violently, the culms could split. And splits, even virtually invisible hairline examples, wouldn't allow for anything close to the vacuum required to haul up a meter or so of soil at each run. No. The culms had to be solid, through and through. Pinhole air gaps were going to be tricky enough to seal properly with his homemade goop. With the proper tools and enough trial and error, of course, he could make it all work—he could eventually engineer the hell out of it even under these primitive conditions. But he didn't have the proper tools. Let alone the time to try to manufacture them. He didn't have much time at all.

If today was indeed Gregorian March 1, 1296, it provided him merely six weeks for drying culms, trimming out the diaphragms, cutting the joinery for the bamboo sections, and manufacturing his vacuum pump. And a handful of experimental trials along the way. All of which eventually hinged upon the quantum entanglement process. And what if he had the date wrong? He had carefully tracked the sun path—the so-called day arc—and the foreshortening shadows at each of his test installations. But without his sextant and his transponder and access to the databases and a high-resolution computational bead upon his true space-time coordinates, he risked floundering within the margins and missing the target.

So much work. Coupled with cumulative error. And a lack of proper engineering trials. Hell, in the absence of proper mechanics-of-materials data or any information on soil composition, to say nothing of the bamboo's polar moment of inertia[41] or its radial strength, he could only pray that his culms would endure the repeated application of a vacuum strong enough to move, what? One hundred nine cubic meters of soil? It was insanity. And it was his only chance.

---

41   The measure of a shaft's ability to resist torsion.

CHAPTER 20

FRIDAY

VIXY SWIPED IRRITABLY AT HER forehead and scowled at her device. "God, it's hot. And humid."

"Yeah," said Neutic. "Hey, if we're not picking up any tracing technology, then maybe we've got it wrong—there's a chance they aren't even looking for us."

"Those mothmen? What would they be doing here, then? I mean, it's not like we can rely on my transponder for anything, apparently. And maybe they're blocking the trace somehow. It's all weird as hell. But they're tracking us, I know it. You saw them, especially that older one."

"Like we're animals. You're right."

Vixy bit her lip. "Somehow, I pictured Cambodia filled with nothing but jungle. But these open spaces? It must be farmland. But that isn't rice."

"It's millet, I think. It was a staple food in ancient Cambodia. I mean, now. And they allowed their cattle to graze on the early growth."

Vixy cocked her eyebrow at him.

Neutic shrugged. "All that reading I did on India, something about millet being their largest crop and how common it was in the rest of Asia. It has more protein and fiber than rice."

"It may as well be sticks and stones for all the good it's going to do us. We're going to have to start worrying about food soon. And water. I suppose we can purify that river water if we have to." She tapped at her transponder. "This must be the Siem Reap River, right?" She shaded the display with her hand. "Which runs north and south and Angkor Wat is, let me see, just west of it. Angkor Thom is north of Angkor Wat. But where are we, north or south of Angkor Wat? God, this sucks—my device can't locate us."

"Hmm," said Neutic, peering at his own device. "Siem Reap. I'm not sure that name was in use then. I mean *now*, sorry. But . . ." He trailed off.

Vixy frowned at the water. "But what?"

Neutic squinted into the distance. "Those mountains. It has to be the Phnom Kulen range. Which are north. And it means this must be the Siem Reap flowing south."

"At least your device can access data," said Vixy, "even if it's just archival. But that's only because it's tapping the internal memory. This thing?" She wagged her transponder in front of her face.

"Hmm," said Neutic. "It's showing Angkor in two locations, see? And these large blank rectangles, I don't get it."

Vixy peered at Neutic's display. "That has to be Angkor Wat, there, to our east. Unless we've got this completely wrong. And there's Angkor Thom, the city, like I said, with all the faces on the towers."

"Angkor Thom?" said Neutic. "Okay, you're right, that's it, there. To the north, then."

"Built I don't remember how long after Angkor Wat that Angkor Thom was constructed. Hell, I was studying China, not goddamn Cambodia, as an undergrad. Who cares, anyway? Let's just assume this is showing us to be west of Angkor Wat. These big rectangles, I don't know, except that I remember something about the Khmer having reservoirs."

"For irrigation?" said Neutic.

"I think so. I don't know. God, we've still got to find a place to bivouac for the night. And wait for the TDC to somehow track our coordinates so we can goddamn communicate with Captain Chase. If we've got to resort to an EIB, then we'll be stuck in one spot—we'll have to wait until they send someone after us. I can't believe this.

We're already a damn liability. And Mr. Z. is on his own in Bombay. If he made it there."

"And meanwhile the mothmen are up to something here, apparently," said Neutic. "Maybe something to do with the Cosmic Clock?"

"It wouldn't surprise me," said Vixy. "Nothing would surprise me." She suddenly appeared wilted and fraught. "I feel like I already need a shower and a change of clothes."

Neutic appeared flummoxed.

"Don't mind me," said Vixy. "Yes, the goddamn mothmen. Who knows? Angkor Wat could be, I don't know—it's an enormous mythological monument, that's for sure. But why are we here? I'm just not fucking prepared for any of this."

———

"It's muddy as hell," said Vixy.

"Suspended solids." Neutic probed the water with the slender tip of his purifier gadget. "Low-level bacterial pathogens. Human and animal coliform." He glanced up and down the river. "Makes sense, I guess. If humans and animals are upriver."

"Which makes me crave a shower even more." Vixy scanned the length of the road, her hand to her trek goggles, modifying the magnification. "Jeezus, there's nothing on this road, no people in the fields, nothing. Wait! Look!" She gestured north. "Just around that bend in the road, coming our way."

Neutic adjusted his own lenses. "An ox cart. Carrying, what? Sacks of grain or something?"

Vixy adjusted the straps on her pack. "It looks to be all trees alongside the river. And not dense. I'm thinking we ought to keep to the trees, or the edge of them, at least. So we can stay out of plain sight and still get a feel for where we're headed, right? Because I don't trust our cloaking mechanism. Look—I've got no cloak indicator when I try to activate it. Jeezus. I don't trust anything to do with our technology right now."

"Where are we going?" said Neutic.

"Where else?"

"Angkor Wat? The temple itself, you mean?"

"Wat. Temple. Shrine. Mausoleum. Whatever it is now. Yes. I mean, what would Mr. Z. do? If we're going to figure out what's going on, it's as good a place to start as any."

"IT'S FOUR O'CLOCK," SAID VIXY. "We've been walking for an hour."

"The sun is strong," said Neutic. "What I wouldn't give for one of those hats." He gestured ahead.

"The cart driver?"

"Yes. I'll pick one up when we get to Angkor Wat. Or wherever. Along with dinner."

"And I'll buy cigarettes and some nail polish," said Vixy.

They'd crested a slight rise and were surprised to encounter a river widening before them and beyond, nestled against its lush, green banks, a collection of tiny houses—or more accurately, unpretentious huts constructed of what appeared to be dried grasses.

"Stilts," said Neutic. "A meter high, or so. This river must flood like crazy."

"Hmm," said Vixy. "All the rivers. I'm glad we're not here during the monsoon season. Look at those rickety ramps—they must have boats or canoes lashed to the houses so they can get in and out when everything floods."

"Maybe its Siem Reap?" said Neutic. "Or what will become Siem Reap."

"Right," said Vixy. "The 1296 version. It's a crazy tourist town in our time."

There was a small stand of palms mixed with deciduous trees near the bottom of the rise, perhaps a hundred meters or so from the edge of the village. Vixy gestured toward it. "What do you say we rest there, under those trees? We can stay out of sight and maybe see what everybody else is doing for food."

They reached the palms and plopped down beside each other against one of the broad, smooth trunks.

"You look terrible, Neutic," said Vixy. "Are you sick?"

"The heat, I guess. I don't know."

"HDT hangover, I bet. Take a medic tab. Here. It helped me." She broke a ration in half and stowed the remainder in her pack. "I need to eat something. Or I'm going to go crazy wanting a cigarette instead. Well, I want a cigarette anyway. For some reason, I never crave goddamn cigarettes unless I'm traveling."

"Sometimes I wish I smoked," said Neutic, his voice weak.

"Take this energy gel with that tab. Here. Drink it all. And maybe you ought to eat something too."

Neutic shook off her suggestion. "We'll see if this tab helps first, thanks."

A breeze rustled through tops of the trees, and they listened to the strange cackles, trills, and screeches that could have been birds or monkeys or insects, for all they knew. Cottony clouds drifted across the blue sky, and the little village seemed empty and quiet.

Neutic sat staring at the village. It occurred to him that he wasn't at all certain he was prepared to get a glimpse of anyone from the year 1296, indigenous or otherwise. This is what it feels like to be in over your head, he thought.

Vixy fussed with her transponder.

"What's it like in Haida Gwaii?" said Neutic. When Vixy didn't respond right away, he felt self-conscious—they never discussed anything but work. "Sorry. It's no time for small talk. It's just that I've never been there."

"It's peaceful," said Vixy. "Beautiful. They say island life is different. But it's my home, that's all. You know what I mean?" She eyed Neutic. "Are you okay? I mean, do you feel all right?"

Neutic leaned his head back against the tree trunk. His eyes were closed, his cheeks were flushed, and his temples glistened with perspiration. She watched him until he half-opened an eye at her. "I'm okay. Don't worry. I'm not flipping out on you. At least not yet. It's an HDT hangover, I guess, like you said. I still have a bit of a headache. But I'm feeling more like myself. The tab must be helping, thanks."

Music, or something like it, floated toward them on the breeze. The sound of thin, tuneless bells, strange flutelike music, and the patter of percussion instruments—bongos or hand drums[42] of some type—grew louder. Vixy and Neutic looked at each other dubiously.

Around a bend in the road marched, or rather paraded, a group of elaborately costumed men and women, many of them bare chested, others with patterned shawls over their shoulders. All wore colorful, silken fabric around their hips, secured with a belt and variously gathered into leggings for the men and draped as skirts for the women.[43] Both sexes sported necklaces, perhaps of gold or silver, and in some cases broad enough to conceal much of their torsos. Other jewelry, especially amongst the women, included arm bands, bracelets, and rings.

In general, the people were of modest stature, their flesh golden-brown, in some cases paler or a darker chestnut hue, and they all possessed gleaming black hair, for the most part knotted near the top and, in the case of the women, with a long ponytail brought forward over the shoulder. Some of the men sported short hair. Everyone was barefooted.

The women themselves were comely—gracefully proportioned, with large eyes, high cheekbones, and full lips—and poised. The men and boys were smooth skinned, sturdily built, and proudly postured, with their shoulders straight and chests out. Everyone seemed cheerful and pleasantly tempered.

More Khmer followed, and still more, until the procession, which indeed bore the celebratory and loosely dignified air of a parade, seemed as if it would never end. A phalanx of young Khmer men attired in hip wraps short enough to resemble loincloths—there may have been more than a hundred of them—bore slender scepters with a

---

42   Skor chhaiyam, a tall Cambodian goblet drum slung over the shoulder with a string so it can be played at waist level while walking. Only the top has skin, leaving a sound-hole at the bottom of a narrowed drum body.

43   A sampot, a rectangular piece of cloth wrapped around the hips, draped variously over the legs and gathered in front in styles indicative of the gender and social class of the wearer.

crooked peak in one hand and a light shield in the other. Certain of them wore short jackets that left their midriffs bare and carried long knives.

"Soldiers?" said Vixy.

Neutic stared as if transfixed. He got up and looked as if he were intent upon approaching the parade.

"Neutic," hissed Vixy. "Neutic! If you don't look at me, I'm going to assume you've got shellback syndrome. And I'm going to inject you with the antidote."

Neutic looked at her. "I just, well, I don't . . . it's all so fantastic. What do you mean, shellback syndrome?"

"It happens sometimes. During a person's first HDT, especially if they arrive into a lot of cultural stimulation. Like this. Without any time to acclimate. Your training was rushed, Neutic, all the stuff about what goes wrong during HDT events, the ill effects and everything—they told me they'd skipped it. Anyway, yes, shellback syndrome. When you encounter people from the past, not just objects or spaces and places. It can cause a kind of overstimulation. Sometimes it triggers a euphoria. Or a trancelike or even intoxicated condition. You feel outside of yourself. It's weird, and it sounded crazy to me until I experienced a bit of it myself in Cairo. Stay here. Take your eyes off the parade and look at me, okay? Now breathe deeply once"—she inhaled to demonstrate—"twice, do as I tell you, Neutic. There. Now, one more time. Inhale . . ."

Neutic grimaced, nevertheless drawn to return his attention to the parade. "It's just that I need to see it all." Then he marched directly toward it.

"Neutic!" Vixy clutched at his arm. "Goddammit, Neutic!" In a single motion, Vixy snatched a hypo from her pack and rushed to tackle him, struggling to jab the hypo into the back of his neck.

"Ow! Jesus, Vixy, what the hell?" Neutic scrambled to his feet and stood aloof, glaring at her and rubbing his neck.

Vixy watched him and waited. "Neutic?"

Neutic seemed perplexed for a moment, screwing up his face, then running his hand through his hair. He focused on a pair of striding elephants.

"Neutic!"

"What?"

She recognized his look of stoic curiosity. "You're back, aren't you?"

He frowned at her.

"Good. You look normal. And you sound normal. You had a spell."

"A spell?" Neutic dug into his pack. "I'm thirsty as hell, I know that." He tore open an energy gel with his teeth and gulped it down. "What do you mean a spell?"

"Never mind. I'll explain it later. How's your neck?"

Neutic rubbed at it. "Something bit me, I guess, I don't know. What is it? And what are we doing out here? We'll be seen. Why are you looking at me like that?"

Vixy gestured at him. "C'mon. Let's get back into the trees."

Safely hidden again, but with a clear view of the road, they settled in again to watch the parade. Akin to parades everywhere, it was composed of one distinctly attired and distinctly themed section after another. Some groups were barefaced and more modestly attired, while others were adorned with elaborate masks complimenting their especially vivid sampots. Some groups seemed especially theatrical or intimidating—thrusting their banners through the air or flashing their swords and knives. Or merely pausing to increase the vitality and volume of their music. The prettiest women and girls were adorned in luminous silks of gleaming red, emerald-green, cerulean, and yellow. They danced as they marched, knees and elbows akimbo and their expressive hands open, so much so that their slender fingers appeared to be bent almost backward.

Next came a contingent of slender, finely boned young Cambodian women, their flowing silken garments displaying an identical floral design. They wore flowers in their coiled hair and bore large candles, alight despite the sun and sweltering heat. Others bore gold and silver utensils—bowls, small vases, gilt knives, and statuettes. A remarkable group of what must have been female warriors followed, naked to the waist and bearing lances and shields.

There were numerous oxcarts, some bearing three or four musicians each, variously slapping at goblet drums, puffing on flutes, or tapping metal chimes—one even possessed a gleaming metal instrument that resembled a trumpet. Carts, some rustic, as if direct from the fields, and others opulent, bedecked with paint and silks and flags and banners, were drawn by goats, deer, small horses, or the occasional oxen. The entire road in both directions was filled with the enthusiastic spectacle.

There were singers too—the young women's keening voices invoked a strange sense of timeless remove and contrasted sharply with the hoarse shouting of the men in step with their drumming. A brassy pot clanged. A slim, aged man, balding, his back twisted and his hand to his mouth, sat beside a percussionist tapping finger cymbals.

Vixy zoomed in with her trek goggles. "That guy, with his hand to his mouth and the bad back? He's playing a leaf! Do you hear it? That high-pitched buzzing? When I was a kid I used to press a maple leaf between my fingers and blow into it. It sounded just like that."

"It's like a dream," said Neutic. "The music."

"Oh, no you don't," said Vixy, scowling at him.

"No. I mean dreamy, or evocative, I guess. The lilt to it and the way it all clashes against itself—all the instruments and voices doing different things and then, when you keep listening and quit fighting it, I guess. It all sounded like noise to me at first. Nothing but an unaccomplished, disjointed racket. I know I've got Western ears and all that, but it sounded primitive and ugly, and now it doesn't."

"Hmm," said Vixy, bending her ear to it. "I know what you mean. It's dissonant. Without a downbeat. And no choruses or any sense of a beginning, middle, and end. But, yeah, I don't know, there's a cosmic quality to it, somehow."

"Cosmic, exactly."

"Look at that," said Vixy. "Their costumes. Those boys and men, in the monkey masks and walking like they're mimicking monkeys—I wonder if that's what's his name . . . the Hindu monkey god?"

"Hanuman? I think you're right. And those girls, they're wearing what, fish costumes? Look at the tails on their behinds, and their headdresses."

"Fish heads," said Vixy. "Look at them moving their arms, like they're imitating waves or something."

There came numerous play actor groups likewise adorned in masks or headdresses and elaborate costumes, their movements outsized, often humorous and just as often fearsome. A group of dragon-masked Khmer men stomped aggressively to the sound of numerous hand drums—they gestured broadly with their arms wide and feet far apart, obviously keen to intimidate. Their masks were wild-eyed, toothy, and snarling, and they brandished knives and spears and ambled forth like monsters or perhaps half-human and half-monstrous warriors.

Vixy and Neutic had not noticed the clutch of villagers, mostly older Khmer and young children, who now bordered the road. The adults giggled amongst themselves and pointed at this or that spectacle. The children stood as if transfixed, and half terrified and half thrilled by the sights, as children anywhere, of any era. And peasants were drifting in from the fields, craning their necks to see, their ears pricked toward the music. The driver of the ox-drawn cart, still loaded with heavy-looking burlap-type sacks, waited wearily beside the road, fanning himself with his grass hat.

"I wonder what all this is for," said Vixy.

She had barely gotten the words out when they saw the elephants. And an astonishing retinue of young men and women bedecked in a new level of opulence and regal splendor.

"Maybe it's the king," said Neutic.

Vixy raised her eyebrows at him and shrugged.

The great beasts, perhaps thirty or more, strode forth two by two and were themselves bedecked like royalty, sporting silken, tasseled blankets upon their backs, jewel-studded caparisons upon their foreheads, and ankle bracelets. The largest animals, their tusks tipped with gold, bore howdahs[44] as well as drivers. The princes and princesses posed stoically upon their upholstered and bejeweled seats. The opulence juxtaposed against the rustic and rural primitivity seemed like a manifest dream, as if the ancient world had emerged from a storybook and become glitteringly real.

Even Vixy appeared spellbound. "Wow," she whispered.

"Hey," said Neutic, "you're not having a spell, are you?"

---

44 A seat for riding upon the back of an elephant or, in other parts of the world, a camel.

Vixy rolled her eyes at him.

At some safe distance behind, trailing a group of energetic adolescents bearing short-handled shovels whose sole job was to transfer the animal droppings away from the roadbed, were a cluster of perhaps twenty palanquins, mysteriously shrouded in silks, each shouldered by four sturdy-looking Khmer men naked to the waist, in turn shaded by courtesans bearing ornate parasols.

Suddenly there was a great burst of drums and rattling of spears, and the whole company came to a halt—men, women, beasts, carts, and all. An enchanting chorus of finger cymbals filled the air, the palanquins were lowered, and the royal occupants, be they princesses or princes or priests, emerged from within their shaded enclosures and posed in courtly formality. They wore shimmering, silken sampots in many hues. Both sexes displayed tiaras of finely beaten gold, the women's many-pointed and intricately rendered, the men's shorter and conical with upthrust brims. Broad, elaborately decorative collars graced their otherwise bare torsos,[45] the ornaments plunging between the women's breasts or adorning the men's shoulders akin to epaulets. The women's cosmetics were elaborate, their dark tresses knotted like the commoners', and their ponytails draped elegantly over their shoulders. Golden arm bands, bracelets, and finger rings were ubiquitous, and also ankle bracelets and toe rings. Many of these women clearly were not expected to walk. In all, the opulence of the royal regalia was eye-wateringly brilliant in the sun.

When, after only a few seemingly magical moments in the direct sun and blowing dust of the road they ducked inside their respective palanquins, the music changed, the spears clattered, and the entire company once again strode forth.

And then, the king. An especially enormous heavy-tusked elephant of imposing bearing appeared. Its tasseled blanket was multicolored, its caparison of beaten gold like a shield, and its howdah gleaming white with brilliant red cushions. The king, crowned in gold, stood precariously upright, one foot upon the platform of his ornate seat

---

45　Sarong kor.

and the other steadying himself upon the animal's broad back. He brandished a long wooden baton, and his gold-sheathed sword was slung upon his side. His driver, straddling the elephant's neck close behind its ears, held aloft a gilt scepter displaying ornate florets like a slender, flowering branch.

Vixy felt suddenly exhausted, as if the spectacle and pageantry of the parade and energy of the Khmer themselves, alongside the strain of her and Neutic's botched HDT and her wonky transponder, was too much. She looked to Neutic, and his face seemed drawn, a bit strained. "Crazy, isn't it?" She was relieved when his eyes met her eyes and they both managed a weak grin.

Suddenly the entire company slowed and once again came to a halt as if a silent signal had been given. The king remained atop his elephant, both hands at rest behind his back, his shoulders square, his sword swinging casually from his hip.

The sun was lowering—it was late afternoon—and the landscape was tinged green-gold. A luminous, pensive quietude pervaded everything and was furthered by the raspy drone of the cicadas and the flocks of sarus cranes raising and lowering their red-feathered heads in the distant fields.

The spell was broken by the horses from the front of the procession trotting back up the road, a retinue of bare-chested warriors running swiftly behind, the points of their spears held high, their chests heaving so that their slender ribs jutted through their sweat-slicked skin as they huffed and puffed their way forward. Gradually, the entire company turned about—apparently this village was the outermost destination of the king—and the music began once again, the musicians now before the king, their music rather less celebratory, quieter, more solemn, the flutes predominant and the drums subdued. When the soldiers and their animals attained the front ranks, the king's elephant driver kicked his heels and rapped his staff upon the shoulders of his beast; the pachyderm flapped its ears and raised its great head, coiling its trunk so that its prehensile tip reached skyward. For a moment Vixy thought the animal would rear up. Instead, it trumpeted as if on cue, a startling, thrilling declaration of the king's departure. The elephant began its march, the king shifted his weight skillfully atop the animal's rolling back, and the parade followed, person by person, animal by animal, cart by cart, until soon enough the rearguard of female warriors rounded the bend from where they had come.

The dust settled, the villagers and farmers dispersed, and it was quiet except for the chirping of the birds.

"Wow," sighed Vixy. It was if she'd held her breath the entire time. She looked round, still swept up by the sense of pageantry and once-in-a-lifetime significance and the feeling that what they'd witnessed had emerged straight from a story book. All duly stifled by the fraught reality of their predicament. They were castaways. And two mothmen were on their tail.

"So, was that Indravarman III?" Neutic tapped at his device. "Hmm, legend apparently has it that his special weapon was a bat of ironwood." He glanced at Vixy. "He was holding a wooden staff or a baton or something, wasn't he?"

"Yep." Vixy merely nodded, staring into the distance. She seemed lost in thought. And weary.

Neutic stored his device and sat down with his back against the tree trunk. He felt weary too. And he felt the afternoon waning and the evening coming on, and with it the worrisome prospect of their first night in this wilderness. So far he'd been nothing but a burden. He ought to be helping. But how? The opportunity to HDT on this mission was a break and strings had been pulled and favors called in—he knew enough how things worked. That he might let the captain and Mr. Z. down, let alone Vixy, and otherwise jeopardize this mission, whatever it was turning into, filled him with stomach-churning doubt. *Courage is being afraid and doing it anyway.* Something Hettie used to say. He would do this for her if nothing else. Have some damn courage. Man up, for shit's sake, and don't make an ass of yourself. He began typing his first journal entry.

"How'd you manage to get clearance for data entry?" said Vixy. She was peering over his shoulder. "For writing? I wasn't cleared for writing."

Neutic looked perplexed. "Captain Chase asked me to keep a mission journal. I figured it was so you wouldn't be bothered with it. Aren't cadets allowed to write?"

"Not on HDT. The influence of writing—it's hazardous, too risky in terms of leave no trace. At least for most of us." She regarded him afresh. "You took the writing psych evaluation?"

Neutic nodded. "Doesn't everybody?"

"Yes. But nobody passes it. Nobody I know, at least. Except you." She raised her eyebrows at him, her attention piercing. "Not even Mr. Z."

The sound of voices interrupted them. A congregation of villagers had arrived at the edge of the tributary where it widened into a broad, slow-moving pool. There were perhaps thirty individuals, mostly women and a handful of aged men accompanied by small children of various ages. They appeared to be preparing to bathe, despite the water's murkiness.

Neutic watched them splash water upon themselves, the children gesticulating, laughing, and splashing about. Before long, they'd finished and drifted back to their huts. The unselfconscious domesticity and quietude of the scene struck Neutic as profound. It was then that he noticed a toddler sitting naked beside the water some distance away from where the women had been.

Neutic got Vixy's attention with a look and nodded toward the child. She raised her eyebrows at him and shrugged. They waited, expecting the child to be retrieved by its mother. They waited and waited, and meanwhile the child crawled around the water's edge, variously struggling to walk upon its wobbly legs and crawling with abandon—a toddler heedlessly exploring.

"Something's not right," said Vixy, watching.

"That shore is too steep," said Neutic. "He'll fall in."

"Look!" said Vixy. She pointed to the far side of the water's embankment, to a section of backwater thick with shrublike foliage that shaded the bright-green lushness of the algae-coated muck at the water's edge.

"Crocodile," he murmured.

Together they watched the dark shape, mostly submerged—a crocodile perhaps the length of a man—glide toward the opposite side of the tributary, toward the child.

The child lay upon its belly and reached toward the water. The bank was too high, the child kept straining, and the nightmarishness of the scene drew Neutic to his feet. He leapt forward.

"No!" said Vixy, grasping at him.

Neutic glared back at her.

"You can't!" she hissed.

Neutic knelt, poised.

"Neutic!"

They were at least twenty meters away, and the crocodile was closing. Neutic sprinted toward the water's edge, saw the child slip and fall and disappear into the water like a sack. With a menacing sweep of its broad tail, the crocodile closed the distance.

He was too late. *Too late!*

Blam, blam!

Neutic saw the splashes of the plasma rounds near the croc's back, and he dove toward the water's edge, sliding across the muddy grass. He snatched the child and hauled himself and the boy, for it was a boy, from the water's edge.

With a thrust of its broad tail, the croc turned and glided stiffly away.

Neutic looked up. Vixy was crouched low, still sighting along the barrel of her plasma pistol.

She beckoned urgently to him. "C'mon, c'mon, dammit! We can't be seen!"

They withdrew, Vixy leading the way and Neutic lugging the child toward a dense copse some distance upriver from the swollen portion of the tributary and the village.

Vixy slumped against a tree trunk with her hands atop her head and her eyes shut tight. She was inhaling and exhaling in long draughts through her nose. "Oh my God, what have we done?"

Neutic, breathless, set the boy down. "There you are," he whispered to him.

The boy pushed himself away and struggled to stand, his eyes like dark saucers. He stumbled backward and plopped onto his behind. His expression drooped into a kind of wary curiosity as he searched the faces of Neutic and Vixy, then he jammed a mud-caked finger into his nose and screwed his face up as if about to cry.

"No, no," whispered Neutic. He tore a ration from his pack and scrunched the wrapper at the boy. The child seemed pacified and Neutic, prepared for the worst, turned to Vixy.

Vixy let out a sigh and blinked at the boy. "Oh my God, Neutic."

Neutic frowned. "I know."

"Do you? I mean, do you really understand what the hell we've just done? Leave no trace. This doesn't even ... I don't know what to say."

"I'm sorry." Neutic looked rueful. "I'm sorry. I couldn't let it happen. It's my fault. If I've screwed everything up . . ." He trailed off, his eyes on the boy.

There was a pause. The boy entertained himself with the ration package and by grasping twigs and hurling them a short distance onto the grass. The silence and strangeness of it all bound them together, and Neutic held out his hand to the boy. "Now what, Friday?"

"Friday?" said Vixy. Her expression was beleaguered.

The boy reached for Neutic's finger, grasped it with both hands, and tried to stuff it into his mouth.

"You know," said Neutic. "Friday. From that famous old story, whatever it's called. Robinson Crusoe or something. This guy is shipwrecked on an island and one day a native discovers him. They can't understand each other. And because he can't think of anything else, he names him Friday." Neutic shrugged.

Vixy's face was blank.

Neutic made a few effortless keystrokes into his device with his thumb. "Yes," he said. "*Robinson Crusoe*. Published in 1719. Considered the first example of realist fiction."

Vixy rolled her eyes. "You and that device. Don't you ever get tired of poking around in it?"

Neutic stowed the device and focused upon the boy.

"God, I can be a bitch," said Vixy. She shed her pack and unzipped a side pouch, producing a sani-cloth. "I didn't mean that, Neutic." She knelt before the boy and wiped his hands and then his face, then stuffed the dirty cloth back into her pack. "Really. I'm sorry. It's just, well . . ."

"It's just that we're screwed," he said. "Because of me. You and Mr. Z. and Captain Chase. All of you took a chance putting me on this mission and now I've screwed it up. The consequences, I don't even know what. But if Friday here should have died? How do I fix this? Or minimize the influence? I mean, I can get him back to that village, right? I'll take him."

"No, just wait." Vixy sighed and sat back on her heels. "There are leave-no-trace violations and then there's this." She shook her head and stared at the boy. "But we can't just knock upon doors over there and ask if anybody is looking for their kid. Nor can we let him alone to fall in that estuary again. God, I don't know."

Neutic put his hands on his hips, puffed out his cheeks, and sighed. He peered into the village. "I don't get it, nobody's out looking for him? No distraught mother? Maybe children disappear all the time around here, I don't know. Maybe he's orphaned? I don't get it— there's nobody in sight."

"Orphaned," said Vixy. "Expendable. God knows. And it's getting dark."

"I'll set up the shadow tarp," said Neutic. "We can bivouac here, can't we?" He began rummaging in his pack, withdrawing the components, and looking into the trees for a suitable space.

"Kids are noisy, Neutic," said Vixy. "That worries me." She frowned at Friday. "He could be bawling his eyes out right now."

"Right," said Neutic. "But the shadow tarps have noise cancelation, don't they?"

"Yes, but we can't keep him shut up in there all night. I mean what if . . . what if he . . . ?"

"Relieves himself?" Neutic scratched his head.

"Oh my God," said Vixy. "Where are your mom and dad, Friday? Or somebody who gives a shit? About your shit. We can't take care of you. We can't, Neutic, we can't take care of this kid." She stood up and helped Neutic unfold the tarps.

"I'll take him back," said Neutic. "It's getting dark." He picked up Friday. "Nobody will see me. I'll just leave him—"

"No," said Vixy. "I mean, I don't understand why he was left alone out there to begin with. We can't keep him. But it seems worse, somehow, for now at least, to just leave him." She frowned at the boy in Neutic's arms. "No. Let's just keep him with us for the night. God. And then tomorrow we'll figure something out."

CHAPTER 21

THE PALE CRIMINAL

The meaning of the legend is that you cannot play safe: an unforeseen combination of opposites that seemingly exclude each other can overpower even your strongest defenses.[46]

FENG DROPPED HIS SONIC SHOVEL and collapsed against the stone wall of the shrine. Digging like this made his heart race, and sweating made him nauseous. And his poor hands, for heaven's sake, they were raw. Look, a blister! He clenched his fist. It was all he could do to keep from swooning at the sight of it.

Chung, breathing hard, looked up from his own digging and swiped at his sweaty face. A dark smear of dirt clung to his forehead. "You are not well?" He shoveled angrily, jabbing at the soil. "You are half as old as me, Advisor, and likewise doing less than half of the work."

Feng turned his back on Chung and dug into his robe for his device. There was a message.

---

46 Heinrich Zimmer, *The Art of Indian Asia: Its Mythology and Transformations*, completed and edited by Joseph Campbell, Bollingen Series XXXIX, 3rd printing (Princeton: Princeton University Press, 1960 [1955]), 149. Republished with permission of Princeton University Press; permission conveyed through Copyright Clearance Center, Inc.

The way is clear. THE BALL?

It meant the end of the cursed emperor. As he and the empress had planned. He expected to feel relieved, even elated. Instead, he felt as if he could not breathe, as if there were not air enough upon this entire planet—enough air anywhere—for him to properly breathe again. Again, he almost swooned and reached for the wall. He had murdered the emperor.

No. Not him. She did it. He merely advised her. She herself delivered the fatal dose. But what if she betrayed him? What if she accused him? His sudden mistrust surprised and sickened him. What was happening to him? Had he not looked forward to this moment, when the empress would be free to accept his affections? But now he doubted everything. Yet it had to be done. The empress's quaint devotion to the Way was beside the point. It was the emperor's own incompetence and bungling that had foretold his demise, had it not? It had. Nevertheless, he could not shake the sense of something within him having gone missing. As if he could no longer recognize himself. *In the name of heaven, what have we done?*

Chung pressed a damp cloth against the back of Feng's neck. "Try to collect yourself, Advisor."

Feng gasped at the chill.

"Breathe, you fool." Chung repositioned the cloth upon Feng's forehead. "Sit back and rest. For the love of heaven, you fail to pull your weight, but if you die here on the spot, you will leave the entire job to me. And I will put your corpse in this hole. Breathe, dammit."

Feng sat back fitfully.

"He is dead, you know," said Chung.

"What?" choked Feng. How could Chung possibly—

"My precious cricket." Chung returned to his excavation and thrust his shovel deep into the soil. "Because I was not there to nurture him. Hence, the emperor has his champion and General."

Feng's initial panic took a moment to subside. For once Chung's impossible ignorance was a blessing. The stupid old soldier knew nothing at all. How could he? Feng peered into the hole they had managed to excavate and glanced around at the tiny rock-walled enclosure, the epicenter of the temple. He lay his head back and breathed quietly, determined to collect himself. But also to abandon their worthless project.

"We have sweated in this hole all morning and there is no sign of the golden ball. No diamagnetic suspension frame either. Nothing but stinking Earthen soil. We are too late. The ball is gone."

Chung dutifully shifted another shovelful of earth from the hole and affected a cheerful tone. "How is it, do you think, Advisor Feng, that I know that my cricket has been defeated by the emperor's?"

Silence from Feng.

"Because last night I dreamed it." Chung shoveled several loads of earth in quick succession.

"Nonsense!" snapped Feng. "The emperor himself told you. With his psi, of course."

"Hmm," said Chung. "Direct psi-communication with the emperor? Does he routinely communicate with his advisors in that manner? Do you yourself receive such communications? I myself would know nothing of such things."

Feng eyed Chung suspiciously.

"Whew!" said Chung, and stood leaning upon his shovel. "Perhaps the ball is indeed gone, as you say. Stolen. This place is a ruin, after all. And ruins are pillaged." He gestured at the disheveled stone blocks surrounding their digging. "The soil here was particularly soft, wasn't it? Easy to dig. Too easy, perhaps. Unless you happen to be an engineer." He tossed his shovel aside in disgust and hauled himself from the hole.

The feeble Feng could not rouse himself enough to be insulted. He was only just managing to assimilate the magnitude of his predicament. The emperor was dead, he and the empress had succeeded, and the path to her heart and the throne had finally opened. But what about the ball? He could not return a failure.

"No?" said Chung. "You disagree? Look here. These ancient carved blocks that comprised the center of this floor. Compare them to the blocks in the corners. Do you see any significant moss upon one side?" He hefted a corner block to expose its underside. "Or the dark stain of the soil that you see here? No. These center stones have been shifted. Tossed about and replaced, perhaps many times since they were first placed. With the intention of doing exactly as we have done. Digging for treasure."

"Deeper," said Feng. "What if the ball is buried deeper than some peasant tomb raider could manage?" He struggled to get to his feet, clutched at his sonic shovel and jabbed pitifully at the earth beside the nearest pile of blocks.

Chung snatched Feng's shovel from his hands and stood over him. "For once I agree with you, Advisor. That the golden ball has vanished. It would be purposeless to dig deeper. We must devise a new objective. Beginning with the idea that gold cannot be hyper-dimensionally transported. So say our scientists. So say your engineers, correct? But are we so certain? What if the molemen, or the time detectives—"

"It cannot, you fool!" hissed Feng. "No gold can go. You comprehend nothing of the science. You are unfit for anything besides wielding a shovel!"

Chung squinted into the shrine's entryway as if capable of seeing past the gloom. "You lay upon your backside, gasping like a fish in the bottom of a boat. It is you who are unfit!" He spit into their shabby hole, snatched up their shovels, collapsed them both, and shoved one into his robe. He glared sideways at Feng and flung the other into the advisor's lap.

Feng cowered. "Argh! How dare you—"

"Get up!" barked Chung. "We are leaving." He limped determinedly from the shrine.

Feng listened to Chung's halting steps and the clack, clack of the old mothman's cane upon the staircase. He had half a mind to return to their HDT nexus on his own and leave Chung behind. But as soon as he could no longer discern the sound of footsteps or the clack of a cane, he knew he was alone, and panic struck him. He scrambled toward the doorway and hurried down the rough-hewn steps. "Chung!" he hissed. "Advisor Chung—wait!"

When Feng scurried from the main entrance of the temple, he clutched his robe around his face, wincing at the withering heat. He squinted, raised his hand against the glare, and looked about wildly for Chung. There. Straight ahead, the cripple limping along. But the old warrior's vitality was uncanny. Were they all this way, these ancient soldiers with legs and arms like ironwood and constitutions like horses? Did they not feel pain, discomfort, or fatigue? Or this infernal heat?

He hurried after Chung, comforting himself with thoughts of the empress. She was beautiful. And her power was a seduction he could not resist. Her ruthlessness too, somehow. His fear of her only sharpened his devotion. She coveted the golden ball and the idea of engineering the Cosmic Clock to their own means. Find it, then. Chung could do the heavy work and sniff it out like the dog that he was. He himself merely had to bide his time and endure the old mothman's repulsiveness.

They were making directly for the main entrance, in plain sight of the villagers, had there been any. Not only did this so-called temple city more resemble a shabby slum, but very few monks availed themselves of the mostly decrepit huts and shacks. And it was very likely the claustrophobic heat within the temple and the shrine itself, open to the sun as it was, dissuaded most of these Buddhists from attending to their rituals or prayers or what have you. And the mere handful who indulged their curiosity enough to try spying upon him and Chung possessed such feeble minds that his own relatively meager psi-abilities sent them away with nary an effort. Nevertheless, to be traipsing across the central western entrance road!

"Chung! Why west? We ought to remain hidden. Look there, you fool!" He gestured at the two saffron-robed monks approaching, each of them striding lightly in their flimsy sandals and garments blowing in the breeze and paper parasols resting upon their shoulders, the very picture of insouciant ease. Damn them and their sunshades.

Chung merely plodded ahead.

"*Chung!*" Feng hissed. The monks were still beyond earshot but closing on them. "We must leave the road—we must hide!"

They had traversed perhaps half the distance from the temple outskirts to the causeway over the moat and were approaching the two so-called libraries—small stone structures that flanked the northern and southern sides of the road. He watched Chung detour toward the northern structure and skulk into a doorway. Feng scurried to catch up. "What are you doing? They have undoubtedly already seen us!"

Chung waited with his head bowed, listening. "Shh. Stay hidden." Then he waddled from the library into the path, half doubled over and leaning heavily upon his cane.

Feng peered out, baffled, as Chung stumbled, fell to his knees, and sprawled onto the road. Chung lay still and the two monks rushed toward him.

They were slender, heads shaved, their skin the strange golden brown of their race, but otherwise indistinguishable from any other Khmer—these humans all appeared the same to him. They knelt to peer into Chung's face, chattering at him in their ugly language. Oh, brother monk, what is the matter? Oh, can we assist you? Or some such feeble nonsense. Why bother engaging his autotranslator?

But what happened next seemed to Feng a nightmarish, impossible thing. Chung, still prone, abruptly rammed his cane into the solar plexus of the closest monk, then leapt to his feet and delivered a savage blow to the temple of the other. Both men crumpled. Chung then tucked his cane under his arm and with a demonstration of considerable strength, snatched each monk by the arm and hauled them both toward the library. "Get their parasols!" he said.

Feng hurried out and back.

Chung had already stripped the men of their garments. He heaved their bodies into the darkest corner of the library and thrust one of the robes at Feng. "Put it on. Move quickly. Leave your clothing here."

"But—"

"But nothing," said Chung. He had already stripped and was donning one of the robes—the cut and color was far more accurate than the hackneyed copies they had been wearing. He adjusted it carefully, grasped his cane, and stepped into the sunlight, ducking beneath his parasol. "Hide your face and head like this."

Feng struggled with his own garment, then fumbled with his parasol.

"Hurry," said Chung.

Again, Feng did as he was told. It wasn't as if he could think of anything better to do. "What if the monks awaken? What if—"

"They will not awaken. We will proceed to the village. What is it called?"

"Siem Reap?"

"Yes. We will follow the river. The time detectives will have done the same. They may have known the ball was hidden there. Which is one explanation for why they avoided the temple and bivouacked where they did while we toiled within the shrine. If I understand anything about these simpleminded humans—ack! It matters not. We must eliminate the options. If the ball is not in their possession and they have not destroyed it or hidden it themselves? Well, we cannot track them on your silly device, can we? So, we scour Siem Reap, and if I'm wrong, then we investigate Angkor Thom."

Feng followed along, a little dizzy from his exertions, and fumbled with his device. "The ball is there," he said. "In Siem Reap."

Chung stopped them short and scowled at Feng. "What?"

Feng proffered his device. "You see? A message from the empress herself."

Chung squinted at the display. "What does it say?"

"Exactly what I told you. 'The ball,' she says, 'is in Siem Reap.' And she suspects the time detectives are there too."

"Then she thinks like I do," said Chung. "Or she has divined it."

"Let us assume," said Feng, "that she has divined it."

"You continue to underestimate me, Advisor Feng. But clearly it is your primary purpose under heaven. It serves to keep me humble. Meanwhile. Hmm. Now I'm convinced we ought to have killed Mr. Z. when we disrupted their transport. He will come for them. He may already be here. Ack! You have been allowed your little machinations, Advisor Feng. Now it is my turn. We must hasten to that village. And prepare for a fight."

CHAPTER 22

ACT OF TRUTH

"Why in hell," said the captain, "didn't you communicate this to somebody as soon as you discovered it?"

Robbie Chitlins withered under the captain's black-eyed scrutiny, and his first inclination was to reach for the door. He nevertheless stood his ground. "I . . . I don't know, sir."

The captain glowered at him.

"Miss Velure's transponder, I'm sorry, sir. Somehow, I figured since the device came to me, you know, in the lab, instead of me having to request it from HDT engineering, where it maybe should have gone, I don't know, it's just that I could see right away it was different. For a transponder. I mean, my training is in biological forensic pathology, specifically anatomical pathology, but my side interest—"

"Never mind your side interests, Robbie. What are you trying to tell me?"

"No, sir. Exactly. I mean, yessir. I'm sorry, sir. I should have said something to somebody, right away, absolutely. It was stupid of me."

"Robbie," said the professor. Her voice crackled over the intercom. "Your name is Robbie Chitlins, correct? You are an acquaintance of Herman Neutic, are you not?"

"Yes, ma'am. Neutic, I mean Herman Neutic, we know each other from college, yes, ma'am."

"I'm Professor Wilhelm, Robbie. The captain and I, we under-stand that you were doing what you thought was right at the time. Despite the delay it has caused by you not coming forward sooner."

Robbie watched the captain thrum his fingers upon the tabletop.

"Is this all of it?" said the captain. "The transcriptions? Have you rendered the entire series?"

"Of encoded messages? Yessir. Oh, yes, I have, definitely. I mean, I think so."

"You think so?" The captain tapped at his console, and a headshot of the professor, the background obfuscated, materialized upon the wall behind him.

"No, sir. I mean, yessir. I mean, well, it seems to me, sir, from what I know about glyphs and off-planet languages—off-planet languages being—"

"A side interest of yours," interrupted the captain. "Yes, you told us."

"Well, you see, Captain"—he glanced warily toward the profes-sor—"well, besides the matrix of coordinates, the hyperdimensional locators, and the astrophysical references, there happens to be all the dialogue. Moleman speak. It has to be. Back and forth with somebody named Cog. Or someone whose initials are C.O.G. I have it all right here." He rummaged in the pockets of his lab coat for his device.

"Yes, Robbie," said the professor. "We have a copy of your anal-ysis, thank you."

The captain glanced at the time. "That will be all, Robbie."

Robbie's earnestness deflated like a balloon. "Sir, if you need me to, well—"

"That will be all," repeated the captain. He nodded at the door.

Robbie turned to open it.

"Thank you, Robbie," said the professor.

"Yes, ma'am."

When Robbie had gone, the captain sighed and adjusted his eye patch. "Good that Neutic passed along the kid's analysis," said the captain. "It amounts to a partial transcript of Five's correspondence from his time in Giza. Also data pointing to how the molemen in-tended to engineer the Cosmic Clock Component. Robbie also happens to be the one who noticed the tattoos on that T.E. terrorist, by the way. All that Egyptian hieroglyph stuff, anyway."

"Yes," said the professor. "The syncretized scarab and taijitu imagery. I agree with Mr. Z. that it must have something to do with the Scarab Cult. Speaking of which, have you discovered anything more about it?"

"The Scarab Cult? No. Hell no. That's Z.'s business. You know, the intrigue and the loose ends and the wild goose chases. Most of that stuff he digs up is beyond me. How he does it. Speculations. Intuitions. He's got a hell of a knack for intuitions. But the imagery. Scarabs. Yin and yang symbolism. I suppose it's all interesting syncretism—is that what you folks call it? Mythological-wise? And I'm all for mythology when it gets me the hard facts in spite of itself. You know what I mean, Professor, I know you do. But we need a serious dose of hard facts right now. I don't need smoke and mirrors. I need a hill to climb. A guy like me doesn't retire from the army looking to decipher esoterica, if you know what I mean."

"Hmm," said the professor. "I understand, Captain. How is it that you took the job of director at the TDC? Isn't there a lot of bureaucracy? And procedures and protocols to abide by? And meetings? And getting backed into a corner with a bunch of, as you say, esoterica?"

"Time crimes are a lot of minutiae, sometimes, I'll give you that. Scientific. Technical. Even ideological. But, you know, crime is crime everywhere, and it comes down to money or passion. Or both. Meanwhile, whether or not I'm any good at this job, I like knowing what's happening on the ground. I like having direct reports in the field. Like Z. And Vixy. And Neutic. They have a range of experience amongst them and that keeps me . . . engaged, let's say. Besides paying my bills, thank you very much." He gave the professor a flinty look. "Which reminds me. I'm still waiting on your decision."

"I know," said the professor. "I'm not saying no, Captain. Not yet. But I'm in the middle of publishing a manuscript. And I have my students. And, well, I'd rather do one or two things well than many things poorly, as they say."

"I get it. We can use your help at the TDC, that's all. The offer stands." He checked the time again. "Your transport arrives . . . when?"

"One hour. At least that's what they told me."

"That's three o'clock, my time," said the captain. "No, they'll be there on the dot, Professor. VIP treatment from the TDC, nothing less."

"Is that a sales pitch, Captain?"

"Take it however you want, Professor. Maybe."

"Hmm, well, meanwhile, I want you explain to me this business with the moleman transponder. From Giza. And what of Mr. Z.? Your message said something about Mr. Z. and Haida Gwaii? That he's in pursuit of Émile Laron? On his own? On top of chasing the man all over Bombay, and Elephanta Island? My God, Captain. Can't somebody be sent to help him?"

"Not until the trouble with Vixy and Neutic is resolved. Their HDT fracture. We can't risk sending another detective into a compromised HDT window. Pure protocol, no exceptions. Meanwhile, with psychos like Laron, I'll admit that Mr. Z. is in a hell of a scrape. Things got crazy at the Shiva caves, I know that. And the jetty. Laron and his goddamn crony, the same goon as from Eranos, Shields is his name. A career nightmare. His criminal record is splattered all over the cosmos. Tough guy stuff. Murder. Extortion. Anyway, there was gunfire, I heard it myself. Z was hot on Laron's tail headed back to Bombay when he cut out. We're tracing them. Z, at least. From Bombay he HDT'd to Haida Gwaii, of all places. He drafted Laron's coordinates, followed in his HDT footsteps."

"When?" said the professor. "When in Haida Gwaii? Isn't that where Vixy is from?"

"Vixy is from Old Massett in Haida Gwaii, yes. But Z is in the nineteenth century." He glanced at his console. "Late nineteenth. 1889 or so—there's some fuzziness because of Laron's damn obfuscation technology. But we're countering it, and engineering is telling me we'll have them pinpointed within the hour. Knowing Z, he won't quit until . . . well, when a crackpot like Laron is on the run, and then cornered? Because Z will eventually corner him, I have no doubt—he's like a cheetah on a gazelle. And he has endurance. So I guess he's more like a sled dog. Whatever. Z will catch him. But let's just say I don't foresee an arrest."

The captain glanced at the image of the professor. She had a way of gazing off camera when she was lost in thought. And playing with her jewelry when she was anxious. Particularly a silver band upon the ring finger of her right hand that bore a large cut stone, brilliant white, perhaps a diamond. Just then, with the video feed, he couldn't see her hands, but he had no trouble imagining them. And mostly he never noticed jewelry on a woman. But somehow the professor always wore interesting, classy things. Rings on her fingers, bracelets on her wrists, now and then a slender chain on her ankle. And, of course, her necklaces like crazy works of art.

"When you say that you don't foresee an arrest, Captain, I'm fairly certain that I know what you mean." She stopped turning her ring. "I apologize for so often appearing naive. It's just that . . ." She trailed off.

"It's just that crime and criminals aren't your business, that's all. Mr. Z. can handle himself, even alone. Him taking out Shields already speaks for itself. Like I said, if I could send another TD, I would. But that HDT fracture, it scrambled Vixy's and Neutic's coordinates like nothing I've ever seen."

"HDT fracture? What is that?"

"The transport was broken apart—Vixy and Neutic were separated from Mr. Z., intentionally as far as we can tell, by way of an outside influence. Z ended up in 1954 Bombay as planned, but Vixy and Neutic? It's looking like Southeast Asia. At least according to what transport engineering is telling me." He tipped his head back to peer at his display through his ocular. And we've only got a partial date stamp. The prefix is second millennia. Thank God it's Earth, that's all I can say. Otherwise . . ." He shook his head.

"Where, exactly, Captain? You can't tell where exactly within Southeast Asia? I don't understand. You said their coordinates, Vixy's and Neutic's both, were scrambled? But not Mr. Z.'s? Scrambled by whom? I mean, how? How were Vixy Velure and Herman Neutic still together but not Mr. Z?"

"We haven't locked on the geographical coordinates for Vixy and

Neutic. We're drilling down, and we'll get there, we'll find them. You have to understand, three-space isn't two-space. The calculational magnitude and coordinate complexity, the increase in resolution and the plus or minus—the margin of error—between three-dimensional and hyperdimensional coordinate targeting, we're talking geometrical values. It's what we do. But it takes huge resources. And time. Meanwhile, all three transports—Vixy, Neutic, and Mr. Z.—were verified quantum-locked and encrypted. Unassailable. With the standard boomerang return in the event of a glitch. Glitches happen, but the technology compensates. Usually, at least. All the fail-safes were in place. Nevertheless, Mr. Z. went through, and Vixy and Neutic, as a pair, it's as if their quantum were decoded and spliced into an alternate wormhole. I say spliced, but we've no evidence of a data breach, let alone a hyperdimensional entanglement. Or a slashed transport weave. But their HDT was hijacked, that's for certain."

"Hijacked. I'm sorry, Captain, it all sounds like technical mumbo jumbo to me. You're telling me that somebody intentionally altered their HDT coordinates? Vixy and Mr. Neutic's. Even with all the precautions and fail-safes that ought to prevent such things. So Vixy and mister Neutic are lost in second-millennia Southeast Asia. Which allows for centuries of error regarding their space-time coordinates, does it not? They could be lost in the jungle. And the civilizations within that historical window aren't going to be anything as sophisticated as Bombay, which I assume they were provisioned for? And don't tell me they've no transponder, either. For heaven's sake, Captain."

"Vixy's transponder is with her and operational, we know that. Partially operational, at least." He held up his hand defensively as if to account for the professor's impatience. "I've yet to get a direct feed, and we're getting an alphabet soup of transport error data coming back, but we can track the geography of her device at this point. It's not like Egypt, I know what you're thinking. No, she's in possession of her transponder, it's HDT capable, the thing works, and that means we can likely repair it remotely and find them. And get them back."

"What about Mr. Neutic's device? Can't that—"

"Neutic is the one with the non-HDT device this time. The lead on this transport was Z, then when we lost Z, it became Vixy. Vixy's device is a full-on TD issue, fully HDT capable. Neutic is a cadet. Cadets are not issued—"

"Cadets are not issued HDT-capable devices," said the professor. "I understand, Captain, thank you."

"We'll find them, Professor. Every minute that passes, we get closer to deciphering their exact hyperdimensional coordinates. Meanwhile, on top of everything, with this goddamn Great Conflict heating up, the hyperdimensional traffic—authorized and unauthorized—is doing likewise, and it complicates all the tracing and puts more demand upon all the resources at the TDC, and for that matter, the T.E. too. I'm sure you can understand. Hell, the IMC is busy with the politics, aren't they? But on my end, time crime surveillance authorizations are harder to come by, the dragnets are going twenty-four-seven, the data processing is at full tilt, and it all just gets stickier to operate."

"War of ideologies," murmured the professor.

"Pardon me?"

"War of ideologies, Captain. Between the molemen and the mothmen. But it's rather a war of mythologies. Because as Mr. Z. would perhaps agree, a mythology goes deeper than any ideology. Ideologies interpret and attempt to influence the practical present. Mythologies communicate our sense of the eternal. They stand outside of time. At least the best of them do. And they are as much personal as cultural. But to your point, it's just that there's so much at stake. Between the molemen and the mothmen. It goes without saying that their war now symbolizes the battle for Time itself. The autonomy of Time. Its freedom versus its enslavement. The argument—the war of ideologies that pits Time's linearity—the mothmen's so-called Arrow of Time, which is commensurate with Earth's own Occidental traditions—against the belief that it is a round, a wheel, a circularity. The cycling eras. You call it a time crime, the molemen's engineering hubris. And I dare say the mothmen's insistence upon a linear perspective will prove likewise. If they obtain the means to engineer their space-time reality, that is."

"Money will start a fight," said the captain, "but mythology will start a war. That's what Mr. Z. told me once. And goddammit, I believe him. Right? And I say ideologies will keep a war going, and wars require huge amounts of manpower and money to run. You know what I mean. You can concern yourself with the mythologies, Professor. That's your business. But I'm keen to follow the money. Which ends up being the power. On the ground and in the air and all through the HDT events. It takes heart to believe in something, I get it. But it takes money—resources—to get anything *done*. Money. Anyway, it brings me to the point that we've no goddamn clue as to who is goddamn financing the goddamn Scarab Cult, excuse my French. But we're working on that too, and we'll follow the money all the way to Mega City One or the Mothman Realm, if that's where it goes, and back again. To the damn Scarab Cult and the gates of hell, I swear.

"Meanwhile," the captain continued, "I can tell you that Vixy and Neutic, they're both professionals. Especially Vixy, she's more or less fully trained as a time detective—she's got the TD designation in the palm of her hand if she'd only grab it. Neutic? Well, I need to rely on that young man's smarts and his adaptability. He's game as hell. He's like Z in that way. They're both learning real fast what it means to be a time detective, that's all."

"What it means to be a time detective," said the professor. "And when that young man discovers that a faction of the Scarab Club, maybe even Laron himself, likely caused the death of his twin sister? Her name was Hettie, wasn't it?"

The captain nodded grimly. "Exactly. Had that intelligence arrived prior to their HDT, I'd have put him to work where I could keep an eye on him. Without a doubt. I wouldn't have risked sending him on his first damn HDT with anything like that on his mind, Christ almighty. Which brings me to this damn thing." He dug into his briefcase and deposited a metallic device upon the tabletop. "It looks like a deck of cards painted flat black, doesn't it? But if you were here to see it up close, its asymmetrical. Not like a deck of cards. This the transponder Vixy brought home from Giza; the one she got ahold of from that moleman, Five. The one we had Robbie in here talking about. Anyway, what we didn't get to—because Robbie doesn't have the clearance and or the experience—is there was a message in this thing. Part of which came from Robbie's poking around, I'll give him that. And a group of transponder technicians at the T.E. took a week between them to extract the rest. What was left of it, at least."

The professor peered at the device. "What was left of it"

"You can't tell from looking at it, but this device, this moleman transponder, suffered a partial self-destruct. More likely a remote destruct that partially failed. From Mega City One. You know, any highly sensitive military equipment, you don't leave it behind still operational. You don't want your technology used against you. Or being reverse engineered. The point is, the data in this thing was partially burned. Torched. It looks immaculate. But this thing is wrecked inside, intentionally or otherwise, just enough to keep most of its technology indiscernible and inscrutable. We couldn't reconstruct this thing in a lifetime of trying. It's a technological mystery. But we found some typical transponder type of functionality and used it. Or abused it, what have you. And we extracted a very unsettling tidbit about Bruggs and Laron and their ties to the Scarab Cult. Via the molemen."

"Tidbit?" said the professor.

"Something about the Scarab Cult being past their usefulness. In the eyes of the molemen, that is. So the molemen not only think they can play patty fingers with the mothmen as they see fit, but they seem to believe they can play fast and hard with the Scarab Cult at the same time. Playing the ideologies against each other, or what have you. And gaining an advantage, of course. Which means I'm going to continue to need your help with the mythological ramifications. You know, all the psychospirituality and, how do you say it?"

"Are you referring to functionality?" said the professor.

"Functionality, that's it. How when a mythology becomes dysfunctional in a society, they seek to fix it. Which is the mothmen's MRI in a nutshell, as far as I see it." The captain hefted the device as if determined to evoke something of its nature. "And this Five character. On the moleman side. I'd like to discern something of *his* functionality."

"His personal mythology?" said the professor.

"That's right." The captain rose from his chair and strode across the room to shut his door. "What makes him tick." His tone was quieter. "Now. This Scarab Club. I'm certain all that media hype about the so-called Star Power Cell claiming responsibility for that raid at Parzival University was bogus. Propaganda, who knows? Anyway, it was, what, six or so years ago, now. Hell, you were there, at Parzival, weren't you, Professor? During that whole business? A guest lecturer or something."

"I was a visiting scholar, yes. At the end of my time there."

"Well, that the target of the assassination attempt was the university president? Bullshit. Plain and simple." The captain flopped into his chair. "Pardon my French again, sorry. But the Star Power Cell was just a scapegoat—just another radicalized cluster of jihadists with blood on their hands that the GIA[47] was happy to have an excuse to neutralize."

The professor pursed her lips.

"Mr. Z. and I dug through the report. I followed the money, as usual. Analyzed the logistics. The timing, all the security video— mostly indecipherable garbage—and the witness statements. Mr. Z. did his thing, following his nose, appealing to the mythology as he sees it. All of this we did with an eye and an ear and an open mind toward anything that might smack of a Scarab Cult connection. In the end, nothing stood out. Least of all a motive. But there's always a motive for a terrorist attack. And it struck both me and Z that this raid was so messy. Incompetent. Botched. And that a little clip of video showed these terrorists—there were only two—just before they were shot and killed by security, stumbling and firing into that classroom almost blindly."

The professor narrowed her eyes at him. She turned the ring upon her finger.

"It points to you," said the captain. "They were after *you*. Back then. Just like at the T.E."

---

47 Galactic Intelligence Administration. See Glossary.

They stared at each other in silence for a moment.

"Now," said the captain, "the Scarab Cult? Who knows? But mind control. Psionics. That's what's it's called, right? Psionics and remote terrorism is mothman territory. This Scarab Cult, whatever their motivations are besides money—all this business with scarabs and tattoos and Egyptian hieroglyphs—has something against *you*, Professor. Something about who you are and what you're doing with the IMC and your publishing. What you stand for. Mr. Z. is as convinced of it as me. It might be connected all the way back to your lineage—to who was it, Richard, did you say, and, and"—he snapped his fingers at himself—"Hellmut! It could go all the way back to their work with the *I Ching*."

The professor turned away and raised her eyebrows at the words. "Symbolize."

"Pardon me?"

"Symbolize, Captain. You said that whoever they are is interested in what I stand for. What I represent. What I symbolize. What does my work symbolize? I think I know the answer to that, but it's likely that I don't see it the way others do."

"Time."

"My work symbolizes time?"

"*You* symbolize time. You are time, to them, at least. At least enough that it drives the mothmen to pursue you, what with their obsession with linear time and all that. Occidental style, like you said."

"The Arrow of Time."

"Right. Unidirectional. They won't have it any other way. Hence this war with the molemen over control of space-time. Now this side project of the mothmen, namely you, Professor. I've been a fool to think we've been keeping you safe. That's why I enlisted Mandrake Artoor to help me authorize a full-time security force to protect you."

The professor appeared aghast. "Security force? My God, Captain, are you kidding? For me? I couldn't bear it. No. I couldn't for a moment tolerate being followed and watched and escorted—no, no, no." She threw her hands up, her bracelets clattering.

"It's not an option, Professor. It's done. We need you safe. And the security team—you won't even see them, you won't know they're there. It's all approved and paid for—the IMC and the TDC are splitting the bill and the T.E. is supplying the manpower." He got up and turned to look out the window, peering down at the street.

"Don't tell me you've got security people waiting down there outside the front door for me." The professor uncrossed her legs and grasped the arms of her chair, glaring at the captain over the top of her glasses.

The captain sat down again. "Professor. I'm asking you to expedite your decision. To help. Officially. It's already been approved by way of Mandrake Artoor and the IMC all the way up to the viceroy. You'll be paid by the hour at a rate that doubles your current salary. You'll be contracted to the Time Detective Contingent as long as this thing with the mothmen indicates an emergency. Until we've shut it down. Until it's over."

She glared at Five's device as if it contained some sort of answer. "I've no shortage of commitments, Captain. And I'm quite unaccustomed to having my duties dictated to me, even by way of the viceroy. It's one thing to be recovering from an attack and . . ." Her eyes flashed and she raised her chin at him. "But on behalf of Mr. Z., who no doubt can take care of himself. And Mr. Neutic. That raid at Parzival that you say was aimed at me, well, Herman Neutic's sister was caught in that. On behalf of Mr. Z. and Vixy and Herman Neutic. I will do my best to help you." She grasped her cane, pulling herself up with it, and glared down at the captain from the video display.

"Thank you, Professor."

CHAPTER 23

LOTUS BUDS

One must rise by that by which one falls.[48]

"FINALLY," GASPED FIVE. ANGKOR WAT. He stood sweating at the edge of the jungle, a stone's throw from the western entrance road, and unshouldered his sling. Damn sled. Damn bamboo. All heavier than hell, despite his trying to divide the burden into two trips. Hauling five culms, each two and a half meters long, as well as his vacuum pump and fittings on a makeshift sledge was a backbreaking, exhausting, miserable ordeal.

He adjusted his trek goggles against the glare of moonlight. A short distance to the east was the moat, one hundred ninety meters wide and spanned by the broad causeway. Then a thirty meter or so apron of land before the three-towered central gopura—as the gateway entrance was referred to when this was a Hindu temple— received the entrance road itself. Galleries, of modest architecture in comparison to the main temple, ran between the towers, and farther to the north and south were the elephant gates, as he called them. He had, on more than one occasion, watched one or two of those enormous mammals bearing supplies or provisions through those entrances. Otherwise, he knew from having traversed the

---

48 Tantric dictum.

distance himself that the remainder of the wall amounted to a mere laterite[49] barrier, sound but lower and unremarkable, interrupted only by lesser gopuras at each of the remaining three cardinal points. Three point six kilometers long, in all and enclosing perhaps eight hundred twenty thousand or so square meters of land.

He squinted at the moon. "Under cover of night, my ass," he whispered to himself. It was as if the damn thing was ablaze. It illuminated every detail and cast stark shadows as if it were the middle of the day. His only advantage was the late hour—although he could hardly be assured all the inhabitants of the temple village would be asleep. So be it. He could have stolen an ox cart and an ox to haul his culms and equipment, and he could wait for a moonless night too, so it would be dark enough to obscure his movements. And he could give this crazy idea up entirely and resolve himself to spending the rest of his damn life here.

He slurped from his canteen, admiring the gilt gold peaks of the quincunx in the distance, its central tower two hundred thirteen meters high. The towers themselves represented lotus buds, of course—the symbol of transformation and rebirth so common within Indian mythology. The plant, as he recalled, was a form of aquatic herb, a water lily, its buds originating under water but blooming upon the surface. A pleasant-enough image. The Egyptians loved their water lilies too, but nothing like the Hindus. *The bud of the lotus symbolizes the approach to the fully flowered realization of the Atman, the universal Self.* That he'd managed to recall that from his studies surprised and pleased him. And assuaged something of his frustration, fatigue, and disappointment. For Angkor Wat, the sandstone architecture of it, struck him as roughshod, understated, and primitive. At least compared to the geometric boldness and efficiency of, say, the Giza pyramids. Nevertheless, the geometry and astronomical accuracy and symbolism were there to behold if one knew what to look for—all borne of moleman influence, of course.

---

49 A claylike soil rich in iron and aluminum oxides, formed by the weathering of igneous rocks in moist, warm climates. Sometimes used for building.

He regarded the central tower. Within it, the central shrine, his goal. Well, his preliminary goal was getting this sled of material to his hiding place at the eastern entrance. Clear across the other side of the temple. Why couldn't there be a bamboo grove on *that* side?

Anyway, one thing at a damn time. Two hundred thirteen meters high, yes. At least according to his scale hypsometer[50] readout. He yanked off his goggles and tapped the clinometer sensor. The laser rangefinder was functional. But the two-axis NEMS[51] had become unreliable recently, perhaps suffering the effects of the stifling humidity. So be it. Common sense told him it was accurate enough.

He donned his goggles and zoomed in. The carving style was elaborately extravagant and impossibly delicate. But then the entire construct, as he recalled, was intended to tempt the gods of the equally extravagant Hindu universe into residing here. Specifically, Vishnu. The sustainer of the universe. Was that right? Yes, Brahma the creator, Shiva the destroyer, and Vishnu, the sustainer. The Trimurti.

Otherwise, to his tastes, gilding the towers in this way seemed an extravagant waste of precious Earthly gold. Gold with trace impurities found only upon this planet. The same gold that could get him home. He scanned what he could discern of the temple boundaries, much of which along the northern and southern lengths were obscured by untrimmed trees and viny overgrowth. The evidence of impending decrepitude. Eight hundred twenty thousand square meters, yes. That translated to eighty hectares or so. Perhaps nine of which he estimated were devoted to the terrace upon which the symbolic temple-mountain itself—Mount Meru, was it called?—towered above all. What it amounted to in engineering and architectural terms was just another enormous mausoleum. Or tomb. Or so-called house of eternity. For a god-king who had been laid to rest, if only

---

50 An instrument to measure height or elevation. Five's version utilizes trigonometry.

51 Nanoelectromechanical system. A class of devices that integrate electrical and mechanical functionality on the nanoscale.

by way of his ashes, at the bottom of the shrine's central shaft. The casing of which had long since been destroyed by looters seeking the cache of valuables buried with the king, and subsequently filled in again by the Hindu priests and Khmer engineers or whomever tended this place over the years. It struck him that the statue of Vishnu residing somewhat incongruously within the southern tower of this western-facing gopura may have originally had its home within the central shrine. And why not? The current Buddhism could never fully obscure the Hindu origins.

More stone was moved to build this monument than for the Giza pyramids combined. That's what the legend was, at least, and it made sense, now that he'd become familiar with this place. It was huge. So huge and sprawling that if he had not chanced upon the golden ball within that damn cemetery, he could have searched within the temple grounds for literally the rest of his life and never come close to finding it.

We taught them a few things about quarrying and structural engineering and primitive, large-scale hydraulics, that's all, General Ten-Square had once said. *Nothing on the scale of the later Egyptian pyramids, of course. But enough to bamboozle the Khmer king and his court into believing we'd come down from heaven or what have you; that our engineering team was the damn divine Trimurti or some such supernatural or spiritual nonsense. Khmer. Egyptians. Whomever. Humans in general. All of them so credulous. So gullible. So many of them so eager to interpret molemen engineers as avatars of the gods. I had to be convinced,* the general had continued wryly, *but I'm a believer, now, pun intended. A believer in the power of mythology and religion and spiritual gobbledygook to get things done and faster—and more efficiently and effectively, with greater precision in engineering terms—than outright authoritarian strongarming.*

The general had laughed, then, laughed at what he had suggested was the simpleminded, divinity-seeking, magic-cherishing, supernaturally inclined nature of the Khmer and the pharaonic Egyptians and every other race upon any other planet in any other damn galaxy that failed to comprehend the authority of science and engineering and insisted instead upon the existence of something Other. *With a capital O,* as he put it. *Kissing their fingers at the moon. The joke is on them, and they bring it upon themselves. We select the pyramids and the temples for their minerality and geometry and the sites themselves for their technologically efficacious geology, and in the end to simply symbolize our technological prowess over the absurdity of their so-called beliefs. Here is your symbology on the scale of Mega City One, you ignorant backward primitives. We mock them, and why shouldn't we? That's half the point, isn't it? That our engineering makes a mockery of all ideologies and philosophies and petty mythologies that have hitherto jammed up the well-being of the cosmos and everybody in it.*

The general could talk, when he got going, that was for certain. Five paused to listen to the sounds of the night. He never thought he could ever miss the old fellow, but now he did. The sound of his booming, obnoxious voice. The way he pounded the tabletops and clenched his fists and shouted at things.

Meanwhile, in this place, especially at night, the cacophony! The crickets and their kin, to say nothing of the croaking and trilling amphibians and whatever else that crawled and crept and slithered and otherwise proclaimed the imperative of its unhinged drive to procreate. Of course, he had to admit that it was hardly less deafening during the day, what with the yowling monkeys and screeching birds. But the sonic exoticism of these tropical nights was a dark mystery that evoked a supernatural menace on behalf of everything outside the modest reach of his campfires. He couldn't imagine ever getting used to it. He was unsettled even now, wide awake and busy as he was. Oh, for the quiet, friendly nights upon Mega City One! How he longed for home!

Over the temple spires, the bats swarmed, as likely pouring from the nooks and crannies within the temple itself as the nearby trees. These little monsters must be feasting upon the night's flying insects. He had learned to listen to them echolocating on their nightly forays.

They only vaguely resembled the much larger, ghastly corpselike versions that hung upside down like black-winged ghouls from the high branches of trees. In broad daylight! Those creatures were truly nightmarish. And because of their size and vicious-looking maws and talons, he'd assumed they were birds of prey. But they consume nothing but fruit, and he had seen them dip their long tongues into certain flowers, perhaps seeking nectar. But he had concluded that anything with furry bodies and leathery, featherless, articulated wings that roosted upside down was a bat, echolocation ability or not.

And he had caught sight more than once of the Khmer killing, cooking, and eating them. Bat flesh? Would these Khmer indeed eat anything?

He cocked his ears, listening to the animal's shrill echolocating chirps and clicks even from this distance. They hunted en masse, flooding the crepuscular sky almost like clockwork, swooping and diving and darting about with their herky-jerky individual flights, and within an hour or so they returned to their caverns and their unseen slumbers. That he had learned so much about life upon this planet only made him feel more alien and alone. The Khmer. The bats. The fish and fowl and everything alive and dead here *belonged* here.

He did his best to recall all he'd learned of the Angkor Wat complex. It had been the second choice for the Cosmic Clock Project. Behind Giza. It had remained a backup well into his initial months of training as a cadet, when the project had finally committed itself to the Giza Plateau and the Great Pyramid. For a time, then, they'd taught him both systems, both plans. All the calculations and contingencies. Concurrent data uploads. Hardly difficult. In fact, he could still recall his response to a test question. What was it? *Compare the essences of the two complexes, Angkor versus Giza.*

> The Cambodian temple tomb combines two major features of Khmer architecture: a pyramid and concentric galleries. Via the galleries and shrine, the Angkor version promotes a center of continued governance, active worship, and a living, celestial presence. The dead king's remains thus already reside within his heaven. The more ancient Egyptian pyramids, on the other hand, were permanently sealed against the presence of the living and, while likewise demonstrative of ruling authority, the pyramids were resurrection machines designed to

transport their dead kings and all of his or her treasures literally to heaven.

You are the only cadet, Cog told him, *who failed to compare the geology, engineering, and architecture and who also responded exclusively in prose. No dimensions, no calculations, no diagrams. Nothing but mythology.*

And, once again, Cog had covered for him. That type of slipup—interpretation versus technical analysis—had been the undoing of many a cadet's career. Except it hadn't been a slipup.

Illicit reading, Cog told him. *Most cadets are guilty of it in some way or another. But don't give them this kind of an obvious excuse to kick you out of the program. Your father, your family, they could never live it down. You are privileged, Five. Do not squander your opportunity.*

Twenty-four point six nine meters. Five repeated the data to himself for the umpteenth time. Because it helped him focus. The king's ashes and the entanglement nexus for the golden ball were exactly 24.69 meters below the floor of the central shrine. And precisely plumb to the zenith passage opening at the apex of the central tower.

He forced himself to review each step of the plan. Cross the moat. Pass through the gopura. Traverse the central road to the western entrance of the temple proper. Don't get seen by the villagers. Pass through the western gopura of the first tier of the temple proper, cross the open space, scale the staircase to the second tier, follow the corridor, scale another staircase to the third tier, and finally penetrate to the inner temple tower. Then back again to his bivouac, if necessary, for more components—he could only guess at how difficult it would be to haul the culms up the staircases. He would carry as many as he could as deep into the temple as he could. Otherwise he'd have to scramble to get everything into the shrine piece by piece. And avoid detection of his equipment. Or evidence of his work. Or, for that matter, himself.

Once everything was inside or near enough the shrine, he would vac-bore and purge the spoils. Vac and purge, vac and purge, until he'd installed the culms and the shaft casing was stabilized and aligned. Then do his best to obscure evidence of his presence and replace the pavers and the Buddha statue and otherwise camouflage his digging. Finally, retreat to his bivouac and await the day of the zenith passage. It had to be clear that day. Or at least during a reasonable window on either side of the moment of the zenith passage or he would be doomed to wait three months to try again. Oh, the weather upon that day must be clear—it *must*!

He felt tired and anxious. So much left to do. But the noisy nights were finally coming in handy. He could lug his sled overland and never disturb a soul. And likewise toil away within the temple and not be heard.

For now, he just had to get this load all the way east to his new bivouac beyond the moat. On the damn opposite side of where he was now. Stage all the parts and equipment. Get that done. Then camp. Rest. Leave the ball and the vac-boring for tomorrow. Those measurements must be dead on. He had to be on his game. Everything must be within tolerance. Or he wouldn't get home.

CHAPTER 24

WOLF, BALANCER

"You were rescued." The young med-tech, attired in blue surgical overlays, squinted at the rack-mounted equipment, twisted a knob, flipped a switch, and adjusted a bundle of loosely coiled poly tubing, one end of which terminated, as far as Cog's druggy perspective allowed him to ascertain, at a manifold connected to the racking. The other end disappeared, disconcertingly, somewhere beneath his own bedsheet.

The presence of the med-tech, the dark smears on his overlays of what must be blood, the medical machinery, and the awful tubing was dismaying enough. Worse, however, was that Cog did not feel at all connected to his own body. "I can't feel anything," he croaked. He couldn't even feel his voice in his throat.

"Heavy anesthesia," said the med-tech. He grasped his overlays and with a quick motion stripped a layer away, top to bottom. Now he was wearing aquamarine versions. "No sensation from your chin down. Don't be alarmed."

Cog watched the med-tech crumple the coverings into a ball, thrust them into the incineration portal and turn to scrub his hands in the sani-sink.

"You're only a boy," mumbled Cog.

The med-tech approached his bedside. "I am thirty years old, sir. My name is One-Dash-One. I am your med-tech. For now, at least."

One-Dash-One lowered his examination visor, peeled back the bedsheet, and perused the bandages that encased his patient. Some seeping of the wounds, especially in the extremities. The monitors indicated adequate blood flow and an elevated core temperature on behalf of the immune response. But he never trusted the monitors. Too many other med-techs did, because doing a manual scan was boring and time-consuming and nobody had any time to spare. Except when your patient went into decline because the monitors were glitchy, and then you're in the shit alongside your patient, and you deserved to be. So he scanned this patient's body head to toe like he did all the patients. Now, only four hundred left before his shift, another double, finally ended and he could go home and shove a crappy fabricated dinner down his gullet and go to bed and get up after, what, six hours? And do it all over again. Fuck this war.

He ran his fingers delicately along the flesh-restoration conduits, sensitive to the internal fluid flow and temperatures. Then along the shoulder, torso, other arm, other shoulder, and finally the legs and feet. He swept the bedsheet back into place and looked the patient in the face. He glanced at his device. It said his name was Cog. Private Cog. "You are not paralyzed, Private Cog. And your flesh will return. You've been fortunate."

Cog lay still, listening to the quiet hum of the medical equipment and the echoey murmur of activity throughout the ward. The soaring height of the ceiling and the expansive yet lean architectural supports indicated this was perhaps a repurposed manufacturing space, space-train hanger, or athletic auditorium. Such was the nature of this Great Conflict, then. Unexpectedly bloody. Demanding upon the infrastructure. Costly in all the ways of war. "Fortunate," he murmured.

"Yes." One-Dash-One leaned over to peer intently yet dispassionately into Cog's eyes, propped each of the eyelids open for a moment with his thumb, and returned his attention to the equipment. "Fortunate. Most soldiers with your injuries understandably wake up thinking they're paralyzed because they can't feel anything and can't move. For some of them it's indeed the permanent circumstance. But you only require minimal bionic augmentation. We've already installed the preconnectors. If your DNA—-" He interrupted himself to dab at Cog's face with a swab. "If your DNA doesn't reject the flesh-restoration technology. But so far you are responding very well to biological preseeding. Above average, I'd say."

The emotional detachment and the practiced, second-nature economy of the young moleman's examinations, well, Cog had seen it before. It was the manner of the battle hardened. It wasn't the military discipline that turned boys like this into molemen. It was merely the stoic resolve and day-after-day physical endurance required to make it through the outsized horrors and exaggerated demands of the job. "What time is it?"

"Thirteen hundred hours, sir, twenty-one minutes." One-Dash-One twisted a display into Cog's line of sight. "There's a clock here. Can you see it?"

Cog's inclination to nod failed him.

"When it's difficult to speak, we suggest one hard blink for yes and two hard blinks for no. If you have visitors they'll be forewarned. It takes getting used to, obviously."

Cog practiced his yes. "My wife. Has she, I mean, does she . . . ?"

One-Dash-One touched a display. "It says here she's been notified. She'll likely be on the next transport, along with the rest of the scheduled visitors. You might see her this afternoon." He turned to leave. "Oh. I get many questions about the toilet, as it were. Don't worry. Your processes are being managed. Okay? Including your nutrition. It's a direct feed. Time will tell when you get to enjoy a more normal existence, I'm sorry. Let's say six weeks. I've got my rounds to finish. Somebody will check in on you. Meanwhile, try to lie still. Sleep helps."

"Wait."

One-Dash-One paused near the foot of the bed and looked back.

"What happened to me? You said 'rescued.' From what?"

"I'm not authorized to tell you anything until you've been debriefed." He seemed about to depart but instead stepped closer and lowered his voice. "All I know, sir, is that Strategic Command responded to the firing of the Big Gun and the destruction of the mothmen's super-dreadnaught attack ship with a reconnaissance force. They scoured the battlefield for survivors, dug you up from underneath the rubble and at least half a meter of earth. You were the only one." He shrugged. "They're saying that you saved the satellite planet and maybe Mega City One, too. I swear everybody thought it was over. For all of us. They're calling for your reinstatement. As a, what was it?"—he glanced at his device—"lieutenant. Anyway. You're a hero. Lucky you."

Without another word, med-tech One-Dash-One turned away and Cog strained to watch him out of the corner of his eye. But he couldn't move his head more than a few centimeters and instead resorted to staring at the ceiling. Again. Better off dead, he thought, and struggled to forestall his visions of the long ordeal of recovery that awaited him. And what about his wife? The strain upon her. To be a damn physical burden after all these years, after all this striving for . . . what? A career? To end up a decrepit hero? He was nothing but a middle-aged foot soldier. He was aging out. Now, he was wounded out.

He closed his eyes, breathed as deeply as he could, tried to feel something in his arms and legs, his hands and feet, to sense something of his extremities. Nothing. Nothing but a vague sense of confinement and the nagging anxiety that he would never be the same. He opened his eyes and groaned. Good, he felt that somewhere in his guts, at least. He swallowed with some difficulty. For shit's sake, take it like a moleman. Try to maintain some damn dignity. Others were worse off. He resolved then and there not to complain. At least out loud. Meanwhile, he was stuck here for six weeks—was that what the med-tech said?—lying here like a damn Egyptian mummy. He scoffed at himself. Earth. Egypt. And the Cosmic Clock Project. It seemed a million lifetimes ago.

It suddenly struck him: what of General Ten-Square? He couldn't recall a thing from the battlefield. I'm the only survivor? From my entire battalion? The general, killed?

Wait a minute! What about Five? Their last communication had been promising. What with the uncanny luck of Five obtaining that mothman transponder and . . . ? He suddenly felt exhausted. Drowsy. As if thinking itself was a physical strain.

He closed his eyes, holding to his visions of the past, of the general as Cog knew him. Of Five and his predicament. And his wife. He looked forward to her arrival, now. He felt he had to see her soon. Otherwise he was trying to convince himself why he had any reason to live at all.

———

"I WANT MY HUSBAND EXAMINED immediately," said Mrs. Cog. "And not by a technician or a nurse. By a doctor."

"Yes, ma'am. I'm sorry, but the doctors do their scheduled rounds and AMTs—assistant med-techs—like myself are responsible for monitoring the status of the patients. If we notice that something isn't right—"

"His temperature is high. All you have to do is feel his forehead to know that. Fever indicates infection." She glowered at the AMT. She was a heavy-hipped girl with plain, thin lips and a tassel of blondish hair that did not particularly flatter her complexion. "What is your name?"

"I'm just an AMT, ma'am. Corporal T-Four. But these numbers, from what I can tell, you see here?"—she pointed at a display—"Do not indicate anything out of the ordinary."

"Feel his forehead," insisted Mrs. Cog. "Can't somebody check his circulation? I mean, look at his complexion. Something isn't right."

T-Four gathered the trash container, tipped it into her collector, and shoved her cart into the aisle as if to move on. "I'm sorry, ma'am. This ward is very full. Technically, it's over capacity by almost one thousand beds. That's what they tell me. The doctors, well, there aren't enough doctors to do anything but respond to legitimate alarms. And they do their best to do their rounds. Otherwise, ma'am, your husband's condition is being monitored at Central Medical. He'll be okay, ma'am."

"Or he won't, and nobody here seems to give a damn." Mrs. Cog averted her gaze and straightened her skirt. "My husband is Lieutenant Cog. He is the one who single-handedly saved the satellite base and Mega City One. He is a hero. Lying here. Suffering. I want you to get me a doctor this instant or I will have your job, young lady, and you will be scrubbing potatoes in the mess kitchen if it's the last thing I do." Her voice cracked and held back a sob.

The AMT lowered her head and hurried away. Then she stopped abruptly, turned about to face an oncoming moleman in surgical scrubs, and clicked her heels together, saluting.

Mrs. Cog stood, watched the youngish med-tech approach, and stood her ground.

"Good evening, ma'am. Mrs. Cog, isn't it? I'm the med-tech. My name is One-Dash-One." He glanced sideways at the ATM. "Thank you, Corporal. Dismissed."

T-Four shot Mrs. Cog an imperious sideways glance and trundled off.

Mrs. Cog scowled at her.

"Mrs. Cog, I've been responsible for monitoring and reporting to the doctors on behalf of your husband's condition."

Mrs. Cog looked the young moleman over. She found him intelligent looking, with friendly but tired eyes. He was lean, but it wasn't anything some good home cooking wouldn't cure. "Thank you, Mr. One-Dash-One. You are a med-tech, did you say? There aren't any actual doctors to be found? None of the soldiers are being treated by doctors?"

"I am a fully trained med-tech, Mrs. Cog. Which means I've received all the training associated with becoming a doctor myself. I complete my internship in a year's time."

"And this job, caring for these wounded soldiers, counts toward your internship?"

"Yes, ma'am."

"Well. That's fine, I'm sure. But in the meantime, you are a med-tech, and you can understand my concerns. Especially given the extent of my husband's injuries."

"Certainly, ma'am. All cases are ranked in order of severity, as you may have expected. Unfortunately, given the situation, there are only so many doctors, and they are fully engaged. There are doctors here who have worked twenty-four-hour shifts, trying to keep up. But we are, all of us, honored to do our part." He seemed relieved when Mrs. Cog appeared mollified. Or rather distracted with responding to the condition of her husband.

One-Dash-One had seen it all before, of course. The loved one on the edge of their chair, or standing stiffly at the bedside, wringing their hands, doing their best to ignore the strange equipment and the dreadful spaciousness of the ward and the misery of the other patients. Doing their best to recognize that a sense of molemanity still existed in the universe. He watched Mrs. Cog gaze into her husband's face. The families suffered as much or more, in their way, than the soldiers themselves.

He approached Cog's bedside and bent to examine his patient's face, placing his hand gently upon Cog's forehead, sensing the temperature of the flesh and verifying his intuition against that of the monitor readout. Sometimes, he was capable of a bit of playacting, if he was convinced it would help. Pay a little extra attention in ways that seemed especially attentive and inquisitive and belied the duties of the monitors and instruments. Conjure some emotion and portray a doctor as nonmedical folk saw doctors. That was, sometimes, as superheroes. Or saviors. Or damn magicians. Doing magic tricks. Instead of beleaguered caregivers laboring to cheat death and disease and mostly one step behind it all and with the devil himself at their heels.

This Lieutenant Cog, at least, was not dying. He scrutinized the dressings again, urging himself to move on. So he could complete his rounds on time for once and get the hell home and maybe enjoy a full night's sleep. A full night's sleep. He didn't even remember what that was.

"Hmm," said One-Dash-One. "Yes, Mrs. Cog, you are correct. His temperature is indeed elevated by two degrees, as opposed to what the monitor has recorded. I will have this machine recalibrated immediately." He tapped at his device.

"Do you mean there is infection somewhere?"

"If it were infection, ma'am, we would likely see a more significant fever and telltale swelling." He gestured at Cog's prone body. "Swelling can be internal, of course. In any case, a temperature increase of one or two degrees more often indicates a natural response to the treatments. Your husband's body and the machines are working very hard to restore his flesh and otherwise overcome his injuries." He tweaked Cog's automated delivery settings. "I've made some adjustments, and if you look here, you will see his temperature is within normal range." He pressed his finger against a display screen.

"No, thank you." Mrs. Cog shifted in her chair and placed her purse upon her lap. "I mean to say, thank you, young man. Mr. One-Dash-One. I wouldn't know what I was looking at. But thank you."

She peered once again into Cog's face. She adjusted his bed sheet, her eyes once again examining, in her way, the bandages, tubing, equipment and all that she didn't understand and didn't want to understand. It was all horrible. "He's so still. He's sleeping, isn't he? He's not unconscious? They told me he would be awake when I visited. Is he sedated?"

"Yes, ma'am. He is sedated on a schedule that allows his body to respond most effectively to the trauma repair functions of his treatment." One-Dash-One glanced at the time. "The schedule of sedation, plasma enhancement, and tissue engineering is modified continually according to his progress—the algorithms compensate for somatic biodata drift and the exponential mitochondrial refabrications that are even now establishing a refurbished anatomical calculus."

Mrs. Cog blinked fretfully. "Refabrications? Anatomical . . . calculus, did you say?"

"I'm sorry, ma'am. All the nomenclature, it can sound very confusing. But your husband's treatment architecture is already showing impressive results." He narrowed his eyes at an indicator and checked the time again. "And, yes, as it happens, your husband should be waking in just a few moments. Let's see . . ."

Mrs. Cog held her husband's hand in hers. "How long until all these bandages . . . I mean, all these treatments . . . oh damn, I don't know what I mean!" She clenched her eyes shut and turned her ears back, flattening them against her skull in an effort to control herself. She ignored a strident tear that fell from her cheek. "I'm sorry, Doctor. I'm not going to cry. You don't mind if I call you Doctor. Anyway, my husband does not need to see me cry."

"Ma'am, besides broken ribs, a broken collarbone, and a separated shoulder injury, his wounds are to his flesh. The heat and intensity of the radiation from the blast may have, well, let me say that he's fortunate to have been afforded the protection of the Big Gun's armor. Frankly, it saved his life."

Mrs. Cog nodded and dabbed at her eyes.

"He is responding to the treatment as well as can be expected. He was healthy enough to begin with, for a man his age. His vitals are strong. In six weeks, if things keep improving, he'll be off sedation and transferred to a rehab facility. After that, perhaps within six months—mind you, nothing is for certain—he may be sent home."

Cog stirred, and Mrs. Cog squeezed his hand.

"We allow fifteen minutes of visitation, ma'am. Typically." He tapped at a control. "For the benefit of the patients and the ward and the visitors too, you understand. But I am authorized to extend visits, within reason. Thirty minutes, then, Mrs. Cog. Beginning now. Meanwhile, I have the remainder of my rounds to attend to. It was nice to have met you, ma'am."

Mrs. Cog nodded at One-Dash-One without taking her eyes off Cog's face. "Thirty minutes. Thank you, Doctor."

Cog half opened his eyes.

"Cog. Oh, Cog!"

Cog blinked at the ceiling, then glanced sideways at his wife. "Darling. Is that you? Am I awake? Dreaming? Where . . . ?"

"It's okay, you aren't dreaming, it's me. I'm here. We're here together. In the hospital."

An orderly walked past, and the footfalls on the hard floor somehow steadied him. Cog licked his lips. He was parched. He remembered the water dispenser installed closed to his mouth and licked at it. He worked to ignore his panic—the panic he endured whenever he first awoke and could not move. It would pass in a moment or two. Calm yourself, soldier. Calm yourself. For the love of science, don't make it any worse for your wife. Seeing you like this.

He blinked at her. She nodded at him, and he was almost overcome watching her struggle to conceal her emotions. He surprised himself by squeezing her hand—thank the stars! He could squeeze her hand!

Mrs. Cog smiled bravely. "You are in the army hospital, Cog. Well, the field hospital near the main hospital they've set up to handle all the casualties. They brought you here after . . . after what happened."

Her voice sounded strange to him. It seemed so long since he had heard it. "When?"

"Seven days. They found you and brought you here seven days ago. And this is as soon as they would allow me to visit you. You've been asleep. Mostly. That's what they said."

"Asleep." He struggled to comprehend it. Asleep for seven days? Most of it was a blank. Except visits by the med-tech and the ATM now and again. But asleep? No dreams. Nothing. A goddamn blank.

She could see that he had to strain to speak, to even turn his head, and she sought a button or a lever, anything on the bed that could raise him, allow him to sit up, to make him somehow more comfortable. "Oh, but I'm sure you are not allowed to sit up, or anything. I'm sorry, dear. Here." She pulled her chair closer. "That's better, isn't it?"

They looked at each other for a time, searching each other's faces.

Mrs. Cog spoke softly yet with resolve. "It all seems so terrible. But it won't be forever. Soon you'll be home again. We'll be together. We'll take our walks. In the garden. And down to the space-train station. We'll watch the trains there like old times." Her voice broke and she stifled her tears.

They were silent for a time.

"The rationing," said Cog. "They told us civilians had been enduring shortages. Lockdowns. Sheltering drills."

"Oh yes, dear, but it's nothing. Nothing compared to what all of you, the fighting—oh, Cog, none of it matters and none of it will last. Right? Isn't that what the general said?" She stopped and put her face in her hands.

Cog squeezed her hand again. "The general was a good soldier. And a good moleman. He died with honor. Despite everything."

She looked her husband up and down again in despair. She saw the bandages and the white sheet. The tubes and attachments and the machinery. She glanced at the ugliness of the ward, at the beds and the unpleasant lighting, and sensed in her heart the desperate isolation of it all and the loneliness and fear that they all had to endure for who knew how much longer. Perhaps forever.

"Home is still home, Cog. The house is okay. Our house is fine. We have food and water and it's safe there, still. For now. There's none of the bombing that's happened closer to the central precinct." She tapped her wrist and extended her hand so he could see the virtual image. "Look, Cog. I almost forgot. It's you, darling. This is the news headline we received the morning after, after your . . . oh, after what you did to save the city. They'd told us to stay underground. Indefinitely, they said, and we all thought we were losing the war, that somehow the mothmen, I don't know, Cog, it seems incredible they could threaten us like they are doing. Impossible. People were saying it was over, that we were doomed."

Her eyes darted back and forth between the headline and his face, and Cog realized how afraid she must have been all this time, alone. He'd had his duties to keep him busy. His orders. And his weapons and the enemy to fight against, face-to-face. His poor wife had endured absolutely nothing tangible; nothing but months of fear and psychological strain and propaganda and slivers of truth.

"It says here the entire legion was destroyed, Cog. That the satellite planet itself was nearly annihilated—blasted into pieces—before the mothman attack ship was struck. Struck by the cannon. Your cannon. The Big Gun, is that what it's called?" She seemed suddenly overwhelmed with emotion and covered her face with her hands, sobbing, her slender shoulders shaking.

He wanted to reach out to her. "There now, there now. It's okay. Yes. The Big Gun. That's it. It was the only artillery our battalion had left. Anybody would have done the same as me."

"They told us you were all killed. But I knew there was a chance. Somehow, I knew there was. And you survived. I knew it, despite everything."

He made an effort to turn his palm upward, and she grasped it firmly. He whispered to bring her closer. "My dear. Has there been any word?"

She looked round the ward fretfully, as if afraid to respond.

"Fire theft," she whispered, her eyes searching his.

"Fire theft?" Could it be? It was their secret phrase—his and Five's—their code phrase. Part of their clumsy attempts to keep the secrets from the listeners. From all the communication screening. "Fire theft." It was Five's phrase. It meant things were going to plan.

"I haven't told his mother."

"Don't," whispered Cog. They couldn't risk it. His wife understood. Meanwhile, he felt his heart swell. He saw the recognition in his wife's face. The secret hope they shared. For Five. Despite the danger. Despite the surveillance and the monitoring. Despite the shamefulness of their espionage and the threat of the ever-watching eyes. But it was the only way.

A harsh, mechanical voice bellowed from the intercom: "Visiting hours for this evening have ended. All guests must leave the ward immediately. Visiting hours for this evening have ended. All guests must leave the ward immediately . . ."

———

WHEN HIS WIFE HAD BEEN gone for a time and the lights of the ward had dimmed, Cog allowed his exhaustion to mingle with his newfound resolve. The code words worked. And his wife would stand by him. And meanwhile, remarkably, the fire theft was working. Five was somehow making the plan work. He and Five had both survived. Despite everything. He could endure anything now. Any pain. Any misery. Anything.

He lay quietly, thinking and dreaming of the future, until drowsiness enfolded him. Then the image came to him, again. The vision. The last thing he recalled from the battlefield, or perhaps merely the last thing he thought he remembered before waking up here in the ward, he wasn't certain. It was something he couldn't recognize, couldn't make sense of—an image of a living thing. A mammal. Alien. Some four-legged, shaggy beast. Perhaps from Earth? If it was a dream, it was a waking dream. But he never dreamed. He never had visions, even before his injury. Perhaps it was the trauma? And the medications? Side effects? Who knew what it all did to a moleman's mind? All the chemicals coursing through his system. All the bio-engineering and regrowth mechanisms, and dammit it all to hell, he was seeing it now, seeing the damn thing in his mind despite all his efforts to clear it away. It was his imagination. It had to be.

There was a mind-speak tablet beside him, a device he knew wounded soldiers were sometimes capable of utilizing whenever their injuries, physical or psychological, prevented both their speech and their ability to write. He concentrated on the device, and an indicator light glowed green. Testing, he thought. Testing, testing, one, two, three.

The words appeared on the display exactly as he'd thought them. Careful now.

Careful now appeared.

He looked away and attempted to clear his mind, to render it blank. He looked again and the indicator light had gone red—disconnected. Confident enough that he could control which thoughts he intended to render, he looked inward, waiting for the image to return. Perhaps it would transfer to the mind-speak machine. And he could capture it. And show it to his wife. He was convinced nobody watching the data would regard it as anything important. At least he hoped they wouldn't. So be it, he had to take the risk.

He lay quietly, doing his best to relax and think only of his breathing, and inevitably his drowsiness returned. And the image too. He glanced sideways at the machine. What appeared on the display surprised him. Frightened him. For there it was.

CHAPTER 25

MARCH OF THE MOLEMEN

CORPORAL TAG, THE MOLEMAN ATTACK-TECH, alongside one hundred or so of his fellow Strategic Command operatives, divided his attention between the dedicated, task-specific monitor within his work cell and the ten priority displays mounted high upon the far wall of the command center. He twisted the fail-safe on his console and spoke calmly into his transmitter. "Mothman sigma regiment destroyed, sir. Rotary irradiation cannon targeting mothman omega regiment and reenergizing in five, four, three, two—"

"Hold your fire, Corporal." Field Marshal Cygnus narrowed his eyes at the scenes of carnage. He watched the mothman regiments struggling to reassemble themselves upwind of the billowing smoke and the off-gassing residual heat of the crater. "Fools," he murmured. "You leave me no choice." He clenched his fist, hammered at the split-screen toggle switch, and steeled himself. "Fire!"

The explosion rocked the mothman front, tearing a chasm into the land and vaporizing a thousand mothman soldiers in an instant. The shock wave rippled deeply into the remaining lines, and the mothman army fell back.

"Prepare for psionic retaliation," said the field marshal, "and plasma wheel counterassault. They'll try to hit us before the cannon can reenergize. Armor at full. Get those harriers in the air!"

"Psi-defense fully energized, sir. Air strike configuration confirmed—our birds are flying."

Field Marshal Cygnus noticed a flicker in the war displays. "Plasma wheel incoming." He cinched his harness. "Prepare for impact."

The field marshal and the technicians braced themselves. The command pod shuddered, the lights flickered, then silence.

Corporal Tag struggled to right himself. One of his cockpit supports had snapped at the base, and he had to grasp his control panel to keep seated. "Psi-breakthrough at thirty-grid, sir. Delta battalion has been turned. The mothmen have seized their minds. Hand-to-hand combat in thirty-grid, sir, against ourselves!" The engineer turned, his eyes fretful, his brow shiny with perspiration. "Sir! Awaiting your command!"

"Moleman against moleman," muttered the field marshal. "We can't help them, Corporal." He straightened his uniform and brushed the dust from his chest and shoulders. He flapped his ears and straightened his collar. "Open that battalion's coordinates to the hellfire assault—they are lost to us—and redirect the energy conduit to the next battalion in line. Commence air strike."

The engineer balked, his hands still gripping his control panel for support.

"Corporal Tag!"

Corporal Tag appeared not to hear. He was pale and stared blankly at his display.

Field Marshal Cygnus stepped down from the helm and hurried to the forward bridge, tapping and twisting at the controls in front of Corporal Tag. He nudged the young moleman aside. "Coordinates opened. Conduit redirected." He hammered at the controls. "Commencing air strike."

Field Marshal Cygnus returned to the helm. "War deck coordinator." He smoothed the lock of dark hair that had fallen upon his forehead. "Replace the attack technician at the forward bridge. Do it now."

Two uniformed ensigns rushed forward, grasped the engineer by the arms, and hauled him from his seat. They tore the broken cockpit chair away.

"Fix that chair," said the field marshal.

A new attack technician, older, of heavier build, leapt forward and hunched over the control panel, scanning his displays, adjusting his controls. The ensigns deployed tools and within moments had resecured the cockpit seating.

"Status report," said the field marshal.

The tech touched his earpiece. "Plasma wheel damage absorbed and diffused. Arc fires extinguished. Casualties"—he blinked at the tallying numbers on the display—"minimal. Structural damage . . . I am awaiting the data, sir."

The field marshal, intent upon the displays, cocked his ear at the tech.

"Here it is, sir. Armor damage at the belly. Repair contingent not responding. Emergency re-armor contingent deploying."

"Hellfire status?" said the Field Marshal.

"Hellfire engaged, sir. Eighty percent destruction efficiency. Their western flank is crumbling."

"Make another pass," said the field marshal. "Annihilate them."

He scanned the breadth of the two-hundred-seventy-degree battlefield viewfinder. Smoke. Fire. Wrecked equipment. Bodies. In the far distance, mountains. Open plains to the west, an infinite horizon. Seashore a kilometer to the east. "Engage the Orion panzers. Coordinate all units, full advance. Target the neutron catapults. On my mark . . ." He raised his fist high above his head and held it there, poised, tracer lamps illuminating the bright medallions upon his gauntlet. He brought his fist down upon the console with a thud. "Fire at will!"

CHAPTER 26

PLANK HOUSE

THE BLACKNESS AROUND MR. Z. was impenetrable. He blinked repeatedly, disoriented and uncertain for a moment whether his eyes were open or closed. He smelled smoke. And cedar wood. And a penetrating earthiness. He heard unintelligible voices somewhere nearby. He thought twice about employing the weak lamp of his transponder—was Laron near, watching and waiting for him? Just try to get your bearings . . .

He strained to focus upon something, rubbed his eyes as if it would help see into the dark, and stepped forward tentatively only to bash his nose against . . . what? He reached out. Wooden planking. Rough surfaced. The joints wide apart. He extended his arms to the right and left. Open space. He sensed cooler air behind him and turned. Hallelujah, some light! An ovoid opening, more than large enough for a man. He bent to peer out, not keen to reveal himself. A chilly, damp night, perhaps six or seven degrees Celsius. He smelled the ocean. He could discern a planked porch before him and a broad wooden stair. Beyond, a thin crescent moon peeped through fast-moving clouds. There was a stony-looking beach a hundred meters or so out. Were those canoes? Pine forest to his left and right—enormous trees, like old growth. All of it was reminiscent of Vixy's Northwest Coast. Yet different, somehow far more primitive.

Or remote. No concrete, no vehicles, no indication of electric lights anywhere. Where and when was he?

He ducked back inside, pressed his back against the wall, and risked checking his transponder, shading the display.

HDT MAPPING FAILED: RETRY?

Dammit! Laron and his blasted obfuscation technology. Was he here? Or had he managed to escape into alternate space-time coordinates?

Mr. Z. unholstered his pistol, safety on, and shuffled left, still straining to see. There! Down below, dancing light. Flames. He blinked, impatient for his eyes to adjust. Movement. The silhouettes of people—some upright, some seated. A large group—he couldn't guess how many, seventy-five or a hundred, perhaps more? Most in proximity to the flames. The fire danced, the sparks and smoke streaming upward through a large, squarish hole in the ceiling.

His vision continued to improve. The people were broad faced, adorned in what appeared to be ancient garb. The men, some bearded, some not, their hair in topknots, wore breechclouts[52] and long robes, some trimmed with fur, others patterned with designs. The women, their tresses long and shiny dark, wore skirts and ponchos, likewise fur-trimmed, decorated, or plain. More than a handful of men and women sported basket hats of the kind Mr. Z. recognized as typical of the Northwest Coast tribes. Some of the adults wore moccasins, but most were barefoot. Children scurried about or clung to the hands and legs of the adults.

A pair of sturdy-looking men appeared from beyond the firelight hoisting upon their shoulders what appeared to be short sections of tree branches, thick as a man's leg and perhaps a meter long. They tipped their burdens into the fire and a torrent of sparks shot upward.

The people cheered and clapped at the commotion.

---

52 A moderately broad length of fabric brought between the legs and looped over a belt in front and behind as a covering for the crotch and buttocks.

The blaze illuminated much of the space, albeit dimly. He could discern the rough dimensions of the room, perhaps forty meters across at its farthest point, a squarish rectangle comprised of three levels. As far as he could determine, he was alone on the highest tier. Gathered here and there were painted wooden screens, large chests or cabinets, even what appeared to be roughly hewn bunk beds. Communal living. He was certain this was a plank house.

He crept from behind his wooden screen and shuffled across an open space to huddle behind a large chest closer to the action. Where was Laron? Was he here? Ought he to look for him outside? He felt time slipping away.

There was a great commotion at the opposite wall, which was a two-tiered stage of sorts, each tier something less than a meter high and flanked with deeply carved posts—house posts. It struck him as something he'd seen in a photograph of. What was it? A Tlingit plank house? Tlingit, Kwakwaka'wakw, Heiltsuk, Nuxalk, Haida, what have you—he was hardly a damn expert. The house posts and wall between were adorned with images were of broad, toothy faces, grasping hands, bird beaks, wings and fins, and so on—typical Northwest Coast–style abstractions—all deftly carved and painted. But the audience had mostly abandoned the fire for the action upon the stage. Or their anticipation of what was coming.

Men's voices whooped and bellowed. The audience became hushed, and as if on cue came a great stomping of feet and pounding of skin drums—Mr. Z. felt the cacophony reverberate through the floor. The fire had been allowed to diminish, and the gloom only enhanced the sense of eerie anticipation. In spite of himself, Mr. Z.'s own heart pounded. Astonishing. Remarkable. This was unquestionably a potlatch! Perhaps a full-fledged Indigenous Northwest Coast winter ceremony! Why would Laron HDT into this, of all things?

Suddenly, with a startling cry, there appeared torches from behind the screen, and several olive-skinned men burst forth, their torsos shiny with oil or sweat or both, their hands clutching against their faces great, broad masks with the imagery of wild eyes, tooth-filled mouths, or the long beaks of enormous birds. They stomped and roared and leapt about, posturing at times, lunging at the audience.

The spectators gasped and fell back, feigning horror, or perhaps feeling authentic fright. The children shrieked with glee, burying their heads into the legs and chests and arms of the adults, and the adults themselves answered with cheers and shouts and exclamations.

The sense of intensity and mayhem increased with a low thumping of drums and banging of shields. The dancers stopped short, poised with their arms and legs akimbo. More drums, and the dancers stomped and leapt and charged the audience. Clack! Clack! Clack! Their heavy wooden masks split open—faces within faces!

The crowd gasped and cheered and clapped. Children were hauled upon the shoulders of the adults to better see, and the dancers obliged the cheers by opening and closing their masks repeatedly, playing for the crowd.

Mr. Z. retreated into the concealing darkness of the house's perimeter. He shielded the glow of the electronic display with his hand and again rebooted the coordinate trace. It worked! But the results were enough to chill his soul.

Utawas [*modern: Masset*]. *HAIDA GWAII. British Columbia. Property House. 02.20.1839.*

1839? So be it. But it was the idea of Masset, of all places in the world! Laron knew too much about Vixy. And her family. My God. What would lead the man here unless he was keen to wreak havoc upon the past, a past he knew was directly connected to Vixy's present?

The potlatch changed its emphasis. The dancers disappeared behind the stage, for the back wall was a wooden screen of sorts, concealing what Mr. Z. assumed was another entranceway. The fire had been allowed to burn lower. The shadowy confines had closed in, and the audience clustered before the stage. There was an air of anxiousness and anticipation.

An actor sporting a wild mop of hair and wild-eyed expression thrust his face through the opening. Adults and children alike laughed and howled and jeered and pelted him with bits of food. Then other actors appeared and seemed keen to utilize everything from fish carcasses to feathers to furniture to enliven their performance. It was uproarious and unpredictable, a little hazardous on behalf of the actors, and the audience adored it all.

Mr. Z. crept toward the entrance. Laron could not be here. But if not here, then where? Had the man arranged some sort of rendezvous with his henchmen? Was he in hiding within the village? The village itself would be empty—everyone would be attending this ceremony as the single significant entertainment within the depths of wearying winter. If Laron intended something malicious against any one of the Haida here who may or may not be Vixy's ancestor, then this was the place to encounter the terrorist. Nevertheless, Mr. Z. had to do something besides watch and wait.

An intermission of sorts ensued. The drums slowed, and the exhausted dancers dragged themselves into the audience and collapsed on the floor or stood fanning their faces. Others disappeared behind the screen. A handful of men restored the fire.

He had to get out. And just as he approached the exit, he heard activity outside. Native voices. They were entering the house! He'd be discovered! He scrambled for the farthest corner of the upper story, away from the firelight yet in view of the portal door. He crouched against the broad planking and waited.

Several natives, all men, entered. But they were adorned far more elaborately than any of the other guests or even the actors. They sported fur jackets and tasseled blankets, and one man, taller and broader than the rest, wore a headdress with a squarish medallion at his forehead, bright white feathers that thrust upward, and tall, slender barbs for a crown. Long strands of thick twine or braided hair—Mr. Z. couldn't make it out—draped the front and back of his vestments. He wielded a staff a head taller than himself and otherwise carried himself with a regal bearing. Was he a chief?

Another man, only slightly less ostentatious by not possessing a headdress, nevertheless stood out by way of his curiously shaggy robe—of hide or hair or perhaps both—and the carved objects—bone charms and figurines from what Mr. Z. could ascertain—that dangled from his lapels and sleeves. He carried what was perhaps a rattle in one hand—the type of bulbous-bellied bird shape that Mr. Z. recalled from his texts on Haida lore—and a light staff in the other. He alone wore trousers—loose animal skins—that dragged upon the floor and he was barefoot, despite the cold.

Following several paces behind, as if to imply a respectful distance, came a sparsely clad, bony adolescent bearing an unwieldy oblong object that inspired an ostentatious pride in the chief. A slave, perhaps—Northwest Coast Indigenous culture originally embraced the practice. And the object must be a copper—a hand-hewn, roughly rectangular plaque of copper ore deemed representative or symbolic of a chieftain's authority. The metal had no proper utilitarian use, neither could it be termed art or craft. It rather represented perhaps the closest thing to money or financial wealth. The larger the copper, that is, the greater the fortune possessed by the chief—yet it was also imbued with potent mythological energy and significance. It was both symbol and concretized property.

Mr. Z. waited. Or rather vacillated. Should he risk being seen in order to escape? He watched the chief, shaman, and slave, if that's what they indeed were, descend the staircases and assemble in the lower level within the vicinity of the firelight. The chief rapped his staff upon the floor, the crowd hushed, and the only sound became the crackling of flames. Mr. Z. tapped his autotranslator, set it to mute, and tried to discern the ensuing oration.

Then more activity at the entrance screen—armfuls of blankets, furs, knives, containers, and implements of all sorts were carried into the house and carefully organized. All of it was likely to be given away as part of the ceremony. Which may go on and on, into the night and perhaps into the early hours of the morning. For all he knew, it had been going on for days already. If any time were ripe for him to attempt his escape, it was now, with the natives below and attentive to their chief.

Mr. Z. crept along the outer wall of the house toward the front opening, moving carefully past the odd piece of furniture. It was now or never—he'd have to risk someone else coming through the entrance as he tried to leave. He gauged the opening and plunged into the night.

The climate was bracing compared to the sweltering interior of the house. The thin moon was low and shimmered like a blade over the calm ocean. A scattering of pale clouds hurried across the sky. Mr. Z. shivered. He scanned left, right. The smell of . . . ? Seaweed.

He could almost taste it. The shore would be close by. He listened for the sound of men. Nothing. He crouched low, still poised near the entrance but anxious to hide, to get his bearings without fear of being seen. And Laron was out there. Somewhere. If he wasn't, if he'd remained hidden in the house, then there was nothing for it. He looked and listened and breathed the clean fragrance of the seashore. C'mon, Laron, make a mistake. Reveal yourself.

Tall evergreens—the edge of the forest—were to his left. Ahead, the silhouette of another, much smaller native house stood outlined against the moonlit sky—he recognized the slanted roof and the dark, unmistakable spire of a totem pole poised between land and sea. The seashore itself was perhaps thirty meters straight ahead.

He was drawn to it, somehow, and when he made off, halfway or so to the water's edge, he encountered crude wooden decking—long, wide, uneven planks and a roughly hewn, heavily used wooden stair descending to the beach and the glistening black water.

He descended carefully, keen to spy any indication of Laron—whatever that could be. He stumbled when his feet met the rough gravel and uneven ground of the beach and only caught himself by grasping the first thing he reached for—the stern of a large canoe. The thing was perhaps ten meters long or more, broadly and heavily constructed, obviously designed to carry many men, women, and supplies, probably to this potlatch and home again. He steadied himself and hurried along the length of it, running his fingers along the top of the hull as he made his way closer to the water. He peered up and down the ragged shoreline. Laron, goddammit. Show yourself.

A dog barked once, twice, three times, and Mr. Z. crouched beneath the massive, elaborately carved bow. The sound of laughter and loud voices arose from the direction of the plank house. A tiny raindrop struck his cheek, then another his hand—the kind of delicate, sparse drizzle held aloft by the wind, foretelling neither storm nor downpour but nevertheless portentous of change.

The talking and laughter ceased at the sound of a great commotion from somewhere along the beach—a rustling like leaves and an eerie whistling. Many feet scurried along the stones. Then a sharp, short voice, incongruously shouting.

Mr. Z. knelt behind the bow of the canoe.

Shouting, then a strangled, inhuman cry. More voices, louder, and disconcerting shrieks—he couldn't ascertain whether they were all men or if women were amongst them. The commotion grew closer, and finally Mr. Z. glimpsed a gathering of five or six natives, men and apparently boys, all clothed in dark breechclouts and coarse robes. Their faces were painted in lurid white, black, and red, their broad headbands topped with fluffy, feathery, whitish stuff—what Mr. Z. guessed to be bird down. It all amounted to a spectacle of aggression. One man wielded a long, double-edged knife; another hefted a fist-sized stone.

One of them stood out—younger, judging by his slenderness and nimble energy. He was burdened around his neck and shoulders by an unwieldy wreath of what appeared to be twigs or stripped bark. His face wasn't as much painted as smudged and smeared with dirt, his blanket disheveled. He seemed utterly filthy and unkempt, and the others were keen to prod him along, fiercely and warily both, as if he were an animal. And the young man seemed either insane or keen to play the part of an animal, lunging and snapping at his handlers with his teeth barred. An initiation, perhaps? Something tied to the potlatch? They were headed for the plank house.

This, then, was a cannibal dancer. Yes, it *had* to be. Mr. Z. had studied a bit about the rite, an example of the famous adolescent initiation ceremony, an initiation of a young man into one of the secret societies by which the youth had been ensconced for days in the woods near the village, supposedly in the possession of the Cannibal at the North End of the World, undergoing transformation into a cannibal himself until finally he was retrieved and brought forth, ceremoniously and in public, before the people of his village, to be tamed and otherwise cured of his man-eating urges. The boy's cannibal spirit, heretofore empowering his transformation, was now to be driven out, leaving him fit to return to his society as an adult.

But they were coming straight toward Mr. Z.

Mr. Z. ducked around the other side of the canoe. Laron clearly wasn't on the beach. There were other, much smaller canoes strewn across the shore, but none small enough for a man to pilot on his own, let alone at sea. Laron had to be in one of these houses. They would be empty, after all, wouldn't they? But to search each of them? There were perhaps eight or ten such abodes, those he could see at least, stretching down the shore.

He caught sight of something—a man hobbling up the beach stairs and decking toward the plank house. He was draped in a blanket or robe, like practically everyone else, his face hidden, but he wore trousers, and there was something frail and clumsy about the way he moved. Mr. Z. snatched at his pistol and rushed toward him. "Laron!"

Laron wheeled and fired.

Mr. Z. ducked and rolled. Laron looked wildly about, rushed toward the plank house, and plunged through the portal.

Mr. Z. sped after him, but when he came upon the door it was blocked—a heavy wooden screen had been thrust against it from the inside. He pressed his ear to it. He heard a great row—shouting, scuffling, the screen resounding with thuds—and held his breath. What in hell? He pushed against the screen with all his might. Nothing. He foolishly threw his shoulder against it.

"Argh!"

Blam! A pistol shot from within.

Get to the roof! There! Leaning against a rafter, a ladder. He scrambled up, making straight for the fire hole. He scrambled across the planking, choking at the soot and smoke—he buried his face in the crook of his arm to no avail. He coughed and hacked, dropped onto his belly, and crawled beneath the worst of it. At the edge, he held his breath and strained to peer inside. Ack, the smoke! He pulled back, coughing, then tried again. There! Laron himself, teetering at the edge of the upper level, gesticulating, waving his pistol, the bodies of several natives lying beside him. For God's sake, had he shot them?

Laron bellowed uselessly in English, his voice hoarse with delirium and rage. "You want a trickster? You want a transformer? You want a *raven*? I am your damn raven! Here to kill every one of you!"

Someone hurled something. A spear! It flashed past Laron and embedded itself with a thud into the wall behind him. There was a collective gasp and Laron staggered away, untouched. He fired wildly at the crowd, and they scattered, the scene suddenly chaotic, everyone fleeing toward the stage, the stairs and ladders, rushing to escape by the back or front entrances. Soon enough the back entrance behind the screen was choked with bodies, and the front door remained barricaded.

Laron clambered down the steps to the second level. "Mr. Z., are you here? Watch me destroy her past! Vixy Velure! That's right! I will kill them all!" He raised himself and hurled something into the fire—a flash erupted and Mr. Z. ducked away. The sparks and heat surged skyward, illuminating the village like a lightning flash. Impenetrable smoke boiled forth, bleeding through the joints of the roof planking itself.

Mr. Z. scrambled back to the roof edge and flung himself down the ladder. They'd all be burned alive, or suffocated by the fumes. He looked wildly about. An axe? Where the hell was an axe?

There! The people were hacking an opening from the inside—axe blades splintered the thick wood, but it was taking too long. Thick smoke belched from the hole—they'd never get out!

Mr. Z. leapt down the embankment to the beach, searched the first canoe he came to for a paddle, and breathlessly dragged it up the steps toward the Property House door. He gripped the thing hard with both hands, gathered his strength, and drove the paddle blade into the blocked doorway.

The heavy impact splintered a section of the paddle and Mr. Z. went sprawling. He collected himself and tried again, throwing his full weight into the effort, and with a loud crack the screen relented and burst inward.

A hoard of people and black smoke together poured from the opening, and Mr. Z. scrambled aside to keep from being trampled. People collapsed upon the ground, choking, gasping, clutching at the air. There were children limp within adults' arms, and others were laid upon the ground, the women hunched over them, wailing.

Mr. Z.'s eyes burned, and he choked at the fumes. Here and there flames blazed, consuming the walls. Was there anyone still trapped? Mr. Z. could not have entered the house if he tried. The heat and smoke forced everyone back.

When the roof collapsed, and a wall of the Property House with it, it was like an explosion—sparks, flames, a wall of intense heat, and suffocating smoke erupted from the conflagration. Raging flames consumed the entire structure from top to bottom.

Mr. Z. struggled to his feet, his flesh caked in sweaty soot. He whirled about, searching, desperate for he didn't know what. Laron? The injured? He coughed and coughed, finally swooned and fell to his knees. When he looked up, a young Haida girl was before him. Her long black hair was matted, her cheeks blackened with soot.

The child clutched her blanket tighter about her chin, her lips quivering, her eyes filled with tears. Mr. Z. blinked at her, she reached out to him, and another wall of the Haida house collapsed in an awful roar. The spell was broken, and the girl turned toward the sound and flames. When she looked back, Mr. Z. had leapt up and was running toward the trees.

CHAPTER 27

GARDEN PATH

*Henceforth they should experience the inevitable
as the hard to gain.*[53]

PROFESSOR WILHELM HAULED HERSELF ONTO her elbow and squinted groggily at the time. 5:30 a.m. "Captain Chase?"

"I'm sorry, Professor," said the captain. "I know it's early."

The professor swiped at the volume control of her console. She could've asked the thing, but it always made her feel somehow lonely and neurotic to converse with machines. She punched her pillow into a makeshift bolster and sat up. "Where are my glasses?"

"Professor?"

"No, Captain, I've just misplaced my glasses, that's all." She snatched them from their usual place on the nightstand.

"I considered waiting till morning," said the captain, "but I'm looking at a message from Mandrake Artoor—I just received this—and you're copied on it. He marked it urgent. I'm not sure what to make of it—something about his analysis of a string of communiqués

---

53   From Joseph Campbell, *The Hero with a Thousand Faces*, 3rd ed. (Novato: New World Library 2008 [1949]), 247. © Joseph Campbell Foundation (jcf. org) 2008, used with permission.

between the GTA,[54] GID,[55] and the T.E.[56] and about a hoard of data he's trying to connect in some way. The mothman MRI[57] stuff, too, that you folks at the PMC[58] are convinced is driving the mothman military strategy. The TDC[59] isn't on this track at all."

The professor yawned, slid from under her covers, and shuffled toward her closet for her nightgown. Coffee seemed the only thing in the universe that made sense, and she continued into the kitchen, jabbed at the coffeemaker, and waited for the cup to fill. Meanwhile, she donned her glasses and tried to make something of Artoor's message. "Fire theft."

"Fire theft, exactly," said the captain. "Artoor goes on about this phrase referring in real time to a golden ball, in Angkor. Out of the thousands of encrypted military frequency messages we've been working to decode, to claim that 'fire theft' is a euphemism for the golden ball, of all things. Even if that's accurate, I'm not sure his extrapolations get us anywhere."

The professor slurped at her coffee—it was too hot, but the risk of scalding her mouth did something to help jog her thoughts. "Hmm. It's Hellenistic. Greek."

"Fire theft?"

"Yes. Prometheus transgresses the rule of Zeus and returns fire to humanity, for which Zeus tortures him. The hero doesn't always win the boon. That is, sometimes he resorts to stealing it. Trickster figures are famous for this. Raven in Northwest Coast mythology. Stealing the light. But the golden ball? For heaven's sake, that was

---

54 Galactic Time Architecture

55 Ghost Impression Database

56 Tetrahectatricontakaidigon Enclave

57 Mythological Revitalization Initiative

58 Pangalactic Mythology Coalition

59 Time Detective Contingent

the moleman plot that was foiled in Giza, wasn't it? By Miss Velure and that Bedouin fellow. And the moleman, Five."

"Foiled. Or sabotaged," said the captain. "And by Vixy's account, the ball itself remained beneath the Great Pyramid. But Artoor claims to have decoded two separate HDT transmission events—one with a Mothman Realm origin and containing the phrase 'fire theft,' and another with a Mega City One origin but no reference to 'fire theft' at all. But they both share—"

"An identical Earth terminus."

"And the same Gregorian calendar signature. You've read the report?"

The professor tortured herself with another sip of coffee. "No. It's just an intuition. Based upon some of my own . . . let me see if I understand you so far, Captain. Artoor has found two hyperdimensional transmission streams, one from the mothmen containing the phrase 'fire theft' and one from the molemen with no phraseology, correct? Both terminating at Earth?"

"Yes, Earth. Southeast Asia. Time stamp 1296. This is our own TDC data, mind you, that Artoor is referencing. And I know what you're thinking—that the accuracy and precision are both pretty dubious. And you'd be right. The plus-minus is significant. In degrees of freedom and the hyperdimensional phase ensemble. You know, all that phase-space and phase-time axis stuff."

"No, Captain, I'm sorry, I don't know."

"Okay, well. It's the best we can do so far, is what I'm saying. Our analysts at the TDC are working on the geographical resolution. They're working around the clock, in fact. I haven't told Artoor yet. I want to run this by you first. Gold cannot HDT, everyone knows that, Artoor included. Unless there's a new ball. Somewhere in Southeast Asia. We don't know that, of course. But you, Professor, with your psi-abilities. If there's a way for you to see anything. Any information at all. If there is some way for you to scan the space-time coordinates, broad as they are. Using extended mind or remote viewing, I don't know, I'm just—"

"Fishing," said the professor.

A silence ensued, and the professor rushed to fill it. "I'm sorry,

Captain. I didn't mean that, it sounded insulting." She rubbed her forehead, struggling for words. "It's merely that those are two entirely different processes—extended mind and remote viewing—and while extended mind techniques can indeed be effective for orienteering-type exercises, and I do have some competence in that area, it requires that I have previously visited the coordinate. Do you understand me? And remote viewing? Frankly, I have never tried to engage that technique. I would say Mr. Z. is a far better resource."

"Z, yes, well, he and I like to pretend he doesn't pursue that research. It's off-limits for our time detectives, never authorized, too controversial, and all that. He's dabbled in it off the record. I guess that leaves extended mind. If I provide you with the space-time coordinate spectrum. Look here." The captain tapped his keyboard.

"You're calling that a coordinate spectrum?" The professor squinted at the projection. "That's an entire page full of numbers and letters. Hasn't the data structure been parsed?"

"We've parsed it six ways from Sunday, Professor. Computational, psycholinguistic—the algorithms are running as we speak, but the parse forest is hyperdimensional. The syntactical ambiguities . . . the magnitudes of complexity are geometrical. Like goddamn anything and everything to do with goddamn HDT is geometrical. Excuse my French. You know? Well, maybe you don't know, but—"

"Garden path sentences."

"Huh? I mean, pardon me, Professor, what did you say?"

"Garden path sentences. Within syntax analysis. It defines the predicament, perhaps, of your machine intelligence."

"Explain, Professor."

"A garden path sentence is an otherwise grammatically correct sentence that leads the reader in such a way that their interpretation will likely be incorrect. There are many well-known examples but, oh dear, it's early, and this coffee"—she refilled her cup—"give me a moment. Okay. For example, consider this sentence: 'The old man the boat.'" She activated her virtual keyboard and tapped out the phase. "It's all about ambiguity." She continued typing. "Another example: 'The complex houses married and single soldiers and their families.' They sound like poor writing and they're often interpreted that way. But they can be intentionally created to deceive. That is to say, the reader is lured into a parse that turns out to be a dead end or yields a clearly unintended meaning. Hence the idea of the garden path sentence—it's a sentence that leads you down a garden path, do you follow me? And the linguistic phenomenon is, of course, not exclusive to the English language. Consider the ambiguities involved in translation, for instance, and you can perhaps understand, no pun intended, that the potential for disastrous misinterpretation is significant. I can only assume your cryptanalysts are experts regarding such pitfalls."

"Our code breakers at the TDC? Honestly, I don't know. Now I'm wishing I had one of our folks here with me. And I'm thinking we've got to get you more integrated into our program—if I can get around to convincing you. But right now, all this makes me wonder about Artoor's abilities. What he knows and how much. About this linguistical stuff and the code breaking and how our TDC folks operate. Or if he's just speculating. If he's the liaison between your group and our group, the PMC and the TDC, that's not the type of skill set I anticipate out of a liaison. I don't know. I can tell you that we at the TDC are already reaching the point of diminishing returns with this guy." The captain gestured at the data. "This is why this is all I've got, is what I'm saying. And why I'm calling you."

The professor stood up and wrapped her nightgown tightly around her neck. She magnified the data and inspected it for some time. "I don't know, Captain. Comparative illusion trees. Depth charge sentences.[60] Just glancing at this I can see examples of dubious . . . well." She closed her eyes. "Artoor will have employed the

---

60 The term "comparative illusion" has sometimes been used as an umbrella term that encompasses depth charge sentences like "No head injury is too trivial to be ignored." This example is often initially perceived as having the meaning "No head injury should be ignored—even if it's trivial," even though upon careful consideration the sentence actually says, "All head injuries should be ignored—even trivial ones."

same symbology and metaphor filters that I have been trained to use. But . . ."

"But what?"

"I will look at this. That's all I can tell you right now. Sometimes I think people confuse clairvoyance, such as it is in my case, with divination. I'm not trying to be sardonic. I'm not even trying to be ironic. It is simply that gaining insight via occult means is another thing entirely from predicting the future. And predicting the future is something I have never been capable of. Thankfully. No. I'll apply my intuition to these trees and see what I can see. That's all. On behalf of Miss Velure, Mr. Neutic, and of course Mr. Z.'s well-being. But you'll have to give me a day or so."

"Zero-nine hundred, tomorrow, then."

"Nine o'clock in the morning?"

"Yes, Professor. What do you say? I've authorized your access to the file in real time, the techs are continuing to tweak it as we speak—anytime you choose to see an updated copy, just use the link. And if you discover anything, or if you even just think you *may* have discovered anything, contact me. That's all, Professor. Thank you. I'll let you go. Do you have anything for me before I log off?"

"No, Captain." The feed canceled, and the professor stared at the space vacated by the captain's hologram. Dawn seemed forever away, yet here she felt as if she'd already put half a day's work in. No, she'd merely been caught off guard. And the captain's manner was always so forceful and . . . demanding. But then it was his job, she supposed, to be driving hard at things. He had people in the field he was responsible for, after all. Hence, she'd offered to help without reservation. And now, well, now she found herself pondering some of the captain's concerns. And her own. Artoor harbored a cryptanalysis skill set? It was news to her.

She reheated her coffee, sat before her console, and pecked at the keyboard. "Fire theft," she murmured. "And magic flight." That Campbell fellow. It had been years since she—here it was.

> If the hero in his triumph wins the blessing of the god-
> dess or the god and is then explicitly commissioned to

> return to the world with some elixir for the restoration
> of society, the final stage of his adventure is supported
> by all the powers of his supernatural patron. On the
> other hand, if the trophy has been attained against
> the opposition of its guardian, or if the hero's wish to
> return to the world has been resented by the gods or
> demons, then the last stage of the mythological round
> becomes a lively, often comical pursuit. This flight may
> be complicated by marvels of magical obstruction and
> evasion.[61]

"Comical." She laughed ruefully to herself. "If only." The idea of magical obstructions and evasions unsettled her. The time-worn myths communicated at least as many truths about humans, mothmen, and molemen as they did fictions. After all, the fictions were metaphors—within the best myths, anyway. And deft metaphor revealed the truths of life, hence the myths' lasting appeal. And why was she lecturing herself? Unless she were trying to convince herself of something.

If Artoor were correct about a golden ball in Angkor? That was the TDC's area. Time crime and all that. What troubled her was Artoor's discovery, if it was a discovery, that the molemen and mothmen conversed in linguistic ambiguities. The espionage potential, using garden path communications to lead each other astray was one thing. What if they intended to lead everyone else who listened astray as well? She ought to have broached the espionage angle with the captain. But it was too damn early in the morning, and she'd been half asleep trying to keep up with him. Espionage was not her forte. It made her feel naive and gullible. Like a child. The opposite of when she was presented with symbology. The myths, for all their unsettling ambiguity, made sense to her. Because they illuminated the

---

61 From Joseph Campbell, *The Hero with a Thousand Faces*, 3rd ed. (Novato: New World Library 2008 [1949]), 170. © Joseph Campbell Foundation (jcf. org) 2008, used with permission.

human condition. But the knotted unseemliness and deception that Captain Chase and Mr. Z. and the TDC continually ran up against, it was exhausting. And it struck her, dabbling as she was within the world of time crimes and criminals, just how far outside her comfort zone she had allowed herself to drift. Her teaching and publishing? She'd spent a lifetime operating with a certain academic remove from things. And the luxury of thinking it all through and studying further and taking her time with her conclusions. That attack at the T.E.? It was as if she were being called to task. She was being thrust into the moment, into current events, by the mythic dynamics she'd spent her life studying. And she wasn't at all certain she enjoyed it.

"What is most important?" She recalled reading somewhere that the Dali Lama asked himself, aloud, exactly that when he was in the middle of something he felt was crucial and some journalist tracked him down and wanted to ask him questions. He had admitted vacillating, then simply asked himself the question. And then he dropped what he was doing and responded mindfully to the questions of the journalist.

What was most important to her, then? Mr. Z. Helping him. And the captain, and of course Miss Velure and Neutic. But, Mr. Z. It was unsettling to think of it. To admit it to herself. That she cared for him that much. Why? How? She hardly knew the man.

It was true, though. She felt the truth of it in her heart. Sitting there, thinking it through, she had to put her hand to her chest because she endured a pang, a stirring within her, something painfully significant. And strangely liberating too. "Because it's real," she whispered.

Just do your best. Keep your wits about you, dammit, and do your best.

She peered at the captain's data. She needed to shower. Then she'd look at all this. And she may need to have a chat with Artoor too. She tapped at the bedside shower controls and listened for the sound of falling water on the other side of the room. "Meanwhile, heaven help me. Heaven help us all."

CHAPTER 28

THE EMPRESS

"I'm so cold," murmured the empress. She had demanded her divan be situated near the hearth, and she huddled upon it with her silk robes drawn close. Yet despite the roaring blaze, she could not get warm. She sipped her hot tea greedily. Neither could she properly fill her lungs. Ever since last night, when she had watched the emperor die. She had steeled herself to it, the necessity of the Way. But it was too much to bear. His tortured face. And crumpled form. The fear in his eyes. Her heart was heavy with it. Was she cursed? Cursed or not, it was as if she would never breathe again. She hurled her teacup at the fire, and the delicate ceramic shattered against the hearthstones almost without a sound.

"Ridiculous," she hissed. She was tired, that was all. In body, mind, and spirit. There could be no curse. The throne was rightly hers. Vouchsafed by the oracle.

"My Augustness," said her servant.

The girl's voice startled her. And she was never startled by any-one—by the heavens, even her psi was failing her! "Bring blankets," said the empress. "And increase the fire."

When it was done and the servant had gone, the empress felt as if she were alone in the universe. She stared into the flames of the hearth fire. Searching. Longing. Lost. The emperor was gone. Gone!

And she would never be the same. Only burdened. Forever. With everyone and everything. She was a fool! A fool!

No. The Way had been foretold, had it not? She was dutybound to it—slave to it. She poured more tea and slurped at it. She moaned. Finally, she sensed something of the warmth of the flames. Warmth bestowed calm. Calm bestowed reason. She could think.

That worthless rogue Laron, for example. Never more worthless than now, for he was dead. Destroyed, likely at the hand of that maddening time detective. But it hardly mattered. Laron's mind had crumbled at the end, the fool. Attempting to thwart her powers. Alternatively, and maddeningly, the time detective, Z, she could not infiltrate his thoughts. His mental architecture presented an exhausting series of barriers. But he, too, would succumb. In the end. She need only restore her strength.

In the end, no one had failed to yield to her. No one except perhaps the human woman, Wilhelm. Her defenses were formidable. Instantaneously reflexive. And, most perilously, reflective. But the debacle at the T.E. could perhaps be explained by the emperor's meddling. Two minds together are weaker than one; the personalities conflict and the psi-energies are not cumulative. She had warned him. He would not heed her. And they had failed.

Only she herself possessed the power to reveal the Way. And the new mothman empire. Hindered only by the molemen and their cursed golden ball. To destroy the Arrow of Time was to threaten the Way itself. But the ball would be hers. She would unravel the technology of the Cosmic Clock and seize control of space-time on behalf of the mothman race. By her hand the molemen would fall. The Way would be preserved, and the Arrow of Time safeguarded.

She coughed and whimpered at her shortness of breath. And the growing numbness within her arms and legs. And her hands.

The servant girl returned leading an old mothman, sturdy but burdened under the weight of a log carrier, the duffel slung high on his back. The two made quick work of stoking the blaze and restocking the rack of firewood. The old man departed, and the girl tucked another blanket of raw silk around the shoulders of Her Highness, then stood waiting.

"It is said that death comes in threes," murmured the empress.

The girl averted her eyes, performed a short bow, retreated toward the door, and bowed again. "Will you receive Advisor Shan and Advisor Ming-tun, Your Highness?"

The empress nodded, and the girl departed.

The advisors shuffled through the doorway, and the empress, as if to avoid their prying eyes, slid from her couch, trailed her blankets across the floor, and curled herself onto the cushion before her divination table. She touched the low table's wooden surface, drawn to the darkened places worn smooth by her years of manipulating the yarrow stalks and coins. She looked upon the stalks themselves, crooked and imperfect, unassuming. The coins too—their roughly hewn metallurgy was a comfort to her. She knew that some oracles kept their stalks and coins covered by a cloth or hidden within boxes, but she had always arranged them in plain sight. Perhaps because for her, unlike for the others, the Way, which these humble objects expressed, was not a mystery.

She endured the clatter of geta and the irritating rustling of the advisor's garments. She was loath to enter their thoughts.

"Excuse me, Your Highness," said Ming-tun. He rung his hands and fidgeted, glanced nervously at Shan beside him. His heavyset physical bulk was an unpleasant contrast to his mincing feebleness. "I . . . or should I say we . . . well . . . Advisor Shan and I, owing to Your Highness's period of mourning, we assumed—"

She silenced Ming-tun by getting to her feet and regarding him imperiously. The bone-white paleness of her lean, high-cheeked countenance, the immaculate delineation of her mascara and arching eyebrows, the pearlescent luster of her eyeshadow, and the lush, evocative stillness of her mouth. Her lips gleamed vividly, like dollops of fresh blood.

These disorienting effects were at least familiar to the more experienced Shan. In his opinion, the empress had ever maintained her striking combination of natural beauty and imperial reserve, with the result that she oftentimes seemed to him a kind of goddess, an avatar or embodiment of the Way itself. Her headdress alone—an extravagantly vaulted architecture of shimmering black paper adorned with dried flowers of pale pink, purple, and dusky yellow, its ruby-jeweled tassels quivering—evoked both her fragile majesty and intimidating mystery. He had watched many an advisor's composure crumble within her presence, but most of them attempted to conceal their anxieties. To say nothing of their private agendas. He had taught himself to be forthright, to hide nothing, to think openly, for he believed the rumors of her telepathy—her mind-penetrating psionics—to be true.

Nevertheless, when the empress allowed her blankets to fall from her shoulders, Shan was taken aback, and he did his utmost to attenuate his gaze upon the empress's face.

Ming-tun, meanwhile, squeezed his eyes shut.

The empress stood before them in a manner unheard of since before the modern millennia, since before the Bronze Dynasty. Namely, she was without clothing, adorned instead with body paint, her garments illusory, mere effects. The artfulness of the otherwise scandalous demonstration of her sensual power was such that from a certain distance, she might indeed appear to be clothed in an embroidered crimson bodysuit with shiny ebony sleeves when the only textile that remained upon her consisted of an opulent silken shawl, which she held loosely draped about her slender hips and rakish legs. She towered before the two dumbstruck advisors as if she were a goddess manifested from on high, poised upon her geta, an arresting juxtaposition of regal authority and stunning sexuality that destroyed the decorum of the room.

"We have suffered defeat upon the galactic front," said the empress, her tone biting, like intoxicating liquor. "Our ground theater forces are in retreat from the molemen advance." She snapped her fingers, whereupon a virtual keyboard appeared, and the communication console came to life. Upon the far wall an expansive image projected —a war room map several meters wide and extending from the floor to the ceiling. "Within forty-eight hours, our field armies will be trapped between the molemen to the east, the Mencius Mountains to the south, and to the west, the Sunset Sea."

"Yet, Your Highness," said Shan, his voice grave, "by your direction, our navy approaches the coast. Likewise, our aerospace forces are en route from the Mega City One war theater. Be assured—"

"But the aerospace divisions," blurted Ming-tun. "Your Highness, they cannot engage both the army and navy of the molemen with any realistic hope of success. Perhaps if we yield the Plain of Heaven—"

Shan scowled at Ming-tun to silence him. "Be assured, Your Highness, the late emperor's strategies are being implemented to the letter. And in due time, the wisdom and virtue of His Majesty's royal mandates will be revealed. Even now, our psi-adepts are applying their full psychological energies in his name to dismantle the moleman resolve and sabotage their offensive."

Without taking her eyes from Shan and Ming-tun, the empress tapped at the keyboard and the war map image split, shifting to one side of the display to accommodate an additional view. "You will recognize Angkor Wat, planet Earth, as seen from space. You will recall the ruined temple's premium geometry, its optimal strategic coordinates, and the mythic imagery virtually commensurate with that of the Giza Plateau."

"But, Your Highness," pleaded Shan, "such a strategy, to acquire the golden ball, only the emperor himself was expected to implement . . . that is to say, with all due respect, Highness, you are in mourning and cannot be expected to—"

"I am *not* in mourning, advisor. Rather, I am in *power*."

She snapped her fingers twice and the girl servant rushed in, gathered up the empress's robes and redressed her. She stood beside the empress with her head bowed.

"The psi-power of the emperor," continued the empress, "was superfluous, a fact made evident by our failure at the Olympic Theater and now in the face of your military incompetence. I will resolve the threat of Wilhelm and the lesser matter of Mr. Z.'s interference myself. To reverse our fortunes and overturn the tyranny of the molemen, to realign ourselves with the oracle and the Way, to manifest the revitalization of the mothman mythology, we must possess the Cosmic Clock Component. I must have the golden ball. Our fate and the fate of the Arrow of Time are entangled. Codependent. We are now poised upon the fulcrum of destiny. We, the mothmen, comprise the only divine race within the cosmos. The Cosmic Clock must be ours. Control of space-time is our cosmic right. We alone rule under heaven. We alone establish and maintain the balance."

"But the engineering," said Shan.

"But *nothing*," said the empress. She raised her chin at Shan and tugged her robes tighter around her shoulders. "I am the manifestation of the Divinity. The wisdom of the oracle is known to me. The power of the Way flows through me. Are you not a member of my court, Advisor Shan? And you, Advisor Ming-tun?"

Shan lowered his gaze and forced himself to nod. Ming-tun furrowed his brow and wrung his hands.

"Your doubt speaks ill of you both. Your self-concerns are a weakness. You will demonstrate your obeisance to the Way, to the oracle, to the people, and to me by expediting my procession before the masses. Today, when the suns are highest, the people of the Realm shall witness the new authority of the throne in me. Advisor Shan, you will organize the procession. Afterward, you will commandeer every able-bodied mothman, mothwoman, and child from every village, farm, city, and town and transport them to the battlefront. Advisor Ming-tun, you will see to it that our hyperdimensional machinery is maximized in the effort. En masse, our population will establish a mothman shield that prevents the molemen from delivering the death blow upon our forces."

"Your—Your Highness," stuttered Ming-tun, "are you suggesting that we surrender?"

The empress glared at him, and the mothman visibly wilted.

"I require time. Time to obtain the ball. Time for our engineers to establish the diamagnetic suspension frame technology and to establish Angkor Wat as the inaugural lattice point of the Cosmic Clock Project. Time to gain advantage over the molemen."

Shan bowed deeply, doing his utmost to neutralize his misgivings. But the empress's strategy was desperate, impulsive, the risks unprecedented. A living shield composed of virtually the entire populace? The logistics alone were unfathomable. And the behavior, the psychology of the molemen was a mystery. What would prevent them from striking down the defenseless mothmen masses? Meanwhile, the Cosmic Clock Project, he knew, was beyond the nascent engineering skills of the mothmen. "Your Highness, before I beg your leave to expedite your initiatives, may I ask, with all due respect, how it is that possession of the Cosmic Clock Component will avail us a military advantage? Forgive my ignorance, but as you know, the clockwork piece is not a weapon. Moreover, the molemen, as soulless heathens and unholy tyrants, will merely threaten us with destruction to regain it."

The empress brought her hand forth from within the folds of her robe—she was grasping a folded war fan, its ribs enameled in black and tipped with gold. "The Way has been foretold. Now expedite my procession before the people. Suspend all labor, cancel all commitments, and direct the attention of the entire populace of the Realm upon me. I shall be presented upon the Central Road. Appropriate the imperial media. Broadcast the event in real time."

"Your Highness," insisted Shan, "should you rather remain hidden, safe within the inner city, here within the castle grounds?"

Ming-tun bowed and retreated carefully toward the door, as if anticipating disaster. Shan suffered the noisy interruption but nevertheless remained where he was.

The empress regarded Shan with a blank expression and stood poised. Even the tassels of her headdress ceased their incidental quivering so she revealed not a sign of perturbation, betrayed no lack of self-possessed imperiousness. The empress's slender fingers closed around the sturdy cypress ribs of her fan. "Come here."

Shan approached with his head bowed.

"Kneel," said the empress.

Shan knelt.

In a flash she struck the advisor hard across the face, and the sharp thwack reverberated beyond the room into the great hall.

Shan fell forward onto his hands, then clutched awkwardly at his jaw. His silken cap flopped onto the floor at the empress's feet and a dark trickle of blood slid down his cheek.

"Your words," said the empress, "are blasphemy. And your thoughts, for I know them, are a betrayal." She deployed the blade of her fan with a deft flick of her wrist. The metal gleamed in the flickering firelight, and the empress stared at the back of Shan's pale neck. "Get up. Leave me. Or I shall have your head, here and now."

His humiliation complete, Shan snatched his cap from the floor and clambered to his feet. The two advisors backed themselves hurriedly from the room.

CHAPTER 29

THE KINGFISHER & THE COBRA

PROFESSOR WILHELM SET ASIDE HER cane, sat forward in her chair, breathed deeply several times to help herself concentrate, and reached out to the mothman empress with her mind. Not with the intent to communicate linguistically, although she had activated the thought translator should an opportunity present itself. Nor did she seek to establish shared awareness. Least of all to engage in psychic ambush. Rather, she was keen to observe from a distance and assess the empress's psychic endowments benignly.

It was not spying, not exactly. Yet neither was it forthright. The risks of inciting aggression were significant. It wasn't as if she had forgotten her experience at the Olympic Theater. She proceeded with her own personality veiled, her diversionary mechanism at the ready, and her palladia[62] array in full spectrum. It was slow going.

Telepathy did not occur by way of quanta, within which she could have availed herself of the advantage of discreet, merely digital magnitudes of commitment. No. The physics of psi were rather that of seamless, analog continuity, centrifugal psychic gravity and the

---

62 Plural of "palladium," indicative in this case of a source of protection.

spiraling depth of the collective unconscious. Or, especially when the mind was alien, ceaselessly abrupt, labyrinthine redirections. No gaps. No safe havens. No reliable openings for escape. She extended her mind carefully, a trickling rivulet.

And immediately encountered telltale irregularities. Fragments. Conscious affects. Nothing authentic except remnants. Something or someone not the empress but nevertheless wedded to her.

Retreat. Reexamine. Reapproach.

Acknowledge me and respond.

The assault was instantaneous, formidable, merciless. *Thou shalt not.*

The professor reeled, then regained herself, stood firm. *I know you.*

Then, gone. Vanished. No residue, no mental breadcrumbs, no trail.

The professor winced at the afternoon sun angling through her apartment windows, felt the penetrating pressure behind her eyes, and resigned herself to the ensuing headache. The price to pay for a psi-session burdened with such hobbling safeguards. Yet it could have been worse. And she had established awareness. Recognition, even. *I know you,* they had said. Except she could not be certain it was in fact the empress.

She placed a headache tab upon her tongue and swallowed. She hated the psi-killing nature of analgesics. And the bitter aftertaste. Suddenly exhausted, she nonetheless groped at the control console and polarized her apartment window. "Dimmer, dammit."

"Professor," said the automaid, "are you intending to shade the window?"

The professor moaned and jabbed at the Cancel button. "Fuck off." She used the manual control instead, darkened and polarized the shade, and slumped back into her chair. "Where in hell is my damn cane?" Here. Beside her. Such was the nature of a psi-hangover. Muddled thoughts and nagging irritability. So be it. She lay her head upon the cushioned arm of her chair and shut her eyes.

"PROFESSOR, ARE YOU THERE?"

The captain's image flickered. Ever since the IMC installed the high-security veil, all her video signals flickered. The captain appeared even sterner than normal. But as usual, his tie was loosely knotted, and his shirt sleeves were rolled up past his sinewy forearms. "Is there anything wrong? The medi-track indicates your electrolytes are down. Muscle glycogen too. Heart rate, blood pressure, respiration—I'd assume that you'd been exercising, Professor, hard, and you are supposed to be letting us know whenever you do that. But I'm also looking at your EEG. Your delta, theta, alpha, beta, gamma—all off the charts. Goddammit, you know we're still monitoring your vitals. They were about to send a team." He scowled. "You take unreasonable risks, Professor. Just like somebody else I know. What have you been up to? No, don't tell me."

She watched him watching her. "It was the emperor," she said.

The captain looked incredulous. "Changpu? What do you mean? A psi-event? I knew it. Foolish. And dangerous. You could have . . . well . . . dammit, Professor. What do you mean the emperor?"

"The emperor was—or I ought to say *is*—protecting the empress. Shielding her."

"Impossible, Professor. No. The intelligence report confirms the emperor's death. Unequivocally. Zero bio. But we shouldn't do this now—call me after you've rested. Or better yet, we'll wait until I can get there to speak with you in person. I can take the first transport out tonight—"

"No. I'm fine. Please don't trouble yourself. I'm just tired. The emperor's spiritual legacy, his posthumous energy, call it what you will, it's significant, that's all. He is surrounding the empress psychically in some manner. As if he were protecting her." She took another sip of electrolytes and gripped her cane. The cold heft of the metal cap and the sense of the wood's strength helped to restore her. "Meanwhile, the empress is herself weak psionically. Extremely vulnerable. I suspected as much. Perhaps her sensitivity to the oracle, to the energies of the Way—her divinations—leaves her as open as anyone to psi-intrusion. Regardless, the emperor protects her mind, whether she's aware of it or not. God, it was the most forceful retaliatory energy I've ever experienced outside of the attack at the Olympic Theater."

"Because it's probably the same goddamn energy. The emperor's, that is. What am I saying, he's dead. He can't attack you from beyond the grave."

"How else to explain it, Captain? It was him. At first I wasn't certain. But I've been analyzing my session. It's the same psi-signature, mostly the same, anyway, that was the recorded at the Olympic. Those cadets were mostly under the control of the emperor."

"What do you mean, mostly?"

"There was someone else involved, perhaps the empress, but without possessing a sample encounter to compare it to, I can't be certain."

"The empress. Okay. At least she's alive. But the emperor? I mean, psi is one thing, the controversial nature of it all, the subjectivity and all that, the fact that we have to rely upon your experience of the event. That's one thing. But posthumous psi-energy? I don't know, the supernatural and the spiritual and all that, well, it's a long putt, as my old commander used to say."

"Long putt."

"A golfing analogy. A long bet. Something implausible."

"I understand, Captain." The professor groaned and grasped her temples. "I'm not intending to appear silly. Nor facetious nor obscure nor mysterious. It's merely that exercises or experiments in extended mind, as much as extended mind is regarded, typically, in materialist and phenomenological terms, generates results that are inexplicable in those same terms. In short, when I confronted the emperor, it was by way of his death personality. Within the context of Egyptian mythology, for instance, where the concept first appears, the death personality is referred to as ba."

"Death personality," said the captain. "Ba. Wait a minute." He rubbed his face with both hands and inventoried the contents of his empty coffee cup. "Okay. The Egyptians were convinced of a transmigration of souls, correct? An afterlife."

"An afterlife, indeed," said the professor. "Except, arguably, not by way of one's soul but rather by way of their personified vital forces, understood as being confined to the underworld. So ba is a mortuary concept, and ba comes into existence at death. For the Egyptian, there is no internal dualism in man. Ba can be said to be a personified entity, a quality of a person, and a mode of existence. But sometimes, I don't know."

"What?" said the captain. "Sometimes what?"

"Sometimes after a session . . . there are aftereffects. Psychic ripples."

"Dammit, if you're not well, then you've got to say something." He scowled again in his heavy-browed manner. "I'm dispatching a med-tech this instant." He tapped at his keyboard and rose from his chair.

"No, wait. It's not my health. I'm fine. I'm just thinking. There's something . . ." She resorted to pressing the heels of her hands against her temples and shutting her eyes to concentrate. Then the image struck her. "My God. Captain. She's pregnant."

"Huh? Pregnant? Who? What are you talking about?"

"The empress. I've been struggling to decipher all the weird energy of my session. Besides the emperor, there was an intimation of someone I kept insisting to myself had to be the empress herself. But the psychic spectrum wasn't matching up to the residuals from the Olympic Theater. But it just occurred to me what the problem was—I wasn't accounting for the possibility of a third energy. I am telling you, Captain, the empress is pregnant."

"What's going on, Professor? How could you possibly? I mean—"

"It all fits, Captain. I'm parsing the data as we speak, and the mapping fits. I'm sending you the analysis right now."

"An heir to the mothman throne. I don't even know what to make of this."

"But you don't understand. There is something else, too."

The captain stared. "No, you're right. I don't understand. I don't understand anything about it. Not the psi, not the biology, not the politics. I mean, I understand the biology, except—is it male or female? Or how would you know that?"

"I venture to say that the child is male. Again, given the energy spectrum. But, Captain, you mentioned an heir to the mothman throne. This child. It is not the emperor's child."

"Dare I ask whose it is?"

"I don't know."

"I'd like to think it doesn't matter either," said the captain. "But something tells me it's going to. The emperor, prior to the beginning of the Great Conflict, he and his advisors, as far as we know, acquired, via otherwise clandestine Sno-Globe-Con events and who knows what else, as much moleman engineering technology as they could digest. Meanwhile, they were perhaps being covertly schooled by the leadership of the Scarab Cult. It's not a stretch to conclude that, despite our lack of hard evidence. For Christ's sake, for all we know, the Scarab Cult were in psionic control of the emperor all along."

"No," said the professor. "The emperor's death personality is singular. I've studied him and the empress, of course, inasmuch as there was any quantity of reliable history. His telepathy was supposedly formidable. And this force against me was likewise. It was him, I know it, protecting the empress. That's not to say that in life he wasn't in communication with the Scarab Cult or anybody else."

"Right. And by the way, did I tell you that Mandrake Artoor gave the TDC access to the entire galactic paranormal activity database maintained by the IMC? I assume you know about it."

"No, Captain, I don't know. That is, I know about the Galactic Paranormal Activity Database. Certainly. I'm one of the chairs of the oversight committee. But I don't know anything about Artoor giving you access to it without running it by the committee. It's not like the information is confidential. Or that Artoor works for me. But, I don't know, as a professional courtesy, I would have expected him to contact me first."

"Sorry, Professor. I've been trying not to burden you with anything admin related. But next time, well, you see what I mean about Artoor? The man is a study in contradictions. Or suspicions. I don't know what I mean, except that he seems the type that the more you know about him, the less you know. Anyway, no surprise, we couldn't find a thing of substance, anything at all evidentiary, that is, relating to any mothman psi-work, let alone any evidence of paranormal activity. Nothing that points to a time crime. But this thing with the emperor. It's another argument in support of standard externalism, of the irrelevance of the immediate environment. Per that article you sent me." The captain sat up and began rummaging about on his desktop. "Written all the way back in the goddamn twentieth century, isn't it? I printed the damn thing . . . here it is." He snatched up the document. "'The Extended Mind.' By Andy Clark and David Chalmers." He flipped through its pages while donning his reading glasses. "Externalists often make analogies involving external features in coupled systems, and appeal to the arbitrariness of boundaries between brain and environment."[63] He paused, skimming the text with his finger. "The immediate environment is irrelevant; only the historical environment counts. Debate has focused on the question of whether mind must be in the head, but a more relevant question might be: is mind in the present?"[64]

"Indeed, Captain," said the professor. "That is very old scholarship. Nevertheless influential. As far as I'm concerned, it speaks directly to the status of the mothman emperor's personality, now that I think about it. If we're going to run with your idea of his psychic afterlife, let's call it. His body is of the past. His mind, however, is certainly within the present. But now I'm curious about something else. This business of who or what comprises the Scarab Cult—you mentioned leadership. On first impression, when Mr. Z. and Mr. Neutic investigated the tattoos discovered on the Olympic Theater terrorists, it seemed the cult's influence was merely a localized element. Gang culture, if you will. Now, I'm not so sure it wasn't prophetic."

"How so?"

"Bruggs and Laron, as supposed members of the Scarab Cult, may have been plying the antiquities trade as it flourished in late nineteenth-century Egypt. But who within the Scarab Cult recruited

---

63   Andy Clarke & David Chalmers, "The Extended Mind," *Analysis* 58, no. 1 (1998): 9n2. By permission of Oxford University Press.

64   Clarke & Chalmers, "The Extended Mind," 9n2.

them? Laron was a failed painter, a fine artist. Bruggs a scholar turned nascent Egyptologist. What appealed to them about a terrorist cult? Besides money, that is. Or were they coerced into joining? Who knows? It's all too occult. How can this Scarab Cult recruit followers and henchmen and still remain so impenetrably hidden?"

"I was going to pose the same question to you," said the captain. It's part of the IMC's business, isn't it, to remain abreast of all mythologically potent activity in the cosmos? Why in hell is an otherwise two-bit terrorist cell, a run-of-the-mill gnostic cult, running riot under the noses of the IMC? I'm not implying that your people aren't doing their job. The TDC has been behind the curve on this all along if anyone has. Guilty as charged. If it weren't for Mr. Z.'s dogging me about his theories and connections and his cold case files and what I always call his wild goose chases that somehow end up digging up valuable leads, we'd be running around in circles. His observations, as he calls them. And his intuitions. It's all circumstantial evidence, but on the other hand . . ." He threw up his hands.

"His intuitions have been correct?"

The captain nodded. "Yes. Z wasn't keen on Artoor from the beginning, for instance, and here I've been trying to stand behind the IMC's recommendation. Meanwhile, we need Mandrake Artoor in a goddamn meeting. I want him to explain this theory of his to me in person. With you there, if you don't mind. And as for the Scarab Cult—" He hammered at the keyboard of his communication console. "Artoor. I'm starting with him. I haven't received his update, first off—it's not at all like him to miss a deliverable." He scowled at the console display. "Where the hell is the man?" He swiped his fingers at the display and continued typing. "And on top of everything else, there's the Great Conflict. Look here"—he gestured at his display—"I'm being told right here that the mothmen forces are pinned between the Mencius Mountain Range and the Sunset Sea, and short of a miracle, we're going to witness the molemen committing a genocide. And then what? This damn war has been keeping the molemen occupied. We've had time to catch up to their Cosmic Clock crimes. But if they end this war with a bloodbath . . ."

The professor strode across the room and stared out her apartment window at the noontime cityscape, at the busy skyway and ground traffic far below, at the otherwise peaceful unfolding of life and commerce in the city she called home.

Artoor. She imagined the man dutifully negotiating the legions of bureaucrats and bureaucratic entanglements, the overgrown jungle of politics and cultural adjudications she'd spent her career attempting to sidestep as she devoted herself to her scholarship, publishing, seminars, and teaching. Never had she aspired to an administrative or leadership position within the IMC. She despised the idea. Despised being beholden to a boss, to leadership of any kind who were not amenable to her freedom to pursue her work and follow her intuitions. Tenure evaded her because she would not remain committed to a particular university. Neither could she imagine being burdened with managing employees or with the responsibility of a semester's worth of students year after year. She was an author and a lecturer and a scholar, and a teacher after that. Meanwhile, she had never regretted her association with the IMC, even after the incident at the Olympic and her newfound high profile within it. It all seemed part and parcel of the work she needed to do.

But now? Something about the IMC being otherwise blind to the operations of the Scarab Cult had begun to gnaw at her. After all, entire divisions of the IMC were devoted to scouring the cosmos for any and all philological, archaeological, anthropological, ethnographic, and political evidence containing mythological emphasis. It was the coalition's mission to remain not only abreast of mythological activity but to encourage its fully functional cultural permutations, to cultivate any and all nonpolitical investigation and inquiry into the past, present, and future expression of mythology. How, then, was the Scarab Cult allowed to spin a pernicious web of influence and corruption in plain view?

"Professor. Professor, are you still there?"

"Yes, Captain. I'm sorry. I was just thinking, that's all. You've not been able to raise Mandrake Artoor?"

"Not even a code red to his transponder is getting through."

"Captain, it's IMC protocol not to allow psi-activity between members, to protect personal privacy as well as professional integrity. The policy is intended to prevent any number of abuses—well, I'm sure you can imagine. Anyway, Captain, you're right. At least I fear you may be right." She sat down before her own communication console and began typing. "I'm requesting an emergency psi-infiltration request to discover the whereabouts of Mandrake Artoor."

"Wait a minute, what are you saying?"

"Artoor could be anywhere. And anytime, for that matter. Do we know he's not in Cambodia, for example? Or was he in India? Is he to do with the trouble with Vixy and Neutic—their HDT? We need to find him now. If he's pursuing his own agenda, I need to know about it. That's what you've been implying, isn't it? My reputation is on the line, here. I approved the man's assignment to assist the TDC."

"All right now, wait. This is my area. Time crime? Is that what you're implying?"

"I don't know exactly what I'm implying. I don't have any idea what the man's motives could be. By the gods, Captain, if we've been blind and there has been a traitor in our midst!"

"One thing at a time, Professor. Don't get carried away because of something I said off the record." He made a handful of keystrokes. "That being said, I'm blocking all HDT traffic to Vixy and Neutic's coordinates, Artoor's or anybody else's."

The captain was interrupted by the electronic bleep, bleep of the professor's notification alert. "It's the viceroy," she said, glancing at her display. "He's authorized me." She and the captain regarded each other resolutely. "I'm going in."

CHAPTER 30

THE RULES OF WAR

FIVE STOOD WITHIN THE SHADE at the edge of the forest jungle and regarded the dusty intersection of Angkor Wat's main western entrance road and the southern trail to Siem Reap. At this point in history, these were merely rural cart paths, and many hours, perhaps half a day, could pass with nary a traveler disturbing its languorous, green-shouldered juncture of byways.

The quiet scene inspired Five's thoughts, or rather his aspirations, for his homecoming. Would he make it? Would his equipment and engineering be sufficient? Would everything go to plan? "Forty-eight hours," he whispered to himself. "Forty-eight more hours. And then it's go time. I make my break."

He noticed someone approaching the intersection by the western road, someone besides a monk or a threadbare villager leading a shambling oxcart. They were a pair of extremely odd-looking persons, broadly statured for Khmer and adorned in ill-fitting saffron robes that shrouded their heads, torsos, and legs. Almost down to their nimble feet. Except that one of them, now that he was watching, leaned upon a cane and seemed considerably less graceful than the other. If Five didn't know better, he would have sworn they resembled . . . no. Couldn't be. Perhaps they were Chinese?

And what did he care who or what they were? Khmer, Cham, Chinese, so what? In two Earth days he would be home. But there was no harm in observing these fellows, if indeed they were fellows, from a distance. He yanked his trek goggles free, blew the dust from his lenses, and refocused.

His guts churned. Impossible. Pale skin upon their feet and hands. When the steady breeze toyed with the fabric of their robes, they hurried to cover their faces. Not Chinamen. *Mothmen*, dammit. Undoubtedly. Of all the damn creatures in the cosmos! It couldn't be! Yet there they were, clumsily disguised as Buddhist monks. At least he recognized a crappy disguise when he saw one. But why? What absurd coincidence under heaven could bring these aliens to here and now? What could they possibly want? "Unbelievable," he grumbled. There was nothing, absolutely nothing good about it. And to make matters worse, they were coming his way.

"THESE TRACKS ARE STRANGE," SAID Chung. "Biped. But not human."

"Impossible," said Feng. "A monkey, isn't that what they are called?" He swiped at the air in front of his face and swatted at his neck.

Chung glared at him. "Walking upright upon a main road? And of similar size and weight to you or me? Keep your face shrouded, Advisor. Khmer may occupy these fields. Farmers. Or other humans. Like time detectives. Anyone could be watching. Try to imagine. What would a moleman do if he were working within the temple shrine? Day after day. Surreptitiously. Or perhaps late at night, or in the predawn hours, when the monks and all but a handful of slaves and sentinels are asleep?"

Feng frowned and continued to fuss with his garment. He felt revoltingly sweaty. And vaguely nauseous. And he felt another headache coming on. Was he ill? Had he contracted something? Malaria? Or was it the so-called HDT hangover? It was the damn intense sunlight, he knew that. And Chung's tedious bloviations. All of it, draining what remained of his health. He ought not have come. If he never endured another hyperdimensional travel event, it would be too soon.

"I have admitted to you that I am neither warrior nor hunter.

Nor am I some sort of master spy or a detective. What I am is the leader of this expedition. We are here under my authority. What do you mean by asking me petty questions?"

"With all due respect, Advisor, the emperor is our only authority. We are here under his auspices. But standing in plain sight arguing with each other is foolish. I say these are the footprints of a moleman. And what do molemen inevitably do? No, I don't mean to insult you with a petty question. I am being rhetorical, of course."

"They place their faith in the supremacy of their technology." Feng shrugged anemically.

"By the stars, Advisor, you are right! And they will inevitably assume a certain ignorance and incompetence on behalf of any other race."

"What is your point, Advisor, please!"

"I say a moleman's confidence in his own superiority—his elitism—will cause him to be careless, that's all. Hence, perhaps he can be observed and not know it."

Feng squinted into the sun as if it offended him. "He would shelter himself from this infernal light and heat, that is for certain. But what are you telling me? We are not even certain a moleman has managed to infiltrate these space-time coordinates. Our mission is to acquire the ball. And since it is not within the temple shrine, then I say we return home and regroup. Your moleman tracks are a figment of your imagination. Stop making nonsense out of this mission."

Chung spit at the ground as if to emphasize his disagreement. "The emperor sees much that is unseen. Hence, when he commands me to beware of a moleman operative because the molemen would never relinquish the ball, a cherished piece of their own handiwork, to the vicissitudes of time and space, I do not question it. When he believes the molemen will yet seek to dominate the cosmos by way of their Cosmic Clock machinations, I likewise believe it. There is a moleman here. Or my eyes have become as blind and useless as your own."

"Seek him, then. But we have a mere three Earth days to do it. If I can manage to endure it, that is. Seventy-two hours in which to find your moleman or retrieve the ball or both, or we will be stranded here. The HDT window will be shut. And I will not be stranded here, Advisor Feng. Nor will I squander any more time listening to your exhausting diatribes. Let us continue, will you please? Where are these supposed tracks leading us?"

Chung eyed Feng carefully. "The moleman's abode, of course. His thatch hut or lean-to—his haven. It will be unobtrusive and utilizing natural materials."

"We could spend weeks searching this fetid jungle to no avail!" Feng rubbed his face and shook his head. "We must have means, technological means and not simply your nose, to track him, or it is futile. We would do better to spend the night within the shrine ourselves and await his inevitable appearance. All this prompts me to request reinforcements. And technology."

"Reinforcements and technology. How would that make us appear to the emperor? He assigns us this auspicious mission, and halfway into it we are already whining for assistance? Like lazy children? As you say, Advisor Feng, it may seem the prudent thing to allow the moleman to come to us, inside the shrine. But then what, Advisor? Are we to ambush him? Are we to assault him face-to-face in hand-to-hand combat as he walks through the entrance? And hope the golden ball is upon his person, as if he carries it with him for amusement or fashion, like a pocket watch? We could wait for days and never encounter him inside the temple. And if by chance we did, him with his weapons and strength and his desperate ambitions and his lust for the ball itself—of what use would you be in such a situation? Or me, for that matter, an old man with nothing but a sonic shovel and a cane? Against an alien with who knows what defenses and weapons and training? No. We shall discover his hideout. We shall wait for him to take leave of it and scour his belongings for the ball. Only then, when we possess it, will we contact the emperor." Chung wiped perspiration from his chin. "Unless the moleman is himself observing us this instant. Watching us bickering like old women. We will follow these tracks. They lead southeasterly, into that woody section of jungle. And I am betting that our quarry will have taken up residence within an easy hiking distance from the temple but remote from the normal Khmer routes. Does that satisfy you? Come, follow me!"

This old goat will be the death of me, thought Feng. But with nothing better of his own to contribute, he gathered his robe, grit his teeth, and fell in behind Chung.

———

FIVE ADJUSTED THE LATTICE OF woven grass that comprised the camouflage of his hovel and attempted to regard it afresh. The bamboo frame had held up well enough, but after all his comings and goings these past months, the grasses, studded here and there with bits of foliage, were very much the worse for wear. It wouldn't do. Anyone the least bit curious would notice something awry. And then his hideout would be discovered. He ought to have tidied it up long ago. *Complacency will get you killed* was an apt lesson from his cadet days. But now it was too late. Screw it. Mothmen, Khmer, monkeys, what did he care who discovered it? He wasn't going to be here much longer.

Nevertheless, that pair of mothmen. If they kept to their route—easterly through the forest just south of the moat—they would pass within a stone's throw of his bivouac. It was as if they'd managed to somehow track him.

He pricked his ears. As if he could hear anyone coming. Even in midday, this damn jungle teemed with all the racket of a concert hall. Could they be seeking the eastern entrance to the temple? Or him? Or both?

He hefted his pack and moved out, padding along the forest floor, deeper and deeper into the jungle, until he came to his lookout tree, the one with the unusually broad and remarkably twisted trunk. "Try and find me up here, you bastards," he mumbled, and leapt at the first branch. He hauled himself up using his handholds and footholds, having long since learned a few climbing tricks from observing the monkeys. Upward he climbed until he'd positioned himself perhaps ten meters or so above the forest floor and settled into the crook of his usual branch, worn recognizably smooth after so many sessions. He looked out.

Tree climbing both unnerved and emboldened him. It was the only thing about cadet training that he'd naturally excelled at. He'd even earned a merit. The other cadets immediately dismissed his achievement as irrelevant. *Five finally earns a merit,* they'd laughed. *How many trees are there to climb in the Egyptian desert?*

Well, a view like this, even if it was merely Earth, sufficed as justification, so there. From up here the jungle was a pleasingly textured canopy, like a velvety blanket rolling out to the horizon in all directions, its earthy, brownish-green uniformity interrupted only by the jewellike shimmer and geometric intricacy of the temple itself.[65] Far beyond were the blue-tinted mountains, impossibly remote, like the boundary of some other world.[66]

Other worlds. He used to dream of almost nothing else before the Giza mission. Adventures and great deeds in distant lands. Saving the world. Getting the girl. Living happily ever after. The same silly dreams that everyone dreamed. And he'd managed to live at least the adventures-in-distant-lands part. And otherwise gotten what he deserved. If he somehow made it back home, who and what would he be? Where would he go? What would he do? He'd been a child, it seemed to him, even as a cadet in Egypt. Now what was he? Neither cadet nor moleman engineer nor—he didn't know what. He felt old, that's all. And apart from everything. As if he had lived a thousand lifetimes within the wastelands of this alien planet. Cursed.

He may yet break free. It struck him that this may be his last time enjoying his lookout. He could make it all the way home. He could die in the attempt. Or he could manage to get nowhere at all and then what? What if all his engineering and planning failed? Would he climb this tree afterward and look out upon this alien world and still want to live?

---

65   The Angkor Wat temple spires are presumed to have originally been gilt.

66   Five is observing the Cardamom Mountains.

He had chosen this lookout because of the strange shape of the tree but also because it provided a line of sight back to his bivouac. That misshapen sliver of an opening in the canopy, that was it. His makeshift home, such as it had been, for months. He decided then and there that whatever it was the two mothmen intended, confrontation was too great a risk—his stealth was paramount. He was no killer. He felt a pang in his heart. But he *had* killed. That human at Giza, on behalf of Miss Vixy. But no, in technical terms, at least, she had killed the man. He had merely injured the fellow. But he'd had in mind to kill him, if necessary. Likewise, that mothman assassin, if his dart had not missed its mark.

He whiled away perhaps thirty minutes upon his perch, listening to wind in the treetops, gazing into the distance, until his ass began to ache and he estimated that the two mothmen, had they kept to their line and maintained their modest pace, would likely be approaching his bivouac.

He had just decided to descend when he heard something. An unusually keen rustling below, and what had to be voices—yes, voices!—muffled yet unmistakable, from the direction of his hideaway. He scrambled down several branches until he could peer through to the forest floor. There. Mothmen.

He zoomed in and watched them doddering about. The slender one followed behind tentatively or distractedly, directionless if not for the leadership of the ungainly one. Nose to the ground. He was the one doing the tracking.

Five's pulse quickened. Sure enough, the cane-wielder poked at the camouflage. And the other mothman hung back, as if expecting something to burst forth. The cane-wielder finally shoved the frame aside and the mothmen stood at the edge of his hovel, peering in.

Five clenched his teeth and fought an uncanny urge to fight them off, to scramble down the tree and charge them in a blind rage, in defense of the only home he had.

Get ahold of yourself, dammit. Wait. Watch. Stay hidden.

The forest held its breath. At the same time, something caught his eye—a low-slung, unmistakably predatory profile that made the hair upon the backs of his ears stand up. A tiger. He had watched such a beast stalk a small deer in virtual silence, one patient step after the other. Then waiting. Watching. Then charging in a lethal burst of fangs and claws. Ever since, he'd never let his guard down in the forest.

He watched the cane-wielder struggling to lower himself into the hovel, watched him reach out to his companion for support. He glimpsed the tiger skulking through the shadowy underbrush, closing in. Meanwhile, the cane-wielder poked and prodded, inspecting things, and the slender mothman knelt close by, observing, each of them oblivious to their peril. The tiger crouched low.

Five hadn't taken his next breath when the beast crashed from the underbrush, swift and terrible. The slender mothman's cry cut short, and the animal hunched over the body, its victim's pale legs straining and an arm flailing weakly. Then nothing but the limp carcass being torn.

Five shuddered, and the cane-wielder, suddenly agile, virtually leapt from the other side of the hovel, glancing once behind him before scrambling with all available speed into the trees.

The chatter of a gibbon and the insistent, staccato chirp of a bird returned the forest to life. Five breathed as if he had not breathed in an age and crept farther up his tree, loath to witness the carnage and keen to keep out of the animal's sight. What if the beast could climb trees? He sat there, stranded. It could've been him. He gulped at the thought.

Meanwhile, he was homeless again. He couldn't return to the hovel. Because of the tiger, of course. And because the cane-bearing mothman was at large. The mothman would seek help—he may have already sent for it. What if more mothmen arrived? He needed his own place to work, to prep and store his equipment for the installation. He needed all the space and time leading up to tomorrow night to finish his preparations. And, heaven help him, to try to rest.

HE FELT AS IF HE were falling and jerked himself awake, gasping and clutching at his surroundings. Where was he?

In the tree.

How in heaven could he have dosed off? He tore away his goggles and rubbed his face. He scratched at his ears and tried to collect himself. How much time had passed? It felt like an eternity, but by the changed light, perhaps only an hour or so. He peered through the branches toward the forest floor. No tiger. No body. No indication of a struggle.

Get your shit together, Five. Get down and get the hell out of here.

Down from the tree, he found himself drawn to the site of the incident. He looked round warily, cocked his ears this way and that. If the animal had drug away its prey, perhaps it would not soon return. But who knew? Make it quick. He hustled toward the hovel, still expecting to encounter evidence—blood, bones, flesh? Yet nothing.

Something unexpected caught his eye—something glinting within the dirt and detritus of the forest floor. He knelt, and his heart leapt. He snatched at it, wiped the dirt and dust away, and touched the display. It illuminated! The glowing icons and text were indecipherable, of course, but it must be a mothman transponder! To hold in his hands a piece of modern technology, from anywhere and engineered by anyone, filled him with conflicting and thrilling energy—it seemed an astonishing stroke of weird fortune. And his mind raced with possibilities.

Then he panicked. What was he doing? Fool. Shut the damn thing off—who knew who could be listening, watching, tracking, attempting to communicate? He fumbled with it, turned the device this way and that, and found the design familiar enough, allowing for some oddities. He pressed here and there—nothing. He swiped at the display, and the thing went dark. Okay, tap on, swipe off. If the thing was indeed off. Again he looked warily about. Looked and listened. He shuddered at the risk he was taking and shoved the device into his pack.

Now, get to the eastern entrance of the temple. Go. He hastily replaced the camouflage over his dugout—if the mothmen sent reinforcements, it made sense to do his best to keep covering his tracks. He checked his bearings and moved out, keen to get himself safely encamped and almost giddy with the sense of newfound possibilities.

Five had not made three strides from his dugout when he heard something—a feeble noise, perhaps a voice. He made to duck behind a tree trunk, his heart pounding. He glanced at the display on his autotranslator. The thing was working, the icon pulsing.

Again, the voice, closer this time, more assertive. "Help. Me."

He endured an almost overwhelming compulsion to flee and was about to when the cane-wielder himself lurched into view from behind the underbrush.

Five froze. The mothman was breathing hard, his chest heaving. His strange, narrow eyes implacable and the contortions of his face a mystery. Was he afraid? In pain? Would he fight?

The mothman groaned, his blue, reptilian tongue flicking over his pale, narrow lips. His voice was husky and moderately pitched, ostensibly masculine. The phonemes—the sounds that made up the words, such as they were—seemed consonant heavy, with fricatives, glottal stops, a diphthong here and there, and an unpredictable intonation that evoked a percolating or syncopated effect. He sounded like a deepthroated bird and a pot of boiling water, both.

Five snatched the autotranslator from his neck and peered at the small display. *Helping. Required. No hide. Me sighting your presence here.*

It was not quite nonsense. But then his translator had never been programmed to interpret the mothman language. The device was improvising based on cosmos-wide linguistic modalities. The mothman hobbled closer and Five retreated a step.

Helping needed. Moleman assist. No safety here.

No safety, indeed. Five's heart continued to pound. What to do? Mothmen were legendary assassins. But this creature possessed none of the athleticism and fleetfooted acrobatics of the initiate Five encountered with Mr. Z. and Hesso beside the Great Pyramid. Was this an aged example?

He watched the mothman shove his cane under his arm and hold out his hands, palms down. It couldn't be. The cosmos-wide gesture of truce and nonviolence? Five moved to switch his autotranslator to speech mode. But as soon as he opened his mouth to talk, the mothman teetered. His cane fell away, his eyes fluttered shut, and he collapsed in a heap.

Now what? Screw the mothman. Just leave. Go, for heaven's sake, it's your chance!

Instead, he crept forward warily. The mothman was breathing. Shallow, labored breaths. Five dropped to one knee and peered more closely. He enunciated as clearly as he could, in a low voice, aware that his autotranslator would likely falter. "If you are injured, I have no means to help you."

At the sound of Five's translator, the mothman's tiny ears twitched and his fleshy scalp wrinkled. His wide mouth quivered, and the narrow lips parted, exposing the pointed tips of his canines. Five watched the mothman struggle to grip his cane, grinding the tip of it into the soil and leaning hard upon it until he'd managed to prop himself up. He sounded almost hoarse now, and the effort of sitting up was clearly exhausting. Yet he spoke. Five's translator managed a halting translation.

"Injury considerable. Pain miserable. Foot and legs joint and joint incapable."

Five thought he heard something in the forest, scanned this way and that, and cocked his ears, listening hard. It could be anything— deer, wild banteng,[67] a wild buffalo, a boar. It could be an elephant, for shit's sake. Or the damn tiger. Silence. And more silence. This jungle would drive him crazy.

The light was low. Night was coming on. He had to get ahold of himself. He addressed the mothman. He shook his head. If they couldn't manage to understand each other, he'd be forced to leave him.

But the mothman struggled to sit, and Five reached out.

Without hesitation, the mothman clasped Five's hand and with a huff of exertion finally seated himself, one leg splayed awkwardly. He took his hand away and leaned heavily upon his cane, as if to relieve the weight upon his leg.

"I cannot stay here," said Five. "And neither can you. The tiger may return. Come with me or stay. You must choose."

---

67 A species of cattle.

If the alien was weighing his options, there was no reading his expression. Five hefted his pack and turned to leave.

"Wait." The mothman again relied upon his cane and with considerable effort hauled himself precariously to his feet. He touched his knee joint. "Too hurt."

"We must flee." Five abandoned all caution, grasped the mothman's wrist, thrust his own arm between the alien's legs, and squatted to receive the burden—a fireman carry he had learned in cadet training. Painfully aware of the lunacy of his actions, he moved out.

He trudged along, and the mothman clutched his cane, groaning a bit whenever the terrain forced Five to shift his weight. They covered the remaining half kilometer of the southern extremity of Angkor Wat in twenty minutes, attaining the southeast corner of the complex before Five was forced to stop and lower the mothman to the ground.

Five gulped from his canteen, already half empty—he'd no time to collect and purify his daily ration—then offered the remainder to the mothman.

The alien sniffed at it, pursed his lips, and sipped. Five stowed the canteen and watched the mothman lie back, eyes half closed, chest rising and falling.

What to do? His plan had been to enter the temple some time before midnight, when most of the inhabitants of the grounds were assuredly asleep. As if to compound his anxiety, a rumble of distant thunder stirred the atmosphere, dreadfully unusual amid the dry season. Could the fates be conspiring against him? First this preposterous encounter with the mothman, and now the threat of storms in the dry monsoon, exactly when he most required clear skies and a blazing sun?

And what of the alien? Here was an enemy of war. It was legitimate to kill him, expected in some sense. And the smart thing, too. How else to maximize his chances of getting home? If only the injury were severe enough to be life-threatening, then this whole predicament would take care of itself. He glanced at the leg. There didn't appear to be any laceration, any blood. He tried to read the mothman's face, gauge his condition.

As if reading Five's thoughts, the mothman grasped his knee and spoke up in a breathless voice. "Twisted ligamenture." The translator faltered, then corrected itself. "Ligament. Maybe no striped killer beast." The mothman lay silent, blinking blindly up through the treetops, his breathing shallow. "No hope. Leave me. To die."

Their dilemma seemed intractable. "I cannot carry you further. I cannot cure you. I cannot help you." He thought of the transponder, and it struck him that the mothman may have been returning for it, perhaps had even seen him take it. He nevertheless made to examine the injury.

The mothman reached out to prevent him. "No. Bone break."

"I must see it." Five pulled the robe away, exposing the mothman's leg. The ankle and part of the shin were swollen and discolored.

The mothman wiped at his own forehead where a fine froth had formed. He stared hard into Five's eyes, moaning. Or mumbling, he couldn't be certain.

Perhaps he was feverish. Perhaps the mothmen perspired like that. What was he trying to tell Five? That he would have killed him? Was that why the mothman was here? Pulses of soundless lightning danced through the clouds as if to punctuate the keenness of their dilemma. Weather was moving in.

The mothman lay upon his back, breathing heavily with his eyes closed, clutching his cane with both hands.

Suddenly a beeping sound and a vibration—the confounded transponder! His impulse was to reach for the thing, then to ignore it. Too late! Yet there the creature lay, quietly, as if nothing had happened. Five snatched the transponder from his pack and frowned at it. His autotranslator was not equipped to decipher text. And the sense that he was running out of time, and that there was nothing left to hide anyway, that no secret of any consequence could possibly be left to him, compelled him to thrust the device at the mothman. "Tell me what it says."

The mothman opened one eye and tried to sit up. When he reached for the device, Five pulled it away, allowed the alien another moment or two to peer at it, then shrugged and returned the device to his pack. "I need to find food. And fetch water. When I return, I will bind your shin with a splint. Such an injury requires weeks to heal. If I were injured in that way, at least. But a splint will lower the risk of further damage." He scanned the area for a suitable campsite. He was loath to dig a hovel—too much effort, especially for two. He was just as loath to camp in the open upon the forest floor. And if it rained? He spied a cluster of entangled trees. It was as good a place as any. He resolved to construct a lean-to there when he returned. He peered out through the trees, beyond the edge of the forest. Perhaps fifty meters or so to the north, he could make out what he knew to be the moat, and farther into the distance, the distinctive outlines of the temple wall and the stony spires of its citadels within. He cinched his pack straps and made to leave.

The mothman spoke up. "When you have claimed the ball. Kill Chung."

Five, astonished at the clarity of the translation, eyed the mothman. The ball? Kill Chung? Was his autotranslator finally properly deciphering the language?

The mothman nodded at him as if having read his mind. "That is the message."

Of course. They were here for it themselves. They had somehow learned of it. He ground his teeth. Somehow, when it came to the golden ball—this one or the Giza ball—nothing ever seemed sufficient to keep them secret. It was as if they possessed a mysterious power or will to reveal themselves and to mangle the intentions of anyone who sought them. "Are you Chung?"

The mothman once again nodded.

"Then you have been betrayed. But it is of no concern to me. Do you possess your own transponder? Can you HDT home?"

"No."

What did it matter? If the mothman had a transponder, he would have already transmitted for help. If he didn't, well, their allegiances were unavoidable. Their association, such as it was, doomed. Their imperative to remain enemies just that. The mothman would eventually attempt to kill him, no doubt, to reclaim the transponder. If their circumstances were reversed, Five would seek any means to execute his duty—lies, subterfuge, cunning, violence. But it only mattered that his own imperative was more keenly urgent than ever. He had work to do. Every moment lost increased his risk of failure.

What to do? What would Cog or the general do? Or his father? Any of them might justly kill, or at least leave this alien to fend for himself. Wouldn't they? He ought to abide by the rules of war. But he was neither Cog nor the general, nor, unfortunately, anything like his father. This decision was solely his own.

He needed to eat and replenish his water. One thing at a time. He would go to the moat for fish, or frogs or fowl or rodents, whatever it came to. If the mothman chose to remain here, so be it. And if the alien were dead or disappeared when he returned, likewise so be it. He strode away into the trees.

RETURNING WITHIN AN HOUR, FIVE found Chung looking further diminished and frail, huddled pitiably against the base of a tree with his eyes shut and his head resting upon a thick root. Five was compelled to examine the mothman to verify that he was still breathing. Even as Five shuffled about prepping for his campfire, the mothman slept.

It may be a case of shock. Or that the wound was festering and any number of bacterial scourges were ravaging the mothman's body. If the old alien—for Five had indeed convinced himself this alien was an older iteration of the race—was dying, there was nothing for it. All he could do is boil water and try to feed them both.

Five lay the large catfish he'd speared in the moat upon a palm leaf. He scooped several large handfuls of soil from the ground for a shallow fire pit, tended his kindling, and set about his fire-starting routine. He coaxed the flames to life, added more fuel, and brought his attention to the filleting.

"Rain may not come tonight," he murmured, as much to himself as to the mothman. He split the fish open at the belly with his knife, gutted it, filleted the thing as best he could, and skewered it upon two sturdy yet flexible saplings, the ends of which he speared firmly into the ground beside the fire. He considered that the mothman may prefer the flesh raw, but he wanted it cooked.

The skewers flexed under the weight of the fish, poising them sufficiently close to the flames. He held out his hand to judge the temperature. Yes, plenty of heat, the fish would cook quickly. He nestled his cooking pot full of moat water beside the little blaze. Having strained what he could of the debris, he intended to boil it all—pathogen-free water was an impossibility from the moat, the Siem Reap River, or any of the rivulets or ponds. The Khmer may have sufficiently mastered the moleman guidance regarding hydraulics for irrigation and by extension for retaining vast quantities of fresh water, but sewerage had understandably not been part of the Angkor project agenda for the moleman engineers.

As for the smoke and odors of cooking, he'd already decided to ignore the small risk of attracting the attention of man or beast. They must eat and drink, come what may.

He discreetly pocketed the mothman transponder before placing his pack beside the fire. He approached the mothman, offering his hand. "I will help you to the fire."

The mothman opened his eyes and reached out weakly. They hobbled close to the flames, and he settled the mothman's head upon the pack. He used his knife to split a sturdy branch into several flat strips and set about strapping them to the mothman's injured shin as splints. "Tightening these straps will hurt."

When the fish was cooked, Five used his makeshift chopsticks to offer a morsel to the mothman, holding the steaming portion before the alien's face. The mothman blew upon it feebly, opened his mouth, chewed carefully. They sat picking at the remaining flesh of the fish.

"I will make a broth from the bones," said Five. Months ago, he'd managed to confiscate, from the unattended outskirts of a farmstead, a tiny clay tripod and a bowl, which sufficed as a cooking vessel more appropriate for one person. Nevertheless, he now filled the thing with meaty fish bones and water and set it within the embers of the fire to simmer. Soon enough, they shared the broth, and Five watched Chung cupping the bowl in his hands, tipping the last of it into his mouth.

Five then cut open a jackfruit, sectioned it with his knife, and the two men consumed the juicy, yellow, perfumed flesh. When they were finished, Five took care to burn the remains of his cooking in the fire. He went about stripping leafy branches from nearby trees, constructed a makeshift pair of beds within the convoluted roots of their camp tree, and spent the last of his energies gathering firewood to last the night.

"What is your name?" said Chung.

Strangely, it struck him that his name had not been of concern to anyone, including himself, for what amounted to an entire Gregorian year since finding himself marooned upon My Island and this miserable planet.

They each fell silent for a time, resting perhaps an arm's length from each other. The little fire crackled quietly above the rasping of the katydids, the limpid singsong of the crickets, and the other-worldly trilling of the toads. Lightning still flashed, but not as often as before, and no thunder followed. There was a breeze, and Five sensed higher atmospheric pressure, perhaps beginning to clear the skies. The weather was moving away, thank heaven. Now, if only he could return to his work.

"Where," said Chung, "is the golden ball?"

The question somehow seemed inevitable. Likewise, the strangely menacing tone in the mothman's voice.

Nevertheless, the blow from Chung's cane—a jab into Five's solar plexus—came too quickly. He'd expected something less agile, more desperately flailing and weaker, a strike perhaps aimed at his head. Five gasped at the pain and raised his forearm only just in time to protect his temple from the second blow. He scrambled aside, the pain in his wrist excruciating, his hand numb from it, and snatched the first thing he touched from the wood pile and swung blindly.

"Argh!" The mothman dodged the blow and stumbled, rebalanced himself upon one leg, and swung again, bringing his cane hard across Five's knee.

Five flinched and the blow missed its mark—instead of tendon or bone it struck the meat of Five's thigh, gave him time to roll and to swipe his stick into the fire and fling hot coals and ash at the mothman's face.

"Aieee!" Chung fell back, his face buried in his forearm, and flailed blindly with his cane.

Five pounced, tore the cane from Chung's grasp, raised it high.

Chung clawed at the air, unsteady on his one good leg, his face smeared with soot, his eyes shut tightly. "Murderer!" His voice was raw, desperate. "Murderers of time! Transgressors of the Way!"

When I move he'll hear me, thought Five. He grasped the cane with both hands, and Chung flung himself at him, clawing, fangs bared, tongue wild and wretched. Five snapped the cane in two across the mothman's skull and ducked aside, breathless, clutching the broken shaft. Chung dropped like a stone and lay still. Nevertheless, Five drew his knife and stood poised, desperate for it to be over.

The mothman groaned, stirred feebly. "Kill me," he panted. "Do not . . . deny me . . . a warrior's death."

"Your life," gasped Five, "and your death. Is your own."

CHAPTER 31

CHAOS AT THE SPEED OF THOUGHT

MR. Z. SURVEYED THE LANDSCAPE of 1296 Cambodia and puffed at his empty pipe to work through the last of the HDT hangover. He examined the encampment Vixy and Neutic had made. "Yes, I'd say this is a good spot. Close to our new nexus and close, but not too close, to your old one—we might get lucky and catch the mothmen trying to access it. Meanwhile, we're well hidden here at the edge of this forest. And the both of you are right about the traffic at that intersection of the western entrance road and the trail to Siem Reap. It's good to have that in sight. We can move east easily enough when it's time."

"Time to enter the Angkor Wat shrine, you mean?" said Vixy.

Mr. Z. nodded and shoved his pipe into his vest pocket. "I just want to get a sense for how busy this temple city is. Getting in and out of the shrine and poking around inside for the golden ball while not being seen is going to be a touchy thing, even with cloaking technology. Hmm. What I wouldn't give for some tobacco."

"Me, too," said Vixy. "Goddamn protocols. HDT. And LNT." She eyed Friday. "Don't let him get too close to the cloaking radius."

Neutic scrambled to corral the boy. "Look here, Friday." He juggled several yellowish-green objects trying to distract the boy.

"Friday loves these things. Fruit or nuts or whatever they are. And this cloaking radius is brilliant, Mr. Z. Not worrying about being seen is a hell of a luxury."

"It seems like a luxury we're all here together at all," said Vixy.

"Hats off to the TDC technicians," said Mr. Z. "They did one hell of a job tracking you. Your coordinates were in bad shape."

"Did they have anything to say about what happened?" said Neutic. "Why we got so off-course?"

"According to the captain, they've eliminated equipment failure and technical error. Otherwise, the root cause remains a mystery."

"But you've got your suspicions, don't you?" said Vixy.

Neutic glanced at the two of them and promptly dropped a fruit. "Oops!" He feigned dismay at Friday, and the boy giggled at him.

The fruit rolled toward Mr. Z. and he snatched it up. "Areca berry. Remove the husk and inside is the betel nut."

"Betel?" said Vixy. "I should have known that. That year I spent in Guangzhou." She glanced at Neutic. "In China it was like any other taboo drug—people talked about the high, or whatever, as if it were some mysterious, magical experience. But I don't know, Mr. Z., aren't the effects pretty mild?"

"What are the effects?" said Neutic. "Do they smoke it?"

"They chew it," said Mr. Z. "They make a paste of it, somehow, with a lime solution as I recall, and wrap it in a betel leaf."

Neutic was tapping at his device. "A-R-E-K?"

"No," said Mr. Z., "it's spelled with a C. It's the fruit of the areca palm. But the leaf itself is from the betel plant, and all over the world it's referred to as betel nut, don't ask me why. I just know that people have been chewing this stuff for thousands of years."

"Since 500 BCE, it says here." Neutic teased Friday with a fruit and tried again to juggle.

"The Khmer with their mouths all reddened," said Vixy. "That's from betel. Or areca. Whatever. Even the monks chew it."

"And the high, as you call it," said Mr. Z., "I've heard it described as a warm glow, but to me—I tried it once in India—it's more like the buzz you get from too much coffee."

"That would be nice," said Vixy. "We ought to try it. Here, Neutic, what are we waiting for—who needs the betel leaf, right?" She held out her hand.

Neutic remained focused upon his juggling. "Right. Disgraced time detective caught chewing illicit substance."

"Disgraced?" joked Vixy.

"Besides that," said Mr. Z., "it's a pretty significant carcinogen. But then again, what isn't?"

"Life will kill you," said Neutic. Friday crawled into Neutic's lap, heedless of how he interrupted the juggling, and curled up with the first rays of the morning sun upon his face.

Vixy looked blindly through the foliage in the direction of the temple. "This is 1296. Those monks living in the temple village—when did Buddhism take over from Hinduism? *Wat* means temple, doesn't it? Don't look it up, Neutic, I'm just asking. What do these Buddhist monks want with a gigantic monument to a Hindu god? All those famous images, the reliefs of all the Hindu mythology. Do they read them? Do they even care what they mean? Or were they intent upon defacing them, like the pharaohs defaced each other's monuments?"

"A wat in Buddhist terms," said Mr. Z., "is simply a temple that includes quarters for monks, a temple, facilities for lessons, and usually a large image of the Buddha. But here in Cambodia a wat describes any place of worship. So *Angkor Wat* merely translates to *city temple* or *city of temples*, what have you."

"*Wat* is supposedly a Thai word," said Neutic, peering at his device. "Taken from a Sanskrit term. And the current king, wherever he is, Indravarman, he annunciated the name carefully. He's Buddhist."

"Indravarman III," said Mr. Z. "A Buddhist, yes. He just assumed power as of last year, 1295. Replacing Jayavarman VIII, I think, who was a traditionalist—the man reinstated Hinduism during his reign. In fact, he was anti-Buddhist, according to the history. Keen to restore something of the old ways. If you come across any defaced Buddhist imagery here—where the stonework has been chiseled away—it was Jayavarman VIII who initiated it. But I guess we all know that the history of the Khmer Empire is pretty messy all around. Least of all mythologically." He scratched his head. "I don't know, Neutic could look it all up for us, but I'm fairly certain you'd have to go back to

Suryavarman II, who built Angkor Wat, to sort of bookend the golden or classic era of Khmer culture with the era we're in now, which is the beginning of their decline. Angkor Wat was a Hindu temple in the beginning, to be sure. But the archaeological anthropology is still quite lacking."

"Because there wasn't anything besides stone that survived this climate," said Vixy. "No paper or parchment or anything made of wood. The architecture and imagery, like practically everywhere else on the planet, rots away."

"Or gets consumed by insects, yes," said Mr. Z.

"It says here that Suryavarman II died in 1150," said Neutic. "With Angkor Wat unfinished. And on top of it all, it seems like the Khmer were almost continually at war with their neighbors. I guess we're lucky there isn't that to deal with. Right now, at least."

"That's not to say something isn't brewing," said Vixy.

"I tried to brush up on the history before getting here," said Mr. Z. "And the TDC archives have nothing surrounding these space-time coordinates. As a matter of fact, no time detective has ever been here and now. We're the first. Hence, the strict limits upon our HDT window. We've got to work fast, get in and get out. Our influence is too significant."

"That's my fault, sir," said Neutic. "With me and Friday."

"It's pushing the limits of the TDC's contingency plans, certainly, Neutic. That our initial HDT was fractured provides us some leeway in terms of accountability—I was supposed to have led the transport and assumed responsibility and all that, but with what happened, well, hyperdimensional travel has its risks, I'll leave it at that.

"But to your point, Vixy, when you asked what these monks want with a monument to a Hindu god—that's an interesting question. We need to keep in mind the difference between the state-sponsored religion, which amounts to a religion of the elite, as is commonly the case, and the commonplace beliefs of the common folk. Like neak ta, for example."

"Neak ta?" said Vixy. "You mean superstitions?"

"Land spirits," said Mr. Z. "Right now, the Khmer king and his court have already relocated to Angkor Thom. We may get a glimpse of the remains of the king's residence on the north side of the temple when we get in there—there's archaeological evidence for it, but it may already be vanished. Angkor Wat is a relic already, in 1296. But it's likely that all the famous Hindu imagery on the walls here wouldn't have been something the common folk identified with—it probably wasn't used to edify anyone except the royalty."

"No weekend temple sightseeing tours for the masses, sir?" said Neutic.

"Let alone any formalized communication of the mythology," said Mr. Z. "It's possible, unless we see something to the contrary, that only the ruling elite ever cared about it. Folk animism, the neak ta, fuels the day-to-day spirituality of the common folk. Hinduism and Buddhism come and go, but the spirits of the land remain. But I don't know for certain. It's right up Vixy's alley, though."

"Except I've got all I can handle with my Haida research."

"Anyway," continued Mr. Z., "you don't see the Buddhists engaging in anti-Hindu iconoclasm, thankfully. I did read that the Buddhists attempted to modify the central shrine, however—there is some history that indicates that right about now they replaced a statue of Vishnu with that of a Buddha and perhaps walled in some sections of the architecture in line with Buddhist temple design. But we'll have to see for ourselves."

"See for ourselves?" said Neutic.

"We're going to have to get into the temple shrine," said Vixy. "Right, Mr. Z.? Because if the golden ball is anywhere and the mothmen are after it—"

"It may be hidden somewhere inside the shrine, yes," said Mr. Z. "But frankly, I doubt it."

"Because anything of value," said Vixy, "would've been pillaged almost as soon as the temple was finished. There might be some evidence of the mothmen having gotten in there. Or the molemen, not that we could tell the difference."

"Molemen," muttered Mr. Z.

"That's what the captain told us, at least," said Vixy. "When he said you were coming."

"Yes, well, that brings me to the parameters of our mission.

Here we are near your original HDT nexus, in proximity to Angkor Wat, safe and sound. But we've got work to do in that temple. And maybe elsewhere. We'll eat, and I'll go over all of it with the both of you."

———

"When the present determines the future," Mr. Z. declared, "but the approximate present does not approximately determine the future. Sound familiar?"

"No checking your device, Neutic," teased Vixy.

Neutic wrinkled his brow. "It's the definition of chaos, isn't it?"

"I'm impressed, Neutic," said Mr. Z.

"Wait a minute!" exclaimed Vixy. "What did you say, Mr. Z.? When the present determines . . . ?"

"When the present determines the future," repeated Neutic, "but the approximate present does not approximately determine the future. I only know it because—"

"Because it's part of the TD cadet training you just had," said Vixy. "That I forgot a long time ago. But you're talking about consequence research, aren't you, Mr. Z.? And the butterfly effect."

"Within the context of HDT, yes," said Mr. Z. "Consequence theory and the butterfly effect are intertwined. We all study that in cadet training. It's an ancient idea, of course, sometimes referred to as complexity theory or chaos theory. But the idea that the behavior of anything with enough complexity can be described as unstable with respect to changes of small amplitude, that was Lorenz, I think—the professor of meteorology in the twentieth century—who did a lot to popularize it."[68]

Neutic examined his device. "Edward Lorenz."

———

68   Referring to Edward N. Lorenz, "Predictability: Does the Flap of a Butterfly's Wings in Brazil Set Off a Tornado in Texas?", American Association for the Advancement of Science, 139th meeting (Cambridge: Massachusetts Institute of Technology, December 29, 1972).

"That's him," said Mr. Z. "And before that, if either of you recall, by the sci-fi author."

"Ray Bradbury," said Neutic. "In a short story entitled "A Sound of Thunder." I actually remember reading that when I was a teenager."

"But it all boils down," insisted Vixy, "to a minuscule influence here generating a significant influence there."

"That's right," said Mr. Z. "And for complex, otherwise nonlinear systems, even determinant systems—systems without random elements where future behavior is fully determined by initial conditions—they are not, in fact, predictable. Instead, they are chaotic. My point is that this is something I suspect ties Laron's machinations to those of both the molemen and the mothmen. And for that matter to the Scarab Cult's perceived existential mandate. It's the Scarab Cult that is playing the ideologies of the molemen and the mothmen against each other, to foster its own agenda."

Vixy raised her eyebrows. "Existential mandate?"

"Yes," said Mr. Z. "Or divine mandate. The idea that your interpretation is *the* interpretation. Supported by the nature of reality itself. That only your group or tribe properly understands what is real. Hence, your tribe possesses the cosmic authority to exert your will above that of all other tribes. It's my theory that the Scarab Cult seeks chaos as the expression of their divine mandate. A chaos that, strangely enough, requires a caretaker of sorts."

"And the Scarab Cult are their own caretakers, right?" said Vixy. "That's how it always works. And the molemen, mothmen, and whoever else—everybody else threatens their caretaking of the chaos?"

"Exactly," said Mr. Z.

"What about a leader?" said Neutic. "Or would that imply too much order?"

"Right," said Vixy. "Good point. I mean, the Scarab Cult is indeed a cult, isn't it? A cult is a group that doesn't necessarily possess any shared ethnic or national identity, it's just a sinister belief system, right? So, there's bound to be some charismatic psycho for a leader behind it all. It's weird that there's no evidence at all indicating who it is. Or who it has been in the past."

"Well," said Mr. Z., "I think Neutic may be correct. That there has never been a leader precisely because that would express order. Unless order happens to suit their current agenda. It's inevitable, isn't it, with any authoritarian regime, that they appropriate what they think they need to further their ideology."

"Even when it doesn't fit with their ideology," said Vixy.

"Deterministic chaos," said Neutic.

"Yes," said Mr. Z. "Which nevertheless translates semantically to chaos—chaos is chaos with or without attempts at modifiers. Then again, it's a strange, added implication that somehow there is a transitional state between order and disorder, a bounded instability region where the complexity of a system is maximal and toward which a system drives itself, or seeks to adapt itself into, or teaches itself to evolve into. It's a strangely seductive zone where big change, big shifts, and big creativity is fostered."

Vixy yanked an energy wafer from her pack and tore at the wrapper with her teeth, a behavior which immediately attracted the attention of Friday, who reached out. "No, not the wrapper, Friday." She tore off a small piece and presented it to the boy.

Friday gummed the morsel and stuffed his chubby, pliant fingers into his mouth, his chin immediately glistening with slobber.

Vixy looked dubious. "He's old enough for solid food, isn't he?" Vixy returned the men's stares. "You both can stop looking so astonished. Why should I know anything about toddlers? And leave-no-trace protocol or not, he's got to eat, doesn't he?"

"Indeed," said Mr. Z. "And enough of me yammering on about cosmic chaos."

"Cosmic chaos." Vixy grabbed Friday under the armpits and handed him to Neutic. "I swear that describes this mission."

"And speaking of mission," said Neutic, "what is ours? I mean, when you arrived, sir, you told us that Laron is dead. And that Professor Wilhelm is in some kind of psi-communication with the mothman empress. You even said that perhaps Five himself is here in Angkor Wat to acquire the golden ball."

"Or a version of it," said Mr. Z.

Vixy spoke up. "And we were all supposed to track down Laron in Bombay together. To figure out what he was up to. On top of apprehending him on account of his blatant time crimes. But you said that all you discovered was more Scarab Cult nonsense—cultish gatherings, some inexplicable connection to an Indian man—Kashi, was it? That the Laron thing is all just . . . I was going to say chaos. Meanwhile, I'm wondering . . . well, I don't know what I'm wondering."

"We both were wondering why we were hijacked," said Neutic. "Could it all be linked to the Scarab Cult?"

"I don't have any answers," said Mr. Z. "I'm sorry. I can only say that between Earth, the molemen and the mothmen—besides the threat of the Cosmic Clock technology that is ostensibly capable of harnessing control of space-time—there is the damn Scarab Cult playing everybody and everything against themselves."

"More chaos," said Vixy.

Mr. Z.'s transponder suddenly crackled with interference. He fumbled with the controls. "Captain? I'm sorry, Captain, I'm getting interference, I can't understand you. Do you copy? Blast this thing!"

"That's probably the high-resolution encryption the captain told us about," said Neutic. "It puts a strain on the signal." He held out his hand. "Here, sir—I can probably fix it."

Mr. Z. handed over his device.

Neutic performed a few taps, swipes, multifunction press-and-hold operations, and quickly handed it back.

The captain's voice blared forth. "Gold cannot HDT. Did you copy that, Z?"

"Yessir. Loud and clear. You said, 'Gold cannot HDT.'"

"That's right. Gold cannot HDT. Every damn technologically modern and scientifically savvy culture in the cosmos knows that. Us. The molemen. The mothmen. Presumably the damn Scarab Cult. Everybody. Likewise, the idea that entanglement physics does not apply to HDT scenarios. Nothing entangles with anything else outside its own space-time coordinates. Right?"

There was a pause and Mr. Z., Vixy and Neutic all looked at each other blankly.

"Are you asking me, sir?" said Mr. Z. "Because I don't—"

"No, Z, I'm telling you. And right now, you're wondering what the hell I'm ranting about except—and this is why I'm calling you—apparently, when it comes to HDT and elemental gold and entanglement physics and all three together, the frigging molemen seem to be, once again, capable of shattering all scientific convention. Because we've got new evidence—hot off the press, as my great-grandfather used to say—that indicates entanglement physics is occurring at nodes within your space-time coordinates there in Angkor. And, get this, goddamn Giza too! Of all places. Not good. Alongside HDT transmission ghosting traceable to Mega City One. Again, not good. It's goddamn unbelievable, it's so not good. Our tech folks at the TDC are teamed up with a task force at the T.E. trying to unravel the physics as fast as they can. All they can tell me so far is that it appears the molemen have exploited entanglement efficiencies dependent upon subatomic impurities unique to Earthen gold. Which maybe helps explain why the molemen selected Earth as a Cosmic Clock Component lattice point to begin with. But who knows?"

"I don't understand, Captain. This is Vixy speaking. Do you copy me, sir?"

"Yes, Vixy, go ahead."

"Well, hyperdimensional entanglement physics—the research has been going on for millennia, right? And maybe it's just latent technology that the molemen used when they were keen on engineering the Cosmic Clock Component in the Great Pyramid? I mean, who knows what it takes to engineer a Cosmic Clock Component? And maybe it means that the molemen are here too, in thirteenth-century Angkor Wat, trying to reengineer the Cosmic Clock Component."

"Look," said the captain. "I'd say goddamn anything is possible at this point. Including another golden ball being present at Angkor. It verifies that the molemen were not only present during the engineering of Angkor Wat itself—a time crime in itself at least as significant as what they perpetrated in Giza—but that they abandoned Angkor Wat before its completion. We find that ball and we have hard evidence of moleman time crime atrocities in that era. And maybe it was the molemen who hijacked Vixy and Neutic's HDT? This throws everything into question. Anyway, here we are, then, with an opportunity to obtain proof that the molemen themselves were there during the construction era of Angkor Wat, that for whatever reason they abandoned it for Giza. They have to leave the golden ball behind in each location because they can't HDT them. But I can tell you that the Angkor ball wasn't configured as a network node. We haven't discerned any evidence of entanglement physics for that. Not yet, anyway. Neither does the Angkor ball appear to be endowed with an entanglement maintenance herald emitter."

"Entanglement maintenance herald emitter?" said Vixy.

"The signal that indicates the entanglement is active," said Mr. Z. "But, as the captain points out, entanglement physics isn't supposed to be viable hyperdimensionally."

"I remember," said Vixy, "that Five told Hesso and me that the golden ball was just"—she affected quotations with her fingers—"'an X-ray reflector.'"

"The Giza ball," said the captain, "was ultimately machined to X-ray reflection specifications—we can discern that from this space-time distance—but perhaps unbeknownst to Five himself, his engineering protocols likely established upgrade capacity for future entanglement architecture. We're convinced that X-ray communication technology, primitive as it is, was their fail-safe for off-planet engineering. To allow for, at worst, subluminal communication quanta to be packaged over HDT transmission events. It works. It leaves no ghosting. Zero transmission residue. But it's so slow, so outdated, that it hasn't been part of the TDC's surveillance spectrum for about five hundred years."

"That's pretty sneaky," said Vixy. "I mean, I always think of moleman engineering as advanced."

"The future is the past," said Neutic, and shrugged.

"What's that, Neutic?" said the captain.

"Nothing, sir, sorry, I was just, I don't know, sorry."

"No," said Mr. Z., "there's something important to that, Neutic. The molemen, more than anyone in the cosmos right now, may be the savviest manipulators—engineers, in their terminology—of that idea. Anyway, if the molemen had appropriated Earth, the next CCC in the lattice would necessarily have been entangled, via moleman engineering, with the Giza ball. That entanglement would subsequently be teleported to the third lattice, and so on, until all lattice points in the tesseract were thus entangled and the Cosmic Clock became operational. Now, with the mothmen maybe involved in their own CCP—"

"The complexity of the time crime advances by an order of magnitude," said the captain.

Mr. Z. raised his eyebrow and once again puffed on his empty pipe. "Hmm, indeed," he mumbled. "Moreover, if the Giza ball and the Angkor ball *are* hyperdimensionally entangled, the equal-and-opposite relationship between them provides the means to machine and engineer or otherwise configure both balls simultaneously. For the moleman engineers at Mega City One intent upon the Giza mission, this would be irrelevant. But the potential exists. And it explains what Five, if it's Five, is perhaps up to here at Angkor Wat."

"Because," said Vixy, "we're still not certain he's actually here?"

"Well," said the captain, "we haven't discovered evidence of an HDT event with biological cargo vectoring from the Giza region to any space-time coordinates on Earth. Let alone any with a known Mega City One signature."

"He's reengineering the CCC at the heart of the temple," said Neutic. "Just like he did within the heart of the Great Pyramid."

"I'd say yes and no to that," said the captain. "Because we have been monitoring the space-time and compositional status of the Giza ball ever since Vixy told us it existed. At least as much as our hyperdimensional coordinate analysis technology will allow. For Caviglia's chamber and the pit and everything to do with the Great Pyramid, the hyperdimensional coordinates have been stable, minimal flux, but we all know you can't just look into the past like it's a damn crystal ball. Meridians, parallels, hypermeridians, the indeterminacy involved, and all that. But the Giza ball indicates zero delta."

"That's because Five would never reengineer the golden ball," said Vixy. "Unless something has changed. Unless *he* has changed."

"Five? Changed? I think you're right, Vixy," said Mr. Z. "In other words—and I've discussed this only briefly with the captain—it's perhaps that Five is tasked with something else."

"No," said Vixy. "It's that he hasn't changed at all. He's still just trying to get home. Like any of us would be."

Mr. Z. frowned at Vixy and put away his pipe. He regarded her thoughtfully. "Okay. Let's see. Accessing the entanglement potential between the Angkor and Giza ball—the polarization and spin memory data. It would perhaps allow him to engineer an ad hoc entanglement scenario."

"Subject to risky decoherence conditions," interjected the captain.

"Subject to risky decoherence conditions, yes," replied Mr. Z. "But an ad hoc entanglement scenario that nevertheless could force the mirroring and open an HDT window to get him back to Mega City One. A technically roughshod, very risky transport. But if he's desperate enough."

"That angle is beyond me," said the captain, "in military terms, at least. You never leave a man behind. But a traitor? I don't care if you're human or a moleman or Bozo the clown, you surrender your status as such. That is, you sacrifice your personhood entitled to the advantages and benefits of your race. Traitors are to this day executed in many parts of the cosmos."

"Sir," said Neutic, "maybe somebody on Mega City One doesn't consider him a traitor. Those transmissions the TDC intercepted, from Mega City One to Earth and back. I suppose there's the possibility that somebody besides the molemen would be transmitting, but it seems to me that whoever it is, they'd have to possess sophisticated knowledge of how to help him. To even track his whereabouts. Unless he contacted them first, somehow. I don't know."

"Those are legitimate speculations," said Mr. Z. "It's not inconceivable that Five, any moleman, could engineer sufficient resources even within thirteenth-century Cambodia to communicate hyperdimensionally, communication being multiple factors of magnitude less complex than his physical transport. And who he's in touch with, well, even if the captain is correct and the molemen would never tolerate a traitor, who knows if they wouldn't still attempt to bring him back. To justice. Or to, I don't know, a rendezvous with dissenters within their own ranks?"

"Like the Scarab Cult?" said Vixy.

"The facts of our mission, then." Mr. Z. twisted the remaining cloaking spike from the ground and scrubbed it clean of soil. "Gold will not HDT. But it can be cloaked. And both the molemen and the mothmen possess the technology to cloak themselves here in Angkor. Hence, we can't track them, not without more sophisticated abilities than any of us here possess. Not without them attempting an HDT—then the TDC could do it. Likewise, the ball. Nothing like it shows up in any scan, correct, Captain?"

"That's right. Nothing. All this talk of an Angkor ball remains speculation."

"So be it," said Mr. Z. "If Five hasn't penetrated the inner shrine to retrieve the ball, then he's stolen it from Feng and Chung, wherever they are. And if he's done neither, if he's not here at all and the evidence of his communications are all erroneous, then our mission is reduced to verifying that the shrine itself shows no evidence of tampering."

"How so?" said Vixy. "I mean, we can't very well go waltzing into the temple shrine, any of us, and sit and wait for Five to show up. It's not feasible. We'd be seen by the monks eventually. Even cloaked, we'd leave too significant a trace. Wouldn't we? Neither can we wander around the temple city grounds asking if anyone has seen a short, squatty alien with unusually large hands and ears like Mickey Mouse and weird goggles on his face."

"But there's no reason to believe he'd venture far from the Angkor Wat temple complex," said Neutic. "If his plan is to access the shrine, then just like us, he would avoid the busier western entrance and encamp at the east end, beyond the moat, still within the forest so as not to be readily seen, yet close to the eastern bridge—there's a footbridge there, correct?"

"Yes," said Mr. Z. "And you're exactly right, that would provide him reasonably convenient access alongside considerably less risk of being discovered. The jungle on that side is close and thick, for one thing. Most of the activity, the comings and goings of the monks and the delivery of provisions, I suppose it happens almost exclusively via the western gate. Five would move under the cover of night. And unless the moleman prerogative for locating their Cosmic Clock Component within the foci of a major symbolic architectural monument has somehow changed, we'll assume the shrine at the center of the quincunx is where the ball and its engineering components will be." Mr. Z. dug into his shoulder pouch and held a tiny, needlelike instrument between his fingers.

"That's a tracer pin," said Neutic.

"Yes," said Vixy, "and you can bet Five isn't foolish enough to enter that shrine without scanning for bugs like that. Mr. Z., are you kidding? We'll never get video or even bio confirmation of Five with that thing. Even if his technology is limited and he possesses zero cloaking technology."

Mr. Z. twisted the tracer pin between his fingers so its variegated surface glistened in the sunlight angling through the foliage. "If it doesn't work . . ." He trailed off.

"We go to plan B," said the captain.

"Which is?" said Vixy.

"You deploy yourselves in the shrine," said the captain, "and watch. Like an old-fashioned stakeout. I'll clear it with the LNT analysts on basis of an emergency need."

"Yes," said Mr. Z. "It won't be pretty, if it comes to that. With the temple in use and the shrine perhaps most of all. But we don't know for certain how this temple city operates."

"And we're to place these tracers where?" said Vixy. "I mean, besides within the shrine. I assume we're trying to track his whereabouts outside of Angkor Wat, aren't we?"

"At the access points to the only other population centers that Five may risk infiltrating," said Mr. Z. "Namely, the southern gate of Angkor Thom and somewhere along the road to Siem Reap. As close to the main entrance to the village as possible."

CHAPTER 32

SHIELD OF THE SUN

Five hefted the mothman transponder. It was a moleman transponder now. *His* transponder. A thrill ran through him. He had managed to reconfigure enough of the electronics to transform the thing into an HD transmitter. His last conversation with Cog had been heartening:

"You discovered the mothman transponder," Cog had said, "and if I believed in miracles, that would qualify. But that you reengineered it is a tribute to your ingenuity, Five. And your training, of course. Meanwhile, the only advantage to convalescence is the opportunity to catch up on my reading. I've been going through the Sno-Globe-Con transcripts, for instance. Before General Ten-Square was killed, during that time we spent on the front lines together, he supplied me with the access codes. He told me that one of us, if either of us made it out alive, had to make the transcriptions public. The whole crazy business, as he called it, explains how the Great Conflict was inevitable, that the mothmen never had any intention of becoming one of our outposts, at least not willingly. And they had secret technological acumen and manufacturing resources, which explains how they could ramp up so quickly for war. What it doesn't explain is how in hell they appropriated our engineering, especially the Cosmic Clock technology. Nor how they became so proficient in implementing our battlefield technologies. Anyway, I used to think the general was reactionary and impatient, his vision blurred by his ambition, that he'd become a bureaucrat, too distant from on-the-ground operations to grasp the realities. And most often I assumed he was as bullheaded as any other general. And he was, I suppose. But now? I think he knew a lot about the impossible conditions of the treaty with the mothmen—how much we gave away and how little we got in return. A damn scandal, I'd say. It was as if somebody else was pulling the strings at those conferences. Somebody who wanted to sabotage everything. I found a note in the transcripts where the general describes the difference between intimacy-dominant cultures and integrity-dominant cultures. I'd never heard of such a thing. That they find cooperation difficult because they find each other's reasoning inscrutable. And it leads to accusations of duplicitousness on both sides. There's an absense of trust. That's us and the mothmen, right there

"I mean, trust. What measure of trust has ever existed between us and the mothmen? Are they intimacy dominant or integrity dominant? I know we could be described as damn well integrity dominant. Integrity of science, of engineering, of the will. So what does that mean when it comes to diplomacy between us and the mothmen? Guaranteed trouble, I'd say. Hell, Five, what I'm reading in the Sno-Globe-Con transcripts are all these cultural sticking points. And we knew they were sticking points and we knew the mothmen regarded us as—what's the word?—inscrutable. It's not as if the disagreements weren't known to anyone, at least to some extent. It was supposed to be on the agenda to systematically address the perspective of the mothmen and vice versa. But did it happen? We're at war in spite of everything, in spite of every opportunity to forestall it. That's the evidence that it didn't happen. Intimacy or integrity, all of that was out the window. From the beginning we were using each other. More like abusing each other, the general would agree with me. Each to our own ends. Never really understanding the perspective of the other. How could we? Who amongst us spent any time within the Mothmen Realm? We've no idea how they really think, no idea what's important to them—really no idea why they do what they do. We made a gaggle of assumptions, that's all. And got caught up in gamesmanship, each of us trying like hell to gain the upper hand, based upon the idea that the other was ignorant of the truth and fundamentally incapable of learning it. Misguided and doomed to remain so by way of their—I don't know, their genetics?

"Ack. I sound like a damn bureaucrat myself, Five. That's what my wife tells me when I go off on this diplomacy stuff. She's worried I'm not going to accept retirement, that I'm going to use the leverage of the hero thing—all that news media bullshit—to angle for a desk job with authority and get obsessed with changing things from within. As if anyone can change anything about the government or the military or geopolitics without making it a life's work. And even then, it seems an exercise in futility at my age, back from the damn battlefield one too many times. But I suppose that's all mostly beside the point if we damn well manage to lose this war.

"Listen, Five. Forget all my yammering about what could have been and what ought to be. Forget about the damn war. You've only gotten as far as you have because you've listened to yourself, to what you know is right. Despite all the noise. You're no traitor, dammit. What am I saying? Screw the stigma of the Giza failure. If this war has accomplished anything, it's to obliterate anybody's interest in taking sides against anybody but the mothmen. Let's just get you home. Have you been able to synchronize the HDT engine to this signal? To our communications?"

"Yessir," he had told Cog. He had been so glad to listen to the man going on about things, to hear his voice, which had become his only connection to Mega City One. To any chance he had of *getting* home. Because without the mothman's transponder and Cog's engineering help, his own clumsy HDT-zenith-passage idea would have been nothing but a flop. But it had gotten him this far. Now the entanglement was going to work. He had double-checked his calculations then, with Cog still on the line. He initiated a system test. All of it for what seemed already the thousandth time. "Yessir," he had said, "I'm running the simulation again now and everything, even the parallel processing booster, is solid. The numbers are good."

"What about phase drift?"

"None."

"Resolution?"

"Holding strong."

"Parallax, compression, distortion factors . . . oh, never mind, Five. There's nothing more to be done, is there? The engineering is half-baked. The tolerances are a disgrace. But there's nothing more we can do."

Five recalled the frustration in Cog's voice. The man remained the same old stickler for technical detail, for robust engineering. "But the meteorology, sir," he had suggested. "Clear skies. We couldn't have asked for anything better."

"Yes, Five, exactly. Despite the interferences. If the forecast holds. Meanwhile, I don't like it, the jerry-rigged nature of it. There's not a moleman engineer alive that would sign off on this contraption. And on top of everything, we can't maintain these communications. Encryption shrouds are more finely meshed than ever and getting tighter. It's the war. That's why this has to be our last audio. Yes. There are more eyes on me than ever. As high profile as our Giza mission was, it's nothing compared to the media circus publicizing so-called heroes of the Great Conflict. Me, a war hero. They want to make me a general, Five, can you believe it? The irony is beyond me. But the next forty-eight hours are all up to you. And the engineering."

And luck, Five had thought, but he'd been afraid to say it. He had endured a flood of anxiety, for their transmission time was almost up. But for the sake of being able to hear another moleman's voice and talk technology, even if it courted disaster, well, it seemed worth it to keep the line open until the end.

He peered over the edge of the rotting tree trunk that constituted one wall of his bivouac and counted the monks traversing the western entrance road. Eight. Always there were at least a handful of them coming and going, their saffron robes slung loosely across their fine-boned, angular bodies, their pace deliberate and unhurried.

By now he'd become familiar with the speed of life in these tropical climes, how the clinging humidity and savage heat sapped the energy from everything except the bloodthirsty insects and the noisy monkeys and the reptiles and birds and amphibians and whatever else that lived here and kept him up at night with their lunatic noise. He swore sometimes he could hear the damn plants growing. "Sir?" he had said.

"I know, Five. Time's up."

"Yessir."

"Stay strong, Five. Just as you have been. And brave. Forty-eight hours. Just forty-eight hours more and—we've got to break off, Five. I'm cutting us off."

The signal had vanished. And, remembering the painful silence and the sense of infinite longing and exile and homesickness that always burdened him at the end of a communication with Cog, he experienced it again. But he was closer to getting home than ever. Cog had resolved all the issues with the entanglement physics between the Angkor iteration and the Giza ball. He had refined all the calculations; dialed in the meridians, parallels and hypermeridians; and honed the transport pathway. In fact, if he had known, back when he was on his own, how many things he miscalculated and how much of the HDT engineering he bungled and how the entanglement physics would have remained beyond his grasp? Magical helpers, that's all. It was a phrase from his book. Describing the weird fortuities bestowed upon anyone properly immersed within their adventure.

Meanwhile, the Angkor Wat towers gleamed. He sighted the aperture in the central tower's peak, laser located the corresponding zenith point upon the floor of the shrine, and drove his long, iron chisel—pilfered from the temple gallery—into the relatively pliant soil, probing. It was a clayey loam, with perhaps 10 percent gravel. It likely began as alluvial, of course, given the region's floodplain geography, but here the entire depth of material down to the sarcophagus was backfill, essentially homogeneous. There would be few if any rocks or stones larger than pebbles. If the Khmer followed molemen engineering protocols, that is.

If not, well, he had prepared only one extra bottom hole assembly, a BHA, comprised of nothing more than a section of bamboo drill pipe, which doubled as the shaft casing, and a ring of coconut-husk teeth that he had mechanically embedded in the tip. Hardly a match for any quantity of stones or hardened soil. The entirety of his poor drill string was nothing more than interlocking bamboo culms. No heavyweight transition pipe, no drill stabilizers to help the shaft remain plumb, and of course no surface-resonant vibrators to free any stuck objects from the bit itself. It couldn't get any more fragile and primitive if he'd resorted to a damn pail and shovel.

He removed the chisel, mounted the BHA into the torque handle assembly, grasped the opposed handles, and leaned hard, twisting the sharp-toothed bit deeply into the soil, perhaps a third of a meter. A good start. He checked his alignment, verified he was plumb, knelt beside his pump and grasped the machine's lever with both hands. Go! He shoved and pulled, shoved and pulled, building vacuum—the damn seals had to hold—there! Open the valves—whoosh! The soil was sucked up, blown through the waste pipe and—wait . . .

He hurried down the short corridor, following the spoils tube, and peered into the lower tier of the temple. Yes. The soil had spilled onto the lower terrace courtyard. Would it be noticed? Of course it would, eventually at least. Along with all his equipment too, should anyone happen to be poking around in the middle of the night. Such was the risk. Worst case—the idea repulsed him—he would be forced to kill any overly curious monk. Word could not get out that anything out of the ordinary was going on in the shrine.

Work fast. The sooner he completed the shaft, the sooner he could get his equipment out and disperse the spoils. Meanwhile, all this cursed bamboo better do the trick. Again he grasped the pump lever, shoved and pulled, shoved and pulled, building vacuum. Valves and seals holding, good.

He disconnected the torque assembly from the BHA embedded in the soil, installed the first section of culm pipe, reattached the torque assembly, and repeated the leaning and twisting and forcing of the shaft culm into the soil. Now the pumping, now the purging, then the next culm and so on—literally vac-boring his way down— each section of bamboo interlocked into the other by way of his engineered fittings. The bamboo casing prevented the soil from collapsing in upon itself as he bored more deeply—he required a clear sight line for the shaft of zenith passage sunlight all the way down to the golden ball, which he would rest upon the sarcophagus. The ball was the HDT trigger. And the trigger had to be aligned within tolerances. The shaft had to remain clear of debris and dirt—no rocks, no roots, no leaves or twigs—nothing could interfere with the entanglement physics of the Angkor ball with that of the Giza ball. The sunlight had to be strong. It had to penetrate the shaft all the way to the ball. Or he would not get home.

Back to the pump. Shove, pull, shove, pull, establish the vacuum. Lock. Mind the shaft culm, lean and twist, open the valve—whoosh! Suck up the soil, purge the spoils. Again.

In this way, Five vac-bored the first culm section within minutes. It was a strangely quiet, almost discreet process. Except for his own huffing and puffing. A mechanically powered pump would have already finished the job but also awakened anyone nearby too. The impossibly primitive materials he was forced to work with bestowed this single advantage, and the irony was not lost upon him. Just maybe this is meant to be.

He retrieved another length of shaft culm, fitted it to the culm now completely embedded in the earth, checked for plumb, and began again. Lean, twist, vac, purge, repeat. Deeper and deeper.

Five lengths of culm into the process, Five knelt over the shaft, breathless, and wiped the perspiration from his face. Five lengths, 24.69 meters. Exactly. Shaft complete. Straight and true. Two hours had passed. One glitch with that last culm, good thing he had that extra seal and extra diaphragm for the pump. But fixing it had taken too much time. Lingering in this place only increased the risk of being discovered. Stealth, planning, preparedness. Keeping to his protocols would keep him safe. And hopefully allow him a little room for error too.

Now for the ball. He listened this way and that, craning his ears down each of the four corridors. He ought to check to see if anyone was around. No. No time. Just load the ball and get the hell out of here.

He removed his gauntlets, hefted the ball, blew upon it—dust was unavoidable, for shit's sake—examined it one last time, pointlessly. It lacked the immaculate, mirrorlike polish and the beguiling illusion of hyperdimensional depth of the Giza ball. Impossibly crude. "Maybe we're made for each other," he whispered. And now he was talking to a hunk of metal.

He nestled the ball within a sling and lowered it carefully, meter by meter. There. The rope slackened. The ball was resting, or ought to be resting, upon the sarcophagus lid. Rather, it was his coconut-husk slip-bearing that rested upon the sarcophagus, and the ball was nested, hopefully, inside the husk, lubricated with the delicate coconut oil he'd worked so diligently to extract. The ball had to be free to rotate in tandem with the Giza ball's position, mirroring it, until the entanglement was set, and then all would be ready. If there was too much resistance—if the ball didn't rotate freely—then the entanglement would fail and all would be lost. How he longed to be able to see clearly all the way down the shaft, to verify with his own eyes that the damn ball was set properly and not contaminated or out of alignment or . . .

Quit fretting! For better or for worse, he had done his best. The ball was ready for the sun, or it wasn't. He had to have faith, that's all. Faith in the ball, faith in the shaft configuration, faith in the goddamn hackneyed engineering of the entire contraption. And faith in the zenith passage. The day after tomorrow. The day after *tomorrow*! A thrill rippled through him. It had to work! It would!

Now, pack up the ball and get out. He was momentarily tempted to leave the thing in place. No. Don't be a fool. The entanglement had to take place live and in hand, in direct contact with the transponder. He and Cog had gone over that. Besides that, he had to relubricate it. He was tired. Forgetting things.

He hauled up the ball incrementally, carefully rewinding his slender cabling, which was nothing more than a fibrous string he'd laboriously braided from strands of cattle sinew. He capped the opening of the shaft with a coconut-husk plug, arranged the stone pavers back into position, slid the stone Buddha back into position over everything, and did his best to brush away his dirty footprints and obscure the evidence of disturbed soil. He collected his pump, glad to be free of the shaft culms, and set about dismantling his spoils tubing. Culm by culm, he collected the bamboo until he found himself at the edge of the shrine stairway. Dirt. Dirt everywhere, goddammit. Soil on the steps, soil in a sloppy heap beside the stairs on the floor of the courtyard. As if the planet itself had somehow vomited it up right there. What would the monks think of it? Should he get down there and try to disperse it? Yes. But first, get the pump and the spoil tubing out.

Five huffed and puffed his way through his makeshift cleanup, hauling his equipment and each awkward length of culm through the corridors, down each staircase, across the courtyards, across the bridge over the moat, and all the way to his bivouac at the edge of the trees. And so on—three exhausting trips.

Whew. He regarded his pile of culms and equipment and tried to convince himself that he would never have to touch this shit again because the golden balls would entangle, the HDT trigger would work, the sun would shine hard and strong as planned, and—the idea horrified him—he wouldn't have to endure a long wait to the next zenith passage to try again. He'd die if it came to that.

Nevertheless, though his inclination was to fling every section of culm and the damn vacuum pump itself into the woods willy-nilly, he made certain to lay the pieces carefully upon a bed of clean palm leaves and the pump itself atop the culms. Just in case. Then he camouflaged it all with a netting of grasses.

He coaxed his little campfire to life and stood breathless and sweating outside his lean-to, his exhaustion a relief of sorts—it seemed to dull his almost unbearable sense of anticipation. He had done his best. His very best. And it seemed horribly insufficient. Perilously primitive. But he'd finished it. Go ahead and find it, he thought. You Khmer. You mothmen. Somebody go ahead and discover the shaft and the spoils and let all hell break loose.

He slumped beside his fire, gnawing on a miserable hunk of dried fish. He was tired. Sore. His hands ached. That old scar across his finger blazed. He guzzled from his water skin. The work was done. The time had almost come. He pressed his palms together, stretched his aching hands, and cracked his knuckles. He stretched his arms and shoulders, almost whimpering with relief. "Please," he whispered. And was not ashamed to know that he was praying, for the first time in his life, to anyone and anything that would listen. "Please let it work. Please let it get me home."

He flopped onto his mat, sighed heavily, listened to the night sounds, glimpsed the whitish tincture of dawn over the treetops, and fell almost violently to sleep.

CHAPTER 33

HEAVEN SENT

"You know the mythology as well as anyone," said Mandrake Artoor. "And the truth within it." He watched the empress, seated across from him, sip her tea. Her body swayed gently to the clip-clop, clip-clop cadence of the carriage horses. She would not look at him, and he felt both furious and forlorn, as if his time within her graces was running out. "The hero, any hero, will inevitably be vulnerable, even if within one spot only. And that will be his undoing. Anyone can be stopped. Likewise, the moleman, Five, can be stopped—despite his proximity to the divine—insofar as we exploit his vulnerability."

The empress poured herself more tea, sipped, and glanced out the narrow window of their carriage. The crowds along the roadside had thinned dramatically within the last kilometer or so—they were entering the countryside, and only a handful of mothmen and mothwomen, mostly peasant farmers attired in their handwoven smocks and trousers, their faces perpetually smudged with earth, their expressions lean and hard, remained to acknowledge her passing. Some waved impassively; others merely stared as the procession rolled past.

Artoor examined the crimson silk of the empress's gown. The way it draped over her delicate shoulders and spilled onto the floor past her feet. His heart ached at the paleness of her smooth flesh, the slim line of her jaw and tender manner of her hair drawn up from the back of her neck in long enameled pins. He longed for her to look at him. To speak to him with anything like the care and attentiveness she once bestowed. "An impressive outpouring of support, wouldn't you agree? Two million people estimated along the Royal Road. An entire day amongst your subjects. Wasn't it glorious?" He regretted his sarcastic tone the moment he'd uttered it.

The empress ignored him completely. She tipped the last of her tea into her mouth and handed the cup indifferently to the attending servant. These fawning child slaves, he thought. Why must she insist upon interrupting his intimacy with her? How long had it been since he'd been alone with her? Long enough to humiliate him before all the other members of the Realm's court. They barely acknowledged him now.

He watched the empress remove the cap from the enameled cylinder in which she carried her clutch of yarrow stalks, watched her shake them gently and cap them again, then cradle the cylinder in her lap. It was a habit of hers that he once found endearing. Now, infuriatingly, she cared more for her worthless stalks than for him. He felt compelled to snatch the thing from her and hurl it from the window of the carriage.

"Advisor Feng's transponder," said the empress in a temperate voice. "Is it still operable?" She raised both hands to her hood, coaxed it past the long pins and flowers fastened within her hair, and allowed the fabric to fall about her shoulders. Her face was flush, as if her public exertions were still a burden.

Artoor's heart once again ached at the sight of her. Every move she made destroyed him. "Yes. It is transmitting as we speak. We can destruct it easily enough with an immolation command. But allowing the moleman to possess it makes him easy to track." He studied the empress's face for some sign that the sound of his voice meant anything to her. "And more importantly, who better than the moleman himself to engineer the installation of the Cosmic Clock Component? Feng and Chung would have been sorely challenged with the engineering complexities, you must admit."

"You will go to Angkor yourself. And seize control of the component immediately upon its activation. Then you will kill the moleman and refocus the component. On behalf of the Mothmen Realm."

"Me? Kill . . . what do you mean?"

The empress looked Artoor up and down coldly. "Or perhaps you would rather betray the details of this conversation to your superiors within the IMC? Or the TDC?"

Artoor felt his brow dampen. "You know the delicacy of my position—" He bit his tongue. Everything was conspiring to push her away from him. And now he was to become a field operative and an assassin?

"My army is besieged. Destruction at the hands of the molemen is real. Unless . . ."

"Empress, please, the tides of war are not the concern of the IMC. And it was you who gave the instruction to establish a living shield with your own plebs, a careless strategy that inevitably diminishes support for your cause. But it is not too late to change course."

"The IMC," murmured the empress. "A pool of degenerate and naive academics with an influence that reflects their feeble ideologies and elitist agendas. Of what concern could they be to any competent planetary nation? Let alone the Mothman Realm? Your allegiance does not even extend to the Scarab Cult. But your duplicitous nature was foretold to me even before our first encounter." She lifted her yarrow stalks in an ominous manner. "You are exactly the weak-minded and opportunistic bureaucrat that I required."

"Required?" Artoor bristled. "Divination, bah! The great empress of the oracle is how you always perceive yourself. From the ignorant darkness of your planet's isolation, that is. Without the supportive machinations of the Scarab Cult, Empress, I dare say your skirmish with the molemen would never have occurred. The Mothmen Realm, backward and blind, would have been lost to history in a single brush of the molemen's engineering might. And likewise your insignificant bid for mythological revitalization. The emperor himself understood this." Artoor felt himself flush. He had never raised his voice to her. That he could feel his heart pounding in his chest only made him feel more desperately weak. He wanted to strike her. To embrace her. To die on the spot.

The empress maintained her imperial attitude, merely raising her eyebrow at Artoor.

"Empress." Artoor rushed to her side, pressing himself against her upon the velvet seat cushion. "This bickering between us, it is nonsense. I . . . we . . . our union," he stammered, "all that we have shared. You and I, our vision, well, nothing has changed with the death of Advisor Feng. And Advisor Chung, without a transponder, we must consider him as good as dead. But we merely replace them both."

"Leave no trace," said the empress. "It was you who instructed our scientists. And now you would suggest leaving corpses from the present within the past. You are as hypocritical as the enemy."

"Hypocritical? Your scientists have yet to master basic hyperdimensional transport. At this rate, despite having been provided with the essence of molemen engineering, it will be years before HDT cleanup technology is within your grasp. I am merely presenting the reality. You . . . I mean we, together, must risk such hyperdimensional traces or surrender to the inevitable. Yes, the inevitable. That the Realm will fall to the molemen. And the Scarab Cult will abandon you. Unless—"

"Unless you were aware of the vulnerability yourself," hissed the empress. "All along. And you said nothing. So as to advance your own agenda. The mistletoe, was it? Within your little tale? The vulnerability that inevitably defines every strength? This moleman in Angkor—no single alien can possibly better the combined power of the Realm. But you? You have perhaps been my own mistletoe. You are the unforeseen weakness within my strength."

"Weakness? Because I love you? And you love me?"

The empress's expression only hardened, and she closed her long-nailed fingers into ungainly fists. "You will arrive at Angkor Wat within the hour," she said. "You will verify the activation of the Cosmic Clock Component. You will kill the moleman named Five and reconfigure the component to the specifications of the Realm." The empress tugged a tassel beside her window.

Artoor leapt up. "I will do nothing of the sort! I cannot! I am not one of your soldiers to be commanded! I am not your field operative!" He immediately regretted himself. "No. Empress. I am sorry.

Must you upset me like this? Please"—he shot a perturbed glance at the empress's servant—"we shall discuss everything within your quarters, with the facts before us and especially after you have rested. When we both have rested. This day has been arduous—"

The carriage came to a sudden, clattering stop, and Artoor struggled to steady himself. The doors flung open, two armored samurai burst into the carriage, and they seized Artoor by his arms.

The empress gathered her robes and stepped down from the carriage. Her servant hurried after her.

Artoor struggled. "What is this!" He feigned a haughty laugh and eyed his captors with cavalier disdain.

The pair of samurai merely flung him onto the seat of the carriage and sat menacingly beside him.

When the carriage doors slammed shut, Artoor's expression turned to fright. "Empress!" he bellowed. He struggled again, craning his neck to see out the window. "What is this? What is happening? Set me free, you brutes! Empress! Empress!"

There was a jolt and the carriage shuddered into motion. One of the samurai yanked the blinds shut. When Artoor reached out in protest, the other twisted his arm.

"How dare you!" Artoor reached for his device and a samurai swatted it away and stood over him, grasping the handle of his sword.

"Where are we going?" fumed Artoor. "Where the blazes are you taking me?"

———

THE EMPRESS STEPPED OVER THE stone causeway and entered the vaulted doorway of the Royal Outpost.

Advisor Ming-tun shuffled toward her and bowed. "Your Majesty, everything has been prepared."

The empress paused and glanced at her surroundings.

Ming-tun watched her. "All is in order. Guards are stationed. Surveillance encompasses the entire distance of the Royal Road, all the way to these fortress walls. Even beyond, as far as the edge of the plateau."

"Light a fire in my chambers. But first take me to the war room."

The empress's assistants hurried past her, bustling into the main hallway.

"This way," said Ming-tun. "Your Majesty, all eyes are upon the battlefront. The propaganda has been dispersed to all planets of the galactic quadrant. Our subjugation and peril at the hands of the molemen forces is known across the universe. Public sympathy is with us. Sanctions against Mega City One and our request to the Galactic Intelligence Administration to condemn moleman military action as a potential war crime is in the hands of the viceroy—he awaits your response to his invitation for counsel. The T.E. has urged a truce and offered to host political negotiations on behalf of you and the leadership of Mega City One. Humanitarian aid has been pledged by all neutral planets. Against such galactic-wide visibility and condemnation, the molemen cannot possibly advance further."

"Fool," said empress. "The molemen heed neither politics nor public sentiment. They understand only ruthlessness. And they underestimate the ruthlessness of the Way. As for the sympathies and cooperation of outsiders, that, too, is never to be trusted."

"Here we are, Your Majesty." Ming-tun paused and gestured. "The war room."

The empress stood within the threshold, eyed the video displays, the control consoles, the handful of technicians, and the empty chairs of the advisors. She acknowledged the commanders, scientists, and engineers with a nod and noted the empty chair designated for Mandrake Artoor. "Postpone this," said the empress. "I am tired."

"Majesty," said Ming-tun, "certainly, the rigors of your journey have been considerable, but the members of your leadership— they have all been awaiting instruction for hours. Some dignitaries of our farther regions have traveled for days. They are anxious—"

The empress dismissed him with a wave of her yarrow stalks. "They shall wait."

Ming-tun bowed hurriedly and directed them down a narrow hallway, then around a corner. The two of them entered the empress's chamber, where she deposited her yarrow stalks on a side table and made directly for the fireplace. She stood before the blaze clutching her shoulders and took no notice of the video feeds streaming across the large display mounted over the mantelpiece.

Ming-tun waited, watching her from just inside the doorway. "Your Majesty," he said quietly, "what shall our response be to the outside inquiries? To the viceroy. And the T.E.?"

The empress merely stood with her back to him, gazing into the flames.

The fire crackled, and Ming-tun wrung his hands. He took a discreet step farther into the room and spoke softly. "Your Majesty?"

"Time," she whispered. "I require time. Alone. For the *transformation*."

Ming-tun strained to hear her. "Time, Your Majesty? I beg your pardon—"

She addressed him over her shoulder. "Inform me when Mandrake Artoor has been dispatched to Ankgor. He is to be coerced. Use whatever means."

Ming-tun winced. "The adepts, Your Majesty, well, ever since the death of the emperor, you realize that their psi-powers have weakened. We no longer . . . there is no one within the Royal Court possessing the psionic prowess to—"

The empress turned to face him, clenching her closed war fan, a detail not lost upon Ming-tun. He ceased wringing his hands, gulped nervously, and backed toward the door.

"Coerce Artoor or it will mean your life. You yourself will be responsible for his transport to Angkor Wat. Now. Leave me. And inform the dignitaries that I must consult the oracle."

Ming-tun, his face drawn and pale, bowed and departed.

The empress slumped onto a divan within view of the hissing fire. She lay against a large pillow and stared with heavy-lidded eyes at the dancing flames. The Way seemed distant, more mysterious than ever, her precious yarrow stalks a burden. Nevertheless, the oracle must be cast. A memory overtook her, or perhaps it was the memory of a dream. She was a young girl standing upon a stony beach, looking out to sea. The sky was heavy and dark—leaden, like a vast weight over the wind-swept water. Frothy waves curled onto the shore, the pebbles and chipped shells of crustaceans eddied at her feet, but when she knelt to touch them, they were swept back into the sea. She felt drawn to the deep water herself.

"No!" Her father's voice stopped her. Her mother called her name and when she turned to look, the water, icy cold, flooded over her feet, and she sank to her knees into the saturated sand. The water rose to her hips, covered her bosom, then closed upon her neck. She cried out, "No!"

She awoke, aware that she had briefly dozed. The fire crackled and popped, and a yellow spark leapt from the fireplace, flashed against the metal screen, and vanished. If only she could forestall the future. If only the Way were not so merciless. If only she could remain herself.

She felt slave to her exhaustion, slave to the heaviness that had gripped her body at the death of the emperor, slave to the cruel shadow that had crept into her heart. She reached for her yarrow stalks, tipped them half out of the canister, addressed their humble coarseness. "My only friends."

She tugged upon the servant tassel. The girl returned, the same servant from the carriage, her face painted in the royal white, her teeth blackened in the ancient manner, her plain robe of raw silk a humble and self-effacing garment.

"Tianci," said the empress. "That is your name?"

Tianci, before she could remember herself, met the empress's gaze directly. Immediately frightened, she averted her eyes and bowed.

"Your name means 'heaven sent.' Did you know that?"

Tianci shook her head. "N-No, Empress," she stammered.

"Look at me," said the empress. "Heaven sent. You shall perform for me a great favor."

Tianci, head bowed, clasped her hands together and nodded.

"Fetch silk, raw cocoons, from the farm outside this stronghold. Bring the weavers to my chambers. They are to spin enough silk to enclose my bedchamber. Do you understand?"

Tianci glanced up warily.

The empress looked about hurriedly, as if searching for something. Her fan lay upon an end table. "Hold out your hand."

Tianci did as she was told.

With a snap of her wrist the empress deployed the slender blade, opened her own hand, and dragged the razorlike edge across her palm. She clenched her fist until blood dripped heavily upon the floor, then spread the fan upon a tabletop and pressed her bloody palm onto the papery membrane. She held the fan before the fire to dry it, snapped it shut, and placed it within the outstretched hand of Tianci.

"If anyone seeks to obstruct you, show them this. If anyone is foolish enough to oppose you, grasp the fan tightly and think of me. I will come to your aid." She recognized furrows of doubt in the girl's face, read her thoughts, eased them with her own, witnessed the girl's resolve. "Go, now. Hurry."

The empress shut the door, bound her hand within a handkerchief, and returned to the fire. She added wood, sat cross-legged before the hearth, closed her eyes, and prepared to ask the question that was closest to her heart—the question she had cultivated since the death of the emperor. But she paused. For the question had forced upon her its own transformation. Such was the unsettling nature of the Way. She reached with all sincerity into the depths of her wholeheartedness and only then, emboldened with conviction, cast her yarrow stalks. "Must I surrender to the transformation—is there no other way?"

CHAPTER 34

THE WILD HUNT

"An Indian man," said Professor Wilhelm, "named Vikas Kamat wrote this in the year 2002." She read aloud:

> Specially prepared rice balls called pindas were fed to the crows, cows, and the river. The rituals continued upon the tenth and eleventh day of the death. There is a belief that unfulfilled desires of the dead prevent the soul from liberating. This is indicated by the refusal of the crow to eat the pindas. I invited the crows to eat the pindas, saying that crows were my father's favorite birds. The crows came near the food but did not bite. The gathered relatives asked me if I knew of any unfulfilled wishes of father. I promised publicly that I'd continue to run his website, and that I'd preserve his cameras and letters. As if they understood, more crows approached, but none would bite. The crowd exclaimed that there must be something else, and I promised to my father that I'd take good care of Mother. As if they heard my thoughts, the crows ate away the rice balls. My non-believing heart had melted and I once again saluted my father's dedication to my mother.[69]

69 Vikas Kamat, "How I Sent My Father to Heaven: Proceedings of Hindu

The professor scanned the images of her students. Blank faces. "Unliberated souls," she said. "Questions of an afterlife aside, what prompts anyone to interpret the behavior of animals as a means of communicating with the dead?" She waited. This was a private seminar with paying students—the self-motived type, in her experience, who rarely required encouragement to participate. Sure enough, a woman from New Earth spoke up.

"I don't understand."

She was middle-aged, with unruly hair, a plain complexion, and an earthy, forward manner.

"I mean, I thought Hindus believed in reincarnation. Don't their spirits pass directly to their next body? Or next life? Or whatever?"

"Yes," said the professor. Even after all these years of teaching, no matter the class size—and at fifteen students this was a very small class—she found it impossible to remember their names. Somehow her own research and her position at the IMC always preoccupied her, to say nothing of her new duties with the TDC. She felt it was all she could do to prepare a syllabus and adhere to her scheduled lectures. But private classes were lucrative. And with money came shameless compromise. This was her last seminar, come what may, she swore. Now she'd give this woman her due.

"Madelaine," she continued—the woman squinted miserably at her—"in Hindu mythology there exists a kind of middle spiritual ground for the disembodied soul, or preta, of a person who has just died. The dead can spend as much as a year, they say, between worlds, literally neither here nor there. They acquire by way of the offerings and devotions of their children, grandchildren, and great-grandchildren—in Hinduism three generations of the deceased benefit from the attentions of their living relatives—the spiritual motivation or peace of mind to finally leave their previous life behind and become reborn."

"Because they don't want to endure the next life? Especially if they're going to be reborn in a lower form, right? I mean. Like a dog or a cat or an insect?"

Death Ritual," *Kamat's Potpourri*, kamat.com, retrieved 1.4.2017.

"Perhaps. Well, yes. You see, however devout a Hindu may consider themselves—and we see this within any contemplative tradition, any religion—the gap between the formal tenets, the dogma, as it were, and the day-to-day interpretation that incorporates superstitions and magical thinking is oftentimes impossible to discern. It all tends to combine into a very personal spiritual or contemplative stew. There is the religious ideal and the religion of the street. That of the street is inevitably bound to flesh-and-blood concerns, to love and hope and sex and dreams, as much or more than any high-minded concepts of breaking the cycle of reincarnation, for instance. And attaining release into the universal self, the Atman. Do you understand what I mean? And from a certain perspective, the Vedas, for instance, communicate an earthier, less strictly intellectual flavor to the Hindu spiritual perspective. Meanwhile, at death, the departed soul resides under the control of Yama, the Lord of Death, awaiting progress onward."

A young man from the Orion Nebula spoke up: "And the birds in this case, the crows, they are believed to be messengers of Yama?"

"Or the ancestors of the deceased," said the professor. "I know, it can be confusing. It's the case with many unfamiliar mythologies that the inculcated beliefs seem to contradict each other or exist as difficult paradoxes. Think of your own beliefs. There are probably at least several key ideas, aspects of your cultural mythologies, your belief system, your own contemplative tradition, that while you take them for granted because you grew up with them, would baffle someone otherwise unfamiliar with the perceived and often quite literal inconsistencies. Broad mythic themes may travel very well across cultural divides, but the details, the idiosyncratic, local iterations of praxis—the excepted or customary practice of a religion—we find they hinge upon terrors, taboos, and temptations as I call them."

The professor sipped her tea. More caffeine might help. The previous evening's adventures—in particular her psi-work attempting to discover the whereabouts of Mandrake Artoor—had been exhausting. Be concise. Be clear. These poor folks could get apologetics, political correctness, and overintellectualized incoherence from a book. Or from any prepackaged lecture series. They were here to engage the material, not merely listen to her talk.

Meanwhile, with Artoor, she had discovered nothing. No evidence, no hyperdimensional ghosting, no psi-traceable residue, nothing at all to indicate his whereabouts. And to have employed a psychic doppelgänger—an alternative disembodied entity? It only reinforced the idea that he was attempting to throw off suspicion. But in such a clumsy manner? The ruse would be flagged during the IMC's random identity verification scans. Unless Artoor somehow coerced a technician or an administrator to look the other way. Which, if that were the case, was going to be its own problem to rat out. Nevertheless, before initiating an official inquiry—which would catapult the entire internal security force of the IMC into another time-consuming, expensive, and perhaps humiliating public audit on behalf of everyone associated with Artoor's assignment, including her—she was going to do her best to find him herself.

She removed her spectacles, rubbed her eyes, and gulped the last of her tea. She felt the eyes of the seminar students upon her. "I apologize," she said, "if I don't seem as sharp today as I ought to be."

"That's okay, Professor Wilhelm." It was Ellen, the invincibly cheerful young woman from the Magellan Confederation. "At least it means you have a social life."

As if on cue, the professor's transponder flashed and vibrated upon the tabletop. It was the captain.

Mothman body discovered within wormhole to Angkor Wat. DNA at crime scene = Artoor's. I am alerting Z, V, N. Reply to me ASAP.

The professor glanced at the time. The class had run five minutes over as it was. "A social life of sorts, yes, Ellen, thank you. Okay, everyone. Our time is up for this week. Read the next two chapters in my book—about the relationship of the paranormal to mythology—and the journal article by Mr. Z., 'The Unforeseen Third Thing,' which I think you'll find quite engaging. If there are no questions, then? No? Okay, until next week, thank you. Signing off."

She double-checked her encryption setting and called the captain.

His voice crackled forth. "Professor. This won't take long. I've only got a minute and then I'm headed to the T.E. We need you there."

"At Eranos? That's a ten-hour flight, Captain. Are you sure I can't be of help remotely?"

"We've got to have you there. Look, there's a driver en route to your apartment—maybe sixty minutes out—you'll leave Quantico for Lugano airport via one of our quasiteleport aircraft—you'll only be in the air for two hours. Well, besides the air cruiser that will take you across Lake Maggiore and into the T.E. See you there."

"Captain, you said something about a body."

"The body in the wormhole was a mothman, an advisor to the empress. His throat was cut. The blood prevented the singularity from obliterating the evidence, otherwise our transport monitors would never have registered the coordinates. The wound was ragged, unprofessional."

"Captain, *please*."

"Sorry. We're guessing Artoor injured himself doing the job—the man's a bureaucrat, after all, not a mercenary—which explains his DNA at the scene."

She glanced at the time and rose from her chair. "You said there's a driver on the way?"

"That's right. You'll see a TDC watermark on their communications with you. The vehicle is a TDC-issue air cruiser. The chauffeur will be armed. He'll show you TDC credentials that will clear all the biosecurity fail-safes, you know the drill. I'm tracking you in real time. I've got to go."

"And I've got to change and pack a bag."

———

Metamorphoses, cavalcades, ecstasies, followed by the egress of the soul in the shape of an animal—these are different paths to a single goal. Between animals and souls, animals and the dead, animals and the beyond, there exists a profound connection.[70]

---

70 Carlo Ginzburg, *Ecstasies: Deciphering the Witches' Sabbath* (Chicago: University of Chicago Press, 2004 [1989]), 263. Republished with permission

The professor closed the file and stowed her device, content that she had located a reference and a starting point for her next lecture. And something to ponder. She looked to the lake. The way it glittered made it seem magical and eternal. And fragile, too. "Tir na nÓg," she whispered to herself. "Arcadia. Elysium." The sparkling waters, the hilly green countryside, the distant Alps—like a sheltered otherworld, heavenly and eternal.

The air cruiser shuddered and lurched sideways, and she clutched at the handhold, her stomach doing flips. So much for her reverie.

"Sorry, ma'am," said the pilot. "Some turbulence, that's all— it's not uncommon around the lake."

The Eranos campus came into view—glimpses of the clay-tiled roofs and stucco walls nestled within the trees. Moreover, a sense of nameless foreboding. It struck her as if a wild hunt, a soul reaving as the folktales sometimes referred to it, had passed over this other-wise sacred place and wounded it. The wild hunt. In the legends its appearance foretold catastrophe and abduction and war. It was led by a furious host of spectral horsemen, some clutching their own severed heads under their arms, others hauling abducted women by their tresses, all the riders fraught and sinister, borne along by a dark and dreadful power. People would claim to hear it coming and cower within their houses, fearing death for whoever witnessed it. That, or they feared they themselves would be snatched away into the legion of the cursed dead.[71]

The sun slipped behind a bank of gray-bottomed clouds, and an ominous image forced itself upon her. Of a painting she'd seen once. Nineteenth century, perhaps. *Åsgårdsreien.* Yes, *The Wild Hunt*

---

of University of Chicago Press; permission conveyed through Copyright Clearance Center, Inc.

71   The concept of the wild hunt was first documented by the German folklorist Jacob Grimm in his 1835 multivolume book *Deutsche Mythologie*. Grimm commented that "it marches as an army, it portends the outbreak of war." (vol. III, 937).

of Odin.[72] She tapped at her device, keen to search for the image and the artist, but the pilot spoke up.

"Secure your harness, please, ma'am."

She fumbled with the buckles and straps.

"Just sit back, ma'am, place your arms at your sides, feet flat on the floor, relax, and when you're ready, press the yellow button that says *autobuckle.*"

"I'm sorry, Nick"—she regarded his face in the rearview—"that was all in the safety video, wasn't it?" She did as she was told, and the harness made its connections.

Instead of beginning its descent, however, the cruiser suddenly gained altitude, banked, and made directly for the lake.

"We're not going around?"

"No, ma'am. Zero road access to Eranos since the attack. You're right, though—no flyovers of the lake are typically allowed. At least as long as I've been flying. But Captain Chase obtained clearance for us."

The professor studied the young man's face. And he was indeed young, in his middle teens, perhaps. Nick II, surviving son of Nick and Rosa de Cosmos, the chauffer and house cook, for Eranos before—she did her best to force the image from her mind.

"It's impressive that you're a pilot already, Nick."

"I took my test on my seventeenth birthday. They told me I was the youngest in Switzerland. The youngest in most of Italy and Austria too. But I don't care about that, I just wanted to fly."

They soared upward, far above the trees yet below the low clouds. They cleared the shoreline and sped across the expanse of darkened water. The bright, effervescent Mediterranean climate she expected had shuttered itself away. Everything about Eranos evoked paradox. Its timeless, half-lidded seclusion beneath the towering mountains, its aspect of antiquity nurtured by mystery and myth. All of it clashing against a clear-eyed contemporariness, a welcoming of advancement and cutting-edge scientific relevance. If Olga Fröbe-Kapteyn, the

---

72   By Peter Nicolai Arbo, 1872.

founder of Eranos, could see it today, she most certainly would still recognize her creation.

The cruiser dipped toward the water, enhancing the professor's sense of thrilling speed. People waved to them from the decks of their boats, and before she knew it, they'd already traversed the heart of the lake and were barreling toward the opposite shore, which, from what she could ascertain, amounted to nothing but a dense forest reaching down to the water's edge.

Illuminated letters flashed red in Nick's rearview: *CLOAKED*.

"Prepare for landing, ma'am—stow your belongings under your seat, you know the drill."

The lake was suddenly behind them, and they drifted low over the treetops. The cruiser paused over a tiny landing pad nestled within a small clearing. The Casa Eranos's tiled roof and pale stucco facade was visible in the near distance. Nick piloted them down, the treescape engulfed them, and they came to rest with a mild jolt.

The engine wound down but remained running, and Captain Chase, ducking and shielding his face against the cruiser's blustering exhaust, stepped from the footpath at the edge of the clearing. When Nick II gestured to him from behind the windscreen, he strode across the well-groomed lawn, unlatched the cruiser door, acknowledged the professor with a curt nod, and gestured for her bag. Then he extended his arm to her and helped her onto the tarmac.

The professor held her hair away from her eyes and smoothed a wayward lock behind her ear. She tucked her cane beneath her arm, closed her collar against the gusty assault of the exhaust, and held closely to the captain. They scurried from the landing pad arm in arm, the din of the cruiser finally diminishing into the distance.

"You said quasiteleportation cruiser, Captain, not air cruiser followed by private jet, ground car, another air cruiser and"—she glanced at the time—"it's been ten hours of travel."

"I'm sorry, Professor," said the captain. "A cyberattack alert. We couldn't risk you teleporting. That, and with the T.E. relocation complete only as of yesterday, your security requirements, and the code yellow on any HDT, I thought it best to keep it analog. Thank you for putting up with everything. Are you hungry? We've got you in Olga's suite, the best room in the place. And you've got all night to rest before the confab."

The professor stopped short, grimacing.

"What is it?" said the captain.

The professor shook her head dismissively.

"Your leg, my God, I'm an idiot!" He dug into his shirt pocket for his device and tapped at it with his thumb. "We've got hover chairs, for Christ's sake, I'll get one out here right away—"

"Never mind, Captain. It's no trouble. It's just the sitting, that's all. This walking will help."

"It's a couple of hundred meters, I'd say, along this path here and then we come out of the trees and we're at the casa. Is that okay, are you sure?"

She nodded.

"We'll take our time," said the captain.

They emerged from the trees, and the professor couldn't help focusing upon the woebegone hill and the venerable tree, fated now with the horror of inhuman cruelty and tragic symbolism. She paused, regarding it. "People say the autumn is melancholy. But for me it's the late summer, at least in these climes. August. When the light seems different. And the spiders begin spinning their webs. A change comes." She shivered, and the captain grasped her elbow.

"Steady, now, Professor."

"Those poor, innocent people," murmured the professor. "And their son. What he has to live with."

"This way," said the captain, and urged her onwards, leading her carefully toward the broad double doors of the casa. "They've received many prayers. From all over the world. Off-planet, too. We couldn't try to hide or suppress news of what happened even if we wanted to. Better to allow the truth to do its work. And if any place can transform a symbol of death into life again, perhaps it's Eranos."

A pair of armed guards appeared as if from nowhere, one stepping forward briskly to open the door for them, the other falling in behind them and facing the way they'd come, gripping his plasma rifle, scanning side to side across the path and into the trees.

They stepped across the threshold into the large, marble-floored vestibule. The heavy door shut behind them, and the professor's weariness threatened to overtake her. She leaned heavily upon the captain.

"Welcome, Captain, sir," said Bull. The frogman saluted, afloat within his tank, distorted a bit by the thickness of the armored plexiglass, and peered at them with his bulbous eyes from the viewing portal. "And you too, Professor. Ma'am, I bet you're tired"—he winked discreetly at the captain. "A hover chair is on its way, stand by."

Immediately a nimble young cadet rolled out a chair and returned to his post, saluting the captain.

"Thank you," murmured the professor. "Bull, is it? Yes, thank you. I don't like these things, mind you. But I suppose I'm in no position to look a gift horse in the mouth."

CHAPTER 35

QUANTUM ENTANGLEMENT

APRIL 25TH, 1296. THE WAXING gibbous moon, near full and almost directly overhead, gleamed fiercely in the cloudless night, and the towers of the quincunx seemed gilt in silver, not gold. Five paused to collect himself, trying to ignore his moon shadow. Traversing the causeway always made him feel exposed and vulnerable, but the intense lunar light made it worse. If not for the leeches and keeping his equipment dry, he'd frankly prefer to swim across.

But he was talking nonsense. Nobody was watching him. The only significant risk was his being discovered within the temple itself. Meanwhile, this clear sky? High atmospheric pressure was a gift. Belying the meteorological percentages. If it held through the zenith passage tomorrow, then Cog would not be forced to risk invoking the cloud-busting fail-safe. What a predicament! All the work and all the planning—to nevertheless be beholden to this planet's weather!

Calm down. One thing at a time. Tread softly. Watch. Listen. No Khmer to be seen. As usual. It had been the same with his practice runs. The temple village itself was mostly confined to the much larger western acreage. And while it never completely slept—always, there was a monk wandering about, or someone trying to pacify a wailing infant, or the slaves trundling about with their reeking nightsoil pots—this eastern portion of the grounds and the entrance itself seemed rarely visited by anyone. And especially this time of night. Who would have reason to negotiate the temple's steep staircases and the narrow, pitch-dark corridors leading to the shrine?

Mostly, everything within the temple grounds happened within daylight hours and according to a loose schedule. Despite the lack of sun dials or water clocks—timepieces of any kind—the Khmer seemed to measure time by the position of the sun and moon and stars and when it was overcast, which was often enough, by a strange intuition.

What was their interpretation of this celestial temple city? Was it not unbound from time and place within their myths? A local artifact, yes, as real as the humble stone from which it was rendered, but also, as with any mythic symbol, much more than that. It was an expression of the ultimate reality—realer than real as only a myth can be. Hence, supernatural. Or hypernatural. Golden. Untarnished. Sacred. Sustaining.

He couldn't help thinking how they, the molemen, had attempted to win over the Khmer like they had the Egyptians. *You are chosen,* they'd had told the humans. *Selected and set apart from other races by the gods themselves and bestowed with the divine right to rule this world. As emissaries of the gods, we have come to bestow knowledge and power upon you. You, the Khmer and your lands—the very location of this temple-mausoleum—are at the center of everything. Your Vishnu-ite myth is real and true and represents how things really are. Beyond the ever-changing, illusory manifestations and perceived duality of the phenomenal world—samsara in the Hindu tradition. Your myth is true. The temple will become the celestial city here upon Earth. So, build it. All of it. Including the barays and aqueducts to increase the yield of the land. Harvest the bounty, both terrestrial and divine. Grow ever stronger, conquer ever further.*

Thus this enormous temple had been built, at something resembling moleman scale. The hydraulic engineering had indeed bestowed the yields. The Khmer perceived themselves as chosen and blessed.

The CCP, then, was poised to advance into the next stage, that of fully funded CCC operation. But despite all the Angkor Cell's successes, the miserable Khmer, in their primitive and duplicitous way, nevertheless held fast to their superstitious ways and their mysticisms and magics. They cherished their little wars too, over borders and petty differences of ideology. And when the battles proved costly and the molemen refused to intercede, it was as if the spell were broken and no amount of cajoling and pretense on behalf of the Angkor Cell's engineers could restore Khmer faith in moleman superiority. The seeds of doubt had been planted, and the roots of betrayal, like the roots of the ruinous strangler fig and silk cotton trees that choked the Angkor forests, penetrated quickly and deeply. The Khmer no longer trusted molemen, no longer willingly ceded authority to them, and by then there was no money within the project budget to even begin to counter the structural rot. No amount of work hours or bribery or material coercion would have reconvinced the Khmer. That was the argument, at least. That was the story. And the molemen couldn't kill them either; at least not all of them. Not without far too great and far too unpredictable an influence upon the future—an influence that risked derailing moleman ambitions.

Meanwhile, the Giza Cell had demonstrated the efficacy, efficiency, and technical viability of properly covert operations. And the timing was fortuitous—the peak of the Egyptian empire's power, hence the peak of its complexity and ultimate vulnerability, was a thousand years hence from the reign of the pliable, insular, unworldly Khufu. Even Snefru, the previous pharaoh, may have been, in his worldly ambitious way, as difficult to manage as Suryavarman II turned out to be. But by then, the lesson to be learned regarding the confounding nature of human nature was beside the point. The Giza project had won. And the Angkor project had lost.

Five padded along, pondering it all, refreshing the history, what he knew of it, as if somehow rehearsing or refreshing who he himself was. Or whom he had become. For the ideology still moved him. The molemen as masters of the universe, that is. It still stirred his heart. It was just that it cost too much. It was an aspiration that had outstripped its altruistic legitimacy. To transform the universe into a better place for all inevitably, it seemed, required the appropriation of the life and freedoms of too many. Must the universe indeed remain a play of opposites? It struck him that perhaps everything and everyone was entangled in this way; that perhaps the fates of all things were bound to each other akin to the precepts of quantum entanglement that he and Cog were seeking to employ to get him home.[73]

What did he seek to go home to? What was left to him as a mole-man but his failure and exile and shame? Who and what would he be, who and what *could* he be upon Mega City One? Cog himself said the war had changed things irrevocably, that for all the horror and destruction and ceaseless anxiety it caused, it had also cleared the air. Cleared the present and the future of many of the nagging controversies and poisonous agendas of the past. The war had rendered so many things into irrelevant trifles. So there was a crack in the door. An opening. To begin again. And that's all he needed.

He suddenly longed for his book more than ever. To be able to open it anywhere, just as he used to, and read what it had to say. As if it were guiding him. Just to have it with him would be a comfort.

The entrance was not pitch dark, and neither were the galleries—their old wooden ceilings had long since rotted away, and the intensity of the moon's illumination shone from overhead. He stepped across the stone threshold, scanned left, right, and straight ahead, and listened as hard as he could.

The staircase to the second tier, a mere twenty-five or so meters ahead, beckoned. But no. Not yet. He had promised himself to see something of the gallery. He had only this last opportunity. He'd never be here again, after all.

---

73 Within the context of quantum entanglement, two such entangled particles can appear to influence one another instantaneously, over any distance. Quantum entanglement occurs when two or more particles interact in a way that causes their fates to become linked. In other words, it becomes impossible to consider (or mathematically describe) each particle's condition independent of the other. Moreover, two entangled particles often demonstrate opposite values in comparison to each other. E.g., if one is spinning "up," the other must be spinning "down." Likewise, making a measurement "here" affects the other particle "over there" instantaneously.

He turned to enter the southern wing, the open palisade of stone pillars to his left, the bas reliefs to his right. He touched the wall lightly with his fingertips as if to guide him and took a few steps farther in, peering at the first set of images.

Here was the scene appreciated even by the engineers at home for its detail and technical accomplishment. Two meters high and forty-nine meters long, the precision with which the stone was finished may have been influenced by the improvement in the Khmer artisans' iron tools (as suggested by the Angkor Cell engineers), but the arresting results spoke for themselves. Five recalled the buzz of public interest the subject of the carving, the story of the churning of the milky ocean, inspired. For a time, at least, the people of Mega City One found an alien mythology a fashionable pastime. As opposed to their general indifference toward the Egyptian imagery. The pyramids themselves, of course, were highly regarded as a charming example of primitive architectural engineering, but the carvings and paintings? No. It was something about the combination of density, punctiliousness, sweeping grace, and perhaps the ambitious dynamic of the imagined struggle that struck a chord.

In the carving, the devas were pitted against the asuras—gods versus demons, or anti-gods—each host hauling upon one end of the mighty naga named Vasuki, the serpent king. The mythical snake was wound around Mount Mandara—a spur of Mount Meru—which was submerged within the sea of milk. And akin to a cosmic butter churn, the devas and asuras hauled upon the naga, back and forth, back and forth, supported above by Vishnu himself in his many armed aspect and below in his guise of a giant turtle. The two groups sought to manifest the elixir of immortality, and the task demanded that they churn for a thousand years. They succeeded and promptly fought over possession of the treasure.

Five sauntered past image upon graceful image. He examined the refined renderings end to end and then found himself transfixed by the central scene. The sea of milk was illustrated below, the fish and crocodiles torn into bits by the force of the churning. In graceful flight atop everything were the beautiful apsaras.

Suryavarman II, thought Five. That ambitious, perceptive, and cunning little human had apparently welcomed the Angkor Cell engineers as avatars of Vishnu, Shiva, and Brahma. And in the beginning it had been enough to teach the king and his court to wield authority over the waters and transform their agriculture. Then the working of the stone. To motivate the Khmer to build the massive temple according to the geological and space-time requirements demanded an appeal to something greater than even their lust for comfort, material goods, and military might. As within Egypt, the cell had to invoke their mythology and provide the Khmer the means to regard themselves as chosen. By the divinities.

It was said the Khmer carvers insisted upon rendering images of the molemen engineers within both sides of the narrative, as both gods and demons, and that the cell allowed it, encouraged it, so long as the images were not literalized. Something about how introducing accurate imagery of molemen into the past—imagery that would survive for millennia—would increase the risk of space-time anomalies geometrically. The science was still inconclusive, of course, but it was foolish then as now to ignore the predictive power of the calculations.

Otherwise, as in Egypt, whatever it was that damn well motivated the humans to get the work finished was worth it. And the Khmer worked day and night upon this massive undertaking of mythic lore, the largest religious monument upon the Earth. It hardly compared to even the most insignificant edifice upon Mega City One, of course, but it nevertheless expressed the potential for serviceable Cosmic Clock engineering. Angkor Wat could have made a fine CCC. On top of that, there was plenty of gold here.

Five stood upon his tip toes, straining to see. There, Vishnu with a conch in one of his hands. But above it—he zoomed in and maximized the resolution of his goggles—yes, there. The defaced, now barely discernable carvings, mere clumsy outlines of the Angkor Cell Trinity—the three engineers of the Angkor Cell who deployed here in the early twelfth century. Here the Khmer intended to immortalize them, in their way, even attempting to integrate the molemen into the mythology. This little image of a god, some deity even more ancient than Vishnu in the Hindu pantheon. What was his name? Indra! Little Indra, gazing down from his heavenly flight, reaching toward the would-be moleman Trimurti. Even the gesture of Vishnu's sword helped converge the viewer's eyes upon the spot within the frieze.

What an irony. Perhaps the Khmer king was embittered after the Angkor Cell engineers abandoned him. The only portion of this gallery's famous technical finery and aesthetic accomplishment that was intentionally hacked away was this modest tribute to the moleman race.

The mothman transponder vibrated and flashed. That would be Cog trying to contact him. And it meant he had tarried in the gallery and was now behind schedule.

Me and my myths. Such a fool!

He hurried back to the eastern entrance, scanning and listening. When he'd attained the middle pavilion, he paused, stepped gingerly down the staircase, and peered into the expansive, moonlit lower courtyard. A breeze refreshed his damp face and rustled the dry leaves gathered along the stony walls. Assured that all was clear, he scrambled diagonally across the sandstone flooring toward the second-tier staircase, bounded up the steps, paused, looking and listening, and hurried ahead the ten or so meters to the final narrow stair. He ambled up cautiously, entered the quincunx proper, waited, watched, listened, and dashed the last twenty meters to the core of the central shrine.

He hunched within a corner of the darkened space and typed: *Within quincunx.*

Cog responded immediately: *Status?*

Go.

He stowed his transponder and scrambled across the sand-stone pavers. He strained to shift the Buddha sculpture, dislodged his pavers, and brushed away the thin covering of soil that obscured his coconut-husk cap. He snatched it free and aimed his headlamp down the shaft. The shaft was clear!

He unveiled the golden ball, shed the palm leaves he'd used to protect it from soil, and likewise shed his gauntlets. He cradled the ball within the sling, applied a fresh dab of coconut oil, and lowered the ball carefully and quickly, down, down, until he felt the cable slacken. Thank the stars he'd had enough sense to accomplish the preparatory cleaning when he'd done his dry run. Now he could save time by focusing on the entanglement.

He messaged Cog. *Green. Green. Green.*

Cog responded with the entanglement keycode—a series of symbols and numerals and glyphs that, if all had gone according to plan, Cog would have translated and successfully packaged within a transmittable binary quantum. But binary was to proper HDT communication as a grass hut was to a Mega City One skyscraper. The probability of a lossy, otherwise low-resolution transmission, hence an entanglement failure, was absurdly high. But there was nothing for it except to try.

Five clutched his transponder, centered the diaphragm aperture over the center of the shaft, and attempted the piezoelectric drive sequence. Nothing. Dammit! Zero ultrasound response. Five felt his face flush and the perspiration dampen his brow.

Failure. Awaiting resend.

Breathe. Stay calm. They had three attempts. He separated the transponder from the ball's sight line, the sequence parameters rebooted, and he recentered the diaphragm aperture.

Cog's response: *Resending.*

C'mon, c'mon! It had to work. It *had* to. He envisioned the Giza ball in its lightless, subterranean pit, tried to imagine it some six hundred Earth years in the future. Cog had verified its viability or they wouldn't be doing this—it wouldn't be possible. The ball was there, beneath the Great Pyramid, just as he left it. And the entanglement could happen. The potential for mirroring was within acceptable probabilities. He reoriented the transponder against the ball and initiated. Dammit to hell, c'mon!

Cog's response made his heart leap—the first entanglement herald!—and he almost dropped the transponder down the shaft. For shit's sake, idiot, calm down! He clenched his fist to stop his hand from shaking, took a breath, and replied to Cog: *Herald acknowledged. Proceed.*

Two to go. He waited. If the hyperdimensional entanglement was successful, the golden balls here and there would rotate twice more, in opposite directions to each other, in quick succession.

Cog: *Herald 2 is locked.*

Copy. Another herald! Only one more. Five held the transponder in place.

Herald 3 is locked. ENTANGLEMENT COMPLETE.

Five toggled the transponder and separated it from the ball. It was all he could do to type a reply and not fumble the transponder again. *Copy. Exiting.*

Cog's response couldn't have been more apt: *Almost home.*

Five hauled up the ball, wrapped it carefully in the palm leaf, rewound his sling, and returned the package to his makeshift container—a short section of culm that secured the ball snugly. He capped the shaft, donned his gauntlets, replaced the pavers, repositioned the Buddha, hefted his pack and made for the exit.

CHAPTER 36

TARANTULA BROTH

Sanctus bells. Distant, but unmistakable. The insistent brassy clangor of the priest's clutch of polished bells from mass, when he was young.

"Welcome back, Mr. Z."

Artoor's face came into focus painfully. No, he thought. Not this.

"You tried to take a little nap there for a moment, didn't you?" Artoor snatched at Mr. Z.'s jaw with one hand and patted Mr. Z.'s cheek with the other. "Now wake up, old man. We can't allow you to miss the show." Artoor thrust Mr. Z.s head aside and brought his attention to the rope knotted tightly at Mr. Z.'s wrists. He jerked at it.

Mr. Z. couldn't help wincing.

Artoor smirked. "Painful? So sorry." He likewise yanked at the lashing around Mr. Z.'s ankles. "But it's your own fault, isn't it?" Artoor gulped heartily at his canteen and waved it front of Mr. Z.'s face. "Hot here, I'd say. Even in the evenings. I bet you could use a drink, couldn't you?"

Mr. Z. turned his face away.

"C'mon now, Mr. Z., what in heaven were you mumbling about? Something about bells? You're hearing things, now? That's not good. It means you're fading on me, doesn't it?" Artoor yanked Mr. Z.'s head back by the hair and slopped water into his gaping mouth.

Mr. Z. choked and coughed and finally gasped when Artoor backed away.

"There, there, now, Mr. Z., slow down! Take it easy! Show a little decorum! Would you like some more? Here!"

Mr. Z. spit violently into Artoor's face.

Artoor flinched, swiped his sleeve across his face, and struck Mr. Z. hard across the mouth with the back of his hand. "Swine! This is all so tedious. So pathetically formulaic and predictable. This cat and mouse nonsense." He sighed fitfully. "This stoic resolve of yours is getting us nowhere. You can consider it heroic all you want, of course. But look here, Mr. Z. Your friends won't know that you've betrayed them. Meanwhile, all this can come to a quick and painless end, I promise you. Well, perhaps not painless. But it's your choice, how this ends. Now, where is she? Where is Miss Velure? And that other worthless fop of a protégé of yours, what's his name? Herman Neutic? And that pesky moleman? Ha!" His lurid laugh seemed to pain him. "Aliens can be such pests, can't they?" He glowered at Mr. Z. as if to force the answer from him by the force of his will. "Where is the golden ball? Does Miss Velure have it? Mister Neutic? The moleman, Five? Who?" He pressed the flat of his dagger against Mr. Z.'s bare stomach. "I could gut you this instant. Or I could make it less unsightly and a good deal swifter and less painful." He jabbed the point of his knife at Mr. Z.'s ribs. "Straight to the heart. What do you say?"

"Ask the empress," said Mr. Z. He struggled to speak past his swollen mouth. "Or don't you take your orders from her anymore? Perhaps the Scarab Cult, instead? Either way, you're on your own, now. Just like Laron. And look what happened to him."

Artoor fumed and stamped his foot. "Raise him," he growled, and gestured at the two scrawny Khmer men clinging to the rope.

The older of the two was missing fingers from each hand, and his face showed the gnarled deformities of leprosy. The younger fellow's hands and arms displayed the telltale pale patches of the disease. The older shook his head and stepped away from the rope. The younger man eyed Artoor warily but did likewise.

"I said *raise him!*"

Spittle streamed from Artoor's mouth and he swiped at it with the back of his wrist, his fingers quivering and his eyes wild with rage, or fear or desperation, perhaps all of it. Another man, thought Mr. Z., akin to Kashi and Laron, unhinged by—whom? Or what? The mothmen? The empress? Somebody within the damned Scarab Cult? Some collapse of their own warped zealotry or ambition? It couldn't be coincidence. Was it psi, or wild fear? Mr. Z. watched Artoor gesture wildly at the two Khmer.

"Do you not understand what up is?" He pressed his fingers against his autotranslator collar and repeated himself. "Up!" he said, and the incongruous, electronic squawk of the device startled the men. "Or you will not be paid!"

The men's faces twisted with anxiety. Perhaps it was the sound of their own language by way of an incomprehensibly strange device, or perhaps the promise of payment was too tempting, or both, but they grasped miserably at the rope and strained to haul Mr. Z. up.

Artoor leered at Mr. Z.'s futile struggles. He watched the knotted ropes stretch themselves taut against the weight of the stone at Mr. Z.'s feet. "Pull, you miserable lepers!"

Mr. Z., naked to the waist, shut his eyes and stifled a gasp.

"Down!" said Artoor.

The Khmer let the rope out, and Mr. Z. crumpled to the ground.

Artoor stood over Mr. Z., scowling, shining his lamplight into Mr. Z.'s face. He spat at him. "Now. There you are, old man. I'm in charge."

Mr. Z. lay prone. To die here? And at the hand of this despicable lout? He could see portions of the enormous moon gleaming through the openings in the treetops. He could hear the jungle forest wildlife—the yowl of monkeys, the harsh rasp of the crickets, the eerie symphony of the frogs and toads. None of it mattered. Not even the pain. To die, yes. He shut his eyes. If he could only will it to happen.

"What to do?" sneered Artoor. "That's what I would be asking myself in your position. Should I hang on and drag this out? Or should I just spill the beans and give the man what he wants and be done with it? And then I can die like a man not a dog. Whatever that means. Like a dog. Whimpering, I suppose. And cowering. Like you. I'm only going to ask you one more time."

Artoor's lamp had gone out and he bent down to fuss with it, toggling the switch, twisting the lens, swatting at it senselessly.

Both Khmer sensed an opportunity, and they ran, bolting into the shadow of the foliage. Mr. Z. strained to hear them crashing through the brush.

"Stop!" shouted Artoor. He spun wildly, fumbled for his plasma pistol, and fired blindly into the forest.

Blam! Blam! Blam!

Silence. Except for the sounds of the forest.

Artoor lurched toward the rope and hauled upon it himself. The effort strangled his voice. *"Tell me, goddammit!"*

Mr. Z. cried out and was hauled to his knees. But he fought back furiously, sensing Artoor's weakness, and managed to yank the rope from Artoor's grasp.

"You son of a bitch!" Artoor scrambled after the rope, dug his heels in, and put all his weight into the task. "You'll beg me to shoot you. You'll beg me, you son of a bitch! You and the TDC. Sticking your nose where it doesn't belong! Screwing with things you know nothing about!" But he was breathless, and the strain was too much. He released the rope and pounced upon Mr. Z.

They struggled briefly. Artoor, breathless, finally knelt upon Mr. Z.'s chest and pinned his arms. He brandished his blade.

"Now," said Artoor. "It will take you a long time to die, I'll make sure of it. Unless you tell me. Velure. Neutic. The moleman. The golden ball. I'll count to five." He shifted his weight clumsily against Mr. Z.'s struggling. "Tell me and I'll shoot you. That will be my gift to you. How about that? Refuse? And I'll gut you like a fish. It will be medieval. The mess. One. Two . . ."

Mr. Z., exhausted, relented, but not to Artoor. Despairing, he shut his eyes. Peace will come, he told himself. Don't speak. Don't cry out. Peace will come.

"Feel that?" said Artoor. He pressed the blade against the vulnerable flesh of Mr. Z.'s belly. He knelt harder upon Mr. Z.'s chest as if to gain leverage. "Three!"

Mr. Z. felt the blade and feared it. He feared the pain and the blood and the—no. He opened his eyes to the sky. Sought the blinding moon. But could only see the stars. Safe there. Safe. Memories came to him—glorious, unbound, whole. His life passed before him. Everyone dear to him arrived. His mother, young again, as when he was a boy, smiled sweetly at him. His father, whom he knew only from photographs, was there. He took his father's hand.

Mr. Z. could not then hear Artoor's rantings. He could not see the heavy, rough blade glinting, nor feel its ragged pressure against his belly. "Bells," he whispered to himself. For he heard them again. Sanctus bells, ringing clear and hard and beautiful.

Artoor raged. He screamed into Mr. Z's face. "You are wrong! You have wronged the chaos and the cult and you have brought this upon yourself! Upon us all!" He gathered himself for the knife thrust.

"Aiiee!"

Is it me? Am I screaming? Mr. Z. thrust open his eyes and the scene assailed him: Artoor, contorted, his feet off the ground, arms flailing, his face a rictus of agony. A sickening, strangled shriek and the horrible snapping of bone. The eyes staring. The body convulsing once, twice, and dropping in a heap.

Impossible. The unmistakable goggled eyes. The huge, gauntleted hands. The broad, roundish ears and the incongruous shock of hair between them. The short, blocky stature. Moleman. Five? Was that Five?

———

THE LOW FIRE FLICKERED AND smoked. A queer, enlivened silence encompassed the jungle, as if a storm had passed. The golden shoulder of the moon was low and enormous, lording itself behind the silhouetted treetops and the florid spires and parapets of the great temple.

Five swiped his gloves together in disgust and stepped over the body of Artoor to where Mr. Z. lay fallen. He knelt beside the Earthling. What could be done? He muted his autotranslator and spoke directly, inasmuch as he could mimic the sounds of human speech. "Mr. Z."

Unresponsive. He doffed his gauntlet and pressed his fingertips against the man's ribcage. Heartbeat. He leaned close and listened, directing his ears at the body. A modicum of respiration. And blood flow, he could hear it. Significant body temperature, too. He set about loosening the knots binding Mr. Z.'s hands, being careful of the wrists, caked as they were with blood and dirt, and the flesh torn. He untied the ankles and regarded the rope lashed to the stone. A cruelty he could not fathom. Yet, what of it? Who were these humans to him?

Mr. Z. The image of their strange parting in the Egyptian desert struck him. They had stood with the sands between them, exchanging he didn't know what—some intuitive form of communication? There had been Miss Vixy, the female, of course. The image of her still intrigued him. And the Bedouin. Hesso. Was that his name? And Hesso's savage battle with the mothman assassin. Together, he and Mr. Z. had buried the bodies. After that? He recalled resolving himself to . . . he had difficulty describing it even to himself. Oh, the longing he had endured since then!

By the gods, what had happened that he should reencounter this human, of all humans? Here and now? Was he doomed to remain entangled with this pitiful species? As some kind of penance? Or yet another test of his otherwise fraught allegiances?

He started, suddenly gripped by dread. What was that? Something in the trees? Hmm, nothing at all. Yet an unseemly silence pervaded, as if the life of the jungle itself had been snuffed out. Then a low rumble, like a deep tremor within the earth beneath his feet. And black fear. No. Not again. No, it couldn't be. Please!

His limbs seemed leaden, as if he were within the clutches of a nightmare. He couldn't see it. He couldn't see anything except the dimming of his lantern light. But he knew the thing was there. And somehow the jungle was closing in as if the twisted boughs and roots themselves were keen to engulf him. He was paralyzed. And it was there. Beside him. The dark shape. A beast. He opened his mouth to scream and could not.

<hr>

FIVE BLINKED AND FELT THE warm humidity of the jungle upon his face. A dispassionate breeze coaxed him back to himself. The trees were as they had been. He listened to the mild chirping of the crickets and the droning rasp of the katydids. A monkey shouted, and the birds trilled and cackled.

But what of the terror? He had experienced it, hadn't he? Again? The same as in the desert, in Egypt? That was silly. Yet he felt as if his senses were heightened, as if he had survived a trial.

He glanced round. There is something different. Something missing. The corpse. By the gods, the corpse was vanished! Tiger? No, no tracks, no disturbances, no indication of anything dragged away. No sign of anything. It was gone, that's all. What happened?

The human stirred. Five slung off his pack and lay Mr. Z.'s head upon it. He snatched at his waterskin and dribbled liquid upon Mr. Z.'s lips. He dabbed a bit onto the man's forehead and chest.

Mr. Z. coughed, instinctively raised his hand against the attentions, and thrust open his eyes as if he had arisen from the dead. "Hell and blood," he mumbled. He looked askance at the moleman, struggling to focus. He tried in vain to raise himself. He swallowed hard and looked the moleman squarely in the face. "Is it you? My God. Five?"

Five nodded. "You are a pitiful sight, Mr. Z. Compared to the last time I saw you."

Mr. Z. grimaced. "Help me sit."

Five grasped Mr. Z.'s arm, steadying him. "I can boil dried fish." He rose. "I shall cook a broth." He shuffled around the camp, such as it was, until he'd gathered an armful of sticks and dry leaves, then went about establishing a proper campfire.

Mr. Z. watched Five work, rubbing at his arms and legs and despairing at the bloody, weeping, abraded condition of his wrists and ankles. His wounds felt as if they were on fire. His joints throbbed as if he'd been run over. He'd been hanging by his wrists, that was it. He remembered the large stone, roped to his ankles, and shuddered. Artoor, the bastard. The fucking son of a bitch.

Five snapped the wood into small pieces, stripped the bark, and architected a little pyramid of kindling over a clutch of the moss he preferred for tinder. He produced his tiny bow drill, handhold, and fireboard and worked the tools feverishly, blowing upon the smoldering combustibles until he conjured an energetic blaze.

He dug through his pack for his clay cooking pot, filled it with water from his canteen, and set it close against the crackling fire. He darted about in search of more wood and quickly accumulated an armful of fallen branches. He snapped them across his knee into stout faggots. He coaxed the flames into a rousing fire, all the while taking care to adjust the position of his water pot.

Mr. Z. must have dozed, for when he opened his eyes, Five was kneeling beside him cradling a steaming crock, the heady aroma of herbs and fish an almost overwhelming respite. He was ravenous.

Five tipped the steaming broth into a cup and offered it. Mr. Z. sat up, blew upon the broth to cool it, sipped tentatively, then gulped at it until he slurped at the dregs.

Only then did it occur to Mr. Z. "Where is Artoor?"

"Artoor?"

"The human. The body."

"Dead," said Five. He wiped out the clay cup, returned it to his pack, and peered into the dimness beyond the firelight, his ears forward, as if listening.

"Right," said Mr. Z., frowning at the memory. "But where is he? Where is the body?" He sat hugging his aching knees close to his chest. The penetrating warmth of the fire and the broth in his belly were intoxicating, and drowsiness overtook him.

"I do not know," said Five. But he noticed that Mr. Z. was not listening. Hmm. Sleep would assuage the physical fatigue. And if humans were anything like molemen, it would assuage the psychological trauma. He desperately wanted to be on his way. He had so much to do. Yet he could hardly leave the man here alone to fend for himself. What had happened to him?

He watched Mr. Z. try to sleep sitting up. The human's head lolled. Five dug a lightweight bamboo mat, tightly rolled, and two deer pelts, softly tanned, from his pack—they were items he used for his own bedding.

"Lie here." He rolled a pelt and placed it beneath Mr. Z.'s head. "Sleep. I will tend the fire."

Mr. Z. awoke, this time with a start. He sat up fitfully, baffled by the animal pelt around his shoulders. The campfire was a sturdy blaze. "Where am I?"

Five sat hunched before the fire. "You have slept for three hours. The waterskin is beside you."

Mr. Z. drank, dribbled water into his hand, and rubbed his face and neck. He sat up with his legs crossed, and though he did not feel cold, he shivered and drew the deer pelt closer around his shoulders. The shivering itself cleared his mind, and he watched Five intently. He appeared to be grinding something using a kind of makeshift mortar and pestle.

Five tipped the contents into the clay cup he had used for Mr. Z.'s broth and held out his hand. "The water, please."

Mr. Z. passed him the waterskin.

Five used the antler to further masticate the ground material into a paste, added more water, swirled the material as if to suspend the solids, and presented the cup to Mr. Z.

Mr. Z. held it to his lips, sniffing.

"Drink it. Consume as much of the solids as you can manage. It will taste bitter. It tastes bitter to me, at least."

Mr. Z. hesitated. "What is it?"

"It is medicinal. High in zinc and folic acid. For your wounds and blood cell count. Protein also. It is a low dosage for a humanoid mammal of your size and weight. It will not harm you." He knelt beside Mr. Z. "These are for your wrists. And ankles. I will apply it topically." He displayed what looked to Mr. Z. to be strips of cloth. Five blinked at him. "But first you must drink."

Mr. Z. sipped warily at the concoction. He couldn't help screwing up his face at the overwhelming earthiness of the brew. "Bitter doesn't quite describe it." He swirled the liquid and hurriedly gulped it down.

"The Khmer refer to them as apin," said Five.

Mr. Z. shook his head. "I don't know the word."

"Tarantula."

"What do you mean? The broth?" Mr. Z. blanched. "You could have told me."

"Roasted gently, the flesh may be easily ground to a powder." Five quickly snugged the strips of cloth, handmade bandages, to Mr. Z.'s wrists. "I applied diluted venom from the animal too. A tincture of it provides many pharmacological properties. I have found it helpful myself as a painkiller absent of addictive properties."

"Tarantula," repeated Mr. Z. "You were trained in medicine, Five?"

"Only rudimentary techniques useful in the field. Cadet level. And I make assumptions based upon what little I know of your physiology."

"Assumptions, I see, yes. Well, we time detectives are taught our own survival techniques. But I must say, this particular treatment is new to me."

"In several hundred years or so, if I remember correctly, these Khmer, embroiled in yet another of their warring periods, will discover, out of necessity, the nutritional benefits of these tarantula. Some will eat them to survive."

Mr. Z. stood up, draped in Five's deer pelt. He shuffled about, squinting at the ground.

Five wandered up to Mr. Z. and held out his hand.

"My transponder!" said Mr. Z. "My God, Five, thank you! You've had this all along?"

"Only by happenstance. It lay within the leaves. I accidentally uncovered it while making camp."

Mr. Z. was duly astonished. He wiped the dust and dirt away, tapped the device to verify its functionality, and hefted it thoughtfully. He eyed Five for a moment, then slipped the device into his trouser pocket. "I suppose you've become quite resourceful out here?" He gestured at Five's hands. "Those look to be a new pair of gauntlets. How did you weave the fabric? And your trousers and shoes and even your pack—they all appear, well, handmade."

Five didn't respond. Rather, he bent to collect another several pieces of firewood.

"Thank you, Five," said Mr. Z. "For the transponder. And for helping me. For saving my life. Again."

They both sat facing the crackling fire.

"But I still don't understand," murmured Mr. Z. "Artoor's body. Where could it have gone?"

"There are tigers within these woods," said Five. "But . . ."

"But what?" said Mr. Z.

"It was no tiger." Five sighed heavily and poked at the blaze. "There was something here. Something mysterious. That is all I can say for certain, Mr. Z."

CHAPTER 37

HEAVEN IS HARD TO GAIN

"Neutic!" hissed Vixy. She shook her transponder as if to expedite Neutic's response.

"Go ahead," said Neutic.

"Are you at the village?" said Vixy. "God, I'm almost to Angkor Thom and Mr. Z., he's not showing up on my tracker and he's not responding. Something must be wrong. I've got to go back."

"To Angkor Wat?" said Neutic. "We just got to the village. Do you want us to come back?"

"No. You and Friday stay where you are. I'll go."

"Alone? You can't. We've got to stick together. What's going on?"

"I can't explain it."

"If it's about Mr. Z., then don't we need to give him time to respond? I mean, maybe he's . . . I don't know. We should wait."

"No. Neutic. Listen to me. He already would've responded in some way. His transponder isn't transmitting his location. He's in trouble, I know it. I only just got to the goddamn southern entrance to Angkor Thom. I'm coming back." Vixy began retracing her route and broke into a trot. Fifteen or so minutes to the western entrance to Angkor Wat, then another damn five or ten to get into the shrine. God, that was twenty minutes. If she didn't run into any trouble herself.[74]

---

74 The entrance to Angkor Wat is 1.7 kilometers south of Angkor Thom

"We're coming back," said Neutic. "But it will take us an hour and fifteen minutes or so to get to the western entrance."

"No! You've got to stay at Siem Reap. We have to verify that Five or the mothmen aren't hiding out there. If Mr. Z. isn't in the shrine"—the running and talking was making her breathless—"I don't know. If he's not there, I'll head to our east gate bivouac. I'll let you know when I've checked the shrine. If you don't hear from me—oh hell, first thing's first."

"But it will be dark soon," said Neutic. "And if you use a headlamp, you'll be seen. Hell, you're bound to be seen anyway. By somebody."

"I know."

—

DAMMIT, THOUGHT NEUTIC. HE KNEW better than to try to argue with her. And in the end, he trusted her intuition. But if Mr. Z. was in trouble, he wanted to help. He forced himself to focus on his own situation. He was beside the road—for all intents a mere cart path—and half concealed in the tall grass that bordered it. Friday squirmed in his arms impatiently. If he became ornery, then what? The entrance to the village was a stone's throw away.

"This is as good a spot as any, Friday," he murmured. He forced his tracer needle into the bark of the nearest tree and checked his device. Transmitting. Good. If nothing else, they could monitor the traffic in and out of the village.

He brought up his map. Vixy looked to be halfway between Angkor Thom and the western approach to Angkor Wat. But Mr. Z.? In the area of temple shrine, where he ought to be, there was nothing. There was no icon for him anywhere, just as Vixy said. What the hell was going on?

Neutic crouched onto one knee and bounced Friday on the other. The light in the sky was fading; soon enough there would be only the torches of Siem Reap and the stars above to provide any light

and approximately 5.5 kilometers north of Siem Reap.

or sense of direction. He was going to have his hands full trying to investigate the village for any signs of the two mothmen. And he wanted nothing more than to hurry north and help Vixy. But so be it.

Friday himself, meanwhile, was an impossible thing. How simple it would be to sneak into the village, merely to the edge of it, even, and deposit the boy in plain sight of the nearest hut. He could whistle, make some noise, get someone's attention, then flee. Someone was bound to discover the child and take him in. Well, nobody was bound to do anything. After all, why had Friday been wandering around to begin with? Was he an outcast of some type? Were children routinely abandoned by the Khmer? Was there some societal stigma that had been transgressed? Or was he merely a kid playing too close to the water and now his parents were suffering over his disappearance?

Neutic chastized himself. Getting in the way of destiny. Breaking protocol. And it was his fault for thinking that somehow they'd find a way to return home with him. Lunacy. Just leave the boy. That's what Mr. Z. would do, despite the emotional quandary. This was Friday's home. No one would question the decision. Not Mr. Z. or Vixy or Captain Chase. He had placed their careers on the line too—hell, they could be accused of being complicit. With a damn class one LNT violation. Unless he managed to fix it. The encounter with Friday had been accidental, yes. He'd been rash. Crazy rash. And now was his chance to undo a portion of his mistake. Get on with it, then.

"Friday. Look at me." The boy quit fussing and reached for Neutic's face. "Dammit it to hell," he muttered, "what am I doing?" He thought of Vixy, alone within the temple. And Mr. Z. If there were trouble . . . He shed his pack, hoisted Friday into it, snugged the closure with the boy's head and arms sticking out, and started back the way they'd come, trudging north along the road toward Angkor Wat.

———

VIXY BIT HER LIP. How to traverse the causeway, sneak through the gate, and get through the damn temple village all the way into the central shrine? Without getting turned around and lost, let alone seen? The place could be chock-full of Khmer, for all she knew. Who knew who or what was inside, let alone how the place operated? Goddammit, what did it matter? Just get across the moat and see what happens.

She darted across the wide, wooden bridge uncloaked, relieved that it was empty of monks—she could conserve her cloak battery for when she was in the village. Or the temple itself. She paused a stone's throw from the main entrance tower, debating with herself. Use your head. Observe the situation. What would Mr. Z. do? He wouldn't go in through the front door if he didn't have to, that's for sure. Screw the main gate. And screw the other two flanking it. Either of the two corner entrances had to receive far less attention. Now, which one, north or south? Easy enough. The whole southern expanse was less densely overgrown. If she had to exit the temple grounds at the southern entrance for any reason, she could traverse the acreage all the way to their eastern bivouac. North of the temple, the jungle was virtually impenetrable. South it is.

She hustled toward the southwest corner tower, considered toggling on her cloaking device, and peered inside, but it was clear. She hurried through without incident.

So that was the village. Little thatched-roof wooden houses everywhere. Some of them appeared more like huts. Modest abodes all side by side in tidy rows, like an ancient subdivision. Except when she looked more closely, nothing appeared all that tidy. Many of the houses didn't even seem occupied. More than a handful were in a state of obvious dishevelment—some missing sections of their roofs or without roofs entirely. Here was one leaning obscenely, like some broken-down little barn, its roof drooping. Over there, a shabby pile of what looked like rotting wood.

Where was everybody? She couldn't discern more than a handful of Khmer milling about. Temple village to the left, then. Not half as populated as she feared. Pathway straight ahead, following the southern outer wall, and beyond that, the moat. No houses or huts in that direction, and it was dotted with trees. Trees made for cover. She hurried along from tree to tree, traversing the open spaces as stealthily as she could, the temple itself looming ever larger as she approached.

Eventually, just to her left, she came upon the corner of a low laterite wall. It stretched directly north toward the main temple road and continued east. Beyond it, or rather within it, perhaps a hundred meters distant, was the southwest corner of the temple's outer galleries. She could go into the temple right there, at that corner entrance. But the idea of sneaking through the galleries seemed intimidating. She could get turned around, and then what? On top of the risk of an encounter. No, she had to cut the distance from the outer temple galleries to the inner shrine. Enter from the south, then, for a straight shot north to the shrine, no turns. And less chance of being seen.

She placed her hand on the low wall. Clearly it was a demarcation, a boundary, perhaps designating the temple area proper from the domestic space. Or maybe this place used to house the entire king's court? Of all places she'd studied, for all her training in archaeological anthropology, and through that brief year or so she'd spent in Asia during her undergraduate days, Angkor Wat had simply slipped through the cracks. And here she was, ignorant as hell about the place and trying to find her way into the heart of it. God, life was irony. She swatted at the mosquitoes and noticed a cluster of dark shapes darting overhead—bats. And that stench? She looked north. Yep. A stinking pond. Likely rife with human waste. No way she was going that way. Stay south. She peered through the trees. Keep the towers on the left and she was bound to—there! The southern entrance. Perhaps three hundred meters. God, this place was huge! And mostly deserted.

She scurried along, sweating, breathless, fending off mosquitoes and her sense of ghostly foreboding. The towers loomed, the intricate details of their carving somehow lending the temple an aura of Gothic complexity and mystery. The elaborate intensity of the carvings, even from this distance—every surface covered—was astounding. The time and effort it must have demanded. Decades of labor. From the quarrying and logistics to the stonecutting and fitting all the pieces. It was no less an accomplishment than Giza.

And akin to Giza, from a distance, it had all seemed monumental and impersonal. As architecturally remote as any legendary monument or modern mega-skyscraper anywhere in the world. But now, with the towers overhead and the galleries stretching out before her, the temple's remarkable handiwork evoked both the astonishing zeal and tender fragility of its human aspiration. It seemed capable of crumbling into dust before her eyes. Yet it would endure for thousands of years, as if it were indeed somehow celestial and eternal and endowed with the imperishable power and presence of the gods themselves. And demons too.

She stood a stone's throw from the southern entrance, suddenly fraught. She couldn't do this. She couldn't go in there. Mr. Z., where are you? What's happened? My God, if something *has* gone wrong . . . What if she didn't make it out? What would become of Neutic? And Friday?

She compulsively tapped at her transponder, checking for messages. What was wrong with her? There wouldn't be any messages. She tapped anyway. Nothing from Mr. Z. or Neutic. She suddenly felt paralyzed with a sense of foreboding.

It was the HDT hangover, that was all. Part of the psychological effects. Neutic had experienced a version of the symptoms. Now, she was having them. Follow the advice, dammit. Find an object that doesn't seem so foreign in space and time and focus on it. Like what?

She felt outside of herself, as if her body and the entire wild scenario of Angkor Wat and 1296 were not quite real and her own flesh wasn't either. She was too far from home. She wouldn't get back. Ever. She had to get out. She couldn't do this. She had to leave. Her anxiety threatened to unhinge her.

You know this, she told herself. You've had anxiety attacks your whole damn life. Deal with it. Wait it out. It can't last. It can't last two minutes. Her biology couldn't keep this up, and in two minutes she'd be herself again, right here.

But she didn't *want* to be here. Run. Just fucking run! Get to the nexus. Request an emergency transport.

No, what was she talking about? A goddamn emergency transport? That was crazy. Stop freaking out. Don't be a damn coward. Find something, anything—there! The setting sun! Over the darkened treetops. The sun, just like at home. Hold to it. The anxiety will pass, it will pass, it will pass . . .

It did pass. She sipped from her canteen and checked her transponder. No sign of Mr. Z. No message from Neutic. She moved out.

She paused within the junction of the galleries, still a little spooked, but her progress emboldened her. It was just an old temple, that's all. Just stone upon stone and dark stairways and creepy court-yards.

She peered into the courtyard. No monks. Nobody in sight. She scurried straight ahead perhaps thirty meters toward the second-tier steps—just keep moving. Up into the vestibule—shorter, narrower than the last—and out, only a couple steps down, and then she bounded across the short second-tier courtyard and—dammit! What was this? Steps to the third tier, they had to be. But what kind of steps were these? She gasped at the incline. It must be fifteen meters to the top. The steps were broad yet shallow. Impossibly so. No handrail. She'd have to be a damn monkey. She imagined herself trying to scramble up using her hands and feet.

No. It looked worse than it was, that's all. If a monk could do it, she could do it. Hell, Mr. Z. did it, didn't he? She tried the first step, instinctively grasping at the next. She already felt as if she'd topple backward. Be careful. Just stand straight up and take the steps one at a time. Look straight ahead, don't look down, and keep moving.

She gained the top tier, and the narrow corridor into the shrine stretched out before her. The vestibule was open to the east and west, and enough light remained in the sky that she could see out the way she'd come, all across the expanse of the grounds, all the way to the causeway and the moat and the road and the fields and portions of forest jungle beyond. It was heady and unnerving at this height. *Heaven is hard to gain,* she thought, something she'd heard somewhere. And then she tortured herself by surrendering to her compulsion to look back.

"My God," she gulped. How in hell would she negotiate those horrible steps going down, to get out of here?

Just don't think about it. Find Mr. Z.

But how? It seemed crazy that he could even be up here, let alone sequestered somewhere deep within the shrine. It was dark now, almost black within the tiny vestibule and utterly lightless beyond. She was tempted to use her headlamp but instead toggled on her night vision.

Perhaps fifteen meters ahead, a heavy-looking, ornately carved wooden door, partially open. She stepped forward, listening, looking. She couldn't trust her footing with night vision. Suddenly, whoosh! A panicked fluttering all around her. She ducked, her heart pounding. Birds? No. *Bats!*

In another instant the animals had flown free of the vestibule, and the silence engulfed her. It was too quiet, too vacant. Mr. Z., where in hell are you? She almost couldn't resist calling out to him, but she bit her tongue. Something wasn't right. Not right at all. The shrine was empty! She didn't know whether to be relieved or aghast. Now what?

Get out of the shrine and contact Neutic. She toggled off her night vision and fumbled with her transponder. What was that? She huddled against the wall, peering out.

"Aiee!" A mothman lunged at her and lashed out mercilessly with a broken cane.

Vixy only just raised her arm, or he would have smashed her skull. As it was, the blow glanced off her elbow—the pain was blinding. She rolled and scrambled to her feet, snatching at her plasma pistol.

Chung flung a handful of gravel at her face and darted after her, half leaping and half hobbling, and drove his cane into Vixy's solar plexus.

Vixy flinched—"Oof!—and she swung wildly with her pistol, striking Chung a glancing blow upon his temple.

"Argh!" The mothman stumbled back, lost his grip on his cane, and collapsed.

Vixy gasped at the pain in her ribs and scrambled to switch on her headlamp. "What in God's name?" she stammered. "Who . . . who are you?"

Chung lay clutching his head.

Vixy looked down the corridors and listened. There was no way to know if they'd been heard or seen, to know if anyone was coming. "Answer me!" she hissed. The creature's face was vaguely humanoid, certainly, but the deathly pale flesh, the narrow eyes and the mouth that stretched nearly from ear to ear? And the ears, well, she couldn't see any. And were those canines? And a goatee? The thing's black eyes were wild. His saffron robe was disheveled and filthy—he appeared to be virtually witless with pain and fury. Was this one of the moth-men? She clutched her bruised ribs and aimed her pistol at the alien.

The creature lay slouched against the stone wall of the passage-way, his chest heaving. His cane lay snapped in half just outside his reach. He held his other hand up to his face, shading his eyes against the dull glow of Vixy's headlamp.

"Khmer language," said Vixy in a flat tone, initiating her auto-translator. "Who are you?"

The alien responded in a hoarse, breathy, depleted voice that even Vixy understood to be nothing like Khmer. She glanced at the display from her autotranslator: *Off-planet. First Quadrant. Algorithmic estimate.* Which meant that the thing was only guessing. "I am Chung. Advisor to the emperor."

"Then you are a mothman. There were two of you. Where is the other?"

Chung merely stared at her.

A wave of dizziness forced her to her knees, and she put her hand to her forehead. Psi-attack? It was all she could do to keep her pistol aimed at Chung. Her vision blurred, and she struggled to keep her balance. The psi-attack dissipated as quickly as it had overtaken her, and she looked to find Chung somehow several meters away from her, having dragged himself across the threshold of the shrine. In an instant he disappeared into the darkness.

"No!" Vixy leapt after him, lost her footing—the psi had affected her balance—and tried to clear her head. She clamored out the east door of the shrine and ran headlong into Chung. They struggled. Chung lunged at her, and she managed to fall back and use the moth-man's own momentum to hurl him over top of her. She scrambled to her knees, watched the mothman attempt to regain his own foot-ing—he teetered precariously upon the edge of the shrine steps.

She aimed her pistol, but before she could fire, the mothman fell. She rushed to the edge, looked down, and beheld the pale form crumpled at the foot of the steep staircase. She sent a message to Neutic: *NO Z. TROUBLE IN SHRINE. I'M OK. MEET AT EAST BIV-OUAC ASAP.*

CHAPTER 38

ALIEN CONTACT

"Attaboy, Friday," whispered Neutic. The child's eyes were heavy lidded, and his face was puffy with sleep—extricating him from the backpack would only wake him. Best to leave him be. Neutic carefully reshouldered the pack and checked his coordinates.

They had finally rounded the southeastern corner of the temple grounds and were trudging northward through the edge of the forest jungle where the foliage was thinnest, within sight of the moat. According to his display, there ought to be a clearing ahead.

He yanked his trek goggles over his eyes and switched to ninfrared, slang for night and infrared vision. But he couldn't see a damn thing, at least at first. Rather, he couldn't *recognize* a damn thing. The travel agents at the TDC—they were technically deployment coordinators, but everyone referred to them as travel agents—while he was hurrying to pack everything according to their instructions, told him that ninfrared typically required a week's worth of field training to properly use. He had merely been instructed on how to turn the damn thing on and off and then received five minutes of breezily informal "instruction" on the limits of the technology. How the digitized images, for example, were merely interpretations, as the agents referred to them, of the real thing. Not necessarily to be trusted. Depth perception in particular, they had warned him, was tricky. On top of the limited field of view and lack of peripheral vision, which he was experiencing this instant. He couldn't see his hands or feet, for example.

What was that? Straight ahead, peeking through the thick foliage—a blip of intense light and heat. Neutic toggled his lenses back and forth between standard zoom and ninfrared. A campfire, it had to be. But in the jungle, so far outside the temple grounds?

Friday squirmed in the pack and whined.

"Shush, Friday, shush." He headed toward the firelight and the boy quieted—he only seemed to become restless when they stopped moving.

Who amongst the Khmer would set up camp outside of a village? Hunters? Thieves? Outcasts of some type? Could it be the two mothmen themselves? Or more of them? Or molemen, for that matter? He fumbled for his plasma pistol, practiced switching the safety off and on again, tried to prepare himself to use the thing—it wouldn't be anything like target practice. *Aim to kill, or don't draw your weapon.* Such was the advice.

He holstered the thing and plodded along fitfully. The ground was uneven and entangled with roots and brush. Here and there he was forced over the trunks of fallen trees. Slow down, that's all. Deal with it. Or don't, and head for open ground.

Finally, the clearing came into view, indeed illuminated by a modest campfire. He vacillated about what to do with Friday. Keep him in the backpack or carry him in his arms? Screw it. Better that the boy was behind him if anything happened. And maybe he'd stay quiet.

Neutic crept forward. He drew his plasma pistol and toggled the laser sight. Immediately he heard a great crashing ahead, as if something—a large animal?—hurtled through the foliage. Then what sounded like gunshots. Blam! Blam! Blam!

He barely had time to duck behind a tree trunk when two men, one close behind the other, bounded past. "Jeezus—what the hell!" he muttered.

In an instant they had disappeared into the jungle and Neutic stood staring after them with his heart in his throat. They had been shirtless and slightly built—Khmer, if he had to guess. What if they'd been coming after him? Like an idiot, he hadn't even thought of raising his pistol to defend himself. Get your shit together, for Christ's sake.

Then it struck him. Those gunshots. He hurried to unshoulder his pack and examine Friday in the dark. Was he hit? He couldn't see a thing. Friday moaned as if half awakened but seemed unharmed and as drowsy as ever, as if nothing had happened.

Neutic reshouldered Friday and turned his attention to the clearing. The men had no doubt come from there. He armed his plasma pistol and approached, stepping carefully through the undergrowth and roots, crouching low.

"Do not move," said a voice.

Neutic started. The voice was behind him. Or was it beside him? For fuck's sake, where?

"Hands in the air." It was the unmistakable mechanical monotone of an autotranslator. And it was indeed behind him. Neutic waited.

"I said in the air. Slowly."

Neutic raised his arms.

"Identify yourself."

Despite his fears, the blunt demands irritated him.

"Answer me!"

"Wait, Five—don't!"

"Mr. Z.? Sir? Is that you?"

"Yes, Neutic, yes, it's me. Five, please, this man is my friend. Neutic, for heaven's sake, come closer."

Neutic approached and with some difficulty recognized the shirtless man huddled beside the fire with what looked to like an animal pelt wrapped around his shoulders.

"Neutic, this is Five."

A dark shape emerged from the foliage—a short, stocky, seemingly disproportioned figure with enormous, round ears, strange goggles, outsized hands, smallish feet, and flesh that bestowed a faint, crimson-hued illumination. Neutic stood aghast. "*The* Five?"

"That's right," said Mr. Z. "Five, may I introduce Herman Neutic. He is a—"

"He is a human," interrupted Five. "From your space-time coordinates."

"Yes. And I was going to say that Neutic also happens to be a time detective cadet. Neutic? Five is a, well, you can see for yourself."

"He's a moleman," said Neutic.

"And he and I shared an adventure in Egypt not so long ago. Didn't we, Five?"

Mr. Z.'s voice suddenly failed him, and Neutic watched him put his hand to his head and appear to swoon. "Sir!"

Five rushed to Mr. Z.'s side and steadied him before Neutic managed to take a step. The entire scene was astonishing. And incongruous. Firelight gleamed against Five's enormous goggles. His large ears moved akin to an animal's—expressive, deft, ceaselessly attentive. His gauntleted hands, grasping at Mr. Z.'s shoulders, were enormous and thick fingered, implying both immense strength and a curious dexterity.

"Sir? What's going on? You look, I don't know, are you injured?"

"I look terrible, I suppose," murmured Mr. Z. "And I have felt better, I must say. I was in a bit of a predicament a while ago. With Artoor, of all people."

"Artoor?" said Neutic.

"Indeed. But Five possesses some remarkable timing. He came to my aid, to put it lightly." Mr. Z. shivered and hugged his own shoulders.

Neutic doffed his pack, cradled Friday in one arm, and dug clumsily into his supplies with the other. "I'm sorry, sir." He yanked out a pullover. "I've got this." He watched Mr. Z. gingerly don the garment, saw him grimace with each careful movement.

"Thank you, Neutic. That's much better, yes."

Neutic watched Five roll the pelt into a tight package and stuff it into his own pack.

"Those are bandages, sir, on your wrists? For God's sake, what happened?" Then it struck him. "Vixy!"

"What's that, Neutic?" said Mr. Z.

"Vixy, sir, I forgot—she's looking for you!" He glanced at his device. "Or she was. In the central shrine. We lost your signal—you weren't showing on the map."

"Vixy! Vixy, do you copy?" When she didn't respond, Neutic

looked fraught. "I've found Mr. Z. He's okay. Well . . . I mean, yes, he's okay. Vixy!"

A moment passed and his transponder flashed and buzzed. "She's okay. There's been trouble, that's all she says. But she's coming. Meanwhile, sir, I can contact Captain Chase. Or, maybe you've already—"

"All in due time," said Mr. Z. "Don't worry, Neutic, there's nothing for you to be doing just yet. This pullover is a godsend, I'll tell you that. It seems to be cooling down, or perhaps it's just me. Anyway, no, everything is okay, for now, at least. Despite appearances. We'll wait for Vixy. Thank heaven she's okay. I managed to get separated from my transponder and, well, no biolink and the tracking fails, of course. And you both came looking for me, I apologize."

Friday clutched at Neutic's leg, apparently wary of Five, who had his back to them, tending the fire.

"Hello, Friday," said Mr. Z. He gestured for the boy to come near.

The boy obliged and Neutic followed. He glanced at Five.

"It's okay, Neutic," said Mr. Z. "I think we can all agree this is neutral ground, as it were. And at this point, I don't think any of us have anything to hide from each other. Wouldn't you agree, Five?"

The moleman finished fussing with the blaze and sat an arm's length or so away from them. Friday whimpered, but before he began to wail, Neutic grabbed the boy under the armpits and bounced him gently in his lap. "Shush, now. It's okay, Friday. You remember Mr. Z. And this is Five." His tone retained a tincture of incredulity.

Friday gazed at Five warily, with a child's guarded fascination.

Five, for his part, extended his hand to Friday or, more accurately, his broad fist, palm up, and one by one slowly uncurled his fingers, as if performing a drama. He whistled a strange melody too, very softly, which only further entranced the boy. In the palm of Five's hand was a large, round, dull-surfaced object, perhaps the dimensions of a baseball, that both absorbed and reflected the orange-yellow firelight. It gleamed like gold.

The boy sat blinking at Five, his dirt-smudged, tear-stained face glistening in the firelight. He stuffed the fingers of one hand into his mouth and reached out with the other.

Neutic gently took Friday's hand away. "That's not for you, Friday."

Five stowed the object.

"Well," volunteered Mr. Z., "what do you know? I venture to say that right there is the famous, or infamous, golden ball. Or at least an iteration of it. Remarkable."

Neutic glanced back and forth between Five and Mr. Z. "I don't understand. The golden ball. Five has it? And you said something about Mandrake Artoor. And your injuries. What's happening?"

"I encountered Mandrake Artoor, yes. As impossible as that sounds. I'm ashamed to admit that he managed to ambush me." He rubbed at the back of his head.

"Wait a moment, sir. I'm a fool." Neutic snatched at his pack and riffled through it. "I've got a first aid kit. Antiseptics and antibiotics and painkillers. Bandages too. We should probably change those dressings."

"Yes," said Five. He was peering at Neutic's kit. "Give me the boy."

Neutic seemed wary.

"It's okay, Neutic. Five is to be trusted."

Five whistled again, quietly, and tended to Friday as the two men worked.

"Mandrake Artoor," said Five. "He was from your space-time coordinates?"

"Time coordinate, yes," said Mr. Z. "But not space. He was human, and his genealogy, from what I know, was mixed, with origins within this spiral arm, if I'm not mistaken."

"He was an employee of the Pangalactic Mythology Coalition," said Neutic. "I assume you've heard of the PMC?"

Five nodded.

"But you're both talking about him in the past tense," said Neutic.

"Yes," said Mr. Z. "Artoor is dead. It turns out he was an enemy. A double agent. With allegiances to, well, I'm not certain where his allegiances resided. I suspect, from some of the things he was ranting about and my own suspicions, that he was in collusion with the Scarab Cult. And perhaps the mothman empress too. Which may have been his undoing, but whatever was happening and whatever his motives, the man had become unhinged. Akin to Laron, it seems to me. Their symptoms, or what have you—the psychological trauma they apparently endured—leads me to suspect that the empress was involved. Telepathy, perhaps. Or something more sinister."

"And you fought with him?" said Neutic. "Artoor, that is?"

"No, actually," said Mr. Z. "Not to any effect, anyway. Like I said, he ambushed me. I think he struck me from behind—he must have been cloaked—and the next thing I knew he had me strung up like a sack of potatoes. He had corraled a couple of Khmer lackeys to help him. Help him with . . ." He trailed off and stared into the fire.

"A rope around your wrists," volunteered Five, "and another around your ankles. The latter secured to that stone, there."

"My God, Mr. Z.," said Neutic. "I don't get it. I mean, Artoor."

"Let me start at the beginning," said Mr. Z. "You and Vixy and I went our separate ways this morning. I made it to the central shrine easily enough. Well, given that I was cloaked. I encountered a handful of monks, especially along the eastern wall of the second tier. They appear to enjoy loitering there, perhaps because of the morning shade. And that staircase to the third tier isn't for the faint of heart. Would you agree, Five?"

Five poked absently at the fire and replied nonchalantly over his shoulder. "Seventy percent incline. 15.24 meters elevation delta. Challenging for bipeds."

"Heaven is hard to gain," said Mr. Z. "As they say. Nevertheless, there I was, twenty or so meters above ground level, I think it is . . ." Mr. Z. again deferred to Five.

"Twenty-two meters," said Five.

"Twenty-two meters. And I managed to install my tracking needle in the shrine—an unpleasant, claustrophobic attic of a space, mind you, with those unsightly walls that the Buddhists installed. I would have liked to have seen the shrine as it was originally constructed, open to the air on four sides with the image of Vishnu at the center. Anyway, I was poking around a bit in there and I was convinced someone had been digging. Recently. Because things seemed to be, oh, I couldn't be certain. Out of place a bit. Too clean here, a little too dirty there. But of course, while any precious metals or jewels, even within the king's sarcophagus, would have been pillaged almost as soon as the capital city was relocated to Angkor Thom, there was a chance that tomb raiders had tried again. But otherwise, who knew? I left things as they were, to see if whoever—tomb raiders, the mothmen, I even had to consider the molemen—returned."

Mr. Z. and Neutic both glanced at Five, but the moleman seemed content to occupy himself with Friday, allowing the boy to tug upon his fingers.

"Just so long as my tracking needle isn't discovered, we may catch a glimpse. I left the shrine. To return to our camp. And I'd gotten myself down those damn third-tier steps and I was making my way out of the east gate to wait for you and Vixy. As if he'd materialized out of nothing, Mandrake Artoor is standing face-to-face with me. He was armed with a plasma pistol and had in tow a couple of uncooperative Khmer, peasants or slaves he'd commandeered somehow, who knows? Artoor was beside himself. More than that, he seemed neurotic, not quite out of his head—nothing like Laron in Bombay, mind you—but he was raving about how I had destroyed his relationship with the empress. By way of my meddling."

"The mothman empress," said Neutic.

"Apparently."

The three of them sat quietly for a time, staring into the crackling campfire. Friday sat playing with one of Five's gauntlets.

"Torture," said Five. He nudged the embers of the fire with a stick, and a flurry of sparks and smoke rushed upward and vanished into the night.

"Torture?" said Neutic. "What do you mean, Five?"

"Suspending a man by his wrists," said Five, "employing a weight attached to his ankles. With the intention of straining the ligaments. And eliciting information."

"What about you, Five?" said Neutic. "This whole business with Artoor is one thing. But why did you help Mr. Z.? What are you doing here? Is the floor of the shrine your doing? To reestablish the Cosmic Clock Component? Isn't that what the golden ball is for?"

Five sat staring inscrutably into the fire.

"Five," insisted Neutic. "Mr. Z.? Have you already asked him all this?"

"Five's mission, if he has one, is a mystery to me. No. I haven't asked him why he is here. How he even got here. And, like you, I was only just made aware that he possessed the ball. I suppose you ought to know, Five, that the TDC has been tracking HDT traffic between 1296 Ankgor and someone upon Mega City One. Is it you? Are you responsible for the communications?"

Five snatched off his goggles and buffed them clean with a patch of textile he'd produced. He repositioned them unhurriedly upon his face. Then he stood, looking beyond the fire, into the darkness of the trees. "Miss Vixy."

Both Neutic and Mr. Z., astonished, squinted into the darkness.

Then Vixy herself stepped forward, aiming her plasma pistol with both hands. "That's right, Five." The laser sight was a red dot upon Five's chest. "What's going on here?"

CHAPTER 39

THE FUTURE IS THE PAST

"My beloved," the empress cooed. They were beside the energetic little creek that meandered through their private garden. The dark water, mountain-born and icy, gurgled over the mossy stones.

"Yes, dear?" said the emperor.

"Nothing." She feigned bashfulness. "It is just that I am so happy."

The emperor, young and handsome in his new imperial garments, his face and head clean-shaven and his eyes bright, gathered fallen blossoms from beneath each of the three cherry trees. He smiled at her. "Now, hold out your hand."

She obliged, and he laughed when she closed her eyes too.

"But I like surprises," she told him.

"Health," he said, and placed a blossom upon her palm.

She smiled.

Another blossom. "Happiness."

At the moment of the third, she opened her eyes and spoke the word with him. "Prosperity."

He closed her fingers round the blossoms. "May our life together be so blessed."

"Likewise, the Realm," she said. "Health. Happiness. Prosperity. As long as we shall live." She tossed the petals into the breeze then, and they laughed.

———

THE EMPRESS AWAKENED TO THE sound of the low fire hissing qui-etly. The intense warmth upon her cheeks and the tender nature of the fire's glow sustained her drowsiness and preserved the sweet bliss of her dream. She lay with her head upon the silken pillow. "Husband. Emperor." She half expected him to respond.

She sat up stiffly, and the effort perturbed her—she struggled to resist her compulsion to lie back down again and return, somehow, to her dream. She forced herself to look around the room. Tables. Chairs. The unsightly communications console. The horrid video display. The room itself seemed weighted with all the unsightly and fraught imperatives of the waking world. Even her yarrow stalks and coins seemed indecently demanding. "Husband. My Lord. Speak to me. Help me." The fire hissed and the room was still. Waiting. Waiting for a man who would not return.

The sharp rapping at the door startled her, and she scowled. Damn them, whoever they were. She could not even be bothered to pry into their minds. "Leave me be! Do you hear? Go!"

Again, the rap, rap, rapping. And the inevitable muffled, beseech-ing pleas. "Empress! Your Highness! Please!"

It was Ming-tun. She endured the beeping of the keypad lockset, the handle being forced, and the heavy door being thrust ajar.

Ming-tun peeked inside, his expression fretful. "I am sorry, Your Highness! Please! It is urgent!"

The empress enjoyed for a moment the delicious idea of silencing him with her mind. The fawning, duplicitous, dull-witted fool. Akin to all her advisors. She spared him. "Enter."

Ming-tun stepped carefully into the room, his hands clasped near his chest as if bearing precious information. "Empress, I am sorry to disturb you. Very sorry, certainly. But Mandrake Artoor." He wrung his hands and appeared reluctant to continue.

"Artoor is dead," said the empress flatly.

"Killed, they say! And advisors Feng and Chung—"

"Likewise killed."

At this overt display of prescience, Ming-tun's face turned pale and he stared at her as wide-eyed and fascinatedly wary as a child.

"The incompetent fools. I have foreseen it. What of the battle-front?"

"I . . . I do not know, Your Highness. Except that—"

She cut him short with a gesture. She knew enough. The vicissitudes of the Great Conflict, with its wild, multifarious potentialities and infinite complexities, was not something she could effectively foretell. The fog of war, indeed. Nevertheless, seeking efficacy and clarity, she had appealed to the coins. Despite the yarrow stalks having bestowed a more nuanced interpretation of the Way.

She had cast the Creative with a nine in the fourth place. *Wavering flight over the depths.*[75] But she was changing. And she sensed her powers of interpretation dimming. Nevertheless, she sought to combine the twofold possibilities it presented—to exploit the way of the hero and the holy sage both.

"Our civilians," said Ming-tun, "have divided themselves. One group seeks to surrender to the molemen. The other to support the army and fight to the death. Many who desire to surrender, both soldiers and civilians alike, have attempted to flee into the mountains. And the army, attempting to forestall them, has resorted to killing hundreds of our own people."

"So be it," said the empress. "Now, leave me."

"But . . . Your Highness? What are we to do? What shall I tell the generals? The Great Conflict. Are we lost? What is to become of the Realm? Our homes? Empress, please, you must lead us. Why do you not act?"

The empress interrupted his tedious thoughts with her own.

"We are to surrender? But, Empress . . ."

She seized his puny mind.

---

75   Richard Wilhelm, *The I Ching or Book of Changes*, 3rd ed., trans. Cary F. Baynes, Bollingen Series XIX, (Princeton: Princeton University Press, 1990 [1967]), 9. Republished with permission of Princeton University Press; permission conveyed through Copyright Clearance Center, Inc.

The tension in Ming-tun's voice vanished. "By your command, Your Highness. I shall communicate our unconditional surrender to the molemen. The generals shall fly the white flag. Our traitors and deserters shall be abandoned to their fate." Ming-tun nodded in lieu of a proper bow and stared blankly at her.

She dismissed him silently and watched the advisor shuffle obediently to the door and depart. She shut the door behind him and barred it. Then she turned to her tea and slurped at it quietly. When she made to place the empty cup upon the tray, she surprised herself by dropping it.

Her hand was shaking, and she swallowed hard at the strange mineral taste in her mouth. There was no time left. She clenched her hand to steady it, endured a newfound heaviness in her arms and legs, and shuddered at the sense of her own flesh crawling. She steeled herself to the changes and hurried into her bedchamber, locking the door behind her, arming the security jam and scrambling the code. She verified the temperature and humidity, then crept into her bed and enveloped herself within the rich silks, pulling them tightly about her. She shut her eyes.

Let it come. She could feel the blood course through her body in every artery, vein, and capillary. The cloying numbness in her feet and hands and arms and legs. Her palpitating heart. Fear. All the symptoms, as foretold.

Peace would come. Then power. And the ancient salvation of the Way.

CHAPTER 40

ZENITH PASSAGE FESTIVAL

THE DAWN SKY WAS CLOUDLESS and pale. Mist clung to the temple city grounds, obscuring Neutic's view of the western bridge, the moat, and all but the top of the border wall so that Angkor Wat itself seemed to float upon a cloud. But the day's heat was already rising, and the mists were beginning to disperse, drawn away as if by the slow inhalation of the forest jungle, or perhaps the respiration of the great god Vishnu himself.

"Wow," he said, and turned to address the company. "You've got to see this."

"Jeezus," said Vixy. She bounced Friday on her hip and squinted at the scene. "There must be, I don't know, four or five thousand people out there."

"Or more," said Neutic. "And they're still streaming in from the western gate."

"All because of the solar zenith," said Mr. Z. "It has to be. It stands to reason that there will be a festival too. I suppose the festival is the main point for most everyone. It's likely that only the king and his court will have access to the temple ceremony."

"Whatever that looks like," said Vixy. "I mean, it's not like there's room for anybody within that damn shrine. But speaking of the king and his court, they're all in Angkor Thom, right? I wonder when they'll show up."

"Or *if* they'll show up," said Neutic. "If they've moved the capital to Angkor Thom, wouldn't a zenith passage ritual take place there? It's not like it has anything to do with Buddhism. Are we certain there will even be a ritual or a ceremony inside the shrine? All kinds of people celebrate Christmas without ever going to church, even on Christmas Day."

"Hmm, yes," said Mr. Z. He chewed upon his pipe stem. "There's a significant difference between a festival and ritual, you're right. Between a celebration of a mythology, that is, and participation in it. Just remember that a zenith passage isn't integral to either Hinduism or Buddhism. Rather, it's unique to the equatorial regions which actually experience the phenomenon of the sun literally passing directly overhead."

"And sometimes people are just looking for a reason to party," said Vixy.

Mr. Z. and Neutic seemed bemused by her bluntness.

"I'm serious. I mean, it's all about syncretization of the folk beliefs and the formal ideology, isn't it? Like the neak ta you mentioned, Mr. Z. These folks here are going to be celebrating the spirits of the land and all that as much as the drama of the zenith passage, and maybe only a handful of them, if anybody at all, will give a damn about Buddhism or Hinduism for its own sake."

"That's it in a nutshell, Vixy," said Mr. Z. "And whether the king and his court are keen to acknowledge the zenith passage at this point in the Khmer's turbulent history is anybody's guess. Meanwhile, Neutic, there's no evidence that the architecture of Angkor Thom includes any accommodation for a zenith passage—no geometry or sighting tubes that allude to it, at least. Not like here. No. I'm betting that we'll see the king, at least for the main event tomorrow. What will that look like? A formal procession from Angkor Thom? Will there be a ritual inside or outside the temple?"

"I don't know," said Neutic. "From what we've seen of Indravarman III, he likes his parades."

"Hmm," said Vixy. "The kind of guy who wouldn't miss a chance to show off in front of a crowd like this for anything. I agree. The king will be here in all his glory. Elephants. Musicians. Dancers. All of Angkor Thom and whomever else in tow."

"Which brings me to the issue of Friday," said Mr. Z.

"What do you mean, sir?" said Neutic. He glanced at the boy, sleeping soundly upon a bedroll beside Vixy, his thumb in his mouth.

"First of all, we can consider having most of Angkor's population here in one place a blessing. That is, when the festival is under way, perhaps one of us can deposit Friday somewhere within the midst of it. There's even a chance that he'll be recognized, that somebody may have been looking for him all this time and he'll be reunited with his parents or whomever."

"Or he'll just wander around and be left to his own devices," said Vixy. "And be left alone in the temple city when it's all over." Vixy frowned at the boy and hugged her shoulders. "I don't know, Mr. Z. As much as I get that the LNT protocol reigns supreme, it's awful to think Friday may end up being, somehow . . ." She shook her head.

"Collateral damage," said Neutic. "Like they talked about in training. It's my fault."

"We'll wait and see," said Mr. Z. "It's an ugly situation, this thing with Friday, I know. We all understand the importance of doing our best to rectify the LNT damage. We're obligated to abide by the TDC protocol as it stands. Which is ultimately based upon galactic law. But I want to be clear. Responsibility for whatever has happened and whatever *will* happen with the boy, for better or worse, lies with me. You both did your best under the circumstances. Meanwhile, we've also got Five to worry about."

"We're not just going to let him go, sir?" said Neutic. "Five, I mean."

"Yes, we are." He clutched lightly at his wrists, as if the nagging discomfort intensified his quandary. "Except I couldn't sleep last night because something about it doesn't seem right."

"Now you're sounding like me," said Vixy. "I suppose Five had me convinced he was genuinely just trying to get home. He saved your life like he saved mine. But maybe he's not just trying to get home. I mean, I believe that's what he wants most—who wouldn't? But it's as if he's been hiding out all this time too. If anybody at Mega City One wanted him back, then he wouldn't be here. And the Great Conflict, hell, his own race is at war. How can we be sure of anybody's motivations, least of all alien motivations, at a time like this? Even if he's not a tyrannical megalomaniac like the rest of his race. I don't know. It just makes me nervous that of all places on Earth he ends up here, in the same space-time coordinates as Neutic and me. In possession of another golden ball, of all things. And it's not like we can find him now even if we wanted to. God, I just don't like that we don't have the means, somehow, to . . . I don't know -"

"Arrest him?" said Neutic.

"No," said Vixy. "I get that we've no hard evidence of his committing a time crime. It's just that, now, whatever it is he's up to, I wish we had the means to keep tabs on him."

"Those consequences likewise rest with me," said Mr. Z. "We could have arrested him as an operative of the Giza debacle. Or upon suspicion of colluding to initiate an unauthorized HDT. But we'd have our hands full trying to subdue him or hold him. At the same time, the mothmen are here and committing their own time crime."

"Or time crimes, plural," said Vixy. "Unauthorized HDT. Sabotaging an HDT. Suspicion of attempting to engineer a Cosmic Clock Component."

"And attempted murder," said Neutic. "That mothman in the shrine, with Vixy."

"Fair enough," said Mr. Z. "Which is why we still need to do our best to unravel what Five is doing with the golden ball and why the mothmen just so happen to be here and now."

"We ought to have forced Five to relinquish it," said Vixy. "We had him there in the camp, with me and Neutic armed with plasma pistols and Five with nothing but, what, a knife and his bare hands?"

"I was hoping Five would've been forthcoming eventually," said Mr. Z. "Otherwise, I don't understand his strange selflessness, given his circumstances. And his humanity."

"Because he saved your life?" said Vixy. "Once here and once in Giza? And mine too?"

"Indeed. Meanwhile, he must know that we won't allow him to engineer a Cosmic Clock Component, even it takes a whole crew of time detectives showing up besides us to stop him. No. I'm convinced we'll do better, just yet, to allow things to play out a bit. The mothmen have an interest in the ball, and unless they're capable of engineering their own, that means they have an interest in Five. And an interest in interfering with our mission, likewise. They'll inevitably send reinforcements to try to resolve both problems."

"And if the zenith passage has anything to do with things," said Neutic, "then time is running out. At least until August."

"That's right," said Vixy. "And if Five needs the zenith passage as some kind of HDT trigger, he'd be a fool to pass up the dry season for the wet season. The weather here is unreliable enough in terms of sunny days."

"And the forecast for tomorrow is sketchy," said Mr. Z. "But I wouldn't put it past the molemen to engineer the weather itself."

"Five himself, though," said Neutic. He appeared thoughtful, staring out at the temple, where the towers of the quincunx gleamed orange-gold in the long, morning light. "He's a moleman, of course. But he's different, isn't he? Saving your lives. Going rogue in Egypt. What do you think he really is?"

Mr. Z. stuffed a coffee lozenge into his mouth and sucked hard on it. "Besides an exile and a mysterious savior, is that what you mean?"

Neutic scratched at the scruff on his chin. "A savior. I don't know. He's a moleman, an alien mind and all that. They have ambitions, as a race. He's got his own ambitions, or a neurosis or a psychosis or whatever it was that drove him to do what he did in Egypt. To sabotage his mission. It's just that Vixy describes how he saved her, and you yourself describe him helping you bury that Arab man, Hesso, and then walking away into the desert. I can't get that image out of my head. You said he just stood there for a time looking at you from afar, alone, in the middle of the desert. It's like I can see him too, you know? What was he thinking? And what happened that so fundamentally changed him so quickly? Vixy, you describe it like it was some kind of nervous breakdown or something. Or a revelation."

"An enantiodromia," said Vixy. "You know, a psychological reversal. It happened right in front of me. One minute Five was bound for the Red Pyramid at all costs, and the next? My God, he and Hesso are barreling back to the Great Pyramid. To save the world. And then the green flare. And a reversal of everything he was here to do. Of everything he thought he was."

"I just don't get it," said Neutic. "And what happened that he ended up here, of all places? Without a transponder?"

"Maybe he somehow engineered it?" said Vixy. "Maybe he's still sabotaging the moleman mission? If we knew, would it matter?"

Mr. Z. shoved his pipe into his pocket. "The golden ball. Five needs it to get home. The zenith passage—something about that ray of sunlight penetrating the tower, perhaps activating an entanglement of some type, otherwise initiating his transport. That's what he's up to and I dare say nothing else, despite everything. Once a rogue always a rogue, I think. It would very much surprise me if Five had anything to do any longer with the CCP. Unless, perhaps, it was propagating the plan unbeknownst to himself."

"Unbeknownst?" said Neutic. He shook his head dubiously.

"It sounds crazy," said Mr. Z., "that Five could be manipulated in some way, thinking perhaps Mega City One is helping him to get home when they're merely using him to install the component. It would be a roundabout method, overly complex."

"Overly complex is right," said Vixy. "They'd just send another moleman. Somebody who could get the job done. Wouldn't they?"

"Unless the politics prevented it," said Neutic.

"Politics," said Mr. Z. "And speculation. We're going to have to leave most of that to the captain for now. If and when Five transports, the ball will be left behind. Within the shrine. That's the most important thing. We have to assume that's when the mothmen will make their move."

"That means you're going to tell us we've got to watch for any mothmen showing up in the shrine," said Vixy. "Somehow. With the entire population of Angkor milling around at the damn temple."

"Yes."

"And without any help from the TDC, sir?" said Neutic. "The captain or the professor?"

"Given the leave-no-trace resources we've already engaged," said Mr. Z., "they aren't going to authorize any HDT to these coordinates for anything, person or equipment. A return event for us is going to be it."

Vixy snatched her plasma pistol from her holster, checked the action, armed it, and verified the safety. "I assume we're all going into the shrine tomorrow, then? Three of us to watch four entrances?"

"Ultimately, yes," said Mr. Z. "But our cloaking time is limited, and we ought to save it for the shrine. I was going to suggest we plant a tracer at whatever entrance we can't cover, but something tells me that tomorrow the western entrance is going to be simply too high profile and busy with foot traffic, whether they're monks, priests, or the king and his court themselves—a mothman could use a disguise as they did before and, well, let's focus on the northern, eastern, and southern entrances."

"When?" said Neutic. "I mean, when do we, I don't know . . ." He struggled to find the word.

"Deploy?" said Vixy. "Yeah. I don't like the sound of hanging out all day around a temple entrance, each on our own, trying not to be seen, and trying to spy for mothmen. Or Five, for that matter."

"No," said Mr. Z. "We'll stage ourselves exactly one hour prior to the zenith passage. We'll do our best to stay out of sight and minimize draining our cloaking batteries, and otherwise keep our eyes open. If any of us see mothmen or Five, then we'll communicate it and at least know what we're up against in the shrine. At fifteen minutes to zenith, which is . . ." Mr. Z. fumbled for his device.

"Tomorrow," said Neutic, eyeing his device, "the twenty-sixth of April at one minute, eight seconds, past noon."

"Adjusted for solar precession?" said Mr. Z.

"Yessir."

"Good. Fifteen minutes before that, at 11:45, we go in. Straight to the shrine. If you are seen, follow protocol and attempt to escape further interaction. Leave the temple entirely if you have to. This remains our mustering point. If we get separated, return here. Do not return to the nexus alone. We've got to make certain we're all together."

"What happens when we get to the shrine?" said Neutic.

"To be absolutely clear," said Mr. Z., "assuming Five is there, we allow him to transport. The consequences of him remaining on Earth are more perilous, more of a potential time crime, than whatever happens if he leaves. Second. Secure the golden ball. We cannot let it fall into the hands of the mothmen. Understand?"

"And what about Friday?" said Neutic.

"I'm delegating that to you," said Mr. Z. "Hell, let's give ourselves an extra half hour to enter the temple grounds tomorrow—that's ninety minutes prior to zenith. If the festivities are in full swing, that's when and where you will have to deposit Friday. Cloak your-selves, select a portion of the festival, mostly wherever there is something going on that serves to distract Friday—children playing games, cockfights, pig roasts, fireworks, what have you. But we've got to leave him. Do you understand? You are attached to the boy, I understand, believe me. I dare say we all are. But we've got to trust that his chances are best here, among the Khmer." He looked hard into Neutic's face.

"Yessir. I understand."

"And then you'll take your position at the southern entrance. For heaven's sake, Neutic, make certain somehow that Friday does not follow you. I'm leaving all that to you. Vixy, do you want the eastern or the northern entrance?"

Vixy shrugged. "The eastern entrance for you would be a little less walking in your condition. I'll take the northern."

"Done," said Mr. Z.

"C'mon, Friday," said Neutic. "Let's go for a walk." He led the boy toward the exposed roots of a nearby tree, ducking beneath the overhanging mass of tendrils as thick as a man's arm. "Friday," he said, peeking out. "Hide and seek!" Then he ducked into the darkness and disappeared. The boy giggled, waited, then toddled after Neutic. "Oh!" Neutic leapt back out into the open, swinging Friday in his arms. "You found me!" Friday squealed and laughed, and Neutic tousled the boy's hair.

Mr. Z. watched Vixy watching the two of them playing. She's attached to Neutic and the boy both, he thought, despite herself. And she's afraid for them. Something has to go right tomorrow. We need to catch a break. We need this zenith passage to pass without incident. And I need to get her and Neutic home. No mothmen, no conflict with Five, no conflict with any of the Khmer, heaven help us, no gunfire. No more bloodshed. And no more time to grow attached to this unfortunate boy.

CHAPTER 41

SHADOW PUPPETS

Tomorrow was the day, and if Five could only sleep, it would arrive more quickly. Or seem to. But he couldn't get the details of his preparations out of his head. The culms. The vac pump. All the parts and pieces. Would everything work? And the logistics—hauling everything into the damn shrine and avoiding confrontation with any Khmer. Had he accounted for delays? What delays? And what if his diversion failed and he couldn't clear the shrine without . . . it was unthinkable. Yet the potential for his having to literally fight his way home was real.

Nothing would go to plan. Nothing ever did. But would it go to plan well enough to get him home? He felt almost numbed, finally, to all his worrying. He'd done all he could. He'd done his best. If it wasn't enough, then it was too late now.

Nevertheless, he could not help pondering the last intangible. The weather. Cog said the meteorological data for April 26, 1296, Gregorian, in Angkor indicated overcast skies, exactly in line with the percentages for the period, but that he had managed to surreptitiously reallocate an unused atmospheric pressure seed from the geoengineering cache within the Angkor Cell mission. The engineers back then were routinely influencing the weather patterns to accommodate construction demands for the temple and the hydroengineering projects. But Five didn't need Cog's forecasts to know a change was coming—akin to any moleman, he could already feel it in his ears, the drop in atmospheric pressure that signaled the initiation of the cloud-bursting forces. There would be rain perhaps several hours past midnight and then, by dawn, a microlocalized high-pressure system would induce clear skies for the zenith passage. By way of the skies, at least, the way home would be clear.

Home. He was closer to it now than he had been in so very long. What would it be like? What had changed?. With the war on, especially, would there be anything left of the life that he had known? His visions of home had sustained him. Now they afflicted him. That he could neither contact nor visit his mother straight away, should he make it, was a painful reality. It was too risky to attempt to stride through the front door of his old life, as Cog described it. Rather, he would be obliged to emerge as gradually and as anonymously as possible. He would have to be patient and test the sociopolitical climate day by day for opportunities to blend back into normal life. And not as Five, of course. No. With Cog's help he would change his name and abandon all records of his identity, of his past, to escape reprisal or sanction or recrimination. Not that he couldn't endure all that, perhaps, if only he were home. But Cog was right. If his return to Mega City One became immediately known, the potential for controversy and public backlash—to say nothing of the incendiary politics—could harm everyone he cared about.

He surrendered to his restlessness and got up. He sipped absently from his waterskin and looked toward the temple. The eastern causeway was empty. It was late, after all, and all the activity seemed to occur within the larger western acreage. Even before the temple village flooded with Khmer within the last twenty-four hours. They would still be meandering about, cooking over fires, eating, drinking, playing their games, reveling. Was a similar gathering happening at Angkor Thom? Would the king remain there? Or would he arrive tomorrow and ensure the shrine would be jammed with onlookers?

Five sighed and made for the causeway—he had to walk, to move, to somehow clear his head. He crossed over the moat, entered the grounds, and turned south, hugging the outer wall. He'd stroll to the southeastern corner and go back, that's all. Nobody would see him. But he hadn't gone half the distance when the sounds of the village drifted toward him upon the breeze. What if he could get close enough to catch a glimpse of things? Just a glimpse. He crept closer to investigate.

Soon enough, he encountered the mostly forlorn and scattered huts of the temple village's outskirts. Further within, it was hordes of Khmer as far as he could see. Campfires large and small dotted the grounds. Men, women, and children of all ages milled about. There were bovines and chickens and at least a pig or two, from what he could discern. The incessant snap and crackle of tiny firecrackers and the ceaseless buzz of an active crowd of revelers drowned out even the boisterous jungle chorus.

It was exactly like a carnival on Mega City One. Well, no, nothing like it—there were no mechanical entertainments, no thrill rides, no electric lights or amplified music. No conditioned air, no properly constructed tents or tables or chairs, no proper food service. Least of all was there any escape from the mosquitoes and flies and scavenging dogs, felines, monkeys, and birds.

In fact, upon this southern side of the western entrance road, halfway between the library and the temple proper, he spied a robust bonfire just roaring to life as he watched. The bright flames made silhouettes of the people before it, and there was a banner being raised—ten meters or so broad and perhaps half as high. It was erected upon slender poles and the firelight illuminated it brightly from behind—it seemed aglow with pale energy.

He couldn't help but be drawn to it. There was something about the whole affair—the carefree nature of it—that made him feel, for once, utterly unobserved. Nevertheless, he wrapped his cloak about his head and shoulders and proceeded carefully, pausing within the shadows of the domiciles and the occasional tree to watch.

Music flowed. Small hand drums and reedy-sounding flutes or pipes of some type. The bonfire was tended by a handful of youths, and the fumes were redolent of burning coconut shell. Hence the significant heat. Indeed, he could sense the temperature soaring on the blustery breezes that darted across the village grounds.

The banner itself must have been woven of raw silk, surely a fine and costly thing for these Khmer to have created. Or perhaps they'd purchased it from a Chinese merchant?

Five approached still closer, mimicking the meandering pace of the others and careful not to draw the slightest attention to himself.

Suddenly the banner became animated with strange silhouettes—flat figures, akin to cutouts, were held aloft upon rods or light poles. This was a screen, designed to project shadow images. He found himself, along with most of the Khmer themselves, crowding closer.

Shadow puppets. Very large examples in fact, perhaps two meters high and a meter broad, manipulated with alluring dexterity and striking drama by the puppeteers, who thrust them here and there, shook them aggressively against the screen, or feigned violent clashes or tender intimations.

He tried to discern something of the story. Or stories. For there appeared to be military battles and the wielding of swords and spears against obviously enemy forces, then there were clearly more domestic antagonisms: love and loss, births and marriages, and subterfuge and courage. He recognized stylized human shapes, strikingly similar to those upon the temple gallery walls. The warriors and chariots and elephants and palanquins. And the multiarmed gods and goddesses, some resembling monkeys, others winged, many indecipherable to him. But everything, all the scenes were performed at high drama. Which the audience adored unequivocally. They shouted and laughed and delighted in attempting to spur the action.

It was frankly captivating. At least when he finally acquired a feel for the dramatic implications—the drama of betrayals and antagonisms, but also tender scenes of intimacy, kindness, longing, and tragedy. All rendered with remarkable deftness and finesse by such modest materials.

He listened to the tapping of the drums and the warbling of the flutes—a kind of soundtrack to the theater—and when there was an especially aggressive, violent clash between the puppets, a brassy cymbal crashed—bash! There was apparently a narrator too, whose words the audience hung upon as much as the images and the music. They oohed and aahed and clapped and cajoled and shouted and laughed at the action. And quieted, en masse, when the scenes became poignant—after a warrior was run through with a sword or a spear and lay dying, or when two lovers embraced.

Five listened to the sounds of the Khmer storyteller (he could hardly employ his autotranslator) in concert with the simple music that communicated so much with so little. He watched the puppeteers manipulate their stiff, mostly unarticulated figures against the shadow cloth, often standing upon one leg to thrust them awkwardly this way and that, tilting and twisting and at times shaking them against the fabric to force them more fully to life.

The fire roared, and the billowing, aromatic sting of the smoke and the strange, dancing shadows transformed the night into something otherworldly. The puppeteer's contorting and sweat-gleaming bodies and the glowing, wide-eyed faces of the Khmer audience, the dark presence of the forest jungle past the temple walls, all of it worked to conjure a sense of the fantastic.

Five found himself being carried away with the action and the life and the magic of the experience. He watched and listened and almost felt a part of things for a time—the festival reminded him of home—and then again, this seemed a farewell, a goodbye on behalf of the strange people of this strange planet. A farewell on behalf of the planet itself.

He had hated it here. He had been tested almost beyond his limits. He had struggled to survive and to retain his sanity. And he had won out, so far, at least. And tonight, upon the cusp of perhaps his last day upon Earth, he suddenly felt a measure of reconciliation with this planet, and he understood that as long as he lived, there was a part of this experience that had changed him forever and that he could not help but cherish. In this way he stood watching, for a time unburdened from his sins, and took solace in the adventure of life, momentarily free from his nagging torments, come what may.

———

NEUTIC LAY WIDE AWAKE, LISTENING to the forest's nightly orchestra of life, the howls and yowls and rasps and chirping and croaking. And the trills and whistles and whoops. It occurred to him that he was no longer troubled by it. For the past several nights, he had slept soundly enough, finally oblivious somehow to the noise, the humid heat, the biting insects that somehow invaded their camp cloak, the sleeping rough and the strain of their predicament. A person could get used to anything, indeed.

He watched the others sleep, still as stones, including Friday, curled up beside Vixy. That Friday could not remain with them was a given. But the circumstances that had brought them together also seemed a given in the sense that if he could do it all over again, he would still rescue the boy. Try as he might, he just couldn't imagine what type of mindset and ruthless perspective it would take to allow the alternative outcome to have played itself out.

He tossed and turned on his mat. He had been incapable of leaving Friday behind at Siem Reap. Now, he was being ordered, justifiably enough, to lose the boy within the festival crowd. To abandon Friday to his fate in this time and place where he belonged. Even if that time and place seemed unwelcoming, even a threat, to the boy's well-being.

Did Friday belong here and now? Neutic understood the logic. He understood the imperative to protect the space-time architecture. And the catastrophe of consequences that the TDC could only partially mitigate, despite their intense efforts. It was exactly why nobody was to ever, under any circumstances, even toy with the idea of transporting the indigenous. Let alone saving or taking their lives. But this was a child about to be twice abandoned. What had the boy been doing out on his own, unwatched, with the whole of that little village apparently indifferent to him? Who did he belong to? Did he have living parents? If not, did he have any type of caregiver? Was he an orphan somehow being raised by the whole village?

Friday had fattened up a bit since they'd acquired him, even on the meager rations they could spare him. Not even a week ago he had been a boney, grimy, unkempt jungle urchin, susceptible to all manner of disease and trauma and starvation. Now he seemed sturdier, his eyes brighter, his personality less fraught and feral and instead more keenly enthusiastic and personable. In a word, human. Neutic liked the way Friday took a moment to gaze wide-eyed at a person's face before accepting a morsel of food, say, or a makeshift toy—a nutshell or smooth stone. How he examined things—beetles and lizards and crickets and butterflies, even flower buds and the leaves of plants. To say nothing of his interest in practically anything Neutic and Vixy and Mr. Z. wore or had brought with them. He could not help being charmed by Friday's evident talents of concentration, how his little brow furrowed when he inspected his latest find. He liked the boy's smile, and his generally amiable, easygoing attentiveness and calm curiosity. Friday almost never cried. He was neither demanding nor grasping nor stubborn nor otherwise impossible. He responded to affection and seemed generous in his way. If you fed him, or offered a toy, he was keen to share whatever it was in return. They were leaving a trace upon each other, he and Friday, yes. More than a trace.

Neutic got up, careful not to wake anyone, and stepped outside the cloak zone. There was a pleasant breeze—enough to discourage the mosquitoes and gnats, thank heaven—and he stood breathing in the tropical air that always seemed redolent of rain and greenery and a kind of mineral rot, as if the stones themselves were surrendering to an unavoidable decomposition. He noticed, too, the scent of burning wood upon the breeze. And the distant murmur of voices—would the Khmer be staging their festival through the night?

Friday had awakened and was grasping at Neutic's pant leg, looking up at him. He led the boy away from their bivouac, let him pee, and without thinking took Friday's hand and wandered in the direction of the temple's eastern entrance, keeping an eye out for anyone but nevertheless feeling strangely compelled to investigate the grounds or walk under the stars.

"Let's go, Friday," he whispered.

The boy seemed eager to toddle alongside but quickly tired, and at the causeway, Neutic gathered Friday into his arms and marched across the open space between the outer wall and the first tier of the temple, following the galleries south, then west toward the main entrance. He checked his transponder. Yes, Mr. Z. or Vixy could track his position if they needed to. But he hoped they would sleep.

He activated his cloak and sauntered along, and it wasn't long before they encountered the fringes of the temple village proper. He set Friday upon his feet. It was mostly quiet and dark, but here and there were significant groups of Khmer, many clustered around little campfires, chatting and gesticulating, others roasting food over their fires while others stirred steaming pots. Toward the western entrance road, however, was a uniquely grand and dramatic blaze of a bonfire, and he was drawn to it, leading Friday along. He soon spied what he assumed was a banner of sorts—a broad, pale fabric stretched taut between raised poles. There was an enormous crowd pressed shoulder to shoulder before it, watching some sort of shadow play. Were these the famous shadow puppets? He had heard or read or seen something about Indonesian shadow puppets that resembled these, but not exactly. These examples were very large and mostly unarticulated and were being thrust about with great earnestness and effort by hardworking puppeteers.

He loitered, drawn to the performance, embellished as it was by strangely affecting music—drums and flutes—and the nasally, monotone voice of what had to be a narrator.

When Friday saw the puppets, he yelped, apparently with glee, yanked his hand free, and before Neutic could do anything, darted into the audience, disappearing in an instant.

Neutic endured a pang of panic, made to dive into the crowd after Friday, but stopped short, struck by the realization that not only could he not risk being noticed—his cloaking would disintegrate the moment he brushed against a stranger—but this was it, the very opportunity he could not have hoped to contrive. This was his chance to let Friday go. It was as if the cosmos were granting them both this chance.

Nevertheless, he couldn't help feeling he'd made a mistake, for how likely was it that anyone here would take Friday in or pay him any attention at all? The puppet show would end, everyone would retire to their tents and makeshift camps, and sooner or later poor Friday would be on his own again. Would he look for Neutic? Would he be anxious and cry for someone to help him? Would he feel betrayed? Was he looking for Neutic already? It was impossible to endure, the painful sense of utterly selfish abandonment. What kind of a man was he to do this thing?

Turn and go, dammit. Mr. Z. and Vixy would understand completely. They would tell him it had to be done, that the opportunity, such as it was, had been fortuitous. He chided himself, half fearing, half hoping that Friday would reappear while at the same time goading himself to hurry away. Then he glimpsed something strange out of the corner of his eye. Poised some distance from the rear of the crowd, between the shadows and bright luminosity of the shadow theater, was the short yet broad profile of—it had to be. Five!

But what about Friday? He glanced about quickly, searching for the boy, torn as to whether to leave him. He glanced back at Five but, no, now the moleman was gone too!

Suddenly, a horrible squealing startled him. A short distance away, several Khmer wrestled with a small pig. Two men spread the beast's legs wide while a woman stabbed at its chest with a blade. Blood gushed forth. The men lifted the now silent animal higher, straining to hold the pig aloft but with a happy enthusiasm, teasing at each other's clumsiness and laughing, and the woman bent to collect the blood into a bowl.

Neutic backed away. Step by step he retreated, feeling himself an utter foreigner, an unwelcome intruder. Friday was gone. Likewise Five, if that's who it was. The firelight danced, the shadows upon the screen thrust themselves about with a violent and obscene drama that was suddenly impossible to endure. It all seemed nightmarishly foreign and unsettlingly ancient and unknowable, and he knew he must return to camp or risk he didn't know what.

He turned and strode forcefully away, leaving the festival and Friday behind him, his own heart heavy with a sense of failure and loss, of impossible circumstance and a pain and hollowness that he knew already would never leave him. He fled like a ghost of himself into the hollow darkness of the Cambodian night.

CHAPTER 42

THIS IS NOT FOR OUR EYES

"Kill anyone who breaks through," said Cog. "Anyone who tries to stop you. You must be isolated and in proximity to the nexus or—dammit, Five, I don't have to tell you that the shrine has to be cleared for the HDT. Or you'll never make it. What about your diversion. Is it prepped?"

"Yessir." Five paced back and forth nervously as he talked. "Twenty strings of firecrackers—perhaps sixty seconds' worth of noise."

"Did you check for moisture damage? Are the fuses dry? Have they been disturbed at all? The technology couldn't get more primitive. I think now that we may have done better to engineer something more effective."

"Yessir. I mean, no, sir. I mean, the firecrackers, as far as I can discern, are just as I left them last night. Clean and dry."

"So be it," said Cog. "They will have to do. Where are you?"

"Northeast courtyard, sir. Second tier. I'm just waiting."

"Waiting, I know. Me too, Five, me too. Less than an hour, now. And if the diversion fails; if those damn pyrotechnics don't get whatever crowd is crammed into that shrine at least curious enough to get out and look—I just don't know. These Khmer rituals. Their whack-job mythological zeal. Hell, you said the Khmer were lighting fireworks all of yesterday? They may not make anything of more fireworks. They may not budge. That's why I say you have got to be prepared. If you have to throw people down the temple stairs, do it."

"Yessir. I am prepared to clear the shrine. And then I brace the door." He stopped pacing and wiped at his dampened brow. The day was warming, but it was his nerves too. The plan was suddenly flimsy as they rehashed it. Foolish, even. It was all starting to seem impossible.

"Now," said Cog. "Nerves are part of any mission. Be nervous. Be anxious. Allow it. And set it aside. Let the psychology go. Adapt to and overcome every obstacle. Meanwhile, focus upon the engineering. Do you hear? Follow the psychological protocols. You are still a cadet, Five. In my eyes you are still on your way to becoming a moleman engineer, remember that. You have done well to reengineer the moth-man transponder so that we can talk and not have to type, for shit's sake. And you've managed to activate the cloaking function—that may help. It may help even after you arrive home. We're going to use that mothman transponder as a valuable bit of espionage. Your acquisition of it, your reengineering of it, it's all to your credit. It will help smooth things over, believe me. With the Giza Cell authorities. With the members of the tribunal. With the damn media. Just like we talked about. You'll see. Now, look here. Everything is in place on my end. When you arrive within Mega City One, I'll know it. Make certain to immediately scramble your coordinates. Then move out. Get to the rendezvous point as quickly as you can, do you understand? Five, we are out of time. We need to break transmission."

"Yessir."

"Good luck, Five."

"Yessir."

"Cog out."

Five shuffled into the shade with his back against the temple wall. It was all he could do to keep from pacing. Stay quiet, dammit. Stay out of sight. Forty minutes to zenith. Keep it together, for shit's sake. It can work. The plan can work.

He toggled off the cloak, saving power if only from habit. He had more than enough battery for the shrine, and nobody could approach him without him seeing them first anyway.

Cog's call seemed to have transformed him into a jumble of nerves.

He squinted at the sun and into the clear blue sky. The last wisps of high clouds were scattering in all directions. Climate engineering. Cog had made it happen. It was working. All those months of thinking he'd have to rely upon meteorological good fortune, of hoping for a statistically anomalous break in the weather, upon dumb luck. He'd been crazy to believe his transport could happen, that he'd have a chance on his own despite everything he lacked. Crazy enough to make his own luck, perhaps.

He checked the time. Again. He checked the sun's altitude. Again. It seemed to stop in its tracks when he looked at it and to hurtle to its zenith whenever he looked away. He felt his pulse quickening. And mind racing. Stick to the plan. Step by step. Let your nerves go and hold to the engineering.

He pricked his ears toward the village grounds and resisted the urge to investigate. Stay here, stay hidden. There was nothing to see out there, no need to get curious, get distracted. More Khmer, more festivities, more noise, that's all. He didn't care if the Khmer king himself showed up with all of Angkor Thom in tow. Let them come.

It wasn't the Khmer that troubled him, anyway. It was the TDC. Mr. Z., Miss Vixy, and that Neutic fellow. They would never just let him go about his business. In their shoes, neither would he. Would they be keen to the significance of the zenith passage? Yes. Would they try to stop him? Perhaps. If they could manage to enter the temple. And then what? He tried to harden himself against them. And the mothmen too. They and the TDC both may have already deployed more operatives. They could be plotting this very instant to ambush him. If any of them broke through, he would have no choice. By the gods, he wished he could make everything go to plan!

Twenty-five minutes to zenith. He inspected his fireworks one last time, brushed a stray leaf away pointlessly. He caught himself yet again patting his garments to verify he had all his equipment.

Stop it. Stop running through the plan. He knew all there was to know. He had practiced all there was to practice. He stared at the transponder. It was go time. Get to the quincunx.

Five cloaked himself and hopped up the short eastern stair, crouching low, looking and listening. What was that? Footsteps. In the direction of the western corridor, opposite him. He listened as hard as he could, placed his hands against the stone as if to feel any indications. Many footsteps. And the tinkling and jingling sound of metal upon metal. Priestly ornaments? Jewelry? Perhaps royalty had arrived? The king?

He felt suddenly galvanized with purpose. He pictured the scene within the shrine, his rearranging of the floor pavers to cover his work. The dirt and dishevelment that someone would inevitably notice.

He was cloaked. And a mere ten meters from the center of the shrine. The Khmer would come from the west, from the main entrance, utilizing those shallower, broader steps to gain the upper level. But the TDC and the mothmen? He strained to hear everything. They could come from any direction.

There! Khmer! Passing into the western vestibule, yes, but turning left! Why? And how many? He counted four, five, six, then so many more so that his counting seemed irrelevant. His anxiety ratcheted skyward. There was only room for a handful of people within that tiny shrine. Along the narrow corridors themselves, only two people could pass side by side. Sixteen minutes until the zenith. Should he rush into the shrine and try to barricade himself inside before all these Khmer filled the corridors and blocked his way? Or were they merely passing through, performing an obligatory circumambulation or a ritual? After which they would disperse? Hell no. Don't be fool enough to count upon *that*. But this was crazy—the entire quincunx would be jammed!

He wrung his hands. There! The king, Indravarman III himself, it had to be! Five's mind raced. You expected this. Get ahold of yourself. And wait. They're holding to the outer corridors. See if any of them move toward the shrine.

He may have counted twenty-five Khmer, including the king. All of them were bare chested but for their necklaces and arm bands and adorned in shimmering, silken sompot chong kben.[76] Some

---

76 A long, rectangular cloth worn wrapped around the lower body, pulled back between the legs and tucked in at the back.

sported shimmering golden tiaras, none of which compared to the king's towering, pointed headdress. He strode forth confidently, wielding a heavy staff.

Five took a breath. It only seemed like an unmanageable horde because he wasn't used to seeing anyone up here, that's all. Let alone Khmer in all their finery.

The four corridors into the shrine itself remained clear, thank heaven. The Khmer indeed appeared to be circumambulating the quincunx, beginning with the far northwest tower and proceeding in a clockwise direction. Watch and wait, then. More than likely, they would complete their tour and approach the shrine from the west.

Seven minutes until the zenith. He cut his observations short—it was time! He rushed headlong down his eastern corridor toward the heavy door of the shrine, shoved it open, scrambled over the threshold, shoved it closed behind him, and got to work uncovering the shaft. He shifted the Buddha statue against the western door to block it. He hauled up the pavers, likewise shoved them against the other three doors, and returned to the shaft. He swept aside the thin layer of soil, yanked the coconut-husk plug free and reached for his flashlight, keen to check the shaft for debris. What? He'd forgotten it! Idiot! No time to clear an obstruction anyway. Forget it. Things are as they are. Four minutes. No time for fixes.

He unpacked the golden ball, cradled it gingerly now, as if it were as fragile as an egg. No fumbles. No slipups. He reached for his sling.

Suddenly, they were there. The Khmer? Or someone else? He strained to listen. Murmuring outside the door. Then a tentative shoving against his stone blockade. Then more force, and the statue shifted a bit.

A rush of panic and he set the sling aside, grasped his device, verified the signal was transmitting.

Dammit to hell! A long iron chisel like the one he'd stolen thrust violently between the wooden door and its stone frame. They were trying to leverage the door open, heaving at it! Five looked straight up. The sun would come. Two minutes left. He tapped the transponder to trigger his pyrotechnics and listened. Pops and bangs and pitiful cracklings, as if from kilometers distant. It would never distract anyone. Nevertheless, the forcing of the door ceased.

Five snatched at his sling, dropped to his knees over the shaft, fumbled to unwind the pouch, and dropped the entire roll of sinew-cable as if it were a live thing leaping from his hands. He gasped, dumbfounded, as the thing unraveled itself across the floor. Dammit to hell! Then, to his horror, the pry bar again, and the door shifted further.

A commanding voice boomed something in Khmer. He'd disabled his autotranslator, so he couldn't discern it. An intolerable silence. But no prying at the door. No movement, no sound, nothing but the grinding in his guts and the awful sense that time itself had stopped and that the zenith would never come. Now what? He eyed the mess of line, eyed the door, eyed the shaft, knelt there in a cold sweat. He shoved his knife into his belt, made to gather up his line, at the same time trying to cradle the golden ball. Hurry. Less than a minute. There was still time, just hurry!

"Nih minmen te minmen samreab phnek robsa yeung te! Stab preahsaursieng robsa preah chea amcheasa!"[77]

What were they saying? It goddamn didn't matter. The wooden ceiling of the tower was dark. His lonely temple shrine was virtually pitch black. Five knelt beside the shaft, struggling to nestle the ball into its pouch. Please. *Please.* He imagined the Giza ball buried deep in its black pit beneath the Great Pyramid, centuries hence. He envisioned its effect upon this ball, if he could just goddamn get the thing lowered! *Get me home. Get me home. Get me home.*

Thirty seconds.

The door shifted heavily. No! Light poured into the room. It would interfere!

A shout, in English. "Five!"

He couldn't believe his ears or his eyes, for it was Miss Vixy bursting into the shrine and aiming her lantern into his face.

"Five!" she cried. "Stop!"

---

77 Khmer. "This is not for our eyes! Heed the voice of the Lord God!"

"Vixy!" It was Mr. Z. now, grasping hard at Vixy's arm and diverting her flashlight. He stared hard at Five. They stared hard at each other.

"Mr. Z.!" shouted Vixy, "we have to stop him!"

"No!" cried Mr. Z. "Wait! Just wait!"

Time stood still in the gloaming. Then a brightness above. He wasn't ready! Five scrambled onto his rear, cross-legged, doused his hands with oil, cradled the golden ball, squirmed into makeshift position, and did his best to align himself and the ball beneath the central tower. A moment later came the fiery light, a singular shaft of sunlight materializing as if from nowhere, blazing wildly upon the ball.

"No, Vixy!" cried Mr. Z. "Let him go!"

Five shut his eyes, felt the ball twist in his hands, endured the flash of light, then the darkness, then nothing.

———

"Hurry!" said Mr. Z. "Get into formation."

The three of them—Mr. Z., Vixy, and Neutic—rushed toward the grassy, open space.

"Here!" said Mr. Z. "Exactly here! Together!"

Mr. Z., Vixy and Neutic crowded shoulder to shoulder.

"I'm disabling the cloak," said Mr. Z. "Closer, now, get closer. All of us together! Lock arms. Counting down. Ten, nine—"

Neutic turned. "Friday!" He watched with horror and dismay as the boy scrambled toward them, arms out, beseeching. "No, Friday, no!"

"Neutic!" cried Vixy. "Don't! It's too late!" She reached for him.

"Vixy, no!" Mr. Z. held her fast round her waist.

Neutic ran to the boy and in a single motion snatched him up and turned to go back. He saw Vixy's horrified visage, watched her silent scream and Mr. Z.'s desperate, awkward, one-handed hammering at the transponder control.

The flash of silvery light staggered him, he fell to his knees, and when he looked up, they were gone.

CHAPTER 43

PLAIN OF HEAVEN

MAJOR GENERAL AXIO-ONE PEERED INTO the viewfinder and scanned the grassy, treeless expanse of the Plain of Heaven. He tracked the battlefield west, all the way to the pale beach sands of the Sunset Sea, whose waters stretched to the horizon. Soon enough, moleman ships would arrive. A moleman port city would be built. The so-called Mothman Realm would be theirs.

He panned to the south, some twenty kilometers distant, past the tattered ranks of the mothman army scrambling to reconfigure itself and deep into the brownish topography of the foothills of the Mencius Mountains. He zoomed in upon the shabby tent cities of the mothman populace. What type of leader was this mothman empress that she would force the displacement of hundreds of thousands of her own people to be used as living shields? Desperate, certainly. And ruthless. And now her offer of surrender, as if she had suddenly grasped the inevitable.

Get on with it, then. The surrender, that is. He glanced at the attack status clock. Still green and counting down. Less than three minutes. Damn high command to hell. The back-and-forth of the last twenty-four hours had been maddening—one minute he was to initiate the attack and annihilate the enemy, and the next, they were to hold back, waiting. Waiting for what?

He evaluated his eastern and western flanks. Three legions with sixty thousand molemen infantry apiece, each legion composed of ten battalions of six thousand battle-hardened soldiers. Each legion's combined heavy and light infantry were deployed in three lines: four battalions in the first line and three battalions each in the second and third lines. The battalions themselves were separated by a distance precisely equal to their width in an alternating, checkerboard-style pattern. In all, 1.4 kilometers of an indomitable moleman army front. It was a classic, some would say unremarkable and even dangerously predictable configuration. But the weakness of the enemy hardly demanded anything exceptional.

The major general scanned the war displays. He watched his lieutenants riding unperturbed through their battalions upon their battle chariots, their glide-engines belching white steam into the rising wind. He watched the high-flying, black-and-silver standards of the moleman army rippling in the wind, the fabric snapping and popping spiritedly, as if annunciating the moleman victory. And he watched the attack status clock running out to zero. Five, four, three, two . . .

He filled his lungs and projected his voice into the receiver, "Prepare to fire!"

"No! Sir! Wait!"

The major general scowled. "Stand down, Major Cog."

Cog inched himself forward in his glide-chair. He gestured urgently at the central war display monitor. "Sir, I understand the order to attack, but look—the fold, if we wait for it, just a few more moments! You know it is the mothman tactic to hide within the trailing obfuscation!"

"Dammit, Major, there is no evidence of a fold!" The major general hammered at his console keyboard. "See for yourself! All zeros, from the west flank to the Sunset Sea. The attack command is green. The time is now, we can end it here!"

Cog held up his bandaged hand, his fingers still curled slightly from the re-fleshing procedure. He tapped clumsily at the console and peered urgently at his display. "No, sir, look! There! Time warp, to the east!"

An alarm bellowed, the attack command clock flashed red— *STAND BY*—and the war room darkened.

Cog pitched forward in his glide-chair, his safety harness digging uncomfortably into his rehabilitation bodysuit. He winced. "There it is, sir—the mothman battalion. Inbound, just like we suspected. And they've brought two, no, three, helical catapults!"

"And the psi-assault energy is building," said the major general. He leapt into his chair and buckled his five-point. He set his bullhorn amplifier at full volume. "Pull back the eastern legion! Pull it back! Redirect the psi-shield to the eastern flank and prepare those units for a mind assault! Repeat: pull the eastern legion back! Redirect the psi-shield to the eastern flank! Prepare for mind assault!"

"The helical catapults," exclaimed Cog, "we've only a few minutes before they launch their entanglement harpoons!"

"Damn the world!" growled the major general. "The psi-shield is down! Those men will be turned!"

Cog stole a glance at his transponder. Dammit, Five, where are you?

———

"LIEUTENANT COLONEL!" THE HEAVY WIND off the sea snatched Shan's words from his mouth and he tried again. "Sir!" But the lieutenant colonel was upwind, too distant and preoccupied with the movement of the battalion. Shan resorted to keying his radio, his hands trembling with anticipation of the news. He watched the lieutenant colonel respond to the vibration of his own device, glance at it, then turn his horse round and round, searching the ranks.

"Go ahead! Shan? Go ahead!"

"Sir, the moleman psi-shield is down! Over!" Shan raised his communication banner higher and flashed the strobe. "I'm here! Here!"

Lieutenant Colonel Gama forced his horse through the ranks. "Clear the way," he shouted. "Dammit, let me through!" He brought his horse alongside the communication chariot, shouting into the wind at Shan. "It could be another recharge delay. Are the backups at zero?"

"Zero, sir. No legacy energy. The psi-shield is down! Down and static. Their minds are unguarded!"

Lieutenant Colonel Gama nodded so vigorously that his helmet slipped over his fleshy brow. He repositioned it with an impatient shove and yanked at the reins of his stamping horse. He signaled to the frontline warriors to advance. "Three lines! Form rank! Three lines and march!" He yanked hard upon his chin strap and galloped his horse toward the rear of the battalion, beside the ranks of helical catapults. He pressed his radio close against his mouth to be heard. "Prime the harpoons!" He paraded his horse down the line of psi-artillery, impatient for the soldiers to set the braces. "You are moving like decrepit tortoises! Like your asses are clamped to the ground! Double-time, men! Hurry!"

The garrison commander eyed the condition of his catapult, jostled the last locking pin, and wheeled around to address the passing general with a salute. "Sir! Armed and ready!"

"Launch!" The general raised his arm and his voice boomed, and his horse leapt forward as if anticipating the fury of the harpoons. "Fire at will!"

As if on cue, the masts of tall ships appeared upon the horizon of the Sunset Sea. Shan's heart leapt and he circled his chariot triumphantly. At the flash of the harpoons, his horse reared, and he watched the general shake his trident, shouting at the top of his voice, "The empress's ships! All hail her Supreme Augustness! Our ships have come!"

The sky flashed, the harpoons flew, then sonic booms and powerful flashes arrived one on top of the other. Bombardment cannons from the tall ships screamed overhead. A deafening sequence of explosions quaked the battlefield, fire and smoke filled the horizon, and the mothman battalions cheered, raising their flags and banners higher. They watched the terrible projectiles flash across the sky toward the molemen's shore-bound legions, heard the thunderous detonations, witnessed the smoke and fire, and rejoiced.

———

"THIS MAP," SAID THE PROFESSOR. She had pushed her chair away from the table so that she could cross her legs and rested her cane in one hand. With the other she teased absently at her earring. "It's a Van der Grinten I projection. Any cartographer will tell you it's an ancient style of map. From several millennia ago."

The captain tapped his coffee cup on the tabletop and focused upon the behavior of the hologram. "Hmm, yes, well, there aren't many maps of the Mothman Realm to begin with. We dug this up from somewhere. Nobody has had time to come up with anything better. But, look here, I've got the latest on the empress's surrender."

"That it was no surrender at all?"

The captain eyed the professor skeptically. "You've been reading her mind and not telling me?"

The professor rattled her bracelets and scooted her chair closer to the table.

"I'm serious, Professor."

"Of course not. Even if I could."

The captain tapped his keyboard and the map of the Mothman Realm zoomed in.

"What am I looking at?" said the professor, squinting at it. "Those icons in the Sunset Sea. Are those . . . ?"

"Mothman navy attack ships. An entire fleet. And these vectors? Look here." He pointed to a data column at the lower right of the screen. "Look at the caliber. Those are high-capacity shore bombardment projectiles."

"The Mothmen are fighting?"

"Fighting like hell. You can see the molemen eastern flank collapsing—this is in real time. There's not a ground force in the cosmos that can absorb that kind of shelling unprotected. Not even the molemen."

"What is happening? What about the empress's surrender?"

"I'd say all this carnage speaks for itself, doesn't it?"

"They were caught unawares," said the professor. "The molemen. It seems impossible."

"Damn close to impossible, I'll give you that. Which gives me a newfound respect for those lunatic mothmen. And their empress. Look at that." He gestured at the screen. "It looks like we've got a whole new war on our hands."

"YOU HEARD THE MAJOR!" COG guided his hover chair down from the command platform, shouting at the technicians. "Reengineer the psi-barrier! Protect the eastern flank! Target the mothman navy!"

A shield technician, seated at his controls, froze with astonishment. "But, sir! The barriers—to reengineer them will require—"

"That's an order, soldier!" shouted Cog. "We've got no more than ten minutes before the mothman battalion recovers from the HDT depletion."

The war displays showed scene after scene of carnage, fiery wreckage, smoke, and flames. Yet the battlefield technicians still appeared paralyzed with surprise.

Major General Axio-One delivered his orders in rapid-fire, clipped language. "Engineers! Technicians! Obey that order! Retarget the GIC[78] upon the helical catapults! Collapse the lines! Turn our army around. Retreat! And hope to hell we don't run out of time!"

Meanwhile, Cog sped from the command platform toward the confines of the nearest war room, then slammed the door behind him. He had no time. Indeed, there was no time now for anything, least of all for the tedium of secrecy—it was all now or never. He rapped aggressively at the control pad mounted on the arm of his hover chair until he'd locked onto their radio channel. "Five, do you copy? Five! Are you *here*? Come in, Five! Come in!" He shook the device angrily and resisted the urge to fling it across the room. He widened the bandwidth and listened, frantically tuning. There! A telltale crackling of static. "Five? Is that you? Five, do you copy?"

"Yessir. This is Five."

The signal was weak and broken. Cog pressed his ear close.

"Major malfunction, sir. HDT glitch. My coordinates were scrambled. I am not at Mega City One. I don't know where I am. Except it looks like the moleman army or something. I'm in a field. There is smoke and fire and . . . I don't understand!"

"Five, you are on the Plain of Heaven. You are on our battlefield in the Mothman Realm. Stand by, Five!" Cog thrust open the door

---

78 Gatling irradiation cannon.

of the war room—damn any secrecy now—and forced his hover chair up the ramp to the observation deck. He shouted into his transponder: "I'm locking on to your coordinates." Cog scanned the displays—there, in the bottom left display—the homing signal had locked on Five's transmission—his coordinates were a kilometer east, a half kilometer from the shore of the Sunset Sea. "Five! Hold your position!"

"Sir?" said Five.

Cog wheeled round. "Major General, the psi-shield is back up. On the eastern flank. We've crippled one of the catapults. But the entanglement harpoons, sir, look! Delta battalion. We were too late. Those soldiers have turned, all of them!"

"For the love of all machines," railed the major general, "we are battling our own damn army!" He leaned toward the intercom. "Mobilize the command center. Retreat. Roll us back to the southwest, twenty degrees latitude and hold. Repeat. Twenty degrees latitude on this longitude and hold. We've got to hold them off until Mega City One can deploy the bombardment. And our navy arrives."

Cog glanced at the time. It would be hours yet to clear the meridians and parallels and hypermeridians for the navy transport. Hell, if anything could be cleared at all now.

The floor of the command center shook.

Cog pointed at the war screens. "High-capacity bombardment shells! From the tall ships!"

The floor shook harder, and the major general stumbled, clutching at the console. "Siege protocol!" He rushed down the ramp, calling for his lieutenants, gesturing for an aide to hand him his mech-saber and plasma rifle. "Ready my chariot! Colonel Cog!"

"Yessir!"

"You are in command. Get this pile of junk to the rear!"

Cog saluted and scanned the battle displays. Then he peered at the flashing icon on his device. There! Near the shore of the Sunset Sea—Five. It had to be. "Five! Do you copy?"

Silence. Then static. Finally, Five's breathless response. "Yessir!"

The bay windows of the mobile command center shuttered closed, and the blast shields lowered. The command center was prepping for lift off. Cog glanced round, satisfied that the bridge was empty except for the navigators, communications specialists, the shield engineers and a clutch of turret gunners. Everyone else was deployed to the field per siege protocol. He jammed an earpiece into his ear, adjusted the volume, and spoke as clearly and directly as he could into his device. "Five, a strike team is en route to your coordinates. You are on the Mothman Realm. In the middle of the Great Conflict. You will be armed and ready in less than two minutes. Do you copy?"

"Yessir. I see them."

"Fight, Five! Fight for Mega City One! Fight for your life!"

Indicator beacons in the ceiling flashed red then yellow, saturating the bridge with monochrome illumination. The pilot's emotionless voice penetrated the quiet. "Liftoff in three, two, one."

Cog tightened his five-point harness and braced himself. Siege protocol dictated that the command center capsule retreat from harm's way and preset an HDT escape trajectory to Mega City One. Meanwhile, the capsule was dutybound to remain poised at the rear of the ground war. Many a commander had seen fit to sacrifice him- or herself and their command center crew in the name of honor, and Cog, likeminded, suffered the agony of being pulled to safety while his army risked all. Suddenly exhausted, he slouched into his glide-chair harness.

"Major Cog." A young med-tech grasped the arm of Cog's hover chair. "Your injuries, sir. That is to say, the monitors—they indicate your constitution parameters are sub-stable and falling. We need to get you to a treatment cell. You are risking—"

"I'm risking nothing our soldiers in the field aren't risking ten times over!" Cog winced at the pain in his ribs. His eyes darted from display to display. He analyzed the visuals, inputted the streaming data, calculated the risks and probabilities, and engineered the solutions.

The med-tech's voice was adamant. "Sir, with all due respect. We have reached the safe zone. The HDT portal preset is established. My orders from Mega City One command are to get you inside a restoration cell immediately."

"Casualty data," said Cog. He tried to focus on the sub-display detailing the activities of Five's strike team, but the images were blurred, and he felt lightheaded. He reached for the console, and his hand slipped. He gasped, shook his head, tried to clear his thoughts. "Data. Strike team . . . Five. Five . . ." He collapsed in his seat, head lolling, one arm dangling.

The med-tech yanked the glide-chair's headplate into position, strapped Cog's head to it, positioned Cog's arm in his own lap, and gestured to a nearby nurse to help him. "Let's roll!"

SHAN'S HORSE STAMPED ITS HOOVES at the controlled mayhem of the reassembling mothman army. Lieutenant Colonel Gama's standard could be seen high above the helmeted heads of the frontline warriors, the colored silk rippling in the offshore breezes. "Easy, High Cloud!" Shan shouted, "this fight is not for us!" The horse relented reluctantly, stamping it hooves, its chin drawn hard against its chest, literally chomping at the bit.

Shan shouted above the din of men, animals, and machines. "Close ranks! Conserve your strength! Pace yourselves!" He kicked at his horse, urging High Cloud into a gallop toward the sea.

They attained the shore at speed, crashing into the surf as mothman navy long boats and transport rafts, still fifty meters out to sea, dropped anchor and collapsed their bay doors into the foaming breakers. Teams of soldiers plunged forth into the water, arms and ammunition held high, striding with great effort through the shallow waves.

Shan led High Cloud along the beach, then plunged farther into the water. The horse kicked high at the frothy waves, his blood-sweat streaming down his flanks. Shan waved his banner triumphantly, urging the mothman soldiers onward. He looked farther out to sea, to the tall ships. There! The royal trireme, the high-bowed craft bearing another two thousand warriors and, if the rumors could be believed, the empress herself. Shan reached for his binoculars and made to zoom in, searching for her, but something yanked at his stirrup.

"Advisor Shan! Sir!"

"Yes." There, dressed in full battle armor, his helmet clutched under his arm and his black hair blowing sideways in the wind, was a young mothman, no more than eighteen years old, fresh faced, his eyes gleaming with excitement and expectation. There was something undeniably familiar about him. "Kang!" said Shan. "Is it you?"

The young warrior's eyes blazed. "Yessir!"

"Kang!" Shan slid from his horse, grasped Kang's shoulder with one hand, and clasped his hand in a hearty grip.

The other warriors, some mounted upon horses, others splashing their way toward shore on foot, still others burdened with firearms, spears, crossbows, surged past them. Then came the great catapults, Gatling guns, daisy cutter canons, and hovercraft after hovercraft of ammunition and supplies.

"By the heavens, Kang," shouted Shan, "I never thought I would see you again. Hail to our empress! But Kang, we need provisions. Shelters. Fuel. Our civilians trapped against the foothills—they are starving. Dying of exposure. Is the empress truly here?"

"Our ships are heavy with supplies, that is all I can tell you." He looked to sea. "I must go, sir, my unit—"

"Of course, Kang! Go! Go!" Shan allowed High Cloud to high step through the surf. "Kill the enemy, Kang!" He watched his mothman friend disappear into the fray. "May we meet together in victory before the day is done!"

CHAPTER 44

GHOST OF A CHANCE

"INBOUND," SAID LIEUTENANT GRACE. SHE gritted her teeth and gripped the airlock release, waiting. "Minus one."

"What!" said the captain. He glared at the arrival bay monitor.

"I don't understand," said the professor. "You said they were all in formation."

The intercom blared. "Coordinates synchronized . . . gyrohelm secure . . . boomerang defense primed . . . travelers arriving in five, four, three, two . . ."

Status lamps flooded the arrival bay with pulsing green light, the overhead exhaust fans engaged, the gyrohelm shuddered, then a blinding flash. A burst of steam-like transport residue belched forth, drawn immediately upward into the roaring exhaust equipment, and the bay itself went dark.

The black pillars of the arrival bay glistened, the metal pinging with heat, and the unmistakable clang of the boomerang defense slammed against the recoil of the arrival, shattering the aperture and rendering the wormhole a thing of the past.

The lieutenant twisted the airlock release, shoved hard at it, and darted through the aperture door into the arrival bay.

Mr. Z. and Vixy stood upon the platform face-to-face and arm-in-arm—standard HDT posture for a dual return. Two med-techs attended them, draped them in decontamination blankets, and hurried them from the arrival bay platform toward their respective glide chairs upon the conveyor.

The lieutenant waited for Mr. Z. and Vixy to disappear into the airlock on their way to medical, and when the all-clear flashed, she made for the HDT control desk and waived the captain and the professor inside.

"Attention HDT Rescue," said the lieutenant. She spoke into the console. "This is Lieutenant Grace at arrival bay 42. Requesting lost man status. Deputy Cadet Herman Neutic."

"Entanglement data unavailable, Lieutenant," said the voice. "There is a decaying HDT fold obfuscating the back trip."

"Impossible," said the lieutenant. "The transport was locked."

"It's not the bay 42 event, Lieutenant. It's something else. Let me see . . . yes, ma'am, it's a fault within the time-coordinate overlay. The entangled Angkor event is still distorting the event horizon. No amount of resolution will allow us back in until it dissipates."

"It's Five's rogue transport residue jacking everything up," said the captain. "I knew it. All the analog consumed by the entanglement. Who knows where Five ended up? A frigging mess."

"But, my God," said the professor, "what about Neutic?"

The lieutenant again leaned close to speak into the console. "Initiate lost man protocol. TDC Deputy Cadet Herman Neutic. Transport ID seven-zero-one-one. Priority one. Full resource. Maximum net deployment. Rolling scan. Repeat. Full resource, max net, rolling scan. Tighten the resolution against Mothmen Realm interference."

"Copy, Lieutenant," responded the voice. "That's full-max, rolling, with Realm screen on fine. The event cone for Deputy Cadet Neutic will remain under continuous surveillance until sixteen hundred hours tomorrow. Entanglement heralds are keyed to your transponder, Lieutenant."

"Key them also to Captain Chase."

"Copy that. Heralds duped."

"Probability of retrieval?" said the captain.

The lieutenant tapped at the console keyboard. "Thirty-eight point six percent, sir. Plus or minus 0.5 percent."

"I'm off to Rescue Command," said the lieutenant. "Something tells me we'll hit zero probability sooner than later—I'm going to forestall abandonment protocol with an appeal to the committee chief. And verify the analysis is running on the updated processors. We need to sense hairline fractures that may lead us to a ghosting, a trace, even a shadow of entanglement. Then we can backtrack to him."

The captain tapped at the console. "Mr. Z. and Vixy are already being cleared from medical. I assume you want to attend the debriefing?"

The professor appeared ambivalent.

"C'mon, Professor. There is nothing you can do for Neutic now. He's not adrift in elsewhere. He's still in 1296 Angkor."

When the captain held out his arm to her, she grasped it and the two of them made their way from the observation theater. "I don't know," she said, her voice heavy with emotion. "I don't know, I had them all, all three of them and the boy, too . . . I had them within my grasp—I had them in mind, do you see? If I could have brought them all in—"

"It couldn't be helped. There was no warning. Something must have happened close to the moment of transport. A fracture. It looked like Neutic tried to reenter the singularity, Friday in tow. I don't know. He may have endured an MPH[79] trauma."

The professor clutched at the captain's arm.

"We'll see. He may be all right. Meanwhile, we've got to rely upon T.E. security and the HDT technicians. And on top of everything, that goddamn crazy, ad hoc moleman transport—it jacked up everything, made a mess of the coordinates into and out of Angkor."

---

79   Referring to meridians, parallels and hypermeridians—see "Hyperdimension" within Glossary.

CHAPTER 45

METAMORPHOSIS

THE HOSPITAL ROOM WAS DIM, illuminated almost entirely by the glowing displays of medical equipment and the single modest reading lamp beside which Mr. Z. was examining his documents. Vixy lay sleeping in the armchair across from him, curled up with her head upon a spare pillow. Nurse Quick shuffled quietly back and forth amongst the equipment, device in hand, checking the data, and here and there making tweaks and adjustments to things.

"Hettie," murmured Neutic. "Hettie."

Mr. Z. looked up and Vixy sat up with a start.

Nurse Quick made to place her hand upon Neutic's forehead but Vixy pushed past her.

"Neutic," whispered Vixy. She watched him staring past her, seeing yet unseeing, and her eyes filled with tears. "Oh, Neutic. You son of a bitch." She grasped his hand. "You're home."

Neutic's expression softened. "Vixy."

Mr. Z. set his aside his notetaking and rose from his chair to peer at Neutic over Vixy's shoulder. He frowned at Nurse Quick.

She acknowledged Mr. Z. with a glance. "He's going to be a little out of it," she said quietly. She turned her attention to the monitors and spoke up. "Mr. Neutic, you are home, indeed. And you have made an impressive recovery already."

Vixy looked hard at Neutic. "But he'll be fine, won't he? I mean—"

"Yes, Miss Velure. Second-degree HDT trauma can be touch and go for some people. But Mr. Neutic's vitals are normal across the board. When he arrived, let's see"—she glanced at several displays—"well, his Glasgow Coma Scale was worrisome, quite low—four when he arrived. But he rebounded within an hour. He flew right past the worst of it. See this?" She jabbed her finger at a display, lowered her reading glasses and squinted at it. "Brain function parameters are right as rain. No lasting trauma to his brain stem or reticular activating system. Age and genetics matter a great deal. And the preventatives you TDC folks ingest. It all helps lower the risk. But I'd say Mr. Neutic is blessed with a robust nervous system. The doctor can explain everything in detail."

"No," said Vixy. "I understand. I mean, he never let go of Friday's hand." She appeared suddenly exhausted, sitting heavily upon the edge of Neutic's bed with her shoulders hunched, her tired gaze fixed upon his resting countenance. Neutic's eyes were closed again. "He's only sleeping, then?"

"Yes, ma'am," said the nurse. "He will require sessions of what is referred to as true sleep for a while yet. It's all up to what his body requires of itself. Including nutrition—he'll need a proper meal tonight. You can visit him tomorrow. The doctor will be through here on his rounds this evening, and meanwhile, I'll be seeing to Mr. Neutic myself. I dare say it won't be long until he's discharged."

Mr. Z. placed his hand upon Vixy's shoulder. "Vixy. It's time you got some rest yourself. You heard the nurse. He's going to be okay." He coaxed her from the edge of the bed and draped her jacket over her shoulders. They exchanged wordless acknowledgments with Nurse Quick. Mr. Z. snatched his papers from the side table, shoved them into his case, and they made their way into the hallway.

They encountered the professor and the captain in the waiting area. Vixy donned her jacket, hugged her shoulders, and stared at the floor.

"He's out of the woods," said Mr. Z. "Sleeping now."

"Oh, that's good," said the professor. "What of the boy?"

"Already discharged," said the captain. "The kid came through it like falling off a chair. You never know. The resilience of a child's physiology helps. Anyway, Friday is quarantined for a day or two. It's unprecedented, of course. There'll be an investigation. All the way up and down the chain, you can bet." He scratched at his chin.

"It's not Neutic's fault, Captain," said Vixy. "Friday would've . . . I don't know, but—"

"The boy would have disappeared into elsewhere if Neutic had not hung onto him," said Mr. Z. "And if Friday had been left behind to begin with, I don't know. I was spouting protocol when I ordered Neutic to find a way to leave him. And he did. He obeyed orders. Meanwhile, a man does what he has to do. An impossible position for any of us to be in. Clearly there was a Cornelian dilemma.[80] But it's all in the report."

"That's right," said the captain. "And it would've been up to you, Z, to file any charges of insubordination. Since you didn't, there won't be a hearing. But a duty to avoid under leave no trace? I've read your report, Z. From Vixy's description there isn't any avoiding a failure there. Neutic will likely face discipline. The child's future is another matter entirely. A past-life transgression—bringing a kid from thirteenth century Angkor into the present—it's . . . like I said, it's goddamn unprecedented, at least within TDC history. Now it comes down to whether a deportation is warranted. The Time Guard will want to weigh in. But as crazy as it sounds, we've got bigger fish to fry."

"The golden ball," said Mr. Z. "It's missing from Angkor."

"Which is a goddamn scientific impossibility," said the captain. "What else can go wrong?" He shut his eyes and put his hand to his temple.

"I've got my theories about the golden ball," said Mr. Z. "Meanwhile, I'm convinced the psi-shield threat ought to be our priority. Professor. You said the empress metamorphosized. You're certain?"

"I'm not certain of anything, Mr. Z., I'm sorry. Except that I lost

---

80 A Cornelian dilemma (*dilemme cornélien*) is a dilemma in which someone is obliged to choose one option from a range of options, any of which reveals a detrimental effect upon themselves or someone near them.

psi-access to her—what little I had, which only ever amounted to an indefinite sense of her presence, anyway. And that was several days ago. Or more. Heavens, I don't know, these past few days have been so . . ."

"Crazy," said Vixy.

"But you indicated that you've regained it," said Mr. Z. "Your sense of the empress."

"There is a psi-energy that I perceive; that I can sense, yes. But the spectrum is too intense. I don't dare attempt to breech it. Hence, I can't engage her. Certain psi-strengths are beyond me, and it's all I can do to block or simply evade them."

"Or reflect them intuitively," said Mr. Z., "like at the Olympic. Or be harmed yourself. I understand."

"Be harmed," said the captain, "or be killed, Z. Isn't that what we're talking about?"

"There was the mothman surrender by way of the empress," continued Mr. Z. "Coinciding with her sudden disappearance, physically and psionically. And now a new psi-force. More powerful. Too powerful for even the professor to evaluate or investigate. I just need to be certain that what I think has happened has indeed come to pass."

"Yes, Mr. Z.," said the professor. "The psi-presence of the empress is off the charts, let me put it that way. And expanding. Exponentially. Or geometrically. I don't know. It is impossibly unwieldy, this strength of hers. Which makes me wonder how she herself can, I don't know—"

"Wield it?" said Mr. Z.

"Or live with it," said Vixy. "What does it do to a mothman? To metamorphosize?"

"That's exactly it, Vixy," said Mr. Z. "If the empress indeed pupated and completed the histogenesis, then we must assume, if anything like entomological science can apply here at all, that there will be a period when she is at rest, awaiting a trigger of some sort. Temperature, light, something chemical—hormonal, what have you—that would initiate her emergence."

"Emergence," said the captain.

"From her cocoon," said the professor. "Yes. There is something called the imago, as I recall—where the new moth emerges essentially helpless, with a swollen abdomen and shriveled wings. It has to pump its wings full of fluid. It takes time."

"Hemolymph," said Vixy. "The fluid is called hemolymph. I studied this stuff as a kid. The butterfly or moth pumps fluid stored within its abdomen into its wings and depending upon the species, it can take hours."

"Distributing the hemolymph can take hours if we're talking about standard entomological biology," said Mr. Z. "I'm just wondering how long we have. Because who knows what the timetable is for a pupated mothman? Or mothwoman? It's not as if we have any records of such a thing. Nevertheless, if she's helpless, as you say, physically and psychologically and cognitively too, that gives us a window of opportunity."

"Only if we can find her, Z," said the captain. "Not to throw cold water on this. I mean, something has to be done. These psi-powers of hers, well, it's out of my lane. But unless the professor can track her, I don't see what chance we have. And the golden ball too. We've got that to worry about. It would be just like the molemen to engineer a way to hyperdimensionally transport gold. And quantum entangled gold at that. What I'm saying is that damn Angkor ball is gone. How can it be gone? And who has it? Five? Where is Five? The mothmen were after that ball, weren't they? They appropriated all that moleman HDT engineering technology, enough to get a start on their own HDT capabilities, and they wanted that damn CCC too. We suspected they had ambitions to build their own Cosmic Clock, and now we know. Would the empress, with all her newfound psi-powers and all that, could she have influenced Five's HDT?"

"And now she has the golden ball?" said Vixy. "Is that what you're saying?"

"Hmm," said Mr. Z. "The TDC and the T.E. are working as we speak, to establish psi-defenses, correct, sir?"

The captain nodded. "I know what you're thinking, and I've already got the professor lined up with assisting with that effort."

"Good," said Mr. Z. "Meanwhile, we've got to find the empress. Fast. We've got to find her while she's still vulnerable and stop her.

Before she accumulates enough psi-power to engage in, who knows? I fear she may have even greater ambitions than restoring the Realm."

"Like getting her hands on the ball and controlling space-time?" said Vixy.

"Exactly," said Mr. Z. "Professor, there is something else about the empress, isn't there? Something only you could possibly have discerned at this point."

The professor hesitated. "Her pregnancy? It was prior to her pupation. But. Oh, Mr. Z., I suppose there is the potential that I made a mistake. But . . ."

"But we have to run with the idea that you are right," said the captain. "That the empress is pregnant, and not by the emperor."

Vixy couldn't help scowling. "First of all," she blurted, "that's gross. Second, I don't know how to even ask this, except, could it, whatever it is, survive a metamorphosis? I mean, jeezus."

"Progeny," said Mr. Z. "I dare say the answer to that is critically important. And beyond all of us, for now, at least." He was eyeing the professor, watching her turn her ring upon her finger. "And when you said Artoor had served his purpose, Professor. His purpose being . . ."

"Oh my God, no," said Vixy. "Mr. Z. You don't mean—"

"Yes," said the professor. "An aspect of Artoor lives within the empress. It is part of her psi-signature. Not the consciousness of Artoor. I don't know exactly what it is. And I don't know what such a thing implies."

"Alien-human interbreeding," said the captain. "That's what it implies."

"Hercules," murmured Mr. Z.

"What's that, Z?" said the captain.

"Hercules," replied Mr. Z. "Perseus. Helen of Troy. Minos. All children of Zeus. From his relations with mortal women. Alexander the Great's mother even claimed that Zeus had fathered her son, and Alexander was alleged to have believed it." He chewed upon his pipe stem. "There is myth, there is metaphor, and there is life imitating art, isn't there? And then there is this. By the gods, I don't know what else we're in store for."

"Monsters," said Vixy. "That's what."

EPILOGUE

Aboard a space train, with cocktails nearby, Newton-Joules, a monocular nonbinary being, tapped the future-scope with its long, painted fingernail. "Fourth Quadrant, you say? A significant measure of order is propagating. Or is it? Am I reading this right? The charts are so dense. Since when is it okay to submit hyperdimensional charts and graphs?"

"They aren't hyperdimensional," said Unisex Seven, a four-armed humanoid with lustrous, pewter-toned skin. "If there is hyper anything it's your own knack for hyperbole. Exaggeration is a fetish with you. Or something." She scowled at her displays, shoved her hand into the bowl of crisps, and began popping them one by one into her mouth. Crunch. Crunch. Crunch. And so on, talking with her mouth full. "Order. A significant measure of it. Propagating. Yes. It most definitely is. See here?" She gestured with her crumb-covered fingers, careful not to touch the screen, then blew onto her keyboard, just to be certain she hadn't dirtied it. "The yellow, blue, and green. Or is that purple?" She scowled. "It doesn't matter. It's like I've been telling you. I swear, I file my reports and nobody fucking reads them."

Newton-Joules rolled its cyclopean eye. "It's the Time Detective Contingent messing with everything. Again. That Z character. His investigations. Hence, his influence has distorted the outer veil. And that weird-ass chart you're looking at—the chaos calculator? Well, it doesn't show the veil. But my chart does. Look here."

Unisex Seven leaned over and scowled at Newton-Joules's display. "Hmm. He's a busybody if I've ever seen one. Let me see." She swiveled in her chair. "What serial number is your chart? I can't find it."

Newton-Joules seemed not to hear.

"Newton-Joules!"

"What?"

"What do you mean, what? I asked you, what is the serial number of your chart?"

"The multiquadrant? It's an EG515, just like everybody else's." Newton-Joules sighed and peered out its window. "I wish to Zeus I could be home. In my little hovel. With my turtles. And stuff."

"Z," said Unisex Seven. "That pesky little pale-skinned humanoid Z. He has cost us two of our disciples."

"Hmm, yes," said Newton-Joules. "Bruggs. And . . . who else?"

"Laron," said Unisex Seven.

"Right," said Newton-Joules, "but Laron wasn't a disciple. Neither was Artoor. More like, I don't know, mercenaries. Or something."

"Contractors," said Unisex Seven.

"Hired guns, whatever. And you see where that got us. Earth pisses me off."

"We're still talking about Earth?" said Unisex Seven. "Must we? As if that nasty little rock matters? We ought to encourage that yellow dwarf of theirs to go nova, shouldn't we? It would clear that portion of the spiral arm of life and maybe inspire the kind of unrest in the neighboring arm that would go a long way to getting us somewhere. There are several planets looking for a fresh start, after all, and that would do it." Unisex Seven flashed her eyes, which were sapphire blue with fiery orange irises, and strikingly large for her race, and she sneered at her reflection in the space train's window. She smiled deliciously at herself and sipped her cocktail.

Newton-Joules watched her out of the corner of its eye. "Hey, Unisex. What if I told you that you are a vain bitch?"

"Ha!" Unisex Seven plunged her third hand into the bowl and hurled a handful of crisps across the cockpit.

"Hey!" shouted Newton-Joules. "What the fuck are you doing?"

"Well, what does a bitch do?"

"Throw food at people, you think that's being a bitch? It's being an idiot! You slob!"

The cockpit door slid open and Kit, the assistant, shoved his fuzzy, multi-eyed head inside. "Psst. The commander's coming." He noticed the crisps strewn upon the floor. "What the hell is going on in here? You guys are screwed." He flapped his ears, tipped his head back with a haughty air, smirked at them, and disappeared. The door was still sliding shut when the commander himself snatched at it and shoved it wide open.

Newton-Joules and Unisex Seven sat bolt upright. "Yessir!" said Newton-Joules.

"Oh my God, yessir!" said Unisex Seven.

They watched the commander, multiarmed, blue skinned, with a forked tongue and a muzzle full of pointed teeth, take in every iota of the cockpit with his glaring, red-rimmed eyes. Newton-Joules and Unisex Seven each typed deliberately, afraid to take their eyes off their displays.

"Oh my God," said the commander. He toyed with his braided beard and his voice was unnervingly deadpan. He tossed a packet at Unisex Seven, and even with three of her hands she fumbled the thing before finally clutching it close to her chest. The commander appeared nonplussed. "Newton-Joules!"

"Yessir." Newton-Joules stopped typing, its hands poised nervously above the keyboard.

"The data in Miss Unisex Seven's lap is for the both of you. Download it, digest it, report to the primary conference car in twenty minutes."

"Me too?" said Newton-Joules.

The commander glared at Newton-Joules.

"Me, yessir. Of course, sir."

"You both are being assigned a little field duty. No more of your playtime fun here on the space train. You're both going to have to start earning your expense accounts. Do you hear?"

Newton-Joules and Unisex Seven were careful not to look at each other. They'd talk later.

"Quadrant Four is a fucked-up mess," said the commander. "The Great Conflict. The molemen. We all assumed they'd just roll over the mothmen. Well, the empress. She's full of surprises."

"She pupated," said Newton-Joules. "Didn't she?"

"What have you been doing, Newton-Joules, nosing into the officers' secure database again? I'm having your passwords pulled. Anyway, her psi-strength has gone off the charts. I bet you didn't know that, did you? Despite your hacking."

Newton-Joules furrowed its brow and began pecking at its keyboard.

"No, you didn't," said the commander. "But you may have, if you could read your charts underneath all those crumbs."

"Crisps, sir," said Newton-Joules.

"Crumbs," insisted the commander.

"Sir," interrupted Unisex Seven. "A mothman pupation, if I'm not mistaken, well, there hasn't been one since . . . perhaps, I don't know—"

"A millennium," said Newton-Joules.

"One point one millennia," said the commander. "And this freaky empress has smashed the first ten psi-veils within all four quadrants. If you'd been scanning properly—you know, doing your job—you may have noticed."

"Scanning," said Newton-Joules. "No, sir. We haven't been scanning while the train is passing the double black hole, per the directive. Nevertheless, sir, ought we to raise the reflectors in Quadrant Four?"

"Raise the reflectors in *all* quadrants," said the commander. "And if either of you are the type that is inclined to pray, then I would say this would be your moment. Because it appears that the mothman empress is on her way to becoming a goddamn manifest, living, breathing goddess. Or as close to it as any of us is ever going to witness in this lifetime."

"Sir," said Newton-Joules. "Reflectors raised."

"Fine," said the commander.

Unisex Seven folded her arms. "How strong is she, Commander? The empress? I mean, the Scarab Cult, any of us, we're not in any danger of—"

"Succumbing to mass mind control? Hell yes, we are," said the commander. "If there is any veracity to the computer modeling, she could theoretically seize control of every mind in the cosmos. Nobody will be safe."

"But what about the molemen?" said Newton-Joules. "Their engineering. We can coerce them into countering anything the mothman empress manages to conjure up. Can't we?"

"Nobody would have doubted that the molemen engineers with their Cosmic Clock nonsense and their ambitions to control space-time were the most important threat to our chaos management. But . . ." The commander checked his timepiece and stepped into the hallway. "I have to go."

Newton-Joules and Unisex Seven glanced warily at each other and spoke at the same time. "But what, sir?"

"But things have changed, that's all. Good luck with your field trip, folks. You'll need it. We all will. Time is short. Far too short for what needs to be done. And that son of a bitch Mr. Z. and the TDC? Well, they are going to help us get what we want. And then, mark my words, they are going to fucking get what's coming to them."

THE END

GLOSSARY

Consequence Research Project (CRP): A transcoalitional, pangalactic research project funded by HDT licensing and certification fees, tolls, fuel taxes, government grants, commercial development authorization fees, and research stipends. Interested parties include, within the Fourth Galactic Quadrant, the PMC, the T.E., the Time Guard, the GTA, and myriad commercial and private entities. The mission of the CRP is that of a nongovernmental watchdog intent upon ascertaining, via the application of rigorous scientific standards, the impact of HDT activity upon the Cosmic Time Architecture.

Cosmic Clock Project (CCP): An engineering scheme initiated by the molemen to gain omnipotent control of the CTA by way of cubing the sphere—originally a metaphorical concept referring in ancient times to the squaring of the circle, but in the hands of the molemen a hyperdimensionally expanded technological reality. Earth is to be established as the inaugural planetary lattice point comprising the major cosmological components of the tesseract—the so-called clockwork pieces—of the CCP.

Cosmic Lexicon Project (CLP): The CLP aims to compile and define into a single, searchable, crosstranslational database all words in all languages across the universe, continually monitoring for both written and verbal usage so as to segregate contemporary, archaic, and obsolete usages and iterations. Funding is both public and private.

Cosmic Time Architecture (CTA): Reality as such, in hyperdimensional terms, incorporating both n-space and n-time. See *Hyperdimension.*

Emergency Immolation Beacon (EIB): A hyperdimensional SOS. Namely, an unrestricted, trans-hyperdimensional signal burst that necessitates a self-destruct command on behalf of a TDC-issued transponder. It is the only remote command that will override the security buffers, physiological fail-safes, and genetic identity links that bind a transponder to exclusive use by its end user. As such, an EIB command requires chain-of-command series of authorizations.

Galactic Intelligence Administration (GIA): A venerable, cosmos-wide, labyrinthine, pangovernmental intelligence network consisting of field agents, operatives, and an enormous, far-reaching infrastructure of overt and covert programs, policies, committees, and attendant political oversight. Controversial from its beginnings, the funding for the GIA is allocated by way of semiannual, usually bitterly contested subgalactic hearings whereby current programs are subjected to public scrutiny. Its mission is to safeguard the so-called Free World, and it inevitably struggles against a lack of political unity.

Galactic Law (GL): The substance and legitimacy of Galactic Law draws upon normative jurisprudence (as opposed to analytic jurisprudence, legal positivism, and legal realism, which reject origins and definitions of law as anything beyond that which people establish in a subjective manner) and therefore acknowledges the existence of objective, psychological, and therefore biological archetypal origins. GL, in other words, is understood as inherent within and a natural expression of the behavior of free individuals in their compassionate state and expresses an intuitive, pancultural, pantemporal, arguably objective realization of n-manity (where n = any cognizant race or individual, e.g., *hu*manity) and ethics. It is officially established within the Fourth Galactic Quadrant legislature. It may be appealed to by any resident entity demonstrating a pursuit of life, liberty, and happiness.

Galactic Paranormal Activity Database (GPAD): Maintained by the Pangalactic Mythology Coalition, the database is far from comprehensive and limited to psionic energies and brain wave functionality calibrated closely to those of humanoid populations. Moreover, it is known that much humanoid psi-activity is shrouded or otherwise psychically encrypted, the parsing of which outstrips the resources of the IMC.

Galactic Transparency Alliance (GTA): An organization of nations pledged to abide by the oversight and inspection authority of the Time Guard, Pangalactic Mythology Coalition (PMC), and the protection and stability of the Cosmic Time Architecture. The GTA contributes annually to the funding for consequence research.

Ghost Impression Database (GID): HDT events leave behind traceable forms of space-time evidence—transport residue, wakes, ghost impressions, etc.—that diminish in intensity following the event. Ghost impressions are unique examples of such evidence because they do not propagate or disperse from an epicenter or generation point but rather remain as subtle, impermanent impressions in the fabric of space-time. The GID is a log of such impressions and therefore plays its part in the history and analysis of HDT traffic. It has been continually compiled and reviewed for centuries from the very first attempts at hyperdimensional travel. It is a tool in the responsible, ethical oversight of and attention to the integrity of the CTA against threats known and unknown (though not yet recognized or understood as such).

Great Conflict: A general term describing any of the interminable series of pangalactic wars (or world wars) that have inevitably if not cyclically strained societies' ability to transcend its arguably innate biological compulsion toward organized violence and conflict.

Hyperdimension: Also, *hyperdimensional* and *hyperdimensionality*. Of or relating to a space-time manifold of more than four dimensions (normally perceived as three dimensions in Euclidean space and one dimension in time) and incorporating the mathematical concept of *n*-space. As an example, a 0-sphere is a pair of points; a 1-sphere is a circle; a 2-sphere is a sphere in three dimensions and a 3-sphere is a three-dimensional sphere in four spatial dimensions, otherwise known as a hypersphere. Stereographic projection may be used to visualize the hypersphere's meridians, parallels and hypermeridians (MPH). Alternatively, a 2-square is a cube in three dimensions and a 3-square is a tesseract. Time, normally perceived within three dimensions—past, present, and future—may also be expressed, akin to *n*-space, in terms of the hyperdimensionality of *n*-time.

Hyperdimensional-hyperspectral (HDHS): Referring to the propagation of the electromagnetic (EM) energy spectrum into hyperdimensional physics. Sub-hyperdimensional, so-called traditional EM is comprised, in order of increasing frequency and decreasing wavelength, of the following bands: (1) radio, (2) microwave, (3) infrared, (4) visible light, (5) ultraviolet light, (6) x-ray, and (7) gamma ray. The expression of HDHS radiation values, by definition, employs hyperdifferential and hyperintegral calculus.

Hyperdimensional Obfuscation Fold (HDOF): The fold flattens space-time, the engineering mechanism of which requires vast quantities of fuel—energy—which can, for example, be supplied via the consumption of a white dwarf, of which several hundred are located within range of the latest Sno-Globe-Con coordinates. See the chapter "The Agony of the Moth."

Hyperdimensional Travel (HDT): Also referred to as *hyperdimensional transport* (referring typically to cargo) and *hyperdimensional transporter* (the machine or instrument that enables it). HDT is an otherwise generic term for any device that allows for hyperdimensional (time and space) travel. There is no universally standardized design and myriad examples exist throughout the cosmos, although only several reliable, Time Guard–sanctioned, tested, and approved manufacturers exist in any particular space-time coordinates.

Pangalactic Mythology Coalition (PMC): An ancient (established late Golden Age), perpetually paradoxical (ostensibly by design) assemblage of otherwise intellectually and spiritually intrepid, preternaturally open-minded thinkers of all biological configurations and vocations. The group, although galactically vast, has remained intentionally leaderless and theoretically anti-institutional throughout its history, electing by true majority a viceroy tasked with directing the activities of each contingent.

Mythological Revitalization Initiative (MRI): Theoretical nomenclature to describe the process of intentional, formalized cultural mythological rebirth. Preceded by cultural mythological schism, disorientation, disintegration, or collapse.

Origin Analysis: A technically sophisticated examination of the provenance, source, or point of generation of an inanimate object. The science hinges upon the influence of space-time upon the subatomic and subtle body nature of an object—otherwise identical versions manufactured in different space-time coordinates, for example, will present different OA evidence, as will any otherwise identical objects with different space-time residence profiles. Take a thing from here to there, in other words, and its OA nature may or may not be traceable depending upon the sophistication of the analysis and the influence of obfuscation technology.

Pangalactic Archive (PGA): A venerable institution, one aspiring to integrate the lending, archiving, and research functions of a typical academic library with the archaeological, anthropological, ethnographical, scientific, and mythologically exploratory fieldwork and scholarship of the galaxy's most elite, well-funded, and rigorous museum research programs.

Tetrahectatricontakaidigon Enclave (T.E.): A peripatetic, quasi-governmental body with embassy qualities that physically relocates whenever security threats diminish its functionality. It represents the core 432 cultural components (thus the polygon descriptor portion of its name) present within the known universe. The institution resembles both the American Pentagon, in its guise as a powerful yet bureaucratically hindered department of defense, and the United Nations (established in the twentieth century in New York City), in its role as a life-affirming and otherwise benevolent peacemaker in line with Galactic Law.

Time Detective Contingent (TDC): A cantankerously autonomous division of the Time Guard that recruits, trains, and employs a renowned, some may say notorious cache of time detectives in both exclusive and freelance capacities to prevent and investigate crimes against Time—time crime—otherwise defined as an unwarranted appropriation, transgression, stoppage, deflection, hindrance, warpage, overlapping, obfuscation, abuse, or tyranny of or related to the Cosmic Time Architecture.

Time Guard: A perpetually autonomous organization with unpublicized ties to the T.E. It has comprised, throughout its obscure history, an elite group of specialists, including time detectives, Time Lords, et al. The study of the origin and history of the Time Guard is ancient and obscure enough to have developed into its own field of official academic scholarship.